K. D. MILLER

To the survivors, whether it be the zombie apocalypse or just getting out of bed every morning.

Never stop fighting.

Trigger Warnings

- LOSS OF CHILD
- MENTION OF CANCER
- ATTEMPTED SA
- DEATH AND GORE AND, WELL, ZOMBIES

IF ANY OF THESE THINGS ARE TRIGGING TO YOU, PLEASE PROCEED WITH CAUTION.

CHAPTER ONE
MELODY

"ONCE UPON A TIME, the world was perfect." I scrunch my nose. "Ok, so maybe *perfect* is a gross exaggeration, but there weren't flesh-eating corpses wandering around, so it was exponentially better than it is now. It really is crazy how quickly the world fell apart though. Within weeks, a third of the world's population was gone." *Snap.* "Just like that. We hardly had any warning at all, it was like the news broke and a few days later, everyone was dropping like flies—only to rise again and go fully dental on anyone within arm's reach. Who knows what percentage is left now. World-wide communication went to hell when the bombs were dropped to contain the worst of the outbreak. Of course, that didn't make a lick of difference in the grand scheme of things other than killing hundreds of thousands of innocent people, but, hey, hindsight is twenty-twenty, right? But because of that genius move, we haven't had an actual update in, oh, what's that been? Seven years? Eight? It's hard to keep track anymore."

I cock my head at the Bloody pinned beneath the overturned shelf in front of me. I glance between the picture on the desk of a middle-aged man standing next to a teenager in a baseball uniform holding a trophy and the thing on the floor. I think it *might* be the same guy—the principal of this preschool, I guess, since that's what the plaque on the door of this office says—but it's really hard to match up the proud, beaming face of the man in the picture with the rotting, crimson-stained one writhing on the floor snapping it's black, dripping fangs at me. I shrug and continue on.

"Well, you know what that's like. I'm sure every day is the same to you, huh? Wake up, wander around looking for a tasty person to sink your rotting teeth into, wander around some more, screech and moan a bit. Lather, rinse, repeat. That's gotta get old pretty damn fast." I clean my nails with the tip of a knife as the Bloody struggles, trying desperately to reach me. I ignore him as I hold my hand out in front of me to inspect my work and then sigh, looking down at him.

"I don't know how much of this you already know, Bubba. It kinda looks like this town was out of the social loop long before the social loop got blown to hell. No offense, of course. It looks like a nice town —or like it used to be, at least. So, anyway, long story short: the world went to hell for reasons still unknown, and you became—" I gesture to what equates to a reanimated corpse from the depths of someone's nightmares "—this."

He claws a gray, decomposing hand into the floor as he tries to drag himself free, dying for a little taste. I shake my head in frustration. It's true that no one has any fucking clue what actually happened to land us here, not really anyway. All anyone ever seemed to know was that people got sick—no idea how or why—blood started oozing from their eyes, nose, and ears, a high fever spiked, and then their body temperature dropped drastically. Soon after that, they flatlined.

But the problem is that they didn't *stay* dead. Oh no, they rose again, usually pretty quickly, but they came back...different. Changed. Wrong.

All remnants of the person they used to be were just *gone*. Their eyes were vacant, and no higher thought processes seemed to exist anymore. No speech. No reasoning. No recognition. You'd tear out your best friend's throat without a second thought once you turned— because you had no thoughts. The only thing left is the basest desire: the hunger for blood and flesh.

I've seen the transformation more times than I care to remember, and *unsettling* is one way to describe it. *Fucking creepy* is another and far more accurate one.

Their skin quickly turned gray and sallow, and started to rot and fall off within a few months usually, and their eyes would shift into a weird milky white, almost totally opaque. But blood still poured from their eyes, noses, and mouths—bright red at first, then more of a black viscous goo as time went on, so they were forever stained with streaks of the stuff—hence calling them "Bloodies." Zombies, the Undead, Groaners, Biters, Screechers, Chomps, Rotters—there are a thousand names for them. No matter what you call them, they're bad news and contagious as fuck. One bite is all it takes and you're done for.

Some people at the beginning thought it was germ warfare. Others thought something in the food supply would explain how widespread things had gotten so quickly. Aliens, secret government experiments, the hand of God ushering in the End of Days—the potential causes are endless, really, and I figure each one is just as plausible as the next. The think-tank kind of minds who would have figured it out once upon a time are mostly dead now, and the ones who might still be kicking are more worried about staying that way than solving a mystery that doesn't fucking matter.

I don't particularly care what it was or how it started. Knowing the how and the why makes no difference now, so no reason to worry about it. I just focus on survival, on the here and the now, and only glance to the past through squinted eyes. There's way too much pain and loss looking back with anything more than that.

I shake myself and continue my one-sided conversation with my new friend.

"It was rough times in the beginning, Bubba, not gonna lie. First, we had to figure out how to even kill something that was already dead. I mean, what a mindfuck, right? But eventually we figured out a shot to the head, removing the head completely, or fire did the trick. After those of us still on a human-free diet figured out how to fight back against the Bloodies, other people became the bigger threat. Desperate times make people do desperate things. You can't even imagine the things I've seen, Bubba." *The things I've done*, I add silently. I shudder, recalling memories I'd rather leave buried.

"But even so, human nature led survivors to band together in groups. We aren't solitary creatures, after all. Hell, even you guys instinctively gravitate towards each other and form moan-screaming, Bloody herds. Now, not all groups are good. There are some out there that you wouldn't believe, Bubba. Slavers. Cannibals. Religious nut jobs making ritualistic sacrifices. It's *crazy*. Thankfully, those have been...we'll say *eradicated* around here, and the good ones left have started to rebuild the world! Well, sort of. I don't know what the rest of the planet looks like, but we have four different secure settlements in this area now, all working together to survive. We call it Haven." I roll my eyes dramatically and Bubba lets out a guttural moan as he strains towards me.

"I know, I know, it's a bit cheesy, but I kind of like it. It holds promise, ya know? Hope and all that. So, we've got," I tick them off on my fingers as I list them for Bubba, "The Cove, which is where I live. It used to be this uppity neighborhood with a giant stone wall around it to keep the lowly riffraff out or whatever it was rich people were concerned about, but it's really great from a defensive security standpoint. Next is Red Leaf which was a working farm before the end of the world and they've flourished in the years since humans and pollution have taken a nosedive. We pretty much all just call it The Farm. They supply us with a good chunk of our food and the rest of us send workers there in month-long shifts to help out. Third is Greenbriar—it was a small community college once upon a time, so it's set up pretty well for housing people. And lastly, is FOS. FOS is..." I purse my lips. "Well, it's a mystery actually, but together, we all make up Haven. We've got running water, electricity, crops and livestock, trading between the settlements. Hell, we even have an evil dictator ruling over us, so just like old times again!"

Another groan from the Bloody makes me sigh and rise from my perch on the desk. I stroll over to Bubba, curling my lip at his disgusting visage. Black, sludge-like blood oozes slowly from his mouth, nose, and ears, and his flesh is completely rotted away in many places, tendons and bones clearly visible. He snaps his teeth as those cloudy eyes fix on me, seeming to burn with hunger.

"It was fun catching up with you. Best wishes in the afterlife,

Bubba," I say somberly. "I know this wasn't your fault. You didn't ask to be a monster, but, well, I can't let you just run around being one. Sorry." With that, I plant my blade deep in his skull, the blade dragging across bone, and his struggling ceases almost immediately.

"Mel?"

"In here!" I call as I straighten and wipe the gunk from my knife. Jonah jogs into the room and arches a brow when he sees the Bloody at my feet.

"You alright in here?"

"Yep, fine. I was just filling my friend, Bubba here in on the state of the world. He's been a bit out of the loop for quite a while by the looks of him."

Jonah chuckles, brushing his brown curls away from his face. "Anything good?"

"A few things, yeah. How about the other rooms?"

"Jackpots!" he grins, cheeks flushed. "Seriously, certified jackpots. Good idea trying this far out in the country."

"You should know by now never to doubt me." He rolls his eyes and I wink as I tuck a few books I'd found in a desk drawer into my bag. Jonah brings in a few boxes and we load up the rest of the supplies from the office. We cart our loot out to the truck and I let out a whistle when I take in everything already in the truck.

"Jackpot is right," I say with a grin up at Nathan as he takes the box from my arms and adds it to the back of the moving van. "Man, when I'm right, I am *damn* right."

"Big score for sure," he agrees with a smile, giving me a fist bump. I survey the truck: a ton of canned food, bottled water, and other snacks —expiration dates have become vague suggestions at this point. As long as the cans aren't dented and the stuff inside the packages isn't fuzzy, it's usually good to go in our book—gigantic boxes of paper towels, tissues, and toilet paper, and a ton of cleaning products. I have a feeling that the school had just restocked supplies when the world ended based on how much unopened stuff they have. There are also a few big boxes of diapers, children's clothes, books, and toys, and I'm already dying to see the look on the kids' faces when we drop them at the school.

I head back inside with the rest of the group and, after several more trips, we've stripped the building nearly to the studs and the truck is almost completely full. Exhausted but excited, I jump in the cab of an old Tacoma with Jonah while Destiny and Jamie take the supply truck, and Nathan, Laura, and Miguel hop in the van. Jonah slaps the roof of the truck and calls out the window.

"Be safe. Stay together. Make it home."

Everyone cheers at our little motto and Jonah turns back to me, smiling as he starts up the truck. No one can bring people together like Jonah. As our caravan of merry thieves bumps slowly down the road, maneuvering around abandoned vehicles and debris, I stare out the window.

The small country town is what I'd call quaint. It probably only had a population of a few thousand back in the day. We drive through what appears to be the heart of town, passing a small church, a feed store, a mom-and-pop restaurant (all already scoured on this trip), and an empty playground with rusted swings rocking gently in the breeze. I try to imagine what life here might have been like. Slow, probably. Nice.

A couple of Bloodies lurch against the fence of a baseball field as we pass. *Not so nice anymore, though.*

"So, what books did you score?" Jonah asks. He knows that almost anywhere we go, I always manage to find a book or ten to bring back. I'd pretty much single handedly stocked The Cove's small library. I figure what's a better time to escape reality than after the end of the world, right?

I smile and dig through my pack.

"Let's see, we've got a Spanish-English dictionary."

"You already speak Spanish," Jonah points out.

"Verdadero." I shrug and set the book aside. "A romance novel. Ooo, the good kind! Check it—shirtless guy on the front!" I wave the book in the air, showing off the cover. "This one is mine. You can have it when I'm done." He chuckles at that, but I know he actually gets a kick out of reading them too. "Annnnd an *Alex Cross*. Fourth one I think, maybe fifth. I can't remember."

"Oh dibs!"

"All yours. I've read them all anyway."

"Of course you have," he says, rolling his eyes. Anytime I'm not on a supply run or taking out Bloodies, chances are I'm reading. "Wonder if Patterson is still out there somewhere."

"Who knows. Maybe he's written a hundred more books on an old typewriter in a cabin in the mountains somewhere. Now *that* would be a cool score. Not that I would take Mr. Patterson out and steal his books or anything, of course," I add, "I just mean, ya know...if we got there and he was a little more crimson than we remember, all those unpublished books would be fair game..." Jonah laughs and shakes his head.

"There is something wrong with you."

"I'm well aware," I assure him with a grin. Jonah knows all my dark and twisty curves, all my sharp edges—and the softer ones that I usually hide—and loves me through it all. I really don't know what I would have done, or who I might be be, without him. We'd been neighbors and best friends long before the end of the world and had gotten through those early days of chaos together. We've seen each other through the worst times in our lives, saved each other time and time again, and I can say without a doubt that I wouldn't still be standing if it weren't for him. I love him more than any other person alive. He's my family, plain and simple.

We had been on our own for almost three years before we found a good group to join up with out on the road. There were seventeen of us at that point...and the *six* of us that were left ended up at The Cove about a year ago. It had taken us all a while to feel truly safe after being on the road and the run for so long, constantly struggling and fighting to stay alive, but now The Cove is home and I'm anxious to get back.

The trip home feels like it takes weeks, but really it's only four days and we thankfully don't run into any issues along the way. I straighten as we hit the turnoff, eager to be behind the high, secure walls and back in an actual bed again. The long private road leading in is still beautiful, though not exactly manicured these days. Tall grass and towering oaks line the street on both sides, along with abandoned cars at strategic intervals that can be moved to block the road within a few minutes if necessary. Guard stands had been built into trees every few yards, and I give small salutes to those on duty as we pass.

I'd become the unofficial head of security after our arrival. I didn't want the *actual* title, but I was happy to help behind the scenes and thankfully Kurt, the official head, wasn't pigheaded enough to not want my opinion. I've improved their existing security measures tenfold in the last year, and am proud of all the progress we've made. Everyone that has found their way to The Cove has been through enough. They deserve a place where they feel as safe as possible, and if I can help give them that, then I feel like I have at least some purpose left in this world.

Only about half of the homes in The Cove had been finished prior to everything going to shit, but that actually worked out in our favor: the empty lots had been converted into gardens or animal pens, helping with food production. Dismantled cars had been moved to line the outside of the wall surrounding the entire community, with metal spikes and wooden spears attached facing outward to stop Bloodies. Barbed wire topped the stone wall now too. Bloodies can't really climb for the most part, but they aren't the only threats in the world these days. At my suggestion, more platforms like the ones in the trees had been built at intervals along the length of the wall and each one is manned twenty-four-seven.

We approach the gate and wait for the guards to roll the reinforced metal gate aside. As we drive inside, I catch Bret's eye, and with the look he gives me, I instantly know something is wrong. I go on alert, ready for whatever might be waiting as the caravan makes its way inside and pulls around the grand circular entrance to the community, two entwined palms standing in the middle with the ornate sign reading *The Cove* still standing stately between them. I leap out before Jonah even comes to a full stop.

"What's going on? What happened?" I demand, body tensing and my hand flying to rest on the grip of the pistol at my hip.

"We've got visitors," Bret says, irritation clear in his voice.

"Fuck," I grit, but relax, knowing that there's no real threat. *Visitors* means that the dickhead who'd dubbed himself leader of the free world—or the leader of Haven anyway—and his goons are here.

Austin Traeger is a ruthless, heartless, annoyingly *likable*, son of a bitch. I know, I know, it doesn't make sense, but it's true. When he isn't displaying mangled bodies to remind everyone what he's capable of, or taking hostages back to FOS to use as leverage—*you obey my rules and I don't torture your loved ones*—he's...charming? I know that's true of many sociopaths, so I take it with a grain of salt, but it's that charming quality that wins so many over to his side. They're happy to overlook the fear and pain, all the terrible things he's done, because it means their safety and, really, "he isn't so bad most of the time." Yep, that's a direct quote from more than one Covey since we arrived. I have no idea how he first managed to take control over everything—he was already HMFIC long before Jonah and I arrived—but he's kept his grip on it just fine since then because he's not afraid to get his hands dirty. My money says he actually likes it, maybe even gets off on it.

We've had a handful of short, I'll call them *professional* conversations since our group joined The Cove. I was introduced to him as a part of the security team, so our interactions have mostly been in connection with that—questions about our security measures, his suggestions for improvements (which I'm annoyed to say were good ones)—stuff like that. He'd quietly offered me a place at FOS after one of our meetings. *Offered*, not *demanded*. I didn't know what the hell to make of that, and of course wouldn't go there in a million years, so I'd declined as politely as I'm capable of. Which is to say, not very—but he'd only smiled and nodded, as if he couldn't have forced me if he'd wanted to. He hasn't brought it up since, but every time our paths do cross, he gives me a look that tells me the offer stands and I give him one back saying my answer is the same. Then, the matter is dropped. It's weird as hell, honestly, but I try not to think about it too much.

I try not to think of Austin Traeger at all, really.

Because I can admit that deep down, in a dark, dangerous part of myself, I know that some of my dislike for him is because we're *too* similar, that Traeger is everything I could have easily become if it hadn't been for Jonah. I've never been much for thirsting for power, but...I could see how pain and hatred could drive me to become like him, to lose all my humanity and bring as many people with me as I could. Except I wouldn't try to be likable in the process and could do a hell of a lot more damage than he could ever imagine.

I shake the thoughts away, focusing on what's going on now. Whenever Traeger makes his rounds to the settlements, his men come in first and sweep for weapons, confiscating every single one until he's gone. Weapons aren't allowed for anyone within the walls except for those on guard duty, and everything is supposed to be stored in our armory—aka the garage of one of the houses—whenever it isn't in use, so really it's mostly just double checking no one smuggled anything they shouldn't have, which is a very punishable offense, and securing everything from the guards. His own men take watches whenever they're here.

But Traeger has his men sweep every house, just in case. He knows all too well that some people would gladly sacrifice the hostages in his compound in order to take him out. The greater good and all that.

Sure enough, three of Traeger's men arrive within a few minutes to disarm the group from the run. I endure the frisking with gritted teeth and glare as I hand over my pistol, rifle, and knives.

"I'm going to want this back," I say to the man now loaded down with my arsenal as I toss my favorite hunting knife on the top of the pile. He's tall and leanly muscled, with dark brown skin and a shaved head. He actually smiles at me in response, showing off very nice pearly whites and dimples, and inclines his head. I quirk a brow in surprise. This guy actually seems alright, especially compared to some of the other members of Traeger's personal security detail that are straight assholes. He has a genuine warmth about him that I don't expect, and when he inclines his head, I narrow my eyes. He looks so familiar...but I have no idea why. I know I've never seen him on these visits before...but I shrug, deciding to deal with it later. I'll figure it out eventually.

I walk away, feeling uneasy and naked without any kind of weapon within arm's reach. Knowing that I can't actually *use* one on Traeger or his men even if I had one doesn't make me feel any better. Another settlement had tried to fight back in the early days of Traeger's reign of terror, and it had ended...badly. Really fucking badly. He'd wiped the *entire* thing off the map and delivered heads on pikes to the other settlements as a friendly reminder of what would happen if they ever tried something similar. Even still, I know there are some people who would risk retaliation if it meant killing him—if they knew where the hell to find him most of the time, that is.

No one actually knows where Traeger's settlement, FOS, is. People have tried to follow him, but all attempts have failed. So, a direct assault on him and his is out of the question—and really stupid, to be quite honest. He's got a crazy big arsenal, more hidden outposts keeping eyes on all of the roads between the settlements and the surrounding areas than anyone can possibly imagine (from what I gather, anyway), and the ability to crush anyone who tries anything to absolute dust.

And the truth of the matter is that a lot of people don't actually mind having him in charge, even seem happy to have someone else making the decisions for them. They either turn a blind eye to his methods or just accept them, figuring this is just the way of the world now. They're just grateful for the safety of the walls and the ability to finally *live* after so long of simply surviving, and, really, I can't blame them for it. Wasn't I just longing to get back to the safety of The Cove when we were on the road?

And, as much as I hate to admit it, things aren't all that bad under him anymore. The heads on pikes and mutilated corpses were things that were more prevalent in the early days. They still happen on occasion, of course, and members of other settlements are still taken as leverage, but overall, we're mostly left to our own devices. Traeger's men check in periodically, aiding in supply exchanges and stepping in if there are any problems, but Traeger himself rarely visits these days. So, it's mostly easy to ignore everything he's done, especially if you *want* to ignore it. Ignorance is bliss and all that.

Another group of Coveys—the terrible monomer we use for ourselves—come to take care of unloading the vehicles and inventorying the haul and I sigh when I meet Jonah's eyes. He'll need to join the rest of the Council and see why Traeger is here. I don't think we're in trouble or we probably would have been met by a small army of Traeger's men when we arrived, but there has to be a reason why he made the trip himself this time. Jonah had quickly become one of the leaders of the settlement after our arrival, accepting a position on the Council, and I hadn't been surprised in the slightest. He just has that way about him. He's always been one of those people that make other people feel at ease and safe. People just instinctively trust him, and he's ridiculously smart and resourceful, and always keeps a level-head and thinks things through. I'm more of a shoot first, ask questions later kind of person, so it's no surprise I wasn't asked to join.

Jonah is the reason we'd survived the initial wave of panic and violence that spread through the world in those early days of the end. He would argue and say it was me and my special skill set, or that we'd done it together at the very least, but I know the truth: he had saved me in untold ways when I was a walking zombie of sorts myself, and he's the only reason we're both still standing. If not for him, I'd be six feet under or a walking pyre of vengeance, burning everything in my path to the ground.

"Want me to come with?" I offer. I won't be allowed inside the Council meeting, of course, but I can stand guard outside and I'm more than capable of fighting my way inside if something goes south.

"Nah, it's alright. Go on home and wash up—you stink," he says, wrinkling his nose. He only grins when I shove him. It's true, and we both know it, but still.

"Dinner?" I ask.

He hits me with the smile that melts panties and boxer-briefs alike, walking backwards away from me towards the Town Hall—what used to be the community clubhouse.

"Hmmm. Filet Mignon, medium rare. Loaded baked potato. Garden salad with lite Italian dressing on the side. And a big ass beer."

I laugh and shake my head.

"Spaghetti it is!" I call. He winks and turns to jog away, and I make my way to the house that we share a few streets over. Despite my annoyance at having Traeger and crew here, I feel myself relaxing a bit more with every step I take down the palm-lined sidewalk, seashells and sea glass pressed into the concrete here and there in decorative patterns. The Cove has a very beach town aesthetic despite not being on the coast. We're only a few hours off, so I suppose that was close enough for the developer to take that vibe and run with it. Our house is an adorable little number with sky blue siding, deeper blue hurricane shudders, and a wraparound front porch complete with rockers and ceiling fans that turn lazily in the breeze.

I mount the porch and surreptitiously glance at the board in the far right corner beneath the flowerpot. I let out a small breath of relief. The line of soil beneath hasn't been disturbed, so that means no one found my secret stash of weapons. It's dangerous having it. Beyond dangerous. If any of Traeger's men ever found it, I'd be dead, Jonah too most likely, no matter how much I insisted he had no idea. He honestly doesn't. He has no fucking clue, but they'd punish him all the same. It's only there for an absolute emergency, of course, but I like to be prepared for any and all alternatives. I have another stash hidden out beyond the walls in a hallowed out tree, just in case.

I do a quick but thorough inspection of every room to take inventory. I know that Traeger's men would have swept for weapons, but I want to make sure the bastards hadn't taken anything else...or rifled through my shit.

"So help me if my underwear drawer looks disheveled..." I mutter to myself as I toss my pack on the bed. I pull out the ragged, stuffed dog, petting his worn, gray fur before giving him a soft kiss on the head and setting him on the pillow.

I strip down and hurry to the bathroom for a much-needed shower. We'd been out on the run for eight days and though I'd done a quick rinse in a stream on the way back two days ago, I feel unbelievably gritty and grimy. I can rough it with the best of them, but I've admittedly gotten pretty spoiled since coming to The Cove. Running water is one of the best parts of the place. Not just running water, but *hot* running water.

We're very lucky that the apocalypse happened after solar panels had become all but mandatory across the country, and these self-sustaining, eco-friendly communities were all the rage. Cruelly ironic that when humans were finally getting serious about saving the planet, the planet said *too little, too late*. The planet is doing much better now, living its best life really, with wildlife and plant life flourishing and taking back what used to belong to them—but mankind? Not so much.

I unplait my braids and shake out my long, dark brown strands, though there are a few strands of silver shining through these days. It's such a relief to be safely back home where I can literally let my hair down. I always keep it up or braided when we're on the road and I suppose it would make more sense to just sheer it off, but until shampoo becomes too scarce, I'm keeping it long. I know it's stupid, but Mitch had always loved it long and I like to keep that part of myself for him, even after all this time.

I grip the sink and lean towards the mirror, studying my reflection. I hardly even recognize my own eyes. Mitch had always told me how full of life they were, how the gray sparkled with mischief and confidence and sensuality, how he could get lost in them for hours. Now, they're as hard as slate, that sparkle all but gone. *He'd be so disappointed*, I think, a lump forming in my throat. He'd understand, of course, after everything I've been through, everything I've had to do, but it would still hurt him to see me this way. So hardened.

Even with the insanely intense and serious job I'd had before the end of the world, I was always the one cutting tension with jokes or off the wall comments, never letting any situation become too tense. I could resurrect a deadened room just by entering it. I was the life of the party, the good time girl who thought any situation could be solved with dirty jokes, a bottle of Jack, or a good old-fashioned dance party.

That's who I used to be.

Now, I can't even remember the last time I'd *really* laughed. Like make your sides hurt, crying, can't breathe, almost pee your pants kind of laugh. I cut up with Jonah and Mull, sure, but even that isn't how it used to be. There's a part of me that's just…missing now. Or maybe it's still there, but it feels like it's encased in a three-foot block of ice that I don't think anything can thaw. I know that some of it is due to the state of the world. I'd had to harden myself to survive and do what needed to be done, but that wasn't all of it.

No, the ice had come the day I lost Gabby.

I turn away from my reflection, not allowing myself to travel down that path. If therapists were still a thing, one would tell me that avoidance is not a healthy coping mechanism. But most therapists are either dead or having other people for dinner Hannibal Lecter style, so I really didn't give a shit about what they might say or think about how I'm dealing.

I step into the steaming shower and scrub away a week's worth of grime. By the time I'm done and putting on some lotion that Jonah had found for me—something with cucumbers that smells amazing— I feel much better and the past is locked firmly back in the past where it belongs. I dress in short cut-offs and an old, nearly threadbare LSU baseball t-shirt that I've somehow managed to hold onto all this time. I pad down the stairs just as the front door opens.

"Oh, that was fast. Did El Douche get what he wanted and leave already?" I ask in a hopeful tone, snorting at my own hilarity, but the humor dies as I come around the corner into the kitchen. Jonah is standing there, shaking his head—and Austin Fucking Traeger is smirking beside him.

Shit.

"*El Douche* is here for dinner," Traeger says, thankfully sounding amused rather than murderous. I cut my eyes to Jonah. He gives me a stern look, arching a dark brow. I know exactly what he's wordlessly telling me: *behave, Morales.*

"Nice to see you again, Mel," Traeger says in a deep voice. His eyes dip briefly to my braless chest and I run my tongue over my teeth in irritation. I'm not modest by any stretch of the imagination, but if I'd known we were having company, I may have decided to cage the girls for the evening. He pulls his gaze back upwards quicker than I expect him to, actually, and I'm surprised that his stare didn't feel invasive or skeevy. He shifts his gaze to my hair, to the long, damp waves hanging over one shoulder.

"The great and powerful Oz remembers my name? Should I be honored?" I reply automatically, before biting the inside of my cheek.

"Mel…" Jonah warns, somewhere between real irritation and exasperated amusement. Traeger chuckles and pulls his eyes from my hair, leaning back casually against the counter.

"It's alright," he assures Jonah. He has a drawl, probably from southern Georgia or maybe South Carolina, I think. It's…pleasant. Annoyingly so.

"Cool it," Jonah whispers as he passes me on the way to the

butler's pantry. I roll my eyes, but go about grabbing pots to start dinner. I know for a fact that Traeger's eyes drift to my ass as I bend over, but I won't give him the satisfaction of letting him know I care. I don't actually, not really. Being stared at isn't anything new, especially in the apocalypse where women are often seen as a rare, very in-demand commodity.

Rumor has it that Traeger has an entire harem of women back at FOS, trading sex for protection. The thought of it makes me want to puke—and castrate him—but there's not much I can do about any that. All I can do is let him know that, even if I really should be, I'm not afraid of him. I straighten and turn to stare at him openly right back, silently challenging him as I arch a brow and cross my arms over my chest.

His dark blonde hair is a bit longer on the top than the sides, enough that he could run his fingers through it and leave it with that messy look that's admittedly a favorite of mine. He has that stubble-that's-a-step-above-a-five-o'clock-shadow thing going on. And yeah, it looks damn good on him, alright? He smiles, showing off straight, white teeth that gleam against his golden tanned skin. Ruggedly hand-some. That's how you'd describe him. Ruggedly fucking handsome. *All the pretty hiding the monster*, I think to myself. Psychopaths often use their good looks to their advantage, like a poisonous flower—beautiful but deadly.

He's tall, six-four I'd say, and judging by his muscled arms and chest, there's apparently a gym at his luxurious secret hideaway. He's in dark jeans and a plain white t-shirt with a blue plaid button-down thrown over the top, sleeves rolled up to his elbows. I narrow my eyes as I study the tattoo on his right forearm. He has others, I know, snaking down his biceps and peeking up under the edge of his collar, though they're covered at the moment. I've never really paid much attention to them before other than to know they exist, so definitely don't know what any of them are. I'm surprised to find that this one is a quote from *Les Misérables*. I frown. *Interesting.* I add another note to my mental profile of the man, begrudgingly admitting that he prob-ably isn't just the dumb redneck I liked to think of him as most of the time.

I let my gaze travel back upwards and our eyes lock, the deep green of his boring into mine for a long moment. The hanging lights over the island catch the deep golden flecks around his irises, flaring out like a sunburst. He inhales quietly, his jaw ticking, and I force myself to swallow. The kitchen suddenly feels very small, the distance between us shrinking, and I suddenly...*want*. I want things I haven't in a long time, all kinds of things that make me seriously deranged for wanting.

What the fuck? Sure, it's been a while since I've gotten any and he's extremely handsome, but he's also a possible psycho who likes to put severed heads on spikes like he's a fucking Lannister for crying out loud.

"Mel, where's that scotch?" Jonah calls from around the corner, pulling me from my thoughts, the weird, tense moment with Traeger all but forgotten. I whirl towards the pantry, mouth gaping.

"You're giving him the Macallen?!" I'd found it hidden in some corporate VP's office on our last run and it's *mine*. Of course I'm fine sharing with Jonah, but sharing it with the prick? Come on!

Traeger arches a brow at that. "You drink scotch?"

"When it's good," I shoot back, annoyed and not even trying to watch my tone. I can't quite read his look, which is rare for me, but he eventually just shrugs.

"Mel?" Jonah asks again expectantly as he enters the kitchen. I huff in irritation and stomp to the cabinet in the dining room, pulling out the bottle and cursing under my breath. I shove it into Jonah's chest with too much force as I make my way back through the kitchen, making him grunt.

"One glass each. That's it. I mean it, Cothren," I add sternly. He rolls his eyes but his lips curl at the corners—I only use his last name when I'm irritated with him and for some reason, it always makes him laugh, which either diffuses my irritation or increases it tenfold, depending on the day.

"Or I could just take the entire bottle. Call it the El Douche Tax?" Traeger chimes in.

Jonah and I both turn towards him. I'd almost forgotten he was there for a second. I clench my jaw and narrow my eyes, and my irritation seems to amuse Traeger as much as it does Jonah. I kind of hate them both at the moment. Traeger smiles an easy smile and holds up his hands.

"I'm joking, I'm joking. Geeze, does she ever lighten up?" he asks Jonah, hiking a thumb at me.

"Yuck it up, couyon," I mutter. He arches a brow at that while Jonah pours the drinks, but I turn away to work on what promises to be the world's most awkward dinner.

CHAPTER TWO

MELODY

TO MY DISMAY, Traeger stays in The Cove for three more days. He inventories our stores, has meetings with the Council, mingles with the townsfolk. Shakes hands, kisses babies, the whole freaking deal.

Now most of the town is gathered around the small community park. Unfortunately, this part of the neighborhood hadn't been finished before the Bloodies started trying to snack on everyone, so what would have been a playground and covered picnic area was mostly just an open grassy space with a small collection of children's toys that we've scavenged over the years—a few balls and jump ropes, a seesaw that's seen better days, and a handful of bikes—and the half-finished pavilion. There was a swing set at one point but it broke during a storm about a year ago.

But that's all changing today. Apparently, one of the main reasons for Traeger's visit was to bring one of those huge wooden playsets for the kids. His group had come across it in a broken-down delivery truck and decided that The Cove should have it. Why, I have no fucking clue. Maybe Traeger has multiple personalities and one of them is a philanthropic saint who truly just wants the world to be a better place.

I have to admit that the playset is pretty sweet. It has swings, three slides, and even a tunnel running between the two separate playhouse areas. This would have cost a pretty penny back in the day, that's for damn sure. The Cove has about twenty kids and they're all chomping at the bit with excitement. It's so strange to think that so many of them have no idea what life was like without Bloodies, that this is just how the world is for them. But despite never seeing one before, they all instinctively seem to know that the giant structure in front of them equals *big fun*. As much as I might dislike the man, I'm grateful that he's here giving them this gift. They deserve a chance to just be kids.

To my utter surprise, Traeger had even helped put the thing together. And not just a ceremonial hammering of the first nail either—he'd put in real manual labor, sweating and gritting along with the others. *What is his game?* I wonder, not for the first time. Sure, he uses violence to keep people in line, but he also uses his charisma, playing the role of friend-to-all savior when it suits him. Is that what this is about? Playing up that side of the coin? Trying to make even more people fawn over him and happy to fall in line?

Well, it seems to be working.

I watch from a distance behind the crowd as Traeger twists the last screw, dusts his hands off, and shoots the crowd a winning smile. He throws his arms out wide in invitation.

"Well, go on. Give it a good test drive!"

The kids squeal and scream and sprint for it like rabid ferrets. Traeger...*plays* with them. My brows rise in surprise as I watch him chase them around, lift them up, and let them crawl all over him. And all the while, he has the most genuine smile on his face. I cock my head as I study him, trying to read beneath the smile and adding even more to my mental profile. Sure, sociopaths are skilled at hiding the monster beneath charisma and "normal" social behavior, but I'm pretty damn good at spotting it. But with Traeger, I...can't. I blink in surprise as I realize that he isn't pretending to enjoy playing with the kids, delighting in their squeals and laughs. He genuinely enjoys it.

A shrieking giggle pulls my attention away from Traeger lifting a little boy up to the monkey bars while three others climb all over him for their turn. I watch as a little girl in pigtails shoots out of the bottom of the slide with a look of pure joy on her adorable face. My heart gives a swift, painful twist as memories assault me: *Black hair sticking on end as she came down the tube slide; huge grin as she laughed like a hyena; Leo clutched in her arms; her little voice calling, "Mommy! Watch!"*

I squeeze my eyes shut and try to swallow around the sudden knot in my throat. I force the memories away, and after a minute, they fade into the darkness again where they belong. Or really that's not quite right. They don't belong there, but that's where I have to force them to stay. When I open my eyes again, I scan the crowd. Half out of habit and half to have something else to focus on as I wait for the pain to ease. Jonah is up front with the rest of the Council, talking animatedly as they watch the kids play. Almost everyone is smiling, enjoying this moment of levity and joy that's letting all of us forget about the state of the world for a little while. Some people rush forward to shake Traeger's hand and smother him in thanks as he disentangles himself from a gang of six-year-olds.

But there's one person who isn't happy or full of gratitude.

No, Kevin Abercrombie is staring at Traeger with absolute murder in his eyes. It's a look I've seen too many times, one that I know means that we only have a few seconds before everything goes to hell. His body is tense, sweat dotting his forehead, and I immediately go on alert, reaching for weapons that I don't have. *Fuck!* Kevin begins to move through the crowd towards Traeger, cold determination in his eyes.

"Oh shit," I whisper when realization sinks in. Traeger had killed Kevin's oldest son just before our group had arrived at The Cove. Story was that it had been an example killing, a Traeger Special to scare the rest of The Cove into compliance, and now apparently Kevin planned to take his revenge. I search for Jonah as I make my way towards Kevin, desperate for some backup to intervene and stop this from turning into a very, very bad day, but he's not where I saw him a minute ago and I don't have time to find him.

Kevin's one of the teachers at the school and an overall decent guy who has a sick wife to take care of. He doesn't need to do this. Traeger's punishment would be death or, if Kevin is lucky, forced imprisonment at FOS—either option left Sandy without her husband and caregiver. Hell, the punishment could be to kill half the settlement if Traeger really wanted it to be. *Fuck, fuck, fuck.*

I grit my teeth as I press forward, trying to make my way through the thick crowd and cut him off. If I can reach him before he reaches Traeger, I can get him out of here with no one knowing what had almost happened. There'll be no punishment, no retribution, no one the wiser. But I have to stop him quietly and not cause a scene.

"Fuck," I grate under my breath as I try to move faster, but there's so many damn people. I cut my eyes from Kevin to Traeger and the guards he has stationed around the playground. My pulse races and dread settles in my stomach when one of them seems to sense something off. Before he can do anything and before I can get there, Kevin pushes through the last line of people standing between him and Traeger. He raises a tiny pistol, the kind you saw women pull out of their purses in movies. I don't know where in the hell he got the thing, but I know damn well that things are about to go very, very badly.

"This is for my son!" he yells as he squeezes the trigger. A shot rings out and Traeger jerks backwards, spinning to the side as he falls. His men are on Kevin in an instant and have the gun out of his grasp before he can get off another shot.

Absolute chaos erupts. Screams ring out, children start crying and frantically running for their parents. Traeger's men begin barking orders, keeping everyone in the area but pushing them back from Traeger and Kevin, guns raised and trigger fingers at the ready. Kevin is slammed to the ground and his arms are yanked roughly behind his back.

Oh God, did Kevin kill him? Though I have no love for Traeger, I hope that Kevin failed. Not only would his men retaliate even if he's gone, word has it that his second in command, a big brawler looking fucker named Jett, is even *worse* than Traeger. He's too afraid to try to take Traeger's command by force, but if the seat was open for the taking? Oh yeah, he'd grab it and the result would be bad for everyone. As loathe as I am to admit it, Traeger's evil seems to serve a purpose at least. From the rumors I've heard about Jett, his is just for evil's sake.

The familiar man from before rushes to Traeger's side, but before he can do anything, Traeger sits up on his own. His bicep's pouring blood and will definitely need a few stitches, but it doesn't actually look that bad, at least from where I'm standing. Kevin had only winged him. That's good news, but this situation is far from good. The atmosphere is tense, feeling like a powder keg about to blow. All it would take would be one small spark, one act of aggression or one wrong word, and this park could become a shooting gallery. *No. No, no, no. There are children here. Please. Don't do this.*

As if reading my mind, Jonah presses to the front of the crowd, hands raised. I keep my eyes trained on the various guns pointed our direction, not daring to move, but the need to go to Jonah claws inside my chest. I hear his calm, quiet voice in between the cries and soft comforting words from parents to their kids.

"Please. Let the children go. Whatever you're going to do next, don't let the children see it."

Traeger studies Jonah for a long moment, and then nods to one of his men.

In a surprisingly gentle voice, the familiar guard from before says, "Take the children home. Everyone else stays put." Parents quickly scatter with their kids in tow, and the group that remains waits in tense silence. Traeger glances at his arm, at the blood running down his fingertips and dripping to the ground. I try to remain calm, but my mind is whirling trying to take in everything that's happening and trying to plan for what might come next. My body is tense, and though I don't have any weapons, I ready myself to fight if it comes to it.

Traeger shifts his gaze to Kevin, who's still being pressed roughly into the ground by one of the guards.

"Get him up," he says, voice cold as steel. An icy jolt of fear skates up my spine and my heart thunders in my chest. They haul Kevin to his knees and I wince at his bloody cheek and broken glasses. All of that fire and hatred from before has seeped out of him. Now, he simply looks broken. Defeated. Is it all setting in now that the haze of rage has subsided? The wife he's about to leave behind alone? The children he loved to teach that he'd just terrified and could have even gotten injured or killed? The friends he'd endangered? Attacks on Traeger and his men were *not* tolerated. Simple as that. We could all be punished for Kevin's actions.

Kevin's lip trembles as Traeger stalks closer to him.

"Now, I don't take too kindly to being shot at, as you can imagine."

He rears back and punches Kevin with his good arm. I force myself not to flinch but quiet gasps ripple through the crowd. I see some of the others turn their faces away so they don't have to watch. Kevin's head snaps to the side and the hit would have toppled him if Traeger's men weren't holding him up. Another punch sends blood spraying from Kevin's mouth with a grunt of pain. Traeger turns his back to us and takes a deep breath, bending his head to one side, and then the other, as if stretching before running a race or something.

When he turns back again, he says quietly, "There are rules..."

I suck in a breath as he slips a huge hunting knife free from the sheath at his hip, turning it slowly as he eyes Kevin coldly. Something about his demeanor is off somehow, but before I can figure out what, Jonah lunges forward and my heart stops beating.

Jonah stands in between Kevin and Traeger, hands up and palms out in a peaceful gesture.

"Just wait, ple—"

The butt of Jett's rifle hits him in the cheek with a sickening crunch, and he goes down hard, blood flying from his mouth. My world tilts and my blood goes cold, but my vision? That goes fucking *red*. All of my instincts and training switch immediately into the *GO TIME* position, and I'm a different person. I want to kill the son of a bitch who had just hurt Jonah. No, not *wanted* to. *Will*. I will kill Jett. Maybe not this very moment, but it will happen one day, it's as good as done. I'm not one to make idle threats. When I set my mind, that's it, there's no going back. I've always been that way, even as a kid. It had driven my dad crazy and was probably why I'd been so good at my job. If I was given a target or a task, once I set my sights on it, nothing could stop me from completing it, no matter how badly the odds were stacked against me.

There are very few people left in this world that I would do absolutely anything for, would cross any line to protect, and Jonah will always be number one on that list.

So, yeah, Jett's days on this earth are fucking numbered. It's now a cold hard fact, and that very dark, very real part of me that exists—though I like to pretend that it doesn't—is *delighted* by the idea of taking him out. I haven't always been this way. I'd had to do plenty of things that toed the line of right and wrong, some that flat out ignored the line, to be honest, but it had always been in an effort to help and protect people. And I'd taken that burden on easily, I'd been happy and proud to do the hard things to keep the world safe, but I'd never enjoyed it or looked forward to it.

But then the world ended and we were fighting for survival, and when I'd lost Gabby, I'd lost my humanity. Or almost had, anyway. Jonah kept me mostly afloat, but when it comes to protecting him, to protecting the people in this world that can't protect themselves, I'll let myself dip beneath the waves into that dark abyss, the one where my hands are permanently stained red and where screams and pleas for mercy echo.

"Don't move, you piece of shit," Jett spits at Jonah. He digs his fingers into the ground and groans in pain, and Jett boots him in the stomach, maybe cracking a rib or two, just for the hell of it, and that's all I'll allow to happen.

"Stop!" I scream, sprinting forward. One of the other FOSers tries to grab me, but I easily duck out of the way, spinning beneath his outstretched hand, and place myself between Jett and Jonah. I see Traeger eyeing me in my peripheral, but whatever he's thinking, I don't really give a shit. All I care about is Jonah and ending Jett's worthless life. I keep my eyes locked on Jett, calculating his every twitch, his every breath, readying myself. I run through six different scenarios in my mind of how this could go, where I'll strike first, where I'll defend and dip and duck, where and how I'll make the final blow. He has a gun but that won't matter much, not with him so close. I can strike before he has time to raise the barrel, and I'm fucking ready.

Jett's lips pull into a cruel sneer, a sick glee dancing in his muddy brown eyes, and I have his number in a nanosecond, no profile necessary: this man enjoys hurting others, but *especially* women. He gets off on it. With what looks like joy, he raises his gun again. I don't cower. Oh no, I bow up as I arch a brow and jut my chin, shifting my stance subtly, ready to act within a breath.

"I fucking *dare* you," I spit quietly.

Traeger roars, "Enough!" stepping closer to our little standoff. Jett reluctantly stops himself from doing anything, but the look in his eyes tells me that he plans to finish this at some point. I give him a look back that tells him I'm looking forward to it. Jett has no idea who he's just fucked with, but I'm more than happy to educate him. He narrows his eyes at me, clearly irritated that I'm not afraid of him, and I decide in this moment that when his time comes, it won't be quick. This fucker deserves to suffer a bit.

"What in the fuck is going on here? Have you all lost your god damned minds?" Traeger doesn't yell, but his voice is loud enough to be heard by the crowd and rings with absolute authority. Even I feel it and know enough to take it seriously. I tear my gaze from Jett to face Traeger. He seems to have forgotten about his wound, the blood running freely down his arm, dripping off of his fingers and splashing quietly on the asphalt. "Now, someone is going to pay the price," he adds, voice cold and sharp as a blade.

I clench my jaw. *Fuck.* I've made it worse. I hadn't thought it through, but I *had* to stop Jonah from being hurt. I can't let them suffer because of me. I have to diffuse this somehow...Gears start turning and a plan snaps into place. A really terrible, stupid, awful plan. A plan that will rip my heart out, but...it would be worth it if it keeps them safe.

Decision made.

I shift my shoulders back and take a deep breath.

"I'll go with you."

Traeger narrows his eyes.

"No, Mel!" Jonah rasps from the ground, spitting blood before continuing. "I won't let you do this."

"Not your choice, J," I say without taking my eyes from Traeger's. I keep my voice firm and even, but the words threaten to break me completely. I point to Kevin. "This man has a sick wife who needs his care. I'll go with you as collateral or a hostage or whatever the hell you want to call it. I'll be your pound of flesh—as long no one here will be harmed for this little...misunderstanding. Kevin *will* be punished by the Council, but there is no need to shed blood over this." I glance at the puddles of scarlet staining the ground. "*More* blood," I amend. He studies me with those green eyes that seem to see far too much as he stalks closer, and I force myself not to move an inch.

"And why would you be a good pound of flesh?" he asks quietly, a cool challenge in his voice. "Jonah would be the better choice. He's a leader here. I take him, I punish the community for this *misunderstanding*." He's right. Jonah *would* be the better choice, but I refuse to let that happen. *Think, think, think.* The obvious answer is to offer up my body, but I'm not ready to just throw that out there quite yet. Instead, I narrow my eyes. Traeger deals in power and strength. Might makes right and all that.

"You know I'm the unofficial head of security, and I'm the best shot in all of Haven. Hell, probably the entire country at this point, dare I say the world. You take me, you weaken their defenses—" I grind my teeth at the thought, but know they'll be ok, "—and gain my expertise in your arsenal." Jett snorts and I flare my nostrils, clenching my fists at my sides.

"I-it's true," a shaky voice says from behind me. "She's the best we've ever had and the one you want with you on any run. I've never seen anyone fight the way she does. We have ex-military guys and cops here, and she kicks all their asses. And she can cap a Bloody at three hundred yards." *Eight hundred,* I correct silently.

"God damn it, Mull," Jonah grits from where he's managed to pull himself up to his knees. Mulligan gives me an apologetic look, but I nod, letting him know that I understand and appreciate the assist. He sighs quietly and shifts his stricken gaze to Jonah, to the blood coating the side of his cheek. *He loves him as much as I do.*

"See. I'm better than anyone you have." Jett lets out a mocking laugh at that and I shoot him a killing look, running my tongue over my teeth before glancing back to Traeger. I would swear I see a hint of amusement in his eyes. "I'll cooperate, I won't put up a fight. I'll... *behave*," I grate, hating how the word tastes. "Just...please. Take me." I hesitate for the briefest moment before steeling myself and adding quietly, "I'll do *whatever* you want," making my meaning crystal fucking clear.

"Mel," Jonah whispers, half shocked, half pleading. We'd all heard the rumors about Traeger's compound, about the hell people endure there, especially the women. I might have just offered myself up to be the village bicycle for a bunch of psychos, but for Jonah, I'll do it. I'd do anything for him.

"You wanted me there before," I say, reminding him of his invitation. "Has that changed?" I hold his gaze, searching for...I don't know what, but whatever's there, I can't get a read on it. *Why the hell can't I read him?* I've rarely encountered anyone that gave me this much trouble. He finally leans in close.

"This is a one-way ticket, Melody. You have one chance and one chance only to change your mind." He says the words so quietly that only I can hear. "Let the old man pay the price and you can stay here with your people. Simple. Why ruin your life for his?"

He pulls back and straightens, and I have to crane my head back to meet his eyes. I hold his stare for a long moment, trying to dig through the layers of his words. Is he serious? Is this some kind of test? Is he mocking me? I honestly can't tell, but I know that my fate is already sealed. As much as I long to stay with Jonah, I won't let Kevin, and by extension, Sandy, suffer for this. I understand all too well the darkness that losing a child leaves inside of you, the rage that slowly eats away at your insides like a poison. I can't blame him for his actions here today. If I'd had the opportunity to end the one who took Gabby from me, I would have done it a thousand times over, but there are some-things you can't fight against, no matter how hard you want to.

I lift my chin defiantly.

"I stand by what I said." His eyes widen ever so slightly. "Do we have a deal or not?"

After what feels like an eternity, he finally nods. Without taking his eyes from mine, he calls to the others, "She comes with us."

"No!" Jonah groan-yells in denial.

Ignoring him, Traeger continues, "Kevin here will get ten lashes and spend six months under house-arrest. If he's let out before then, I *will* know about it," he says, the threat clear in his voice. "No other harm or retaliation will come so long as this punishment is upheld." He returns his gaze to me and adds, "And so long as you *behave*." His lips curl into a crooked grin that's somewhere between bemused and cruel. "Better go pack your things. We're leaving in an hour." He snaps his fingers at one of his men. "Get me the fucking Doc."

CHAPTER THREE

TRAEGER

GETTING FUCKING shot was not on my agenda for today. I grit my teeth against the pain, my entire arm burning with it, but sit still as Doc patches me up. The bullet just grazed me, so I really can't complain since it could have been much, much worse. I'm lucky that Kevin is a shitty shot.

"You're really bringing her back with us?" Jett asks, sounding like a petulant child. I know damn well why he doesn't want Melody at FOS. My second in command has been hiding things, but it's all coming to light now. He doesn't know the extent of my knowledge, but I'm sure he knows there are rumors going around about him. Whether he thinks I'll think of them as just that—rumors—or if I'll ignore them since I trusted him enough to put him in a position of power, I'm honestly not sure, but I can tell he's trying to be on his best behavior around me lately. Overcompensating and all that.

I give him a look now that tells him that I'm watching him closely and he clears his throat.

"Do you have a problem with that?" I ask, putting that calm, unwavering authority in my voice that serves me so fucking well when I need it to.

"No, no, of course not, sir, I just…I was worried about her making trouble, that's all."

Fucking liar.

"I think she'll behave herself when the safety of the people she cares about is on the line."

Jett looks like he wants to argue, but holds his tongue.

"You're the boss," he says nodding.

"You're god damn right I am."

He chuckles a bit and I grin at him, playing my part.

"What's the verdict, Doc. Am I going to live?"

Doc concentrates on his work as he finishes sewing up my arm, but glances up at me from under the rim of his thick glasses.

"For now." His lips curl at the corners and I smirk at him. Doc Hastings and I have…history. He knows my secrets and I know his, and he's one of the few people in the world that I count as a true friend. No one would ever know it, of course, but that's how it has to be. Everything is calculated. Everything is planned. Everything happens the way that it happens for a reason. I've worked hard to build this house of cards and it's finally mostly solid, the cards becoming real walls that don't threaten to topple at the slightest breeze. It's been hard and exhausting, but worth it.

"Glad to hear it." I turn to Jett. "Go help Johnson get everything ready. We'll be heading out soon."

Jett nods and heads out. Once the door closes, Doc sighs and punches me hard in my uninjured arm.

"Austin, what the fuck?"

"Hey, I didn't ask to get shot," I say defensively. He runs a hand through his hair, the dark brown streaked liberally with gray. "But I'm fine, so it's no big deal."

Doc looks at me like I have a dick growing out of my forehead. It's still hilarious to me that he's always gone by Doc—short for Murdock—but then ended up being an actual doctor. One of those happy little twists of fate that make me smile for some stupid reason.

"No big deal? If Kevin wasn't such a horrific shot, you could be *dead* right now."

"Some people might see that as a blessing," I point out and he gives me a dry look. "Can't really blame them." I try to shrug but it sends a searing pain radiating through my arm. I hiss in a breath through clenched teeth, and Doc lets out a long, measured exhale, looking so very tired and far older than his forty-five years. He wraps a bandage around my arm and shakes his head.

"One day," he mutters quietly, "one fucking day, it'll be enough." He gets up and washes his hands before rummaging through one of the cabinets. He hands me some pain pills and a cup of water, giving me a stern look until I down them. "Until then, be more careful for fuck's sake."

"Again, I didn't *ask* to get shot."

My arm is throbbing like a son of a bitch, but I try to ignore it. Hopefully whatever he's given me still packs enough of a punch to dull the pain a bit. We've got a long drive ahead and I don't need one more thing to worry about during it. Doc leans back against the counter and crosses his arms, studying me. It's a look I've seen a thousand times and as much as it drives me crazy, I also kind of love it. When he looks at me that way, it's like I'm the old me again, the *real* me. He's the only person on this planet who knows that guy anymore.

"So, you're really taking Mel?" There's a hint of disapproval in his voice.

"It was her idea and I gave her ample opportunity to change her mind." Both of these things are technically true, but at the end of the day, it's still my choice, my decision, and my fault. I know she won't soon forget that, but maybe one day, she'll understand.

"Uh huh…"

I sigh and heave myself up from the chair. He hands me small plastic bag with a handful more pills in it.

"Two pills, twice a day for the next week. I'm not too worried about infection on this one, but just to be safe. And these," he holds up a second baggy, "should help with the worst of the pain."

I tuck the bags in my back pocket and wrap him in a one-armed hug.

"Please try not to get yourself killed," Doc says, slapping me on the back but being careful of my arm.

"I make no promises," I tell him with a grin.

CHAPTER FOUR

MELODY

I DROP down beside Jonah and brush his shaggy hair from his forehead to inspect his cheek as Mull kneels on his other side. I don't think the bone is broken, but there's a nasty gash.

"This needs stitches," I sigh.

"I'll get him to Doc Hastings once he's done with Traeger…and Kevin," Mull says and we both wince, remembering Kevin's punishment. But given what happened, he pretty much got a slap on the wrist and everyone should be really fucking thankful. Mull slings Jonah's arm over his shoulder and helps him stand.

"How could you be so stupid?" he hisses at Jonah.

"I'm sorry," Jonah says, leaning heavily into Mulligan's side. "I just…reacted." Mull kisses his temple roughly, muttering something about Jonah being a lovable idiot. I've always been so happy that they'd found each other here, that Jonah found his second chance at happiness, but I'm even more grateful for it now. Jonah will need him when I'm gone. My eyes water, but I force myself not to cry. Not yet. If I start now, I'll never stop and I'll never be able to do this.

I look to the crowd that's still standing around looking a little shell-shocked.

"Chloe, go get Sandy. Tell her what happened and what's coming down the pipe for Kevin." Chloe was young, maybe seventeen or eighteen, and her eyes are still wide with fear as she stares unblinking at the puddles of blood all over the ground. Traeger's, Kevin's, Jonah's. So much blood spilled in such a short amount of time.

She's been at The Cove from the beginning, her family having been one of the first people to move into the neighborhood before the outbreak, so she's been spared from the worst of the violence of the world. I don't want to call her sheltered, but, well...if the shoe fits. She's a sweet kid though, always eager to help out around town and watch the kids.

"Chloe" I say again, gently gripping her shoulders and turning her away from the blood, forcing her to focus on me. "It's ok. Everything is fine, I promise, but Sandy needs your help. Can you help her for me?"

"I..." She shakes herself and swallows hard. "Yes, yes I can do that. I'll wait with her until...until they're done with him." She runs off and I head back home with Jonah and Mulligan. I feel like I'm walking in a dream, like nothing is real. I'd agreed to leave my home, to leave *Jonah*, and go live God knew where with Traeger and be subjected to who the hell knew what.

I don't really remember making it home or up the stairs, but the next thing I know, we're in my room and I'm packing up my things, feeling numb.

"I won't let you do this, Mel. I won't," Jonah protests from the bed. We got his cheek closed up with some butterfly bandages for now, but the sooner he gets to Doc, the better. He needs to take a look at his ribs too. *Fucking, Jett.* I grit my teeth and strangle an innocent pair of socks in my hand. The one good thing about being carted off to FOS will be having ample opportunity to off that bastard.

"It's already done."

I put my small wardrobe, spare boots and sneakers, and toiletries into a duffle, tossing in a handful of books and topping it off with Jonah's hoodie that I always steal.

"I'm taking this," I say thickly. Jonah lumbers off the bed and wraps me in a tight hug. I told myself I wouldn't, but I can't help it. I let the tears flow and allow myself a moment to break down. I clutch onto him like I've done so many times in our lives. I can't believe that I won't have him in my life anymore, that I'm actually leaving. How can I possibly do this without him? I haven't known a life without Jonah in almost twenty years. There's no way I can have one now, it just isn't possible. He's a part of me. And not just any part, the very best parts. Without him, I'm…I don't want to think about what I am without him beside me, keeping me afloat and pulling me back when the darkness starts to look too tempting.

But I have to do this. If this keeps him safe—and not just him, but everyone at The Cove—then I'll do it. I'll serve my time and survive somehow so long as they're alright. I pull away and sniffle, patting Jonah's chest.

"Maybe he'll let me come visit."

"Maybe," Jonah says through tears, giving me a sad smile. We both know he never will. I'll never come back to The Cove…probably never see Jonah again. Hostages never came back again. Letters could be sent to prove that Traeger was holding up his end of the bargain, but no one was ever allowed to come back again.

My heart feels like it's breaking in a way I didn't think was possible. I know that in this world, anyone can be taken at any moment, but Jonah has been such a fixture in my life for so long, I've always had this notion that somehow, that didn't apply to us. We defy the odds, transcend them. Our bond is bigger than Traeger or banishment or the entire fucking zombie apocalypse. *I will see him again,* I vow, right here, right now. *I will fucking see him again.*

I fill my canteen with water and put a few more protein bars in my backpack before adding the stuffed dog to the top, as I always do, along with a small photo album, and zipping it tight. I shoulder the pack and Mulligan grabs my duffle. I almost laugh at the sight. I'd always been the over-packer on every single trip, cramming three weeks' worth of clothes into suitcases for a two-day trip, sitting on them while Mitch struggled to get them zipped. Now, my entire life fits into a single duffle bag and a backpack. *Oh how times have changed.*

When we reach the front door, two of Traeger's men are waiting. I roll my eyes—did he really think needed an escort to the gallows?—and give them a double barreled salute as we pass by. One glares, the other chuckles. They trail behind us as we walk to the gate where

Traeger's little cadre is all loaded up and ready to leave. They're just waiting for their war prize.

My pulse starts to race as fear trickles in past the walls I'm trying so hard to keep up inside my mind. I have no idea what I'm walking into here. There are so many rumors about Traeger and his men, and about their compound—some horrific, some only mildly awful—but there's no way to know for sure. I try to mentally prepare myself for what might come. I'd been trained to withstand much worse than they can dish out. I *had* withstood much worse than they can dish out, I'm positive about that. I absently roll my right shoulder, remembering when it had been pulled from its socket and punched repeatedly. *Fun times.* So, I know I can survive whatever's about to happen, and somehow find my way back to Jonah, but that doesn't mean that it's not going to be painful as hell.

When we hear the vehicles, I stop and throw my arms around Mulligan's neck, squeezing him tightly.

"Take care of him for me, Mull," I whisper, nose burning with tears again, but I won't cry now. I had my moment with Jonah back at the house. Now, I need to be strong for him.

Voice rough, he says, "I will. I promise."

"I'd never be able to leave him if you didn't love him so much."

Mulligan squeezes me tighter and shudders, his big body shaking mine.

"You know I love *you* too, stupid."

I pull away and pat his bearded cheek, giving him a watery smile.

"I love you back. I mean, Mullody isn't complete without you." We both laugh at the terrible "couple" nickname we'd come up with for ourselves not long after he and Jonah got together, much to Jonah's chagrin. Cheap vodka may have been involved in the decision making, but it had stuck like glue. Mulligan and I become fast friends, feeling as if we'd known each other our whole lives. He worked his way into my tiny little bubble with Jonah almost instantly, and I'd been all too happy to expand it to encompass the burly man.

My heart splinters as I step away from him, but I know that it's about to shatter completely because next comes the impossible goodbye. I don't know how to do this. I can't. But...I have to. I know this was the right decision: this place needs Jonah. It doesn't need me. I've gotten them secured and safe. The rest of the security team can handle it now.

I hug him hard despite how much I know his ribs must be killing him.

"Mel, *please*, we can figure something else out." His voice breaks and it nearly does me in. I somehow keep the floodgates closed as I pull back enough to kiss his cheek.

"It's ok, Jonah. I'll be ok. I can handle this." I hold his gaze for an endless moment, memorizing every fleck of gold hidden within the brown of his eyes, the smile lines fanning out beside them, the small scar just above his left brow from a million years ago when he thought an eyebrow ring would look sexy—spoiler alert: it did *not* and it got super infected.

"Thank you for saving me," I tell him, putting as much love as I can into the words.

He huffs out a hoarse laugh. "You saved me way more."

"You know what I mean," I say. "You pulled me out of the dark place, more than once. I couldn't have done it on my own. I love you."

"I love you too, Mel." He pulls me in for another hug and whispers low in my ear, "I'll find a way to get you back. I swear."

I pull back and eye him.

"Don't you dare do anything stupid, Jonah Cothren. I swear I will kick your ass if you do." He laughs lightly. "But I will find a way to see you again, J. I promise. This isn't goodbye, just...see ya later."

He smiles at me through his tears and tucks a bit of hair behind my ear. And it's too much. I can feel the tiny bit of control I have left crumbling away, and I have to turn away before I completely lose it. I kiss his cheek and turn away, all but running towards the truck where Traeger's waiting by the open passenger door, assuming that's my assigned seat for this little road trip to hell. I can't look back or I'll never leave, so I jump in, throwing my pack at my feet and trying desperately to breathe. My throat feels thick, like it's closing up, and my heart's beating way too fast. I close my eyes and squeeze my hands into fists so tightly that my knuckles throb.

Traeger hops into the driver's seat and it isn't until we're nearly to the gate that my eyes fly open. I don't care if it destroys me, I have to see him. Jonah *has* to be the last thing I see as I leave this place. I spin and push up to my knees in my seat to stare out of the back window. I put my hand to the glass and Jonah raises his, as if we can touch. He leans heavily into Mulligan's side and I tell myself over and over that he'll be ok, they both will. *They have each other, they'll make it.*

But who do I have now?

Everyone I love is taken from me eventually.

I watch until the gate closes behind us. I lean my forehead against the cool glass for a long moment before finally turning back around. I settle into the seat, and though I hate the idea of letting Traeger see me like this, I can't stop the tears. I'm not allowing myself to fully feel the enormity of what's just happened or having a complete breakdown yet, but I let the tears silently fall as I stare out the window, feeling numb and dead and broken. Jonah is my light. Jonah is what keeps me from falling into the darkness, or when I do start to tumble, he pulls me out again. Can I do this without him?

I really don't know, but I guess I have no choice but to find out.

To my surprise, Traeger isn't a dick about it. In fact, he doesn't even say a word. He silently hands me a box of tissues and lets me say goodbye in peace.

CHAPTER FIVE

MELODY

EVENTUALLY, all of the vehicles pull off into the parking lot of an old fruit stand. My tears have long since stopped and I've come to terms with the situation as best as I can for now, but even after I was done crying, neither of us said a word. A little over an hour of complete silence next to a possible psycho who gets off on violence and pain. I should have used that time to study him without any distractions or a way for him to stop me, but I hadn't had the energy. Instead, I'd just stared out the window with my arms crossed. At least I know that FOS is northeast of The Cove, so that's more than I knew yesterday. Silver lining.

Now, he turns to me.

"If you need to go, now's the time." I shake my head, still not speaking, and he nods his in return. "Alright. I'll be back."

He exits the truck and I go back to staring out the window. Part of my mind catalogues everything, as it had been trained to do all those years ago, but that's second nature. I barely even register that I'm doing it and don't have to put much energy into it. Without thought, I count the men standing outside in loose circles, noting which ones go out behind the wooden building to take a piss and the exact amount of time each of them is gone, and the number of weapons each of them have strapped to their bodies. I map out plans of attack in my head, who I would take out first and how. I can see it so clearly in my mind it's like playing with action figures. Of course, I won't actually do any of it, but my mind prepares my body just in case.

I open my door and slide out to stand beside the truck, figuring I might as well stretch my legs. I have no idea how long this trip is going to take, so I better take the break while I can. I twist this way and that and stretch my arms over my head before pacing back and forth.

The familiar man approaches me. A guard? I sigh and stop my pacing to lean against the side of the truck.

"Does he really think I'm going to make a break for it already?" I ask.

The man laughs. "Just protocol, that's all. And you look like maybe you could use a friend," he adds softly. A friend? Here, among Traeger's men? Impossible. But as I eye him, I sense such sincerity from him, that I can't find it in me to turn him away or be a bitch like I would have done to almost anyone else in this moment. I tilt my head, studying him and trying to figure out why the hell he looks so damn familiar. Not in this world, but in the old one. I didn't know him personally, I know that much but...maybe he was a weatherman or something? I feel like I've seen him on television...

And finally, a lightbulb goes off.

I narrow my eyes and ask, "What's your name?"

"Wynn," he answers easily and my eyes widen.

I fucking knew that I knew him! Wynn Landry. I want to smile, but I'm not sure when I'll be able to do that again. *Maybe never.* Even so, something about seeing this man here makes something inside me relax a fraction. It's like having a piece of my old life back again some-how, as strange as it sounds. It's not like we were friends or anything, but still. He's a part of home in a way.

"You were one hell of a running back, Wynn Landry," I say a bit smugly. I cast him a sidelong look and my lips actually do tilt up slightly when he jerks in surprise.

"How..."

"I'm originally from Houma, and I graduated a few years ahead of you at LSU. Go Tigers," I add with a wink. He grins at that, the wide smile splitting his face and making his brown eyes sparkle. He's a handsome guy, that's for sure.

"Christ, it's been a long time since I've heard that," he says with a laugh, running his hand over his short hair. He eyes me. "Not much of an accent being from Houma." His own accent is still fairly thick and it makes a pang of homesickness go through me that I haven't felt in decades.

"That is a long story," I huff out. He doesn't press for more, just nods, as if he knows I'll tell him at some point, like he knows we're going to be friends or something. Hell, maybe it could happen. If I'm stuck in hell, at least I'll have a fellow Tiger there with me. We talk football for a bit, reliving the glory days of Saban and Miles.

"You were about to start playing for the Saints when the world went to shit, weren't you?" I remembered the news of his trade being big excitement for everyone in Louisiana, a very *small town hero coming home* kind of vibe.

"Yep. I was actually there house hunting when…when everything happened," he finishes quietly. I can tell by the flash of pain in his eyes that he lost people in those early days. I vaguely remember him being married, I think a cheerleader maybe? It was a really cute story…She must not have made it. I want to tell him that I understand, that I'm sorry, but before I can say anything in response, some signal I don't see has all of the men returning to their cars and Traeger heading back our way.

Wynn leans in and says in a low voice, "It isn't as a bad as you're thinking, I promise. Everything will be alright." I arch a brow at that, but Wynn just gives me a smile and nods to Traeger as he walks away. Traeger inclines his head in return and approaches the truck.

"Ready to go?" he asks, holding out a red bandana folded in the shape of a…

I straighten and narrow my eyes at him.

"Oh you've got to be shitting me."

"Standard procedure I'm afraid. I like my secret hideout to remain secret." I glare at his outstretched hand. I could argue, but since I'll know where we're going even without sight, I decide to let it go. Act like I'm *behaving* and all that. I still don't like it, but I can deal with it.

"Whatever," I mutter. Traeger takes a step towards me and I inhale sharply as he leans close to tie the bandana into a knot at the back of my head, his big body practically surrounding mine. I drop my arms to my sides and clench my hands into fists while he works. It's unnerving having him so close, in an almost intimate position. He tenses for a moment, but quickly finishes and steps away.

"There we go," he says. I grit my teeth but let him guide me to the passenger seat by my elbow.

"Think I can manage from here, thanks," I spit before the asshole tries to help me up into the cab, most likely with a grip on my ass. He chuckles lightly which only makes me grind my teeth harder. My jaw is already sore from it and I have to force myself to relax. I climb in and he closes my door. A few seconds later he slides into the driver's side.

"Can we just get this show on the road already?"

"As you wish," he says and I can hear the smile in his voice. *That bastard better not be quoting my favorite movie,* I think. *Better just be a coincidence.*

We drive, and drive...and just for a change of pace, we drive some more. I know for a fact that we've doubled back at least three times and seem to be taking as many detours as possible. *Shit.* Traeger isn't messing around with the whole secret location thing. By the third hour, I have no hope of being able to backtrack or tell you how far we've actually traveled or even in which direction.

Traeger thankfully doesn't try to make small talk, and instead just puts on music and quietly hums along. His taste in music is eclectic but actually mirrors my own, so at least I have that going for me. Just as Johnny Cash fades into Breaking Benjamin, a voice crackles through Traeger's walkie.

"Sir, we have Bloodies ahead near checkpoint Echo Fourteen."

"Take care of them," he says, that cool authority in his voice. Echo Fourteen? I'm burning with questions about his checkpoint system, how they're manned, how they're kept so hidden, all of the security measures in place, but of course I don't let a single one of them past my lips. Not like he would actually answer any of them anyway.

"Of course sir. I'll let you know once it's clear."

Traeger slows, puts the truck in park, and then, we wait. After a few minutes of silence, he says quietly, "I'm sorry."

"Save it," I spit, and he exhales roughly.

"You'll come to understand."

I huff out a humorless laugh. "Fat fucking chance, couyon."

"What part of Louisiana are you from?"

I cross my arms, annoyed that I still have this ridiculous blindfold on and that he's figured out even this small detail about me. Telling Wynn was one thing, but I don't want Traeger knowing a damn thing about me. I'd learned long ago to hide my accent for work, and eventually, it all but disappeared. I still have a faint drawl these days, but bits of my home accent and diction sometimes creep in without me realizing it now that I don't *have* to hide it, usually when I'm drunk or pissed. *Well, that explains why I've slipped with him twice already,* I think. Traeger seems to have knack for pissing me off.

I should probably watch my tongue, but I really don't care. I go ahead and let the full Cajun in me come right on out when I snap back at him.

"It's a small town called None of Your Fucking Business, bout twenty clicks south of Go Fuck Yourself. Ever heard of it?"

To my surprise, he chuckles, and I know he's filed something else about me away in his mind.

"Fair enough. *For now,*" he adds, that authority seeping back into his deep voice again. Not quite a warning, more of a promise. After that we go back to letting the radio do all the talking. I feel like he's watching me, so I try not to fidget. I want him to know that he has no effect on me whatsoever.

Eventually the *all clear* comes through the walkie and we start up again. Several more hours of driving pass before we finally turn off onto a rough, bumpy road before stopping again.

"You can take that off now," he tells me. I yank the damn bandana off and blink several times as my eyes adjust. It's still light out, but the sun will be setting soon. "We're stopping for the night."

He hops out of the truck and stretches his arms.

"Goodie," I mutter dryly as I open my door and get out. I stretch too, moaning quietly as my muscles unknot. I glance around and realize why the blindfold wasn't necessary for the night: we're in a small clearing completely surrounded by trees, no distinguishing land-marks to be seen. The vehicles have been pulled around to form a barrier between the tree line and the center of the clearing. Some of the men are unpacking sleeping bags and bedrolls, even a few tents, while others start a couple of fires. *They've done this before.* So, this must be a typical stopping point for them along the way then, and I'll admit, defensively, between the trees and the vehicles creating barriers, it's a good one.

"You can take care of anything that may be pressing that way," Traeger says, nodding towards a small path between two black SUVs.

"Privately?" I ask with an arched brow.

"Semi-privately."

He beckons to Wynn with two fingers. Well, if I have to be escorted to pee, I suppose Wynn is a better option than Jett. He's still throwing murderous looks my way, and it makes my skin prickle. Not in fear, but in anticipation. He'll make a move, I know it. Not tonight, but one day, he *will* come for me—and he won't be ready for what happens when he does. I suppress a smile at the thought, telling that dark, twisted part of me to quiet down.

"Don't suppose I get a weapon to protect myself?"

Traeger smiles at me, and I hate how attractive it is.

"The area has been thoroughly swept, no weapons needed, I prom-ise." His smile fades and his features grow serious. "You're smart, Melody. I'm assuming I don't need to tell you how bad of an idea it would be for you to try to run?"

I nod, telling him I won't do anything stupid, and his smile returns. He jerks his chin, telling me to get on with it then, so I sigh and waltz towards the opening with my shoulders back and my hair swishing behind me. I never leave the safety of the walls with it loose like this, but I hadn't exactly been in the best state of mind when we left The Cove. I'd been too focused on not falling apart and saying goodbye to the only people I love in this world.

I may be a prisoner for all intents and purposes, but I won't act like one. I won't cower and I make it clear with every line of my body that if they want to break me, they better come ready for a long, long fucking fight. Some of the group give me inquisitive glances or incline their heads in greeting. Some glare at me. A handful give me unmistakable looks of wanting. Those are the ones I'll keep in my sights.

"Sorry about this," Wynn says quietly as we make our way out of the circle of vehicles and walk a short distance into the tree line. There's a thick group of bushes a few yards away that will provide a little bit of privacy. He hands me one of the flashlights and a roll of toilet paper.

"Not much room for modesty in the apocalypse," I say as I take the offerings and throw him a mock salute that makes him laugh. I wind my way around the bushes, trying not to get snagged on the prickers. I don't tell Wynn that my modesty had been long gone before the end of the world. I'd been collecting beads at Mardi Gras since I was sixteen and had grown up hunting and camping with my cousins—no ladies rooms out in the backwoods.

Wynn continually makes noises while he waits—coughing, rustling leaves with his feet, talking about football. I actually grin. I can't understand why someone who seems so *good* is working for Traeger. Maybe his family is being held at FOS and he has to work to keep them safe?

When things are all taken care of, we make our way back to the campsite, and Traeger is waiting for us by the truck.

"You'll sleep in here," he says, nodding to the back of the truck. Do I imagine the quick glance he shoots at Jett across the clearing? I spy over the edge and see that a sleeping bag had been laid out inside the bed of the truck. I shrug, grab my pack from the cab, and hop up onto the tailgate. Wynn stands nearby as Traeger makes his rounds to speak to some of the men, probably planning for the rest of the trip. I wonder how much longer we have before we get to FOS. I can't deny that I'm intensely curious about the place, despite the fact that I wish with everything in me that I wasn't going there. It's like getting a chance to check out Area 51 or something. Who wouldn't be a little excited for that?

Food starts being doled out and, to my surprise, I'm handed a can of green beans and some sort of jerky by a short, stocky guy with a long, bushy orange mustache. I take it with a nod of thanks and he bustles along without a word.

"You look surprised," Traeger says as he walks back over to the truck.

"Figured starvation was part of the Hostage Package at FOS."

He gives me one of those inscrutable looks again, studying me in a way that makes me uneasy, but then his lips curl up at the corners as he leans his elbows on the edge of the truck bed.

"You have a lot to learn about me."

"I know everything I need to."

He shrugs and though it's nonchalant, there's a sense of challenge there that makes me narrow my eyes. He straightens and slaps the truck where his arms were just resting.

"Sleep well, Melody."

Things settle down pretty quickly after that as everyone finishes eating and hunkers down to sleep. Sixteen men sleep on the ground around the campfires or in the tents, and the missing four must be on patrol. Wynn and Traeger round out the group of twenty-two, standing near the truck. I won't be sleeping, but I'll pretend to. Maybe Wynn and Traeger will be chatty and I can glean some new information about…well, anything, really. Any intel is good intel.

They talk quietly, but move far enough out of earshot that I can't make out much. I sigh in frustration and roll onto my back, staring up at the sky. The stars shine so much brighter now without all the smog and city lights blocking them out. I try to focus on them and the beauty that I wish so many other people were still around to share with me. I try not to let myself think of Jonah, of how he'd looked as we drove away from him today. Before I can stop it, my mind drifts back instead.

Back to the beginning of the end.

CHAPTER SIX

MELODY

"ARE YOU AT HOME?" *DeWitt asked, voice tense.*

"Yeah. They said they had a bad flu outbreak going around, so they sent us home for now to be safe," I said quietly, stroking Gabby's hair but being careful not to wake her up. She was still acting mostly like herself, but she was getting tired out more easily and more often. I tried to ignore it.

"Flu," he muttered, almost to himself. My brows drew down.

"What's up, Whitt?" I asked. "Are you alright?"

"I'll be at your place in ten minutes."

Apprehension prickled down my spine. Something was wrong. Something big if he didn't want to just tell me over the phone.

"Alright, I'm here." He hung up and I eased Gabby's head off of my lap, settling a pillow beneath her cheek instead. She sighed but didn't wake. I kissed her forehead, made sure Leo was tucked in safe beside her, and went to wait for Whitt on the front porch. He pulled up twelve minutes later and hopped out of the car, barely even putting the thing in park first.

"What the hell is going on, Whitt?" I asked as he jogged up the front steps, urgency written in every tense line of his body. He wrapped me in a quick hug and when he pulled away, I could see how exhausted he looked. Exhausted and...afraid. I swallowed hard.

"Inside," he said on a rough exhale.

Once in the kitchen, I leaned back against the counter and crossed my arms over my chest. He ran his hands through his hair, making the blonde strands stand up at funny angles. When was the last time he had a haircut? I'd known Justin DeWitt for almost a decade, and aside from a handful of times when it wasn't possible, I'd never seen him without a fresh haircut and a clean shave. The more I studied him, the more I realized he looked downright haggard right now. Still handsome, of course, but haggard all the same.

We'd hated each other the moment we met. We were both competitive to a dangerous degree and happened to be each other's biggest competition. That made for a bad combination. We were top of our class at the Academy—me first, him a close second—before both being pulled out for specialized training, where again, we were both in the running for top dog. We'd been placed on the same Ops Team and were constantly at each other's throats. But eventually, we'd been stuck in a particularly sticky (i.e. life or death, leaning towards big time death) situation together, and we'd emerged friends. He'd saved my ass, I'd saved his, and we'd both had nightmares about it for years afterward. We'd bonded to say the least.

Since then, we'd both moved on to new jobs, new departments, new lives, but we'd remained forever close.

"Fuck, Mel. I'm not supposed to be telling you this. Hell, I'm not even supposed to know, but POTUS owes me big time..."

"Whitt, I need you to say more words. Coherent ones. Now." Anxiety was already starting to gnaw at my gut, a numb, cold feeling settling deep in my bones. He took a deep breath and met my gaze.

Keeping his voice low, he said, "There's something bad coming down the pipe, Mel. Big bad. The flu outbreaks aren't flu outbreaks. We've been containing the news as much as possible, but we won't be able to much longer. It's spreading too fast and we don't know how to stop it. We're barely containing it right now..."

"Not the flu? What then?"

"We don't know, exactly. But..." He blew out a long breath, as if steeling himself for what he was about to say. "It's a near-extinction event, Mel." My heart stopped beating completely for a long moment before roaring to life again with an ominous thud, going into overdrive. Extinction?

"What..."

"It's a disease or a virus or hell, maybe the End of Days from the hand of

God himself. People are dying and...fuck, I know it sounds crazy, but they're coming back to life, Mel." I nearly snorted but the look in his eyes told me that this was no laughing matter. No joke. No trick. "And if that wasn't fucked up enough, they're coming back all kinds of wrong. We're talking horror movie shit here."

"What?" I breathed. That just wasn't possible. Like he said, it was something out of a movie for fuck's sake. I looked around the corner at Gabby, making sure she was still asleep. My blood turned icy as worry and cold hard reason warred within me. It wasn't possible. It just wasn't. *But I knew that Whitt wouldn't bullshit me on this. He wouldn't have come with some crazy, half-cocked notion of something going on unless he had proof—or the word from the very, very top.*

POTUS owes me big time...

"I know it sounds batshit, Mel, but I swear to God it's true. I've watched it happen with my own eyes at the research hospital that officially doesn't even exist outside of Quantico. It's...bad." He quickly explained what happened, the symptoms of the initial illness and the insanity that came after. "It's going to start spreading beyond our ability to control the news soon. And when that happens...they're going to take extreme measures to try to stop it from getting too far too fast."

"Extreme measures?" I echoed in question. I already knew the answer, but I squeezed my eyes shut waiting for him to respond all the same, needing to hear the words out loud.

"They're going to bomb the most populated areas. That's where the most cases are being seen, of course, in the big cities. They think if they do that, it'll be enough. It won't be," he added quietly, "but they have to try."

"Jesus," I breathed, my heart thundering in my ears, but entire body feeling numb and cold.

"I don't know exact dates, but it'll be soon. A week, maybe two. Mel, this is...it's bad," he said again. "It's scary. I'm telling you that I'm fucking scared." I met his eyes and saw it there again. Fear. Fear like I'd never seen in Whitt's eyes before. Even when we'd been locked in that cell together, tortured, thinking we were going to die, there hadn't been fear like this...

That forced all doubt away, silencing that part of my mind that refused to accept that something like this could be real. It was real. It was happening. I needed to accept it and move on to the next phase: preparation. That's why

Whitt was there, I knew. To give us time to prepare, to give ourselves the best chance at survival.

"You need to leave. Pack up as many supplies as you can, get Jonah, take that little girl—" he pointed towards the living room and his voice broke, my chest cracking at the sound. I knew how much he loved Gabby too, like she was his own flesh and blood. "—and get as far away from the city as possible. Go to the lake house, and take as many backroads to get there as you can. Once it starts, it's going to go fast. Too fast."

I forced breaths in and out of my lungs. I glanced to a picture on the fridge of our last trip to the lake house, taken just as Gabby's fish made its break for freedom and Jonah was falling off of the dock. It was mostly in middle-of-nowhere territory, deep in the woods on a large lake with the closest neighbor at least a few miles away. Even the nearest real town was an hour, anything closer than that were just mom-and-pop convenience and bait shops. If we needed to avoid people—and fucking bombs apparently—it was a solid choice. But...

"Whitt, I can't. You know I can't."

"I know, Mel." His voice was tight with understanding and pain and misery. "But you have to. You have to take her and just...do the best you can for as long as you can." Now the breaths wouldn't come no matter how hard I tried. The aching in my chest was nearly unbearable. I tried to lock my mind down and compartmentalize everything. I couldn't lose it now. I had to be strong, for Gabby and for Jonah. I had to get them through this, no matter what.

"Look, I know your instincts are going to tell you to warn others, but you can't, Mel. If people knew what was coming..." He let out a shuddering breath. "You have to play this one close to the vest. It's a shit call, but it's the right one, trust me in this. Jonah and no one else, got it?"

"I understand," I said, already making a plan and several back-up plans, a running list of supplies, and mapping out different possible routes out of town in my head.

"What about you? Tell me you're leaving."

"I'm heading to meet my brother and his family down at granddad's old farm as soon as I leave here. Car is already packed." Good. The farm was in Podunk, North Carolina, so they should be safe. From the bombs at least. Fuck, I still couldn't really make myself think about what else was coming. I

knew it without Whitt having to spell it out: widespread panic and desperation and violence.

"Ok, good. Give Lila a hug for me."

He pulled me into a bear hug then, squeezing me so tightly, like it was the
last time he would ever do it. I realized with a cold, sinking feeling that it
probably was.

"Stay safe, Mel." He pulled away and held me at arm's length. In a gruff
voice, he added, "You know I love you, asshole."

My eyes watered. This was goodbye, though neither of us would dare say
it. We shared a look, one that said so fucking much with no words needing to
be spoken.

"I love you too, jackass."

I hugged him one more time because I couldn't not hug him one more
fucking time, and when I pulled away, he gave me a warm smile, wiping a tear
from my cheek.

"Survive, Mel. Do whatever it takes. I mean it—whatever it fucking
takes. Things are going to get really bad before they get even a little bit better,
but I know you can make it through this, Mel. I fucking know that you can."

With that, he turned away and walked through the living room. He leaned
down to kiss Gabby on the forehead, careful not to wake her. His shoulders
shook as a silent sob racked through his body. My heart splintered but I knew
already that this was far from the hardest goodbye to come. He gave me one
last look, a half-hearted smile, and a nod, and then walked away from me for
the last time.

After he was gone, I went back into the kitchen. I leaned over, gripping the
edge of the countertop so hard my fingers throbbed, and took a few gasping
breaths, careful to still be quiet. My heart was racing and I felt like I couldn't
breathe as I really let myself think about what was happening, what was
going to happen. A lot of people were going to die. And some of them weren't
going to stay that way. Our entire existence was going to change in ways I
couldn't even fully imagine. We were going to be fighting for our lives in a
world that wasn't going to make it easy. I had to slide to the floor and put my
head between my knees then before I passed out completely.

I forced myself to focus and get myself under control. I'd had years of
training to be able to keep my shit together in any situation, and this was no
different. Sure, a zombie fucking apocalypse hadn't exactly been on the

curriculum in any of the classes after the Academy, but still, all the same logic and techniques applied. So, I slowed my breathing, inhaling for four seconds, holding for another four, and slowly exhaling for the final four. Over and over until my rhythms all settled back into a normal range. I took all the panic and fear and put it in a nice little box that I compartmentalized neatly in the back of my mind. Now wasn't the time to deal with those. Now was the time to start planning.

I pulled myself up and texted Jonah to get back home as soon as possible. He'd just run out to grab take-out from our favorite Thai joint down the road, but I needed him here. Jonah and his husband, Sean, had lived just a few houses down from us originally. Sean and Mitch had been best friends since bootcamp, had gone into Special Forces together, had been stationed together —and because sometimes the universe is awesome, they had found spouses who were plutonic soulmates too. After Sean and Mitch had been killed in action on the same mission, it had just made sense for Jonah to move in with me and Gabby, and we'd been together ever since.

Not a minute later, Jonah came in the front door. I waited for him in the kitchen, trying to figure out how the hell to break this news to him.

"Hey, I was already turning into the neighborhood when I got your text." He sat the bag of food on the counter. "Are you starving or what?" he added with a laugh. It smelled delicious but I had zero appetite now. He was smiling widely but it faded as he met my eyes. "What's going on?" he asked, voice tense, knowing something was wrong. He immediately shifted his eyes to Gabby, still sleeping soundly on the couch.

"She's fine," I assured him and he relaxed a fraction. I pulled out two beers and popped them open. "You're going to need this," I said, handing him a bottle and taking a deep swig of mine before filling him in on everything Whitt had told me and everything I thought it might mean.

"Jesus," he said, running a hand through his dark curls. But, God bless him, he didn't question it, didn't think I was crazy or had gone down some conspiracy theory rabbit hole on social media. He glanced down at his watch.

"The lake house is solid, but I'll take the trailer and go to Bulk-N-Go now, they're open for another few hours. You start packing up what you can here." Jonah wasn't a Prepper exactly, but the lake house was always well-stocked in the event we got snowed in or the road washed out during bad storms, or anyone ever needed a place to disappear for a while. With my jobs—past and *present*—*there was always plenty of danger and we had friends in the same position. We both just liked to be prepared.*

"Sounds good. *Grab as much as you can, I'm talking load that thing down, J. If anyone asks, tell them it's for the Cobra's training camp." Jonah snorted. He hated the Cobras with a passion, but their training camp was happening right down the road, so it was a legitimate excuse. "Bottled water, protein bars, all the non-perishable stuff you can find: canned veggies and fruit, peanut butter. Oh and honey! Get lots of honey." Memories of my mamaw telling me the hundred different ways she could use honey sprang to my mind. "And toilet paper. Fuck what else...medicine and first aid supplies. And those fruit snacks she likes," I added, shaking my head, eyes watering. "I know it's dumb but*—"

Jonah cradled my face and made me meet hie eyes.

"I will buy out every God damn box of fruit snacks they have. And Oreos too. Our girl will have everything she could want, alright?"

I gripped his wrists and mirrored his steady breathing before mine could get out of control again. Eventually I was settled enough to give him a small smile and a nod.

"Thank you," *I whispered. As always, Jonah grounded me and gave me the strength to keep moving forward.* "After Bulk-N-Go, swing by Outdoorsman and grab extra camping and hunting gear. Ammo too."

He nodded, pulled me into a hard hug and kissed the top of my head before heading out, a determined set to his shoulders. Jonah had worked in the capital for years as a campaign manager before getting tired of the hustle and bustle—and lying politicians, really—and started his own landscape architecture business. He knew how to handle pressure and keep his cool no matter how hot the situation got and I was never more grateful for it than I was in that moment...and I knew I would need it in the days, weeks, years to come.

I started packing things up, letting Gabby sleep as long as she could. When she finally woke, I told her we were taking a surprise trip to "her" house as she always called the cabin on the lake. She loved it more than anywhere else on the planet and had claimed it as her own pretty much as soon as she could talk.

"For really?" *she asked, eyes lighting up. My heart cracked a little, remembering how upset she'd been when I told her that we wouldn't be able to* go up there for a while because the doctors said—I stopped the thought in its tracks.

"For really really," I said, plastering a smile on my face and hiding everything else. I vowed right then that I would shield Gabby from all of it for as long as I could. "But you gotta pack! As much as you can, hurry hurry! I'll time you!"

She screeched in pure joy and I winced, laughing despite everything else going on. The kid had pipes, that was for sure. She ran around like a tiny tornado, racing the imaginary clock I had ticking down, and packed up her unicorn suitcase and her mermaid duffle bag. I watched with a smile on my face as she debated between three different princess dresses and eventually decided on taking them all. I would pack anything essential that she overlooked later, but for now, I didn't dare make her leave anything behind that she wanted to bring. Of course Gabby didn't know it, but we would never be coming back to this house, at least not for a long, long time. I could barely swallow from the sudden lump in my throat.

We were leaving this house, probably forever. The house where Gabby had taken her first steps, where we'd said goodbye to Mitch for the last time, where Jonah and I had held each other together when we'd each lost the loves of our lives at the same time. There were painful memories here, but also so many beautiful ones. I ran a finger along the marks on the doorframe where we kept track of Gabby's height, but forced away the tears when Gabby asked how many coloring books she should bring.

Gabby eventually tired herself out again and I watched her sleep for a long time, Leo clutched in her little hands, despite how much still needed to be done. I didn't know what was coming, but I hated that my daughter was going to be stuck in the middle of it. I felt helpless...and like a failure. Parents were supposed to protect their children, and I hadn't been able to do that for Gabby. The hits had just kept coming and I couldn't fend them away no matter how badly I wanted to. I wiped tears from my eyes, kissed Gabby's head, and got to work.

THE NEXT MORNING, the tailer was loaded down with everything you could think of: food, water, blankets, clothes, extra cans of gasoline, medicine,

camping gear...and an entire arsenal of guns and ammo. After my conversation with Whitt, I had a bad feeling that the world was headed into a dark,
dangerous place, and I wasn't taking any chances.

I glanced across the street to Mrs. Huggins' house. She was a widow and
surrogate grandmother to all three of us, and had been there through some of
our worst days. I worried at my lip with my teeth and Jonah, as always,
seemed to read my mind.

"Go on. One more won't hurt."

I gave him a smile and squeezed his arm in thanks and love and a thousand other emotions. I jogged over and knocked on the door, trying not to bang
urgently like I desperately wanted to. I could hear Mrs. Huggins moving
around inside, slowly making her way to the door. She was eighty-eight and
on hospice for end-stage pancreatic cancer, but she could still maneuver
around fairly well. She was a tough old bird, as she liked to call herself. She'd
refused an in-home nurse, but didn't fight when Jonah and I took turns
coming over to help her out every day after work.

The old woman finally opened the door and gave me a warm smile.

"Melody, good morning, sweetheart! How are you?"

"I'm alright," I said with the closest thing to an easy smile I could muster
up. "Can I talk to you for a second?"

Mrs. Huggins glanced over my shoulder, eyeing Jonah's truck and trailer
as he put in the last of the supplies and bags. She arched a brow at me.

"Going on a little vacation?"

"We're headed out to the lake house, but that's what I need to talk to you
about."

"Well, alright then, come on in, honey."

We settled into her small living room and I laid out what was happening
as best as I could for the old woman. To her credit, she didn't laugh in my face.
Her brows drew down as she listened, gripping the handle of her cane tightly.

"So, will you come with us? Please, Mrs. Huggins, it won't be safe here,
but I promise you we will be out at the lake."

She smiled at me and stood, holding up a finger, telling me to hold on a
minute. I waited patiently—semi-patiently anyway—as she clamored around
in her bedroom for a few minutes. I assumed she was packing up things and
called out offering help, but she ignored me. She eventually returned, holding
an old hat box. I eyed it, half in confusion, half in amusement. I supposed if

anyone were going to ride into the apocalypse in proper Sunday style, it was going to be Mary Huggins.

"I think we need more than just a hat. I can help you pack up, it's no troub —" Mrs. Huggins cut me off firmly, but gently.

"I'm not coming with you, honey."

My heart clenched but she patted my hand softly, smiling as she settled down into the chair again and handed me the box. She nodded towards it and with a furrowed brow, I opened it. My heart sank into my feet and my stomach felt like a bundle of snakes, coiling and writhing around each other. Inside were vials and vials of morphine and bottles of every prescription pain killer the woman had.

"Mrs. Huggins?" I whispered around the lump in my throat. I knew what this meant. I knew what she would say. She gave me a sad smile.

"She's going to need it more than me, sweetie. I've only kept enough to help me take a very nice, long-awaited nap when the time comes." I tried to speak but couldn't. If I'd tried, I would have just broken down into sobs that might not have ever stopped. "I've got Harold waitin' on me anyway. He's probably disgruntled I've made him wait this long already," she added with a wry smile and I huffed out a small laugh through my welling tears.

"And I don't think I'm up to fightin' off whatever it is that's coming down the road. I've lived a good, long life, and I'd rather end it on my own terms." A tear escaped and slid down my cheek, and Mrs. Huggins smiled, cupping my face gently. "You get somewhere safe and...do the best you can. Cherish the time you have."

I gave her a big hug, holding on for dear life. I knew this wouldn't be the last goodbye—or nearly the hardest—that I would face in the months or years to come, but it didn't make it any easier to manage. I finally pulled away and Mrs. Huggins wiped away her own tears and then mine.

"Goodbye, sweetheart. Thank you for making a lonely old bird feel like part of the family. It meant the world to me. Send those other two scoundrels over here for a quick goodbye hug if you don't mind."

I did and while Gabby said her goodbyes, talking animatedly about all the things she was going to do at the lake, I showed Jonah what was in the box. He sucked in a harsh breath, as if he hadn't been allowing himself to think about what was coming either. He wrapped me in a hug and we silently gave each other the strength we needed to make it through this. Somehow, someway, we *would. We would survive, no matter what came for us, but we'd only do it together.*

We got Gabby strapped in, happily playing some strange game on her tablet that involved aliens and unicorns and a giant slingshot, and we pulled away, saying goodbye to the lives we'd known and bracing ourselves for the unknown, admittedly terrifying future waiting for us.

CHAPTER SEVEN
MELODY

"IS THE BLINDFOLD REALLY STILL NECESSARY?" I demand when Traeger comes towards me with it again on the third day. I'm over it big time. There' no way in hell I could possibly tell you where we were, what direction we'd gone, or even how far we were from the other settlements at this point. The secret lair's location would be remaining secret.

I'd forced myself to remain awake all night in the back of the truck in the clearing. Partly because I didn't want to see what kind of dreams might be waiting for me—painful ones, most likely—and partly because I didn't trust these people as far as I could throw them. I'd slept during the drive on the second day, conceding that I was probably safe with only Traeger in the car. The dreams were still there waiting and I woke gasping and clawing at nothing more than once. Though I couldn't see his face because of the stupid blindfold, I got the feeling that Traeger was studying me and I hoped to all things holy that I hadn't been talking in my sleep.

We'd camped out again the second night, this time in the office of Richard P. Johnson, CPA. I'd eyed the door with a snort.

"I know right?" Wynn said quietly, chuckling low. "I mean, his name is essentially Dick P. Dick. His parents must have hated him." I'd given him a small smile before Jett had bumped me roughly as he entered, making sure I knew that he was still large and in charge. I glared and *may* have made a gesture that suggested a certain male appendage was being, uh, *serviced* with my hand and then erupting onto Jett's back. Wynn tried to hide his laugh with a cough.

Traeger ushered me into a small office where I got to camp out in private, again reminding me not to get any bright ideas of trying to escape out the small window—both the room and the building itself would be guarded all night, he assured me. I'd moved the small chair in front of the door as soon as he'd walked out, shifted the bookcase in front of the window, and let myself sleep through most of the night.

Traeger eyes me now in that intense way of his and I force myself to meet it, jutting my chin stubbornly.

Finally, he sighs and hands me the bandana. "I guess we've traveled far enough that you can go without now."

I throw the thing onto the dash as hard as I can and Traeger chuckles. I give him a sidelong glance before turning my attention out the window. The caravan of vehicles pulls out of the parking lot and eventually makes its way to a small scenic highway, thick forests or open farmland on either side for as far as I can see.

"How much longer?"

He shifts to place his right hand on the wheel and rests his left elbow on the open window frame, looking so casual, as if we're just out for a nice little Sunday drive, heading to the movies or something.

"A few hours now," he says, rubbing his thick stubble before dropping his arm back on the window again.

I prop my feet up on the dash and catch Traeger gazing at my bare thighs before quickly jerking his eyes back to the road. I probably should have opted for jeans, but it's still sweltering out and I didn't feel like suffering during this ride any more than I had to. Traeger shifts in his seat and absently traces the base of his ring finger with his thumb. My eyes narrow a fraction. I'd noticed him doing it before too, and I add it to my mental profile on him. A tell of some sort? Or just an absent-minded habit, like me with biting my thumb nail? I scowl when

I realize that I'm doing it now and drop my hand just as a swift stab of pain laces through my chest.

Whitt used to tease me mercilessly for it. I wonder for the thousandth time what might have happened to him. I hope that he made it to the farm and that his family is still there, safe and together. Maybe they found other people—*good* people—and formed their own little version of Haven. I'd tried to figure out a way to contact him a lot at the beginning, even tried Jonah's dad's old ham radio a handful of times in case he had the same idea, but nothing ever came of it. We'd even thought about trying to find his grandpa's place when we left the lake house, but a bunch of Bloodies and other groups and people in need of help had other plans. I still think about him though, still let myself hope that he's still out there somewhere, happy and whole and alive.

I turn my gaze back to the window and try to mentally prepare for what might happen when we arrive. Will I be thrown in a cell? Tortured? Used and abused for entertainment? Jett's cruel smile flashes in my mind and I clench my teeth. I'll endure. I've had worse from better, and can handle whatever they throw at me if it means keeping Jonah and the others safe, but that doesn't mean that I'm excited about it.

Just like the previous two days, Traeger doesn't try to talk, just lets the music play and lets me stew in my thoughts. Maybe this is part of his game. Not speaking and letting my imagination run wild with all the possibilities so I'm a nervous wreck by the time we arrive. Mental warfare.

I decide to stop worrying about what's to come because honestly, it doesn't matter. It will be what it will be and thinking about it won't make a bit of a difference. So, I let my thoughts shift back to Traeger instead. He's bugging me. Or, not *him*, exactly, but my mental profile on him. There are pieces that aren't fitting quite right, and I've never been good at letting puzzles go without solving them.

I think back to the altercation with Kevin, something about it nagging at the back of my mind. I replay it over and over before it finally hits me. When Traeger had pulled the knife, ready to kill Kevin, there hadn't been that sadistic glee in his eyes that I'd expected, no flash of impending pleasure and power. No one else would have noticed, I'm sure, but I'm not anyone else. Noticing details, reading people and seeing them in ways most of the population didn't, had been my job—and I'd been damn good at it.

No, in that moment with the knife, I hadn't seen excitement at all. I'd seen...something else. Something that really doesn't fucking add up. I turn to stare at him with a frown, tilting my head.

"What?" he asks, not taking his eyes from the road.

"Nothing, just..." I purse my lips and shake my head. "Nothing."

"Trying to figure me out?" he asks, that challenging smirk tilting his lips up on one side.

"Nothing to figure out, I've got your number," I say confidently, though it's only about eighty percent true at this point. He quirks a brow and I turn away again to watch the scenery fly by in a blur. I hang my hand out of the window, letting it rise and fall in small waves as the wind rushes by. A flash of a memory of Gabby's small hand doing the same thing hits me out of nowhere and I yank my arm back in, cradling it to my chest.

"You alright?"

"Fine," I say quietly. He doesn't push and we settle back into silence again. After several more hours, a few more detours, and a bathroom break, we finally turn off the main road and pass beneath a tall wooden arch, a carved sign hanging in the middle.

"The Lodge?" I read as we pass below it.

"I prefer FOS," he says with a smirk. I shrug as if I couldn't possibly care less, but why he calls this place FOS is a mystery that I would love to solve. *Just like the man himself.* I scowl to myself. Why the hell does it matter if I figure him out? Why do I even care? I shouldn't. I don't. I may not know everything about him, but I know enough, so I tell myself to just fucking drop it.

The woods are thick on either side of us, dense green foliage and chunks of dark gray rock scattered between the towering pines. Are we close to the mountains? The terrain reminds me a bit of hikes we'd taken on vacation in the Smokies way back when. We cross a wooden bridge over a small stream and I have to admit that it's idyllic. I lean forward in my seat when something finally comes into view: a small gatehouse in the middle of the road. At one point, those flimsy arm-type gates that raised and lowered stood on either side for the entrance and exit, but those had been replaced by giant sheets of metal that roll to the side to allow entry. They're waiting open for us now and as we drive through, I see that a tall wrought iron fence branches off from either side of the road, and, I assume, surrounds the entire place.

Though I prefer the solid stone wall of The Cove, the spaces between the bars aren't nearly large enough for anyone to squeeze through, Bloody or otherwise, and it's too high for anyone to easily climb—not to mention the barbed wire and sharpened spikes on the tops of the posts would be good deterrents for climbing anyway. An entire herd of Bloodies could probably knock the fence down with enough force, but they wouldn't have to worry about anyone slipping through undetected here. A decent outer defense system, I'll give them that.

The Lodge finally comes into view and I raise my brows in surprise.

"Whoa," I whisper. I hadn't actually meant to say it out loud, but I'm too tired and keyed up to give a shit.

"Home sweet home," Traeger drawls.

It's a giant—and I mean *giant*—log cabin with two long wings branching out from the main building. Five floors in the center, three on the outer wings. Who in the hell lived here? A billionaire by the looks of it…Then I realize we're driving through a parking lot and everything clicks into place: it's a *hotel*. Or, used to be anyway. It probably has at least two hundred rooms, maybe more, depending on how big they are. A second large building connects to the main one by a wooden breezeway and the sign over the door reads *The Cast Iron Skillet*. On-site restaurant and bar, I assume. Half of the parking lot is full of vehicles and mismatched storage buildings of various sizes, and a handful of people are milling about in what appears to be a large garden off to the left. A greenhouse stands on the other side where tennis or pickleball courts may have been once upon a time, tall fences still surrounding the structure. Beyond the hotel, a large lake stretches out as far as I can see, trees surrounding the entire thing, and mountains in the distance behind that. Small cabins dot the edge of the lake, and there's a small beach area and dock on one end, a stack of kayaks and paddle boats still sitting nearby.

It's beautiful. *Gorgeous*, really.

I study everything, taking in as many details as I can. I cock my head as I look at the cars in the lot again: on one side, they're all utility vehicles and beat up trucks, but on the other, they're nice. Like, *really* nice. Jags and Bentleys, and I even spy an Aston Martin that I want to slide into so badly I nearly moan. I'd, uh, *borrowed* one once in Nepal and dear God it had ridden like a dream. I have a thing for sleek, fast cars—they're just plain sexy. Bikes too. Anything that can make me feel like I'm flying.

I keep scanning and see that a handful of electric cars and hybrids are thrown in the mix too, but even those are high-end brands.

Now I look at everything with a new eye: the guardhouse, the ornate iron fencing, the high-end cars and ample amenities. This place wasn't just a hotel, it was a luxury resort. *Rustic elegance.* I guess if you're riding out the apocalypse, this is a pretty nice spot to do it. Or at least it looks that way on the surface. I remind myself that plenty of the people here are being held against their will, probably tortured and used as slaves and God knew what else. It might be heaven on earth for Traeger and his right hands, but for everyone else? Who the hell knows.

The caravan parks and I get out of the truck, not sure if I'm about to be tied up or thrown in the stockades. I spy what looks like a whipping post on a platform by the lake, dark stains marring the light wood, and I barely suppress a shudder. I take a deep breath and shoulder my pack, tugging at the straps and trying to fight off the nerves. *For Jonah, for Jonah, for Jonah,* I chant in my head over and over, reminding myself that I can survive anything for him.

My duffle had been thrown in one of the other vehicles and I assume I'll get it back if and when Traeger sees fit. I'd honestly been surprised that he let me keep my backpack. He searched it and confiscated all the weapons, of course, but still—he handed it back afterwards and I decided not to look that gift horse in the mouth. Where I go, this pack goes. Simple as that. I would have gone down fighting if I had to in order to hold on to it.

I eye the group wearily as I wait. Traeger is having a low conversation with a tall, skinny man that came running up as soon as we'd parked. Traeger's little silence game may have actually worked a little bit: the anticipation is nearly killing me. No one has been outright cruel to me or harmed me so far, but again, that could just be part of the game too. Lull me into thinking I'm relatively safe and then BAM—I'm beaten within an inch of my life...or worse. I glance to Jett and find him leering at me, and it makes my skin crawl.

Traeger finally makes his way over to me and I note that Jett quickly schools his features and busies himself with something on his jacket. *Scared of the boss, then?* I wonder what Traeger had done to make him that way? Maybe just his reputation was enough to keep Jett in check. Whatever the reason, I'm reluctantly thankful for it. If he's able to keep the worst of Jett under lock-and-key, then that's a good thing. The other men from the caravan begin unloading the trucks as more people come out to help. Some of them give me looks of interest, but they quickly go back to their jobs, averting their gazes.

"This way, pound of flesh," Traeger says with a sly grin, gesturing for me to walk with him.

"What? No cuffs?" I ask with maybe too much bite.

"Into bondage then? Good to know." I give him a dry look, refusing to admit that it was a good one, and he chuckles easily. I clench my jaw but fall into step beside him as we walk across the parking lot. We stop just before the oversized front doors, each carved with a bear standing on its hind legs. I wonder if there are really bears out here? I glance back towards the forest and mountains in the distance and figure the answer is probably yes.

Traeger turns to me, crossing his arms over his chest and giving me a serious look.

"You're about to be inducted into a very exclusive club, Melody. You're going to learn things that no one outside of this compound knows." *What the hell is he talking about?* "These secrets are held in the strictest confidences. We're talking the highest level of top secret here. Should these secrets be revealed, the consequences would be *severe*. Do you understand?" *Not really*, I think, but I nod. Who the hell am I going to tell anyway? I'm stuck here for the rest of my life.

He studies me for another minute before nodding.

"Alright then."

He pulls open one of the doors and ushers me inside, whistling *Pure Imagination*. I quirk a brow but don't say a word.

The lobby is huge, but somehow cozy, with a towering stone fireplace in the center that soars up three of the five stories. Balconies from each floor form a large square, overlooking the main floor. We're quite a few months away from needing a fire yet, but I imagine that one roaring in that grate would heat the entire space easily when the time comes. People mill about and I'm relieved to see that none of them look too worse for the wear. They're in clean clothes, no obvious injuries, not starving. Hell, they're even *smiling*. I honestly expected much, much worse. Of course, there could still be plenty of people suffering here, rooms turned into dungeons or torture chambers for all I know. I'd learned long ago never to trust outward appearances. Too many secrets lurk beneath the surface of almost everyone and everything, usually dark ones.

A plaque hanging beside the reception desk boasts that The Lodge had been built green as hell. Sustainable materials used in construction, closed-system, echo-friendly plumbing and electricity, completely powered by a nearby solar farm and water energy from the river that runs along the north of the property. *Pretty cool,* I think. *Kudos to whoever created this place. Wonder if they're a mindless undead corpse now.*

A woman approaches, looking me up and down. She's on the shorter side, only coming up to my chest, with pale blonde hair and deep blue eyes. She looks like she might be a few years younger than me, early thirties maybe. It's hard to tell in this world though—fighting for your life can age a person beyond their years pretty fucking quickly.

"Sir, I have two rooms in C block available, six in D block, and of course almost all of E is still open." C block? *God, part of this place really is a prison.* I keep my face passive. If I'm thrown in a cell, fine. If I'm thrown in a dog cage, fine. If I'm tied up outside and whipped bloody, fucking fine.

I. Will. Endure.

"I want her in A block, in the adjourning suite," Traeger says.

The woman's eyes bulge for a moment before she blinks and schools her features. She tucks her hair behind her ear, revealing a long, angry scar from her temple to the middle of her cheek.

"O-of course, sir." She obviously knows better than to question Traeger's commands. My eyes flare and heat radiates through my chest, quick and angry. Had *he* done that to her?

Traeger turns to me.

"Renee will show you to your room. Stay there until I send for you."

That grates on my nerves, but I hold my tongue—barely. My downfall has always been my stubborn pride. It had always driven Mitch crazy, my superiors too. My evaluations usually went something like *Agent is smart, resourceful, and an asset to the team. However, she continues to have trouble with authority figures.* I nearly smile at the memories. I obeyed orders...*mostly*. I didn't always follow them to the letter, exactly, but I did things in the *spirit* of said orders, and almost always got the desired result in the end, so usually they overlooked my "insubordination" as they liked to call it. I called it getting the job done in my own way and not listening to stupid assholes when they were being stupid.

Now, having Traeger of all people tell me to stay put until he calls for me? Like a *dog*? I ball my hands into fists so tight my knuckles whiten, and I bite the inside of my cheek, letting the pain distract me. He gives me a knowing smile, as if he knows exactly how his command irks me, and I blink. Is...Is *he* profiling *me*? I narrow my eyes and he fucking winks at me before strolling off down a hallway to the left of the reception desk. I stare at his back, wondering who the fuck this man is.

Renee clears her throat softly.

"This way."

The man with the bushy mustache that had given me food that first night—Holloway, I'd learned—drops my duffle bag at my feet without a word, inclines his head, and strides off. I blink, surprised they're actually letting me keep my stuff, but heft the bag on one shoulder. I follow Renee as she crosses the lobby and heads down a hallway to the right.

"Well, as Traeger said, I'm Renee, and I know that you're Melody."

"Mel," I interrupt. "Just Mel."

Renee bobs her head, a lock of hair falling back across her face to hide her scar.

"Mel. It's nice to meet you. You came from The Cove?"

"Yes."

"I've heard it's lovely."

I give the woman a nod, not wanting to think about The Cove. We go down an oversized corridor with beautiful hand-scrapped wooden floors and large windows looking out onto the lake, pass the elevators, and head into the stairwell. About halfway up, we pass a woman in a tight, black dress. I blink in surprise. Little black dresses aren't exactly standard apocalypse apparel.

"Is he back, then?" the woman asks Renee. She's pretty, with dark blonde hair and pouty lips.

"Yes," Renee says, sounding a bit exasperated. The woman smiles and shifts her gaze to me, the smile fading a bit as a challenging look settles in her dark brown eyes.

"Who's this?"

"A new resident." Resident? Not prisoner? Not hostage? "Mel, this is Tricia. Tricia, this is Mel."

I nod in greeting and adjust the strap of my duffle on my shoulder. Tricia narrows her eyes as she looks me up and down.

"Wednesdays are mine, so steer clear."

I blink in confusion, but she flounces off, her heeled boots thudding loudly on the stairs. *Wednesdays are mine? What the fuck is she talking about?*

Renee shakes her head and sighs, this time in clear annoyance.

"Sorry, she's…" She seems to be casting about for the right word to describe this Tricia woman, and lands on, "one of Traeger's girls."

"One of his…ohhh," I say as realization hits. One of his girls. A member of the harem. "So, that rumor is true," I say, mostly to myself.

"He'll probably want you as one too," Renee says as she looks me up and down, the same way Tricia had, but while Tricia had seemed challenging and predatory, Renee seems appreciative and admiring.

That won't be happening, I want to say, but I honestly can't be sure that won't be happening. If that's what he demands of me to keep everyone safe, then I'll do it, but...I nearly shudder at the thought of being one of "Traeger's Girls," of having a fucking scheduled day of the week when I'm designated to be his plaything.

I just stay silent and we both let the topic drop as we continue up and up and up. We huff it to the fifth floor, Renee breathing a little hard by the time we reach the door. *I guess FOSers don't take cardio as seriously as the rest of us,* I muse. Too many times in this world, your life comes down to if you can outrun the thing chasing you. Your life can literally depend on cardio. I'd made sure that anyone who left the gates of The Cove could run for at least two miles before needing a break. You couldn't go on a run or to work at the farm if you couldn't run for your life, simple as that.

Renee ushers me into the hallway, and I'm surprised to find that there are only two doors along the right wall. *The suites must be fucking huge.* We stop in front of the door closest to the stairs, and a moment later, a FOSer emerges from the other, rifle in hand, and posts sentry outside. Another enters from the stairs and I know without a doubt that he's about to be taking up his post outside of my room. Renee locks eyes with the man, a small smile playing on her lips and her cheeks heating a bit. The guard inclines his head and gives her a crooked grin. *Well,* that's *interesting.*

Renee opens the door and stands back to let me step inside. My jaw goes slack. It is, in fact, huge, but also *gorgeous.* A small dining area with a solid wood table and six upholstered chairs, an over-sized living room with a plush L-shaped couch facing a large stone fireplace and giant flatscreen mounted overhead. Floor to ceiling windows look out over the lake with another sitting area with two over-sized chairs and a fur rug sitting just before them. What at one point was a fully stocked bar sits just to the side, and rustic looking furniture adorns the balcony just beyond the windows...which I'd bet now are actually doors that can slide into the wall and open up the space to the outdoors completely. I can only imagine how much one night at this place would have cost.

There's one door on the right side of the room. I peek inside and find an empty bedroom. On the left side, there are two doors. One is closed but the other stands ajar, giving me a glimpse of a huge canopy bed of deep red wood sitting atop a crisp white rug on a raised platform. Another wall of windows looks out to the lake and mountains beyond, and I can only imagine how gorgeous the sunrise would be from this vantage point.

Everything is luxurious but not over the top. I almost huff out an incredulous laugh. It's like whoever had designed it had plucked it right from my brain, to be quite honest. This is exactly what I'd always envisioned my dream cabin would look like inside. Light colors, clean lines, oversized furniture you could nap in on a rainy Sunday. I whirl back to Renee who's been watching in silence as I explored the room.

"What is this?"

"It's a room?" Her voice is hesitant, obviously confused by the question.

"I mean, why am I here?"

"This is where Traeger wanted you placed. So, this is where I'm placing you," she says simply.

"But...but I thought...Aren't I supposed to be a prisoner? Shouldn't I be in a cell or a cage or something?"

Renee's lips twitch, but she doesn't answer. Instead she says, "Traeger will send for you soon. Until then, you can shower and rest. I'll have food brought up too."

"But—"

"Patience," she interrupts with another soft smile before heading out of the room and leaving me alone. Once the door clicks shut, I stand for a long moment, dumbfounded. None of this makes a lick of sense. I'm a hostage. A prisoner. A war prize. I'm supposed to be tortured and miserable...so, why the fuck am I staying in the penthouse suite?? Is it just so that Traeger can keep a close eye on his newest investment? Only the best of his men would be put on guard duty on this floor, so if he wants me watched liked a hawk, this is the logical place to put me, I guess.

But it still doesn't explain *why*, not really. I'm sure I'd be watched perfectly fine in a cell. I decide it must be more of his mind games, and tell myself to stay alert. I immediately start snooping, studying every inch of the room for weapons, means of escape, and even cameras. I'd put nothing past Austin Traeger. I find pretty much diddly squat, though. I'm surprised that the doors to the balcony actually open. Guess they aren't scared that I'll fling myself off, at least not yet.

I eye the closed door off of the living room and Traeger's words echo in my mind: *I want her in the* adjourning *suite.*

"Oh you've got to be shitting me!" I hiss as I yank the door open. Sure enough, it opens to an identical door that I know leads into Traeger's room. I jiggle the handle, but it's locked. I could pick it pretty easily, but don't want to push my luck too far on day one. I close my door back and curse loudly when I find that it doesn't have a lock at all. I glance to the main door: no lock there either.

"Ohh no you don't," I say through gritted teeth.

I huff and puff, but eventually drag one of the large chairs from across the room in front of the door leading to Traeger's suite. He could still probably bust through if he was determined to, but he'd at least be slowed down a bit.

I don't know how long it'll be before Traeger calls me like the good little doggie I am, so I decide to take a shower. If he comes while I'm in there, he'll either bust in like the bastard he is, or he'll wait. Either way, I'm showering. I feel gross after three days on the road, so I shrug and head into the ensuite bathroom. It's just as gorgeous as the rest of the place, all white marble with rustic accents here and there. Body wash, shampoo, and conditioner sit in the large, tiled shower stall, but I fish my own out of my pack, wanting the familiar scents surrounding me.

To my delight, the water grows hot after a few seconds. I do my best to quickly scrub away the grime and not linger, but the hot water feels so good on my tight muscles, that I stand there letting it beat down on me longer than I should. Eventually I sigh and get out of the shower. I eye the oversized tub while I dry off, wishing I could take a nice long soak in it. I used to *love* a good bubble bath.

I leave my hair down to air dry and dress in a clean pair of jeans and a black tank top. I'm not cold, but I grab Jonah's hoodie anyway and pull it on like a security blanket. My eyes water and I breathe in his familiar scent, forever imprinted on the fabric. It's linked to so many memories, too many memories. *And now he's just...gone. Forever.* I angrily wipe a tear from my cheek. I won't let myself cry now, not yet. Traeger will be *sending for me* soon, so I can't be in the middle of a breakdown when that happens.

I wander back into the living space and find a tray of food waiting on the dining table. I make my way closer, eying the plate suspiciously. They wouldn't poison me, would they? No, I don't think Traeger would kill me, at least not so quickly. That just seems like a waste of a good hostage and if he planned to kill me, why not just do it on the road? Or better yet, just do it at The Cove as an example for everyone there to see. Why go to all the trouble to bring me back here? No, he won't kill me, but he may make me sick as a dog just for shits and giggles...

I deliberate for a few minutes, watching the plate like it will eventually tell me whether it's poisoned or not. My mouth waters...

"Oh, fuck it," I huff as I sit heavily in one of the cushioned chairs and take a tentative bite of what looks to be chicken, though it could be some other kind of bird I guess. It's fucking *delicious*, whatever it is. I quickly polish off the rest of the meat, followed by the cucumbers, potatoes, and bread. I actually moan in delight as I chew on the roll. Several people in The Cove make bread, but they need to take notes from whoever's doing it here at FOS because *damn*. It's soft and warm and full of flavor.

After my meal, I have nothing to do but wait. I feel like I wait for hours and hours, the sun slowly making its trek across the sky and getting closer to setting. *Is he ever fucking coming?* Without much else to do, I go through everything I know about him again, trying to fit the inconsistencies into the puzzle that is Austin Traeger. I'll figure him all out eventually, it's just a matter of time, but the inconsistencies are admittedly fascinating—and frustrating.

He's known as completely savage and despicable, despite his charming and charismatic personality that he displays the majority of the time. He's killed too many people to count in his quest to gain and maintain his power...so, why hadn't I'd seen that sadistic gleam in his eye when he'd been about to gut Kevin? Then I realize what had felt off about it: he'd seemed *resigned* to it, as if it was a chore that had to be done, not something he was excited about. He'd treated me surprisingly respectfully during the trip to FOS, hadn't physically harmed me or touched me in any way, hadn't allowed his men to do so either.

"Ugh!" I groan in frustration, punching a pillow. It just doesn't fucking track. Was the monster some kind of façade? Or was he just better at hiding his monster and mind games than anyone I've ever met? I decide to stop thinking about Traeger and read instead. I only make it a couple of chapters before I end up dozing off on the couch, more exhausted than I realized it. When I wake to a knock at the door, it's full dark out. To my utter astonishment, the guy guarding my door waits for me to answer instead of just barging in.

"Traeger will see you now."

"And I didn't practice my curtsey," I say with a mocking gasp. The guard's lips twitch, but he doesn't respond as he steps to the left of the doorway so I can exit and turn right towards Traeger's room. It's a short distance from my door to his, but why couldn't I just go through the connecting door? Does he just want to make a big to-do of having me come in the main entrance? So I can be escorted the thirty feet by an armed guard? I roll my eyes.

The guard posted outside of Traeger's room gives me an appraising look before nodding and moving so I can enter. Despite all my bravado, I swallow hard and take a few deep, steadying breaths before I open the door. Will he...expect things from me tonight? Will he demand them? Force them? I remind myself again that I can't lash out or fight back, no matter what happens. I know without a doubt that he'll punish Jonah for anything that I do here.

Because that was the deal, wasn't it? Jonah and everyone at The Cove are safe so long as I *behave*.

I push my shoulders back, open the door, and enter the room. *Holy. Shit.* His suite is twice as big as mine, maybe even three times, and even has a spiral staircase leading up to a second-floor loft overlooking the living space. There are what look to be three bedrooms and a bath-room on the left side, with his master bedroom on the right—meaning we share a bedroom wall. I eye the connecting door with disdain before scanning the rest of the room.

There's a full kitchen and dining area, and a large, fully-stocked bar in the corner, bottles lining the glass shelves behind the stone counter.

A large desk strewn with books and notes sits just beside it in between two of the bedroom doors. A few pieces of art hang on the walls—a couple of Monets and a Degas—and I narrow my eyes: are these... fuck, I think these might be *real*?? I take a step forward before I've even made the decision to move, like I'm going to sprint across the room and touch one of these masterpieces with my own hands, but freeze, locking my muscles in place.

I let my gaze keep sweeping over the space and find mismatched shelves filled to the brim with books lining the other wall. *Hundreds* of them, maybe thousands.

"Surprised?" he drawls as he unfolds himself from the leather couch. His hair is damp, a few droplets falling from the strands and turning the light gray fabric of his t-shirt nearly black. He has a bandage on his bicep from where Kevin had grazed him, but it doesn't seem to be bothering him too much. His tattoos are on full display now, covering both arms pretty much fully down to his elbows. Neither are one solid design, but a mix of things that flow cohesively together to form one overall picture, though the actual items vary wildly: a pocket watch; a cross with some script beneath it; the state of Georgia; a lion's head; a thick Celtic knot encircling his right bicep; a compass; initials and dates. I hate that I'm interested in the stories behind all of them. I idly wonder if the bullet wound ruined the design beneath the bandage, but I can't really tell right now.

I hike a shoulder as if I couldn't care less about what's in his room, but I'm eager to get closer and browse the titles on the bookshelves. I'm in desperate need of new reading material. Not that I'd ever ask to borrow his books, of course, but I could *steal* them...

"I trust you found your room to be adequate." His lips curl at the corners and I narrow my eyes.

"Why am I staying there? Shouldn't I be in a cell or something?"

He doesn't answer, just studies me before making his way to the bar. He adds ice to two glasses, pours a healthy amount of amber liquid into each, and strolls towards me. I tense but don't retreat and he holds out one of the glasses. Though I could really use a drink or twelve, I eye it coldly. He waits, cocking a dark blonde brow and telling me without words that he'll stand there all night if he has to. I roll my eyes and take the damn glass. Whiskey by the smell of it. My brows rise a bit. *Good* whiskey. I take a sip and just stop myself from giving an appreciative *mmm*.

"I like to keep an eye on the new members of our little group," he finally answers, though it seems like a lie to me. Renee had been shocked when he'd told her to put me in that room. Maybe it's reserved for the ones he takes a particular interest in torturing—or using for...other things. I grit my teeth as he makes his way back to the couch, gesturing for me to sit too. I reluctantly follow, perching on the chair that sits opposite the couch. He studies me in silence as he sips his drink slowly. The look is calculating and...intense. *Smoldering* comes to mind, and my entire body feels like a bow string pulled too taut. *From fear,* I tell myself. *Just fear and nothing else...*

I quickly down my entire drink, wincing a little at the burn left behind. If ever there was a time for liquid courage, it's now. Sure, I'd been trained for, and put into, far worse situations, but that is different. I almost always had backup in those days, for one. Now, I'm totally on my own. And it isn't just *my* life on the line if I fuck up. *Jonah, Jonah, Jonah. I can do this for him.*

I decide that since this is happening whether I like it or not, maybe it won't be as bad if I do it on my own terms, if *I* make the move. I can pretend in some delusional part of my brain that this is *my* choice. I take a deep breath and rise from the chair, closing the small distance between it and the couch in just a few steps.

His brows draw together as I lean down to take his glass from him. He lets me and I toss the contents back too before setting the glass on the coffee table. I slide into his lap, my thighs straddling his hips and sling my arms over his shoulders. His hands fly to my hips, holding me in place. My heart pounds loudly in my ears, but my body...reacts. *Oh boy* does it react. *Traitorous little bastard.* It's admittedly been years since I've been with anybody, and even this small contact is enough to set every nerve in my body on fire. I suddenly *need* and I need very, very badly.

No, no, no. I try to remind myself that he's a cold-blooded killer. *You're one to talk,* a part of my mind whispers, but it quickly shuts up as I start to lose my ability to think rationally. Maybe this arrangement won't be so bad after all. I mean, hate fucking is a thing…but even with psychos? Sure. Why not? There are plenty of dark romance books about it, right? It's definitely a thing…

"What are you doing, Melody?" he asks, voice a little gruff. He clears his throat lightly.

"Isn't this why I'm here?" I ask in a whisper as I lean towards him. "To be one of your whores?" Though he hadn't outright said it, of course, I'd assumed, and apparently so did both Tricia and Renee. Plus, I'd caught him stealing appreciative glances at me more than once over the years. I'm not ignorant enough to think that my looks and body weren't part of the reason I'd been such a successful agent before the end of the world. Of course, that wasn't *all* I was, but my looks could be a huge asset—or a weapon, depending on the situation —so why not use them?

Now, I realize, they can be both. The idea of seducing Austin Traeger quickly flits through my mind. I'd taken down bigger targets than him this way, made powerful men fall in love and forget themselves and their agendas. Could that work with him? Maybe I could use my body to get certain concessions from him. *Like seeing Jonah again.* Hope flares. Maybe I can be more than just "one of his girls."

He stiffens and turns his head away just before my lips met his. He gently pushes my hips away, keeping space between our bodies. I pull back and stare down at him in confusion.

"As enticing as that offer is, and as much as I appreciate the sacrifice you were prepared to make," he says, cold sarcasm thick in his voice, "I'm going to have to decline your offer." *Huh? Is he…turning me down? What the fuck?*

"Why?" I blurt. He gives me a hard look, jaw ticking.

"Do you really want to be one of my *whores*?" He says the word like it tastes like vinegar. *No. Yes. Maybe?*

I press my lips into a hard line, annoyed by my conflicting thoughts when I know damn well it should be a firm and unequivocal *fuck no.* He nods, taking my silence as an answer.

"That's what I thought. So, why don't we just get to know each other a little bit instead?"

He glances pointedly down at me, wordlessly telling me that I should remove myself from his lap. I blink and scramble off, swallowing hard. Relief floods through me, of course, but I'm also a bit... indignant. And disappointed. And ok, maybe even a little embarrassed. *He* doesn't want *me*? Seriously? Sure, maybe I'm a little rusty in the charming-men's-literal-pants-off department, but still. It's the apocalypse for fuck's sake, and beggars and choosers and all of that, and fuck, I don't even know what's going on right now.

I don't understand what game he's playing and decide anger and irritation are better emotions to feel right now than anything else, so I push all the other things aside and focus on those. I glare at him as he rises and returns to the bar before coming back with the entire bottle, pouring us both another drink. I take it and sip, eyeing him distrustfully.

"I already told you, I know enough," I say, keeping my voice even, determined to act like nothing had happened. Yet again, he'd surprised me, more inconsistencies to drive me insane. The man who kept a literal harem of women to use as he pleased, and who had taken me as a hostage to again, use as he pleased...*didn't* want to use me as he pleased? I don't fucking understand.

One brow arched, he asks, "Care to enlighten me?" I shrug. "Alright then, how about I ask you some questions then?"

I stand and start to roam around the room.

"I don't think I really have a choice, so go ahead."

"Fair enough." There's a bit of amusement in his voice now. "What did you do before the world ended?"

"A little of this, a little of that," I say vaguely as I move towards his desk. I add honestly, "I worked on a shrimp boat for a while when I was younger." I turn back to look at him. "Also at Hooters for a whole four hours before I got fired for breaking a guy's hand." My lips curl at the memory and I don't miss how his eyes flare at that. I snort and turn back towards the desk, surreptitiously studying the contents strewn across the surface. Notes and maps and statistics and projections and... The Divine Comedy—*in fucking Italian??* I shoot him a look over my shoulder, eyes narrowed. Who the hell is this man?

"Where were you before The Cove?"

"On the road, mostly. We tried to settle into more permanent places a handful of times, but never found anywhere truly safe until we ended up there."

"And when you say *we*?"

I sigh and prepare for the stab of pain that's coming.

"Me and Jonah. I've known him for over half my life. We were together long before the world went to shit, and have been together every step of the way since then." My eyes water so I turn away to pretend to study the art on the wall again. Over my shoulder, I continue, "We joined another larger group a few years after it all started, and what was left of us ended up at The Cove eventually." Anger begins to burn, temporarily chasing away the sorrow. I turn and glare at him.

"And now I'm here, to be tortured via twenty questions, apparently. I personally prefer waterboarding or bamboo shoots under the fingernails. Really has that wow factor, ya know?"

"An expert in torture, are you?" he smirks. *Oh, you have no idea.* I ignore that and wave him on, taking another drink while I wait for the next question. "How'd you get to be so knowledgeable about security?"

Again, I give a half truth. "Married to a Special Forces guy. Picked up a few things over the years. Pillow talk and all that." Mitch *had* been Special Forces, but that isn't where I learned most of what I know.

"Is that how you became the alleged crack shot then?"

"No alleged about it, counselor," I say with absolute confidence. He merely keeps studying me in that unnerving way, so I continue scoping out the place since he hasn't tried to stop me, moving towards the bookshelves.

"See anything of interest?" he asks.

"Well, I expected to find the full library of Dr. Seuss, but alas, I'm disappointed." He chuckles low at that. Really, I'm desperate to borrow half his titles. Some are old favorites that I haven't thought about in years, others I wanted to read but never got the chance to. Some just look cool or sound interesting. He's got a crazy mix of genres too: classics, historical and military texts, epic fantasies and space operas. He even has three entire shelves dedicated to graphic novels and comic books and—

Click.

I whirl.

"Seriously? FOS? *Fortress of Solitude*??"

He smiles a little crookedly and looks...adorable? Fuck me. So, add nerd to the profile. I *almost* smile. I'd been to Comicon on multiple occasions, even dressed as Supergirl a time or two, come to think of it. Then I want to scowl. I don't like that I have things in common with Traeger. I don't like that these bits of information make me want to smile or laugh or get into heated debates about comic legends. I don't like thinking that, in another world, we might actually...get along? Like each other? Fuck that.

"What about family?" he asks next. *Alright, that's enough of that.*

"Enough about me," I snap.

"Ask away," he says in invitation, unperturbed and raising his glass to his lips once more.

"I don't need to ask anything. I told you, I already know enough." It's only a half-truth now that I've been in this room, but I still have mostly him pegged. He gets that challenging look in his eyes again.

"Then, again, I invite you to enlighten me, Melody." The way he says my name...I fight a shiver. *God, what is wrong with me?* I'm going to blame it all on emotional distress. The past few days have been a whirlwind and a mindfuck and my mind and body are reacting in weird ways. That's all.

"Late thirties to early forties. From southern Georgia most likely, not the low country though. Highly educated. At least semi-fluent in Italian. Athletic. Right-handed." His face remains impassive as I speak save a slight narrowing of his eyes. "You were married, but she's gone, maybe has been since before the end. You feel guilty about something to do with her. You worked with kids, maybe a teacher or a coach, but you didn't have any yourself."

"And how would you know that?" he finally asks, interrupting my assessment, his green eyes stirring with...something. Interest? Annoyance? Anger? I hate that I can't read him clearly. He can guard his thoughts and expressions much better than most and that in and of itself intrigues me. Was he just naturally that way? Had he been taught? Had circumstances demanded it?

Before I can stop myself, I say, "Parents who have lost children have a look in their eye, a look that never goes away. You don't have it." That's one thought that can't be hidden, no matter how hard you try or how well you're trained. It's a permanent scar that only certain people know how to recognize—the ones who have identical ones. He studies me too intently at that, so I quickly continue on. The next bit is a lie, but I say it anyway, wanting to see his reaction.

"You're ruthless, savage, and sadistic. You enjoy the power you hold and the pain you inflict to keep it, maybe even get off on it."

He clenches his jaw before he stands and stalks forward, eyes going dark. I remain still as he comes closer and closer. I crane my head upward to meet his gaze when he's only a foot away. He stares down at me, cold menace radiating from him. Real, or forced after my assessment? Right now, he looks every bit the heartless bastard who would stick someone's head on a pike or carve out their heart. I can feel the heat from his body seeping into mine, and again, my own body reacts to his nearness despite the small tendril of fear working its way up my spine. Again, I curse it.

His gaze bores into mine and it takes everything in me not to look away at the intensity of his eyes.

"Is that what you really think?" he asks quietly, voice gone low and rough. I swallow hard. Half from fear, half from…something else, but I don't answer. His lips curl up on one side. This time isn't the playful half-smile he flashed earlier. This one is cold and calculated and sharp as a blade. How easily he slips in and out of the different personas. The question is, which one is the real thing, and which is the mask?

"I think that's enough for tonight, Melody."

I blink and back away, head spinning, and nod. I quickly make my way out of the room, leaving my glass on the dining table as I go. The guards outside give me inquisitive looks, but I don't pay them much attention, rushing inside my own room as fast as I can. I lean my back against the door after I close it, not quite understanding what in the hell had just happened or where I stand on the entire situation.

Austin Traeger…confounds me, and that's not something I'm used to. I replay every single second, trying to figure him out, and heat spreads through my chest when I think about settling over top of him.

I tried to tell myself that I hadn't actually wanted him, that I'd just assumed being his plaything was what was expected of me, so I was doing what I had to...but when I'd glanced down at his lips, a part of me *had* wanted.

A dark, lonely, fucked up part of me had wanted him so badly it made it hard to breathe.

I bang my head softly against the door several times.

"Fuck, fuck, fuckkkk," I whisper. I sigh heavily and finally push away from the door. I change into some sleep shorts and crawl into the luxurious bed. I'm not ready to grieve the loss of Jonah yet, so I just try to think through everything I've seen since arriving and wonder what might be in store for me in the days to come.

Not much time has passed before I hear Traeger's door open and close once more. Was he leaving? No, someone had come inside. I hear low voices, muffled so I can only make out that they're talking, but not the words. A few seconds later I hear a loud thud through our shared wall, in what must be his bedroom. The door hitting the wall maybe? A second later, another thud sounds, though this one is a little softer, more like...*bodies* hitting the wall? Followed by...moans.

Oh my God.

I bolt upright in the bed and tilt my head to listen. Is he...Are they...? Muffled groans and grunts and cries of pleasure fill my ears, and soon enough, the unmistakable sounds of people getting busy, the headboard thudding against the wall just on the other side of mine.

"You have got to be kidding me," I mutter as over the top screams begin. Whoever he's with right now is very theatric.

"Yes, Traeger. Oh God, it feels so good! Don't stop! Oh God, you're so good! Yes, baby!"

I roll my eyes so hard they nearly get stuck. One of the infamous concubines there to earn her keep, I guess. So...why hadn't he wanted me to do the same? And why do I care?! I should be *glad* that he isn't forcing me to do that shit. Him not being a fucking rapist on top of everything else should be a *good* thing. What the hell is wrong with me? I pinch the bridge of my nose, deciding that the whiskey isn't helping my thought process at all.

I lay back and try to ignore the sounds, but I can't. More moans, more pleas, more ridiculous praise and begging for him to keep going. Why the hell are these walls so thin? Did echo-friendly mean zero sound proofing? I turn over to lie on my stomach and slam a pillow over my head, but even that doesn't drown them out completely.

Austin Traeger is apparently very far from a one-pump chump, and it seems to go on for hours. Good for whoever he's with, I guess.

Finally, exhaustion pulls me under into a blissfully dreamless sleep.

CHAPTER EIGHT

MELODY

THE NEXT MORNING, I expect the torture and cruelty to begin, but it...doesn't. Renee arrives to bring me breakfast.

"After today, you'll eat in the restaurant with everyone else," Renee tells me while I eat—eggs, bacon, fruit. I'll give it to FOS: the food is top notch. "We call it The Skillet, but it's essentially our cafeteria now. When you're done eating, I'll give you a full tour of everything."

I eye her suspiciously but just nod and finish scarfing down my breakfast. I'm eager to get a good look at the place, look for weaknesses or potential escape routes should it ever come to that. I dress in dark jeans and a tank, gritting my teeth when I realize that putting on my thigh holster or weapons belt would be useless since I have nothing to put in them. I toss them back onto the bed and lace up my boots, muttering curses under my breath. I couldn't have weapons within The Cove technically, either, but I wasn't surrounded by potential threats twenty-four-seven there.

Renee takes me on the promised tour and the more I see, the more confused I get. Everyone seems...happy. Healthy. Whole. This doesn't make any fucking sense. This place is supposed to be abysmal, the inhabitants are supposed to be all but slaves. Rumor said that disfigurement was often used as punishment—or just for entertainment, that women and men alike were used in unspeakable ways or forced to work themselves to the bone for their master and his goons.

But I see none of that. Sure, I'd been correct that the structure by the lake was indeed a whipping post, but The Cove has one too. That particular punishment had strangely come back in style with the end of civilization, so I can't really be surprised by its presence. Other than that, there are no outright signs of abuse or misconduct. People smile and wave, kids run around and play, they *laugh* for fuck's sake. Couples kiss and hold hands. A younger guy struggles to keep a wheelbarrow upright and Holloway, the man from the team that brought me here, rushes over to help steady it for him, even flashing the guy a smile.

I rub my temples, trying to make sense of it all.

"Everyone has an assigned job," Renee says, gesturing to the sprawling gardens and additional greenhouses that I hadn't noticed before as we walk by the lake. "Some are in charge of harvesting or scavenging or hunting; others are on security, manning the outposts and doing patrols and runs; cooking, cleaning, plumbing, mainte-nance, teaching—everyone contributes and keeps this place running."

I finally can't take it anymore. I turn to Renee, holding up my hands.

"Ok, ok, just stop. I don't understand."

"About the jobs?" she asks, though there's understanding in her hazel eyes.

"None of this makes sense. This place is supposed to be a living hell, but it looks to be the opposite."

Renee gives me an innocent smile and hikes a shoulder. Is she not supposed to give me any straight answers or something? Maybe everyone is brainwashed or driven by fear to act the part of gleeful citizen to keep Traeger happy. It's like a cult or something. I eye her but decide to let it go for now. I'll find out what's really going on sooner or later. I'll find the skeletons.

Renee continues the tour, introducing me to people along the way. When it's time for lunch, I find myself seated at the end of a long row of tables with Renee and a handful of other FOSers in the restaurant, The Skillet she'd called it. I stay alert, ever skeptical, and though I'm not rude, I'm tight-lipped when they speak to me until they mostly give up on including me in the conversation. A guard has been trailing us all day, and another stands just across the room. *Keeping an eye on me? Making sure I don't lose my mind and attack someone or try to escape?* I can't totally blame them for that, I guess. If I was in charge and the situation was reversed, I'd definitely have eyes and guns on any new potential threats for a while, just to be safe.

After lunch, Renee says, "Now, I understand that you might eventually be shifted to hunting or security—or both. A lot of people have multiple roles—but for now, you'll be on harvesting duty."

"Um, alright then," I reply, a little uncertainly. I'd rather be outside than cooped up in the kitchen or doing laundry, so I'm fine with it, but again, I didn't really expect to just...be a part of the community. If I'm not going to be locked in a stockade or starved in a cell, shouldn't I at least have the terrible jobs that no one else wants, the ones that are a grueling or disgusting, as part of my torture?

The rest of the afternoon is spent in one of the gardens collecting tomatoes. A short man with gray hair and kind eyes tells me how to tell if they're ready to be pulled or not, and gives me a wide smile when I select the right ones while he watches. A guard watches my every move as I work, but soon, I find my mind relaxing as I focus on the task at hand. The other people working nearby smile and chat as they fill their baskets, and though I don't respond much, it doesn't seem to bother them, they keep up the chatter all the same.

I'm tired and filthy by the time dinner rolls around, and I practically inhale the stew. Renee laughs a bit and I give her a tentative smile in return. The guard that she'd made eyes at last night comes over, grinning and holding out two cookies. Renee smiles widely, cheeks turning a bit pink, and takes the cookies, nodding in thanks. The guard doesn't say a word, but winks before turning to walk away, taking a big bite of his own treat. Renee hands one cookie to me across the table and I take it gratefully. She taps her cookie to mine in cheers and I can't help but laugh.

After dinner, she escorts me back to my room.

"So, how long are you on babysitting duty?" I ask

Renee's lips quirk. "Just until you get settled in."

So, until Traeger decides that I'm not a flight risk or threat. Got it. I nod and tell her goodnight, but when I turn the knob of my door Renee reaches out to stop me.

"I know you didn't come here willingly, but...you can be happy here, I promise. It's not what you think. I'm...well, I'm supposed to let you come to terms on your own," she says with a little roll of her eyes and my lips twitch at her mocking tone, "but just...trust me."

I study her for a long minute.

"Were you out there?" I just my chin in the direction that clearly means on the road, amid the Bloodies. "Before you came here?" Something dark flashes in her eyes and she unconsciously runs a finger over the end of her scar.

"Yes, I was." She holds my gaze as she says, "And I'm thankful *every single day* that Traeger found me." The vehemence in her tone makes me blink. She's absolutely genuine. I wonder how she and Traeger had crossed paths. Had he actually *saved* her? She seems to have a bit of hero worship going on for the man...so, does she just not care what he does then? The pain he causes? Or is there far more to all of this than I can possibly know?

Someone exits the stairwell then, drawing me out of that wormhole, and my brows rise as a stunning redhead waltzes down the hallway in an obscenely short skirt and tight, glittering crop-top. Her eye shadow is bright blue, her lips bright pink, and she'd gone a little heavy on the blush for my tastes.

"Hey Renee," she says with a thick Boston accent. She shifts her gaze to me. "And we haven't had the pleasure, though I've heard plenty. I'm Destiny." *Of course you are,* I think, and then chide myself for assuming she's a bimbo or a bitch or a combination of both.

"Mel."

"Nice to meet you. The gossip train is running wild about you right now. Did you really try to stab Traeger?"

"*That's* what everyone's saying?" I ask, incredulous.

Destiny laughs. "I didn't think it was true, but you just never know with the folks brought in from the outside." She says it like FOS is some posh country club and everyone *outside* are street urchins. "Well, I've got...*things* to do," she says with a sly wink. *Oh God, is she the screamer from last night?* No, that must have been someone else—I hadn't detected an accent in all of those throaty moans and overly dramatic pleas.

I barely stop myself from rolling my eyes. So, this is a *new* playmate. Then I remember Tricia's comment: *Wednesdays are mine.* Fuck, does he really have a different woman for each day of the week? I thought she'd been kidding. *Jesus.*

Destiny waves and makes her way to Traeger's door, teetering on six-inch heels. She pats the guard there on the chest. She has a very... regal air about her, as if she thinks she's the queen bee since she's fucking the self-appointed king.

Renee rolls her eyes and whispers, "She thinks just because she sleeps with Traeger, that makes her special. Poor thing doesn't seem to understand that that list is a mile long and far from distinguished." I snort at that and Renee grins.

"So, he's quite the man-whore, huh? We'd heard rumors that he kept a harem here, that he...forced women to sleep with him in exchange for protection."

Renee waves that away. "He has no lack of volunteers to be in his bed, that's for sure. I mean, have you *seen* the man? But it isn't forced or some kind of payment for protection or anything like that. Anyone who goes in that room does so willingly and understands that it's all... fun. No strings attached as they used to say."

I'm completely skeptical of that but keep it to myself. He may not physically force them or outright tell them they have to, but it could still be implied that they'd be expected to...service him if they want to remain safely behind his walls.

"So, they just ignore all the things he does? All the blood he spills?" Do they just not care? Or do they care but push it aside to do what has to be done, like I'd been prepared to do?

Renee's expression pinches. "It's...complicated." *Isn't always?* "No one's hands are clean anymore," she adds softly, her gaze shifting to somewhere far, far away from here. I wonder what she's seeing, but I don't dare ask. She focuses again and seems to shake herself. "I'll let you get some rest, I'm sure you're exhausted. I'll see you for breakfast? 8:00?"

"Sure. Yeah. Um, thanks, for today." It had been really nice having Renee to guide me and talk to. I know she was being forced to, but it was nice not having to navigate everything completely alone.

"You're welcome."

I shower, change, and collapse into bed. I've been on security detail or going on runs since coming to The Cove and not taking shifts out at the Farm, so it's been quite a while since I've done manual labor like I had today. I'm in good shape, but my focus is always mostly cardio, and my muscles are already pissed as hell at me for that fact right about now. I'm just drifting off when the sounds started again.

"Nooo," I groan at Destiny's loud chuckle and then screaming moans. I slam a pillow over my head, but I can still hear the screams and grunts and eventually the steady thud of a headboard banging against the wall. I grit my teeth.

Destiny, it turns out, is quite devout. If I hear *Oh God* one more time, I'm going to lose my fucking mind. Come on. Does he really buy this shit?? It's so over the top, it's comical. I eventually give up and throw the pillow to the side.

"Come on!" I whisper-yell to the ceiling. Why does Traeger have to have such damn stamina? I'm tempted to go sleep on the couch when one final scream sounds and the thudding finally ceases. "About damn time."

I quickly drift off to sleep now that the show is over, but this time, the dreams don't stay away.

I DON'T UNDERSTAND what the hell is going on here and I can't get close enough to Traeger to demand an answer, though I'm pretty sure I already know what it is. But no. I refuse to accept that, to believe it. It's been three days, and I still haven't been punished or locked up or seen any signs that this place is the hell we all thought it was. Every day, I've been escorted to meals and my shift in the garden or greenhouse I was assigned to by Renee, still with a guard trailing behind us. Everything has been…fine. Nice even. I really like Renee and Wynn has joined us at our table for dinner every night too.

I might not have been able to talk to Traeger yet, but I've seen him, and every time his gaze locks with mine across the room, his look is so intense that it makes my pulse race. I can't decipher the look. Is he still pissed or upset or whatever he'd been when I'd essentially called him a sadistic psychopath that first night? Is he waiting for me to do something stupid? Is he rethinking my (embarrassing) offer to be his whore? I have no idea, but I decide to do my best to just ignore him until he decides he wants to talk to me again. Maybe that'll be never.

I've had the privilege of running into Jett on several occasions though and it's taken all of my self-control not to kill the bastard each time. He'd blocked my path coming in from the gardens my second day, forcing me to walk around him with a stupid self-satisfied grin on his face. Last night, he'd forced his way in to sit beside me at dinner, continually brushing my thigh with his, even going so far as to grab it roughly when I tried to jerk it away. He'd given it a harsh squeeze, hard enough to leave bruises where his fingertips had been before releasing me, eating and chatting and laughing as if nothing had happened. Wynn had eyed him with thinly veiled contempt and given me a look that asked if everything was alright. I nodded, letting him know I was fine. This place may not be what I thought it was, but I knew that I was still being watched very closely to make sure I was keeping to my end of the agreement and behaving. Having beef with Jett wouldn't be a good idea.

But now, he corners me in a supply closet.

"One of these days," he says quietly as he closes in on me. I don't lash out, not yet, but I tense every muscle as he presses me back against a shelf. I don't think he'll actually try anything here and now, this is just a scare tactic, but I'm ready to defend myself if I need to.

"One of these days," he continues, "I'll get to play with Traeger's new shiny toy." He grips the shelf just above my head as he leans in to whisper in my ear, his breath hot and smelling like an ashtray. "I tend to *break* my toys though…"

I inhale sharply but he only chuckles and pulls away, leaving me alone and fuming and feeling like I might vomit. That's when I realize that my body reacted to Jett with pure revulsion...but with Traeger, it had practically purred. *Maybe because you know Jett is a true monster, whereas Traeger is just masquerading,* my mind whispers. I push the thoughts away and force my muscles to unclench as I try to calm the undeniable *fight* instincts that are still screaming inside me.

BECAUSE I DON'T REALLY HAVE any other choice, I reluctantly begin to settle into life here at FOS. It's been two weeks now and though I'm still cautious and trying to keep to mostly to myself, Renee and Wynn are both already weaseling their ways into my heart. Maybe I'm just getting soft in my old age, but as much as I might pretend, I don't *want* to be alone here. So, I'm happy to have them, but I think about Jonah constantly, missing him like a lost limb. I've cried myself to sleep more than once...at least on the nights when the live-action Skinimax isn't blaring from next door. He thankfully doesn't entertain visitors every single night, but it's a pretty steady rotation, that's for damn sure.

The worst part is that hearing him in the throes sometimes doesn't make me annoyed. Oh no, sometimes it makes me very much...*other* things. More than once I've imagined what was happening on the other side of that thin wall, picturing it as my hand dipped below the covers. One night his deep voice had rumbled "Grab the headboard," and I'd nearly whimpered. Fucking *whimpered,* literally having to bite my lip to keep quiet. Don't even get me started on where my dreams have taken me...

Though I've poked around as much as I can, I've found jack squat hiding in the shadows of this place. No prisoners in horrific living conditions. No one chained up in a dank closet. No one being starved to death in a boiler room. Nothing. Nada. Zilch. I'm fairly certain I understand the game now.

I'm pulling up peanuts now when Kyle, one of the guards, walks over.

"Come with me," he says, not unkindly, but not overly friendly either. I quirk a brow but stand and wipe my hands off on my shorts. He leads me to one of the tall towers that had been erected around the lake without making small talk, but his lips quirk when he jerks his chin towards the ladder.

"Up you go."

I give him a salute and he almost cracks a real smile, I think. I climb up, wondering what the hell this could be about, and my stomach clenches when I reach the platform and see Traeger and Jett waiting.

CHAPTER NINE

TRAEGER

"MEL," I say, nodding in greeting. Something flashes in her gray eyes, something surprisingly not hostile...no, it's actually the *opposite* of hostile, I think...but then it's gone so quickly that I wonder if I actually imagined it. She smooths her feature into an impassive mask, like she doesn't have a care in the world. She glances between me and Jett, her muscles tensing. Does she think we're about to toss her off the tower or something?

Or maybe she just knows what kind of man Jett is. He hasn't been able to hide his disturbing mix of hatred and fascination of Melody very well. He wants to hurt her, that much is clear, but whether it's because she challenged him in front of so many people back at FOS or he just enjoys hurting people, especially women, is anyone's guess. Maybe a little of both. I've got eyes on him that he doesn't know about, and he's still too afraid to make any kind of a move with me around, but I know he's just waiting. He will find a time and a place one day.

And I'll be ready when he does.

I push the thoughts aside, surprised by the hot surge of anger that rears up inside of my chest. My fists clench discretely at my sides. They want to lay into the bastard right here and now, to feel cartilage and bone crunching beneath them, to feel the hot blood coating my knuckles as I teach the prick what it's like to be a victim. I force my thoughts under control and keep my demeanor calm and cool.

"How are you settling in?"

"Could use some better soundproofing in my bedroom," she says pointedly and I can't help but smirk at her. I know she can hear damn near everything through the walls, and yeah, ok, maybe some horrible, sick part of me is glad about it, maybe hopes it'll make her jealous. I think about her straddling my lap that night, how I'd barely been able to stop myself from gripping her hips and pulling her harder against me, from slamming my lips to hers and making her forget about everything else in the world. She'd offered to be my whore and it had sent ice through my veins, effectively squashing the moment, but that didn't mean that I hadn't thought about it since then. Not her being my whore—I fucking hate that phrase—but about her and me and all the things I would die to do with her...to her...watch while she does to me...

I clear my throat and focus on the task at hand. We're up here for a reason.

"But, other than that, it's been surprisingly...pleasant. Mostly," she adds, cutting her eyes briefly to Jett. I don't miss the look. Oh yes, she knows exactly what kind of man Jett is. I'm willing to bet she had him dead to fucking rights the minute she bowed up to him that day. Melody is extremely observant. Too observant. She has to have figured out everything by now, though she hasn't accosted me or demanded answers. I haven't met with her again, but I've been watching and waiting, letting her come to her conclusions and deal with that information as she will. We'll talk soon enough.

"All reports show that you've been behaving." I try to hide my smile when she clenches her hands into fists at the word, knowing that it grates on her nerves. She gives me a saccharine smile.

"I think we've established that I'm smart enough not to do anything stupid."

I hold her stare and quirk a brow.

"Smart enough that I can trust you with a weapon?"

She physically perks up at that, like my old German Shepherd when he heard the word *walk*. His favorite thing in the world. I study her for a heartbeat longer, gauging whether she's going to haul off and shoot me or anything. I decide that I'm safe and nod to Jett. He reluctantly shoves an M4 carbine at her. She transforms before my eyes the second her hands wrap around the weapon. It's like it's a part of her, like she was made for it. There's an undeniable, quiet skill and strength and confidence in her all the time, but it turns into something completely different when she's holding a weapon. Something deadly and beautiful and terrifying. Prior military, I'm guessing, but I know without a doubt that Melody Morales was born to protect people. *As if I needed one more thing to fucking like about her.*

She does a quick, efficient check of the weapon and nods to herself before looking back to me. Don't ask me why that was fucking hot as hell.

"I'd like a little demonstration," I finally say. "You said you were the best shot around. So," I jerk my head towards the fence and the woods behind it, "prove it."

"Bloody at two o'clock, three hundred yards out just beyond the fence," Jett says, a mocking challenge in his voice. Melody glares at him before raising the weapon and sighting down the target.

Without lowering it or looking at either of us, she asks, "And this isn't some kind of weird test? I'm not going to reap any kind of punishment if I fire this weapon?"

"No trick. I just want to see if you can back up the boasting," I assure her.

"So this is a nut up or shut up situation, then. Got it," she says and I can't help but laugh. I see her lips curl up, her eyes still on the target. Then, she flat out smiles like she's in on some joke no one else is. I narrow my eyes, wondering what brought that on.

"Alright then. Watch and learn, boys." She takes a deep breath, and squeezes the trigger as she exhales. One loud bang reverberates through the surrounding air. She lowers the rifle and looks at us with a bored expression, clearly saying *that was child's play.*

I pull up binoculars while Jett uses the sight of his own rifle to check her work. I frown—the Bloody is still moaning and groaning. She...missed? But no, there's no way. She's acting far too cocky for someone that missed her target. I scan around and then I see it. A smile splits my face and I laugh quietly. Jett's dumb ass laughs like an imbecile, loud and obnoxious, because he has no fucking clue.

Gonna regret that, bucko.

"You missed completely. Some hot shot," he scoffs.

I lower the binoculars and give her an appraising look, cocking a brow. Another piece of the puzzle that is Melody Morales. One day, I'll fit them all together and figure her out. I haven't told her she can leave, but I don't try to stop her as she turns and strides towards the ladder. I tell myself not to check out her ass in those cut offs...but do it anyway. Just a quick peek and then I yank my gaze back up again.

I'm pretty sure I know exactly what she's about to do as she nears Jett, and I wish I had fucking popcorn.

She shoves the rifle into his chest and he fumbles to grab it.

"I wasn't aiming for that one, sweetheart."

She smirks as she climbs down the ladder, meeting my gaze for a heartbeat before pulling it away and disappearing from view. Jett's thick brow furrows in confusion and he sets her rifle down and pulls the scope of his own back up to his eye.

"*Sonofabitch*," he mutters when he realizes that Melody had tagged a different Bloody—one that had been standing nearly *six* hundred yards out.

I smile and don't even try to hide it. She is fucking amazing.

And very well may be the death of me.

CHAPTER TEN

MELODY

"TRAEGER WANTS you to have dinner with him," Renee tells me as we jog around the lake together. I've started running every day again, and invited Renee to join me anytime she wanted. She'd eagerly agreed and I'm actually glad to have the company. Me and Jonah and Mull used to run together, constantly pushing each other to go faster and having (mostly) friendly competitions. God, I miss them so much still that it physically hurts, a constant dull ache in my chest. I wonder what they're doing, if they're alright and if Traeger has kept his promise.

"Why?" I ask, reeling back and nearly stumbling.

Renee hikes her shoulder. "When will you figure out that it isn't my place to question him?"

We stop to rest at the far end of the lake, waving to Wynn who's on duty in the nearest tower, before plopping down in the grass. Renee leans back on her hands and kicks her legs out in front of her. I glance at her sidelong and after a few minutes, decide to just go for it.

"Can I ask you something and you give me the honest answer?"

"Sure," Renee says easily.

"Did he do that to you?" I nod towards her scar. "Is that why you obey him without question? Out of fear?" She straightens and gapes.

"No! God, no. He's *never* hurt me." She exhales roughly and turns to stare out over the lake.

"I'm sorry, I didn't mean to upset you, I'm just...trying to understand this place, to understand him. Nothing's the way it's supposed to be. Which isn't a bad thing, but it's just...confusing."

"It's alright. I know that it can be disconcerting at first, to try to reconcile the rumors and what you think you know with the reality of it all." She pulls out a thick blade of grass and begins peeling it into tiny strips. I wait, having a feeling that she wants to talk, but just needs a little time. Sure enough, after a few minutes, she says, "I owe him my life. *That's* why I obey and trust him without question. But it isn't out of obligation, like a debt he expects me to pay. I do it because I want to, because I respect him and believe in him and care about him in a way that I can't really explain. Not like *that,*" she adds quickly as she glances at me, "but it's a really important way."

She takes a deep breath and throws the pieces of grass away. Her entire body tenses and I react in kind, preparing myself for whatever Renee is about to tell me. I know that it isn't going to be anything good.

"He found me two years ago not too far north of here. I'd been with a small group, but we ran into a herd and I was the only one to make it out alive. I was on my own for a week or so, barely surviving—I wasn't built for this world, not to be out there alone, at least," she says with a small self-deprecating smile, but it fades quickly. "I ran into two men and they...they..." She swallows hard and I lay a hand on her shoulder, offering support. I already know that this story is the dark and painful kind. Renee gives me a grateful look and reaches up to put her hand over mine, squeezing gently.

"They attacked me. Tied me up and kept me in an old storage shed in the woods for days while they..." She squeezes her eyes shut and fury tears through me. Renee doesn't have to say the words. I know exactly what those men did to her. There are a few surefire ways to make my cold, unforgiving dark side come out in full force. One is hurting—even *threatening* to hurt—the people I love. The other is forcing anything on anyone who isn't willing. *Tell me Traeger punished them. Tell me he made it slow.*

"I tried to fight back and one of them did this." She points to the long scar on her face. "I stopped fighting after that," she adds quietly. She turns to face me again. "Then Traeger came. He heard them talking about me, *joking* about what they were doing, when they were in the nearby town getting supplies. He followed them back to the shed and subdued them both. When he opened the door and found me, the rage I felt radiating from him terrified me. At first I thought he was just like them, that he was going to pick up where they left off or just kill me. I struggled, screaming against the gag they'd shoved in my mouth. He held his hands up and told me it was alright, that he wasn't going to hurt me. Something in his eyes made me believe him. He was so gentle as he took off the gag and cut the rope from my wrists. He looked at the crusted blood and the burns the rope had left on my skin, and that quiet rage poured out of him again. He helped me stand and eased me out of the shed. He asked if I wanted to kill them, or watch him do it, or turn away, but no matter what I picked, they were going to die. There was no other option in his mind. I couldn't do it myself, even after everything...but I watched." She swallows hard but lifts her chin. "And I didn't feel bad at all as he executed them both."

"Good," I say, my body practically vibrating with rage and wanting to take matters into my own hands, even knowing that justice has already been served. For a moment, I have nothing but respect and appreciation for Traeger. If he responded like that to Renee's situation, I can't imagine that he would ever force anyone himself. *So, yet another thing we had so fucking wrong.*

Renee laughs lightly and sniffles, wiping tears from her eyes.

"I know his hands aren't clean, but I also know that the things he's done are always for the right reasons and that most people only see what he *wants* them to see. He's no angel, but he does what has to be done to keep everyone safe. Not just here, but in all the settlements. The world isn't black and white anymore. It is all gray."

"Fifty shades of it by what I hear each night from my room," I say with a small smile.

Renee laughs out loud, throwing her head back. "Oh my God. Ok, that was a good one." She scrunches her nose. "Can you really hear him?"

"Ohhh yes. More so the girls than him, but yeah. Natasha is the worst. She literally sounds like a cat in heat." I shudder and Renee snorts, slapping a hand over her mouth.

"You are terrible," she hisses.

"I never claimed to be otherwise." I shrug. I bump her leg with mine. "Hey, thank you for sharing your story with me. It...helps me understand things a bit better."

Renee smiles. "You're welcome. Maybe now you'll share some of your story with me. Not right this second," she adds quickly, "but... some day."

"I will, I promise." I glance at the setting sun and sigh. "I guess we should get back so I can get ready for dinner."

"I WANT you as part of the security team," Traeger says when I sit down for dinner in his room. His green eyes had flared with heat for a moment when I'd first walked in. I'd gone with cut-off shorts and a tank top, deciding that being as casual as possible made it feel less like a weird date. But he'd raked his gaze up my bare legs and over my chest, lingering for a long moment on my hair, which I'd let dry in loose waves, and with the way he looked at me, I didn't feel casual at all. My stomach clenched at that look, heat spreading through my chest.

It's obvious that he's attracted to me, so why had he turned me down that first night? Was it truly because he's a...decent human being after all? More and more evidence is pointing me in that direction, it's true, but I still can't quite make myself just accept it.

I quirk a brow. "Seriously?"

"You're obviously extremely skilled in that department, and I like to surround myself with the best of the best."

"You're going to let me just waltz around with a loaded gun?"

"Eventually, yes. You mentioned previously that you were smart enough not to do anything stupid. I'm assuming you still stand by that statement?" I roll my eyes and his lips quirk up on one side. "So, yes. Eventually, you'll get to just waltz around with a loaded gun. For now, you'll just...observe. That's across the board, mind you. No one gets a weapon at first. There's a probationary period for all new members on security detail."

I eye him critically as I sip my water, keeping my expression passive. I'm excited to be back in some type of guard or security role, dying to do more and use my skills, but I don't want to let him know just how eager I am for this.

"I guess that makes sense," I finally allow. "I'll observe for now." He nods and takes a drink, watching me over the rim of his glass. I pick up my knife and spin it slowly in my right hand. "You know, rumor has it I tried to stab you and that's why I'm here."

He watches the knife with amused interest.

"Is that what they're saying?"

I nod. I could throw the knife now and end him in seconds if I wanted, and he has no idea...but as if reading my thoughts, he leans back in his chair and throws his arms out wide.

"If you want to try, be my guest." His green eyes darken as they meet mine, that subtle challenge in his voice again. I arch a brow, as if considering it, but then hike a shoulder.

"Nah, this is too easy. When I kill you, it'll be more...sporting." He snorts and my lips curl at the corners. "When do I start?"

"Tomorrow."

We eat in silence for a few minutes and it's surprisingly comfortable. The food is again delicious. Roasted vegetables, a small salad, and meat of some kind—deer, I think. One upside to the end of the world is that wildlife has absolutely exploded. Animals are immune to the disease, both the initial sickness and whatever the hell spread from the Bloodies to turn you if you got bit. They can still be torn apart by the damn things, of course, but overall, they're thriving. Which means, if you're a halfway decent shot, you'll never starve in this world.

"So, have you figured it out yet?" he asks, popping a tomato into his mouth.

I know what he's asking. If I've figured out the truth about FOS, about *him*.

"I have some theories, but I'm still conducting research before I make my final deductions."

He smiles as he takes a drink.

"Alright then. That's fair, professor."

I suppress a smile and take a few bites of my salad. Bolstered by the strange...pleasantness of the evening, I decide to ask the question that's been on my mind all these weeks.

"I've held up my end of the bargain...have you?"

"Are you asking if Jonah and the others are alright? If I've harmed them?"

"Yes," I say simply.

He leans forward and puts his forearms on the table as he holds my gaze.

"I'm a lot of things, Melody. Some of them not so great, some of them fan-fucking-tastic. But one of those things is a man of my word. If I make a promise, I keep it. I promised that no harm would come to anyone at The Cove so long as the terms of our little arrangement and Kevin's punishment were upheld. You've held up your end, and Kevin is still in his house—" I don't even bother asking how he knows that. I've long assumed he has spies in every settlement reporting back to him regularly "—so I've held up my end. Your friends are safe and will remain that way."

"Alright," I say, nodding. Our gazes lock and suddenly that terrible heaviness settles around us, the same one I felt in the kitchen back at The Cove. I inhale softly and his eyes flare, and I wonder if he'd make the same decision as he did that first night if I crawled across the table right now, if I straddled him in that chair and wrapped my arms around his neck, leaned in and pressed my lips to his...but a knock at the door breaks the tension before I can do anything so ridiculous.

His lips curl into his customary smirk, but it looks like a mask now and I narrow my eyes a fraction. Had I just had a glimpse of the real him? He rises from the table and I would swear there's the tiniest flare of disappointment as he walks to the door. He opens it wide to reveal Natasha and I groan inwardly. *Not the cat in heat.*

The woman gives him a sultry smile and his eyes dip down to take in her tight, skimpy blue dress. It's covered in sequins and cut into a v between her breasts clear down to her navel. She can rock it, I'll give her that, but...Traeger's eyes *don't* widen as he takes in Natasha the way they had when I'd come in earlier. *Interesting. Doesn't matter,* I remind myself, dismissing the errant thoughts I'd had a few minutes ago. *But…it's interesting.*

I toss my napkin down and waltz to the door. I have the strange feeling that Traeger's *trying* to make me jealous, so I make sure to act completely unaffected.

"Can we try to keep the theatrics to a minimum tonight? I'm tired." Natasha looks offended and Traeger looks amused. I just stop myself from winking at him before sauntering out.

THE FURIOUS LOOK on Jett's face as I'm ushered into the Big Boys Club meeting the next morning is an unexpected perk of my new job assignment.

"You can't be serious," he scoffs, giving Traeger a disbelieving look.

"Deadly so, and if you have a problem with it, by all means, let us know." Traeger's voice holds a note of quiet, understated authority that makes me see how he'd managed to gain and maintain his position. Men who talk like that can usually back up whatever claims they make, can handle their business and handle it well. The ones who need the testosterone-filled bullshit theatrics, the ones who need to *show* everyone that they're big and bad rarely actually are. Traeger looks at Jett and waits expectantly, ready to have this out if his second-in-command really wants to.

Jett grinds his teeth, but eventually says, "Of course not, sir."

"Great," Traeger says with a winning smile to the group. There are nineteen members of the official security team in addition to Traeger and Jett, and I'm glad to see that a small handful are women. There are plenty more FOSers assigned to security detail as their job—guard duty, patrols, etc.—but this is specifically Traeger's personal security team.

"Introductions: Mel, this is everyone. Everyone, this is Mel." I cast him a sidelong look. He only calls me Mel when other people are around. When it's just the two of us, I'm always Melody. Could mean nothing, but I'm coming to realize that something rarely means nothing when it comes to Traeger. I get the feeling that every little thing is calculated and done for a reason.

After introductions and a run down of what's going on, things noted on patrols, status of provisions and scheduled supply trips, and areas that need attention within the settlements, I'm assigned to be Wynn's shadow for the next few weeks until I pass initiation, I guess. He grins at me when the meeting adjourns.

"I'm glad I'm with you," I say, fist bumping him.

"Well, of course he wanted you with the best," Wynn says, spreading his arms wide and grinning, those pearly whites shining like he's in a Crest commercial. I roll my eyes but laugh and we make our way out to our assigned spot for the day. We're on guard duty on one of the platforms outside the gate that had been so well hidden, I hadn't even noticed it on our drive in, which is really saying something.

"I heard you capped a Bloody at six hundred yards," Wynn says when we're settled into our perch.

"Maybe." I hike a shoulder with a sly grin.

Wynn chuckles. "Jett was pi-*issed* about it. Dragging his knuckles and beating his chest like the angry gorilla he is." In a cave-man voice he adds, "Me mad! Me manhood threatened! Me smash!"

I laugh out loud at his Jett impression and he smiles.

"Not his biggest fan, huh?"

Wynn's smile fades, his eyes turning serious.

"He hasn't been here all that long. Him and his two shadows, Collins and Bartlett, were all found together and Jett quickly found a place as Traeger's second-in-command. He's a decent enough soldier, but he's a prick, all three of them are. I think he hid it long enough to get into Traeger's good graces, so he's not as dumb as he looks, but now his true colors are coming out. And rumor has it they...take liberties when they're out without the rest of us."

"And Traeger lets it slide?" I spit, annoyed.

"Well, it's all just rumor, I guess," Wynn shrugs, but he seems uncomfortable with the idea of Traeger letting it slide. Then again, he knows better than most how fucked up this world could be now. He'd had a rough go of it until he'd found FOS. Or rather, until the FOSers had found him. Wynn told me that he'd been captured and held prisoner by a feral group a couple of years ago. They'd turned out to be very into cannibalism. I shudder now even thinking about it. Traeger had gotten wind of the group somehow, and had come to shut that shit down, rescuing a tortured and nearly-dead Wynn and a handful of others in the process. I'd reluctantly put a gold star next to Traeger's name in my mental inventory for that one. *He's a certified knight in shining armor, isn't he?*

"I keep my distance from him though," Wynn continues. "We're all supposed to have each other's backs, but I wouldn't trust any of them with mine. Steer clear of them, but especially Jett. Collins and Barlett are mostly harmless unless Jett is there to pull their strings, I think." His tone is serious, as it so rarely is. Has he seen the looks Jett had given me? Or is he just guessing based on the bad vibes he gets from Jett in general? I'm pretty sure it's a combination of both.

"I will," I promise him, though I add silently *until it's time to end him.* I sweep the area with my binoculars yet again, but there's still no trace of anything. Not a single Bloody in sight and no one else skulking around either.

"Is it always this quiet here?"

"Usually, yeah. A handful of Bloodies make their way here every now and then, usually more through the woods on the other side by the lake than on this end, but there's an old rock query a few miles to the east full of abandoned cars. We rig a few to blare their horns on a pretty regular schedule to draw as many of the Bloodies there and away from FOS as we can." I raise my brows and nod. It's smart. Really fucking smart, actually. I should mention trying to create something similar near The Cove to Jonah...then I remember that I'll never actually get to speak to him again. Pain laces my chest and my eyes burn, but I force the tears away.

"Hey, I know you probably aren't really supposed to, but the next time you go to The Cove..."

"I'll let him know you're alright, I promise."

"Thank you. Tell him...tell him I said "you cheatin', bitches!" and he'll know I'm alright, he'll know the message really came from me."

Wynn laughs at my over-the-top Texan accent and I explain that it went way back to the early days of our friendship.

"So, one night, Me, Mitch, Jonah, and Sean—that was Jonah's husband—were playing three-deck rummy. Well, Jonah and I were... we'll say colluding. Some may call it cheating, but that's such an ugly word..." Wynn snorts. "So Jonah was feeding me the cards I needed throughout the game with the husbands none the wiser, right. But after a few drinks, we got a little sloppy in our sneaking and Sean figured out what we were up to. He jumped onto the table and pointed an accusing finger at us and yelled "You cheatin', bitches!" in his thick Texan twang. We all about died from laughing so hard and the phrase just became a thing we all said to each other all the time."

Wynn cracks up and I can't help but join him, laughing at the memory even as the familiar pain settles in my chest. God I miss them all. I miss those days together, our lives, how the world used to be. We finally get ourselves under control and I tell Wynn to float the idea of the car lot distraction to Jonah too. He promises he'll deliver both messages for me.

After a bit, I lean back on my hands and eye him.

"So, level with me here, Landry. Is all of this real? This whole paradise in the middle of the apocalypse thing?" I gesture back towards the compound. "Everyone thinks this place is hell on earth, but being here, that doesn't jive. So, which one is the truth? Are the people just brainwashed and he's really good at hiding the hell from me so far, or...?"

Wynn gives me a knowing look.

"You're smart. What do you think?"

I puff up my cheeks before letting a long, slow exhale.

"I think...that he might just be a genius," I begrudgingly admit. The rumors of his brutality and the horrors to be found at FOS not only keep his power in his grasp, but it keeps this place from being overrun with people wanting in. *So, he's only a monster outside of these walls or when he needs to be.*

I think about all the lives he's taken and all the things he's done: Kevin's son used as an example killing, the other settlement being destroyed in retaliation for an attempted attack, heads on pikes and disfigured members of his group being strung up outside of other settlements to show what happens when he wasn't obeyed. Was it all for show? Is he really just playing a part and doing what has to be done?

And if that's the case…what toll is it taking on him? And why do I fucking care?

I pinch my forehead and groan. Wynn chuckles.

"Is it a perfect system? No. But it's doing the best with what we've got and even though its hard to see it sometimes, it really does keep everyone as safe as they can be."

I don't want to believe it. I want to believe that he's really just a sick bastard who likes being large and in charge and hurting people along the way. I want to believe that he's evil. Because if he isn't…

No. I don't go there. I don't even let the treacherous thought take shape. Instead, Wynn and I start chatting football and life back in Louisiana, passing the time until dinner.

A FEW DAYS LATER, I see an older woman struggling a bit to carry a heaping basket of laundry in from the outdoor lines near the edge of the lake. I supposed there are probably still dryers somewhere deep inside the hotel, but there's no reason to waste the energy on them when the sun can do the job just fine.

I sprint over to the woman.

"Here, let me help you with that." I take the basket and the older woman straightens with a bright smile, her sienna skin wrinkling at the edges of her amber eyes. She's tall and thin, with an easy grace to her movements, like a dancer. Her hair is a deep, chocolate brown, streaked liberally with silver, and pulled into a tight bun on top of her head.

"Thank you, Mel." My brows rise and the woman chuckles. "Everyone knows your name, mija. We haven't had a fresh addition in quite a while…especially one that Austin has kept such a close eye on." She glances over my shoulder and I frown in confusion. I turn to follow her gaze and find Traeger just across the lawn, watching us as he talks to Johnson. He raises a hand in greeting and the woman smiles and waves back. I turn back to her. Hearing someone refer to Traeger as anything but Traeger is so strange. I'd honestly almost forgotten his first name was Austin. Even his nightly visitors scream *Traeger*, not *Austin*.

"You've been the talk of the town, of course."

Her smile is warm and inviting, her eyes kind, and her Columbian accent reminds me so much of my late mother-in-law that my heart clenches in my chest, one of those swift, stabbing pains that comes out of nowhere sometimes. I'd loved Gabriella as if she'd been my own mother. Hell, she'd been more of a mother to me than my own ever had. Mitch had always joked that his mom loved me more than she loved him. And I had always responded with "can you blame her?" I smile inwardly at the memory, but it fades quickly. We'd lost her just before we'd found out I was pregnant, and it still breaks my heart that she'd never gotten to meet Gabby, the granddaughter that had been named for her.

But I do like to think that in whatever life is after this one, wherever we go next, Gabriella *does* know, and that she, Mitch, and Gabby are all together somewhere, safe and happy.

"Oh, well, I'm no big deal," I say to the older woman with a smile.

"It is nice to meet you officially finally. Everyone just calls me Abuela." She smiles, her eyes crinkling again, and I think that she must be older than she looks.

"It's nice to meet you too." I glance back to Traeger only to find him still watching. "So, uh, does Traeger not usually keep a close eye on newcomers then? They don't all stay in the suite beside him at first?"

Abuela laughs, a deep, hearty sound that warms my chest.

"Oh no, my dear." She leans in and adds with a mischievous glint in her eyes, "And he most definitely does not watch every new resident of our little community like *that*." She nods conspiratorially towards Traeger and I just stop myself from turning to look again. My cheeks flush and I rub the back of my neck a little self-consciously.

"Well, I didn't ask for special treatment. I didn't ask to come here." I purse my lips. "Ok, well actually that's a lie. I *did* technically ask, but it wasn't like I wanted to come."

"Is it so bad here?" Abuela asks.

I let out a long exhale and Abuela nods to a picnic table nearby, as if she can sense that this is a...complicated question. We sit and I think about it. Is it so bad at FOS? Though I still don't want to acknowledge that Traeger isn't actually the monster I thought him to be, and feel like a traitor admitting the truth, I can't really deny it any longer. I sigh.

"No, it really isn't so bad here at all."

"Did you leave people behind then?"

"I did. Jonah." I try to breathe around the lump in my throat. "He's the reason I left. I offered myself up to Traeger to keep him safe, to make sure he stayed there where he needed to be."

"Well, that was very brave of you, given what I'm sure you had heard about this place."

I hike a shoulder. I didn't feel brave for doing it, I just knew it was what had to be done. I love Jonah more than anything, but he found Mulligan and had another chance at real happiness, at a real life after all the pain and suffering and surviving. I couldn't let that be taken away from him. And I couldn't let anyone else at The Cove suffer needlessly either. Everyone there had...someone. I didn't. I was the expendable one, so it made sense for me to be expended.

"So, you don't mind him?" I tilt my head towards Traeger. He isn't staring anymore, instead deep in conversation with a couple of FOSers and looking thoughtful.

"Of course not," she says, looking at me like I'm crazy.

"But...you know the things he's done, don't you?"

"Mija, you know that the world has changed. Right and wrong, good and evil—it isn't as it used to be. There are no clear lines anymore, everything is blurred. He has done what needed to be done to keep everyone safe, to give everyone the best chance at life again."

"I understand that. Believe me, I've done my fair share of what needed to be done too, but...he's different."

"How so?" It isn't defensive or angry, just conversational, like she really wants to know what I'm thinking about the man.

"I've killed, but it was always in self-defense or to keep my people safe. He kills just to kill. To prove a point and make people fear him. I get that the fear is necessary to an extent, to keep everything running the way he wants it to and to keep the people here safe, to keep everyone in Haven safe, I guess, but..." I shake my head. I know I'm grasping at straws, but I can't quite make myself just fucking *give in* and accept what I know to be true. So, I'm still fighting. I'm still going to throw everything I have at the wall and see what sticks. My guess? Not much.

"He wiped out an entire settlement," I point out, desperate to have her confirm that he is, in fact, a horrible person, that even if it was a necessary move to solidify his place as a leader and keep the other settlements in line, that it doesn't make it ok.

"Did he now?" Abuela says in that motherly way, likes she's letting me discover the right answer on my own. The old woman places her elbows on the table, resting her chin in one upturned hand. I narrow my eyes at her suspiciously.

"...didn't he?"

"He did," Abuela says breezily, "but not in the way you think. That settlement was a true hell, worse than even the worst rumors you have heard about FOS. The men there were the worst kind of humans left, the rot of the earth. They kept women and children as slaves, used in whatever manner they wanted. Any man who stood up to the others was tortured in unspeakable ways. The people were starved, beaten, raped, tortured, forced to fight each other and fed to Bloodies for entertainment."

My mouth falls open in horror and fire flares in Abuela's eyes, a rage on the surface and pain just below it.

"Until Austin. He did wipe that settlement off the map, and he did deliver the heads of those men on spikes to the other settlements as a warning, but he *rescued* the others. He saved them, gave them a safe place where they were cared for and respected and felt unafraid for the first time in too many years. They were all too happy to keep his secrets in order to preserve the peace and safety they'd found, in order to help others have that same safety, and to keep the same thing from happening anywhere else ever again."

I stare at Abuela with wide eyes. Every word rings with absolute truth—truth of someone who witnessed it firsthand.

"You were there." It isn't a question. She inclines her head.

"That man is not what you think he is. He is not perfect. He can be vicious and cruel and lethal when needed. He does what is necessary, but the lives he takes are never without cause and never just for show, I promise you. He's smart and calculating and shoulders far more than you could ever imagine. He lets everyone but those within these walls think and see the worst of him. It takes a toll," she says sadly. "He'd never admit it, but I know that it does."

"I…" I don't know what to say to that. I knew that Traeger wasn't the sadistic, blood-thirsty dictator he likes to pretend he is, but I hadn't realized that the people he hurts might…deserve it? That he's strategic in the pain and fear he distributes. That he's…I shake my head, not wanting to go too far down this line of thinking right now.

Abuela gives me a knowing smile and reaches for the basket, waving me off when I try to help again.

"I just needed a little break, I've got it now, mija. I'm glad to have met you and glad that you are here." After another brief look to Traeger, she adds in a low voice, "Keep an open mind. Happiness is often found in the most unlikely of places."

She winks and leaves me sitting in stunned silence with too many thoughts roiling in my head.

CHAPTER ELEVEN

TRAEGER

I'M ninety-eight percent sure Melody has it all figured out. Has *me* all figured out. I think I have Wynn and Abuela to at least partially thank for it, but I know she was already halfway to the right conclusion on her own. She's been looking at me differently these last couple of weeks. Less like a monster and more like a man...a man that she finds interesting. Maybe more than just interesting?

I have no idea if that's really there or if I just want it to be, but she's definitely changed the way she acts around me. It's almost friendly. Or at least as close to friendly as she'll allow herself to get with me for now. But I'll fucking take it, because there's an edge to the friendly, a dangerous undercurrent that I want to explore so fucking badly I have to constantly keep myself from crossing lines, from reaching out to touch her, to asking the questions I want to ask. The decision has to be hers. I'm the one who tore her away from her life, from the one person that she loves in this world. She has to be the one to decide if she can move past that or not.

But God I fucking hope she does. With her on the security team now, we've been spending a lot more time around each other and the connection is definitely becoming more defined with each day that passes.

About two weeks after she'd first been added to the team, I decided to take a very small step. Nothing big deal, just a small gesture to test the waters. I'd seen her eyeing my bookshelves that first night and I'd seen her with her nose in one more than once by the lake when she had downtime, so I figured why the fuck not? I picked one of my favorites and left it in her room. No explanation, no big pageantry about it, just a note on a scrap piece of paper tucked into the front.

"–*T*"

I half expected her to toss it out into the hallway, but she didn't. A few days later she returned it. No thanks or discussion, just handed it back to me with a nod. So I did it again, and again, and now it's our weird little thing. I leave her books, she returns them. I switch up the genres, feeling out her favorites. I would have killed to see her face when she found the romance novel waiting for her last week. I annotate my books, always have, and I was floored when Melody added her own notes to mine. It's like a secret conversation between the two of us that no one else can touch. Without saying a word, we talk for hours through the books and the notes.

I haven't had dinner alone with her again, partly because I don't want chatter to start up when there's nothing to chatter about—there's already enough because of her being in the suite next to mine. Probably not my most rash decision, but I'd wanted her close. I can justify it all I want for a hundred different reasons, but in the end that's the only reason: *I wanted her close*—and partly because I honestly don't trust myself to be alone in my room with her without doing something really fucking stupid. But I've found myself at her table for dinner at The Skillet most nights. Every time our arms or thighs brush, it sends a jolt through my entire body. I feel like I'm a fucking teenager again, that rush of terrified excitement and anticipation when you start something with someone. Not that we're starting anything, exactly, but... hell, maybe we are?

I spy Wynn and Melody strolling up to our little game of touch football this afternoon. I'm grabbing waters from a basket under one of the big oak trees and I don't think she's spotted me yet. I like watching her when she doesn't know I am. Ok, that sounded really fucking creepy. I just mean that she still has a barrier that she keeps up around me. It's a hell of a lot less substantial now than it was before, more like a stormdoor now instead of the bank vault door she had in place when she first got here, but it's still there. But when she's around most everyone else, it falls away and I get glimpses of the real girl behind the wall.

Johnson beams, pointing to Wynn.

"Oh hell yes! Landry, get your ass over here! Dibs!" he calls, shoving his long, brown hair out of his face. Her lips curl into a soft smile, like she's visiting some old memory. Probably a bittersweet one, but most of our memories are that way now. Remembering how life used to be when almost everyone from those times is gone, the world completely changed—it's nice to think about it, but it hurts too. A few of us are lucky to have at least a small piece of the past with us still. Melody has Jonah and I have Doc, but most aren't that fortunate.

I make my way towards them.

"Do you still got it?" she asks Landry, shooting him a challenging grin. He gives her a dry look and dusts his shoulder off.

"Watch and learn, cher. Watch and learn."

She snorts while he flexes his arm muscles like a body builder and kisses his bicep, but then smacks him hard in the stomach, making him double over with a loud *oof*. I can admit that I'm envious of their easy camaraderie sometimes. I wish she could be that way with me. *Maybe one day.*

"Well, if you get Landry, we get Mel," I drawl. She whirls, her eyes widening as her gaze skates downward. I'm on the Skins team and with the way she greedily lets her eyes travel slowly over my bare chest and stomach, I'd say she's not mad about it. I let her look, liking her eyes on me. She swallows hard and, gaze dropping lower…lower still…

Landry clears his throat pointedly and laughs, making her yank her gaze back upward, well aware that she'd been caught. She meets my eyes and I quirk a brow, grinning. Surprisingly enough, she gives me a half smile that seems to say *can you blame me?*

"Whatdya say? You game?" Landry asks her.

I look at her expectantly as I hand off the bottles of water to Jack to hand out to the others. She clears her throat quietly and her typical confident swagger settles over her again. The fact that I'd been able to fluster her enough for it to drop for a few seconds makes me want to beat my chest like a caveman. Sue me. She looks pointedly at all of us sans shirts.

"As much as I would love to run around topless on this fine afternoon, I'm pretty sure at least four of the men out here would have heart attacks and die at the sight."

I chuckle low.

"You're probably right about that." I turn to call to Johnson, "We get Landry. You get Mel."

The guys on the Shirts side cheer and she can't hide her smile. Landry gives me a fist bump and then jogs over to start stretching and cutting up with the rest of the guys.

Mel watches him go, looking like she's about to follow, but then she hesitates. I think I know the problem, why she always seems to hold herself back. I know for a fact that Renee has invited her to the socials but she always declines the invite. She thinks if she lets herself be happy here, it's some sort of betrayal.

I lean in and say quietly, "Come on, Melody. You can let yourself have a little fun once in a while. We won't tell anyone." I try to keep the tone playful, but there's a more serious undercurrent. I want her to know that she doesn't need to feel guilty, that she's allowed to find happiness in a shitty situation. It's the best any of us can hope for. Hell, it was the best any of us could hope for even before the end of the world.

"I have fun," she snaps, sounding defensive.

I give her a look that clearly says she's full of shit, but I make my tone light and raise my voice so everyone can hear when I say, "Do you even know how to play?"

I give her a challenging look. *Your turn, Melody. Come on. Play the game. Play with me. Let me in, just a little…*

"Oooh, come on Mel, you can't take that!" Landry calls. She holds my gaze and though she fights it, she eventually smirks, letting the wall come down, at least a bit.

"You'll regret that," she says quietly and it only makes me grin wider.

"Let's do this!" Johnson calls as Mel tosses her button-down to the grass, leaving her in a tank top, and jogs over to the group. Everyone whoops and hollers in excitement. I love days like this, when we can all just pretend things are the way they used to be, that everything is fine and there isn't danger lurking outside the walls. When we can just *be*. I let myself shed this persona I've had to wear for so damn long and, at least for an afternoon, I'm just a guy named Austin playing a game of touch football with his friends. I can just be me, the *real* me.

I don't miss how Melody's eyes can't seem to pry themselves away from me during the game. I'm admittedly showing out a little bit, wanting her attention on me.

"Come on, Mel! Get him!" Eckerd yells as I break free from Meadows and Baker. I sprint down the field, ball in hand, and Melody gives chase. I laugh as she closes in, tossing the ball to Ramirez just before she can touch me, spinning away from her outstretched hand. But I slip just as she lunges for me, and we end up going down together in a heap—with her landing fully on top of me.

Jesus.

She braces herself with one hand on the ground beside my head, the other on my chest. Can she feel how hard my heart's beating? Will she just chock it up to the run down the field? Because that has nothing to fucking do with it. I tell myself not to move a muscle, but that doesn't work for shit, and a second later my hand flies to her hip. It takes all of my self-control not to reach out and slide my other hand to her nape, to tug her down and press my lips to hers, to use my grip on her hip to pull her body hard against mine, letting her know just how fucking much I want her…

Her eyes are wide, pupils expanding while I watch. She's breathing hard, but I'm not sure that's all from the run either.

"Melody," I rasp, and I don't know if I'm asking or begging or praying. Our faces are close. Too close. Not close enough. Her gray eyes blaze as they dip to my lips, and she inhales softly. Does she want to kiss me as badly as I want her to? Not fucking possible. I've never wanted anything so badly in my life. It's a terrible idea. It's a fantastic idea.

And if she doesn't stop looking at me like that, my self-control is going to disappear completely and I'm going to fuck her right here in the grass in front of half of FOS.

"I…" She licks her lips and my hand flexes on her hip, that small movement of her tongue having a direct line to my cock. Her shirt rides up and my fingers brush her bare skin. *Fuck.* She gasps quietly and I groan low in my throat.

"It's touch, Mel! Not tackle!" Landry calls, and she blinks, like she's suddenly remembering where we are and what we're supposed to be. Or not be, I guess. Just like that, the spell is broken and she scrambles away, rolling off of me and bounding to her feet. She clears her throat but to my surprise, reaches out to offer me a hand up. I take it and quickly release her grip as soon as I'm upright. Her eyes meet mine and just like that, the fire is back again, whatever had been burning between us before blazing to life again just below the surface. Before either of us can say or do anything else idiotic, Landry bounds up and bumps her shoulder with his.

I force myself to smooth everything away, smiling and acting like nothing had happened at all. Her eyes narrow a fraction and I know she's noticed the change. Does she believe it?

"Johnson says that's game for today. A few of the guys are due to start their rotations on patrol soon. And not that anyone is surprised, but *my* team won," Landry says, cocky and grinning.

"And now you need a shower," Mel says, shoving him playfully and wrinkling her nose. He hooks his arm around her neck and ruffles her hair in a very playful, big brother kind of way. She laughs loudly, shoving at his stomach, and I blink in surprise. I'm not sure I've ever heard her laugh, not really. She straightens when Wynn releases her, and I catch her eye, quirking a brow. She hikes a shoulder but thankfully doesn't put the wall back up, her easy smile remaining on her face. Fuck it's a good one. It's one of those smiles that would have gotten her out of any speeding ticket, no matter how fast she was going. The kind that would have gotten her free drinks at any bar in the world.

One that would bring grown men to their knees.

"Aw, don't be a sore loser, Mel," Landry teases her.

"Better luck next time," I say with a smile, letting the words hang in the air, making it clear that I'm hoping there will be a next time. She eyes me for a long minute but then nods.

"Next time."

I STARE at the door that connects my room to Melody's. I've almost knocked on it at least half a dozen times since I got back from my rounds and showered. I keep talking myself out of it, reminding myself that I'm supposed to let her make the decision, that I'm supposed to wait for her to come to me.

What if she never does? The thought makes me clench my jaw and push myself off of the arm of the couch where I've been leaning and take a few determined steps to the door. Again.

"Just fucking do it," I mutter to myself. I stop in front of the door and raise my hand, but again, I stop myself before I knock. I scowl and pace back across the room. "What the fuck is wrong with me?" I groan quietly, running a hand through my damp hair. A knock at the main door has me whirling, my heart thundering in my chest. *Finally.*

I cross to the door quickly and throw it open—only to find Destiny on the threshold.

Oh.

Right.

I'd almost forgotten that she was coming by. I don't really want her here. Don't get me wrong, I have a good time with all of the girls, but now that I'm feeling more and more for Melody, I don't want anyone else.

"Hey, you," she says, giving me a sultry smile and leaning forward to run her hands up my chest. "I've been thinking about you all day."

I should tell her to leave. I think about Melody next door, knowing she can hear pretty much everything that happens in here...and wonder if she even cares. I think back to the look in her eyes when she was on top of me on the field earlier, the unmistakable desire, but also

the longing, like she wanted me for far more than just something physical. Was it really there? Or am I just reading into shit because I want it
to be there so fucking badly?

Well, it might make me an asshole, but I decide to do a little experi-
ment. I pull Destiny forward and her body slams into mine.

"Oh!" she says, breathless, and giggles loudly. I nuzzle my face into
her neck.

"Tell me how much you want me," I command quietly. "Make it
loud."

She groans. "I want you so bad, baby. I've been *aching* for you." I
press her back into the wall with enough force to make a loud thud
reverberate through the room. "Hmmm, yessss, Traeger," Destiny
moans again, digging her hands into my hair. I grab her wrists and pin
them above her head. Not because it's sexy but because I really don't
want her touching me. Even kissing her neck right now feels wrong. I
want someone else in front of me. I want my lips on someone else's
skin. I want someone else's moans ringing in my ears.

Come on, Melody. Come on...

I hear her stomping across her room and out into the hallway and I
smile, relived that I won't have to turn Destiny down outright tonight.
I'm going to have to figure out this whole "Trager's Girls" situation
soon enough though. I have no desire to do anything with any of them
at this point and so I need to tell them the arrangements are over. They
won't mind, I don't think. I mean, we have fun and I know they like
the imagined title, but really, everyone knows it was all just fun and
escape.

A second later there's a loud bang on the door. Destiny pouts as I
step away and give her an apologetic look. I open the door and cross
my arms over my chest. I smile at Melody and she narrows her eyes.
I'm ninety percent sure she knows exactly what I'd just done, that I'd
been trying my level best to make her jealous and make her storm over
here like she'd just done. It only makes me smile wider. I have a feeling
this might get very, very fun in a few minutes.

"Can I help you, Melody?" I ask innocently.

"I need to talk to you," she snaps.

I hold her gaze for a second and then call over my shoulder, "Raincheck, Destiny. I need to speak with Melody."

"Seriously?" Destiny says indignantly, but then presses her lips into a thin line. She knows it won't do any good to argue or beg. I'm a little surprised when she glares daggers at Melody as she squeezes past me through the doorway though. When the door to the stairs slams shut behind her, I step back and throw my arm wide, inviting Melody to enter. She storms in, seeming to avoid touching me at all costs.

I close the door and follow her further into the room. She stops in the middle of the living room and whirls. I wait expectantly, silently begging her to finally say what she's really thinking and feeling, to finally tell me what she wants. Or better yet, to fucking *show* me. *Come on, tell me I'm not crazy, tell me you feel it too, show me that this is fucking real.*

"I want to be moved to a new room."

I keep my face smooth, barely smothering the smirk. Oh yes, she's definitely pissed that I had Destiny here.

"Why's that? Is the suite not to your liking?" I ask. I'm going to make her say it.

"The suite is fine, it's the ridiculous low budget porno happening next door every night that's the fucking problem," she snaps. "I'm so over hearing *your girls,*" she rolls her eyes so hard at the term that I'm surprised they don't get stuck, "vying for Day Time Emmys, so clearly faking orgasms just to stroke your ego. It's pathetic—and loud."

"Think they're faking, huh?" I ask, taking one stop closer to her. She takes a step back, but not in a way that makes it seems like she wants me to stay away, more like we're starting a slow, dangerous dance. I can feel that sweet tension in the air, electricity practically sparking between us, my entire body lighting up like a live wire.

"Of course they are," she spits. Another step forward, another step back. Her eyes dart to my lips and back up again. She wets her own. "If you can't tell the difference, then you've got bigger problems than I thought." She makes her voice extra breathy and over-the-top. "*Oh God, Traeger, don't stop, right there, you're a sex God, you're the best I've ever had, you're so* big." She curls her lip in obvious disgust and annoyance. Another step.

"You've got to be kidding me with that shit." She jets her chin but her gaze drops downward again, moving from my lips to my throat, to my chest…lower…

Her back is nearly against the wall now, only one more step to make.

"And you wouldn't fake it, then?" I ask in a low, silky voice. "To stroke my ego?"

She swallows hard and her eyes blaze.

"And reward you for something you didn't earn? *Never.*" I take another step forward and she hits the wall. Our bodies are so close I can feel the heat radiating off of her. Mere inches separate us now and it's suddenly too hot in the room, too combustible. One spark and we're both going up in flames. I won't be able to stop it. I won't *want* to stop it. She reaches out and settles her hands on my hips, and I lean forward, bracing my hands on the wall on either side of her head, caging her in.

"Oh, I'd earn it, Melody," I say in a low, rough voice, my mouth so close to hers that it's torture to keep that tiny bit of separation. "I'd earn it—*All. Fucking. Night.*"

She gasps quietly and shifts one hand, curling her fingers into the waistband of my jeans, tugging me forward. I stifle a groan, even this small contact sending sparks of fire through my veins. I lean in and brush my nose against hers, barely keeping myself under control.

"Tell me yes, Melody," I whisper, and I can feel a shudder roll through her body. "I need you to tell me yes."

I pull back to look at her again, waiting, desperate. Her lips part and I know she's going to say the word that will rock me to my core, the one word I want to hear so badly I could fucking scream.

But before she can say it, another knock pounds on the door. I grind my teeth in annoyance.

"Go away!" I bark.

"Sir, I need to talk to you. It's urgent."

I want to put a hole through the wall. Wilson has the worst fucking time in the history of the world. But if he says it's urgent, it must be.

"You've got to be fucking kidding me," I grumble under my breath, leaning my forehead against Melody's, and she huffs out a strangled laugh. I exhale roughly and somehow manage to push myself off the wall and put a few feet between us. Her chest is rising and falling in quick bursts, and there's the most intense disappointment in her eyes. She looks like she wants to say something, and I get the feeling that whatever had just happened here was far more than two people who wanted a good lay. No, this was something much more than that.

Our gazes hold for a few seconds before Wilson calls, "Sir?" again. I want to tell him to fuck off. I want to let someone else be in charge and handle whatever is happening that needs my attention. I want to be done being this fucking guy and finally have a chance to be the real me and explore this thing with Melody. But I can't. I know I can't. Maybe one day, but that day isn't today.

I run a hand through my hair and accept that we're effectively putting a pin in whatever this was. I hope it's not forever. I hope this doesn't spook her and she doesn't chock this up to temporary insanity and talk herself out of trying again. She glances to the front door and I know that she won't want to go that way and see Wilson. I tilt my head towards the door at the side of the living room instead, the one that connects our suites. She nods and without a word, crosses to the door, flips the lock and throws it open. She pushes against the second door leading into her room, but it barely moves, like something's blocking it.

"Fuck," she grates, throwing her shoulder against the door trying to get it to budge.

"One second!" I yell to Wilson before coming up behind her. I push and meet pretty hefty resistance. She must have put some furniture in front of it. "For fuck's sake, Melody, did you really think I was going to attack you in your sleep?" I ask through gritted teeth.

"You can't possibly blame me!" she hisses quietly. "This place was supposed to be Lucifer's Den-O-Fun, remember??"

I huff out a laugh and shake my head. No, I guess I can't blame her. When she blocked that door, she thought I was a sadistic psychopath who probably raped and murdered for shits and giggles. I nudge her out of the way and take a deep breath before putting my full weight into it. The door and whatever's behind it—a chair, I guess—finally give way and she can step through into her room. She turns to face me and opens her mouth to say something, but seems to have no clue what it might be, so she snaps it closed again. I won't lie, I'm in the same fucking boat. I desperately want to say something, to beg her not to overthink this or change her mind, to wait for me just for a bit, but I don't. I sigh and reach for the door handle, holding her gaze for as long as possible as I pull it closed.

I don't have to wear the full mask here at FOS, not the one that I wear outside in the real world, but I still have to wear a version of it. Only with Melody can I take it off completely. I tell myself that doesn't mean what I think it means, but I know damn well that's a fucking lie.

So, I put on the mask and slip back into the role I have to play before opening the door for Wilson and getting to work.

CHAPTER TWELVE
MELODY

TRAEGER'S GONE for the next week and I can't decide if that's a good thing or a bad thing. I...miss him? No, that can't possibly be right. Except it fucking is. I hate that it is, but it is. I'd gone for a punishing run after our almost...whatever the hell that had been in his room before Wilson came to grab him for something urgent. I'd needed to clear my head and try to figure out what was going on with me, with him, with us. I'd been asleep when they left, but he'd slid a note under my door. Not anything profound or swoon-worthy. Just a simple:

BE BACK SOON.
-T

But the fact that he'd left it meant something, didn't it? And, ok, fine, it made me *happy* that he'd left it.

"Fuck my life," I whisper-groan as Renee and I finish up our afternoon run.

"What was that?" she asks.

"Nothing," I say, shaking myself. We slow to a walk and Renee gives me a sidelong look.

"He'll be back tonight," she says, wiping sweat from her brow.

"Who now?" I make a point to be purposely obtuse and Renee laughs, shaking her head.

"Uh huh, fine, go ahead and act like you haven't jolted every time someone walks into The Skillet every single night since the day he left, only to deflate when it isn't him."

"That's...I was...It's just..." I have nothing and she knows it. I hate that she's so observant and hope to God she's the only one who is. "Shut up," I finish lamely, and she laughs again.

After a few seconds, she adds a bit more seriously, "you could, you know."

"Could what?" I ask, looking out over the water to the mountains in the distance. The sun will be setting soon and the sky is streaked with deep pinks and reds and golds, the colors reflecting off of the mirror-like surface of the lake. *It really is gorgeous here,* I think.

"Could be happy here." I turn to look at Renee. "I know you're still holding yourself back, and I don't know if it's because you feel guilty letting yourself be happy when Jonah isn't here, or if it's something else, but...Well, I'm just saying you're allowed to be happy, Mel. Even if that involves being with someone who may not have been the conventional choice originally," she adds with a knowing smile.

"I...you're right, I do feel guilty," I admit. "Jonah knows that I'm ok, but he obviously can't know the full truth, so I know he's still got to be worried about me being here. If I just move on and act like everything is fine, it's like I'm betraying him or making him worry in vain or something." I shake my head, not able to really explain it quite right.

"But you being unhappy isn't what he would want, no matter what. You've told me enough about him to know that for a fact."

I sigh heavily. "You're right. I know you're right. But I can't be with Traeger, not like that."

"Why not?"

"Because I don't want to be part of a harem?"

"Ok, that's fair." Renee laughs, wrinkling her nose. "But I don't know...the way he watches you, the way he *looks* at you..." She shakes her head and chews on her bottom lip. She does that whenever she's deep in thought. "It's just different. I think the harem would be retired if you said the word, is all I'm saying."

I snort as if that's the most ridiculous thing she's ever said, but a part of me wonders if she could be right. Part of me *hopes* she is.

"Well, at least the asshole has been gone for the week too," she points out, and I nod in agreement. Jett thankfully went with Traeger wherever they ran off to. He still hasn't outright tried anything, but I know he hasn't given up. He's made that perfectly clear on more than one occasion with disgusting remarks said low in my ear waiting in line for lunch, rough bumps of my shoulder, an "innocent" swipe of his hand across my ass when our paths cross. No, he's still very much plotting and I'm still very much waiting for the day it finally happens.

"Will you come to the social tonight?" Renee asks, changing the subject. "Practice that whole being happy thing?" I scrunch my nose and pretend to debate. I'd actually already planned on going finally, deciding it might be a good distraction from…well, everything, really, but I decide to make Renee beg a little. Right on cue, she clasps her hands in front of her chest. "Please, please, *please*??"

"I guess," I say with a martyred sigh, and then grin. Renee actually jumps up and down and gives a little squeal of joy and I can't help but laugh. After a few more minutes, I say casually, "So, speaking of being happy…what's going on with you and Zimmer?"

"A whole lot of orgasms, that's for sure," Renee says immediately, and I nearly choke. Renee grins. "It's semi-serious, I guess? We like each other, and we definitely like *being* together, but we haven't made any kind of official declarations or anything like that." She shrugs.

"You dirty little girl," I tease, bumping her shoulder with mine. "Are you a kiss-and-tell kind of girl, because…I need some dishing…"

Renee smiles a wicked little smile and I whoop, grabbing her arm and dragging her back towards the main building so she can give me all the details while we get dressed.

I SIT at a table with Wynn in what had once been an event space, somewhere that the resort had held weddings and retirement parties probably. Renee is dancing with Zimmer, and Wynn and I chat while we watch and snack.

"This would be a whole lot better with a nice cold beer," I say over the music. It's a surprisingly good mix of 80s and 90s pop and country, and I've found myself swaying to the beat more often than not. The old me would have been dancing to anything and everything, pulling everyone else onto the floor with me, and a part of me longs to find that piece of myself again. The one that had been fun and crazy, the one that Mitch had loved, the one Mitch would never have wanted me to lose. She has to be in here somewhere, doesn't she? I know she is, but she's buried deep, deep down. Or, more accurately, I've got her locked behind a four-foot-thick bulletproof glass wall. I can see her. I have the key to the door. But I can't make myself put it in the lock and turn...

"And fried pickles," Wynn adds, taking a sip of his tea.

I groan, suddenly craving fried pickles worse than I'd craved chili-cheese-fries when I was pregnant with Gabby, which is *really* saying something.

"How dare you," I say accusingly, tossing a peanut at him. "How fucking dare you."

Wynn chuckles. "If I suffer, you suffer. Isn't that how friendship works?" I flip him off, but smile. A pretty woman with pale blonde hair and big blue eyes beckons to Wynn from the dance floor.

"You better go," I say nodding towards the woman. Ophelia, I think her name is. Wynn follows my gaze and a grin spreads across his face, showing off those pearly whites.

"Sure you don't mind?"

"'Course not," I promise. "Get out there. I'll join in a bit."

Wynn makes his way onto the floor and pulls Ophelia close, swaying along to *I Wanna Dance with Somebody*. Abuela slides into Wynn's abandoned chair, smiling warmly at me and I return it immediately.

"You don't dance, mija?"

"I used to," I admit. Abuela is one of the few people that I just can't seem to keep out, don't even want to, actually. I've told the old woman damn near everything: about my life in the Before Bloody era, my friendship with Jonah, losing Mitch and then Gabby, life on the road before Jonah and I had found The Cove, the things I'd seen and done and survived. She knows more about me than almost any other person on this planet.

"You could dance again, you know," Abuela says with a knowing look, and I get the feeling she isn't only talking about actual dancing. "You can always find the music again. *Always*." She lays a hand on my wrist, squeezing gently. I want to believe her, want it in a way I haven't in so, so long. I smile back at the old woman and, as if the universe is testing me, *Footloose* comes on. It's always been one of my absolute favorite line dances, and I smile at the memories of the many nights me, Mitch, Jonah, and Sean had spent at The Neon Moon dancing to it and a thousand other songs, having the times of our lives.

A lot of people clear off the dance floor, not knowing what to do, but Renee, Wynn, and Ophelia remain. Renee meets my gaze and waves me over, mouthing *please*. Wynn doesn't mouth his invitation, instead yelling, "Come on, Mel! Get your ass out here already! I *know* you know this one."

Abuela laughs and arches a brow at me, waiting for me to make my choice.

"Fuck it," I say with a grin, tired of fighting. I lean in to kiss the old woman on the cheek before sprinting onto the floor right before the chorus hits. I tear the clip out of my hair and shake out my curls, and Renee gives a loud *whoop* of excitement. I lose myself in the familiar steps, finally letting a sliver of my old self out of that glass room and push its way to the surface. I throw my head back and laugh as Wynn messes up some of the steps, bumping into me and nearly knocking me into Renee. It had been so long since I've laughed like this, since I've just let myself *be*. Since I've given myself permission to stop punishing myself for things that I know aren't my fault, and yet I've felt the blame for all these years.

I get Wynn back on track and smile widely, looking back towards Abuela, but my eyes lock with *Traeger's* instead. My pulse races at the sight of him, hair still damp from the shower, the sleeves of his button-down rolled up to his elbows in that inexplicably sexy way, his scruff a bit thicker than usual and looking damn good. Without letting myself stop to think it through or, more accurately, talk myself out of it, I raise my hand and crook a finger at him, smiling a flirtatious smile. I feel almost drunk, giddy with finally letting myself enjoy life for a few minutes. His lips curl up on one side, a crooked, sexy smile that yes, I can admit, I've missed for the last week. He quirks a brow and I roll my eyes and shrug, silently saying *your loss*. I turn to keep up with the dance steps.

A second later, he slides into the line beside me, Renee quickly making room for him and giving me a meaningful look. I have no idea if it means that he doesn't normally dance, or if she's just harkening back to our earlier conversation, but either way, I'm glad that he decided to join in. To my surprise, he actually knows the dance and matches me step-for-step, moving his body easily. *Well fuck.* I don't need to find one more thing attractive about him, but here I am, adding another check mark to the list. There is just something about a man who knows how to dance.

The song ends and I grin, turning to Traeger.

"Didn't know you could dance," I say, a little breathless.

"Ditto."

A second later, the opening bars of *Tennessee Whiskey* sound through the room and I swallow hard, a shiver running through my spine. Traeger's eyes seem to burn, and I wonder if he thinks it's as sexy of a song as I do.

"Dance?" he asks, holding out his hand. I glance down at it, hesitating for a heartbeat, but then I decide that even if it's just for tonight, I'm not going to let myself worry or overthink or hold back.

"Sure," I say, stepping towards him and wrapping one hand around his neck, putting my other into his. He settles his other hand on my lower back, pulling me close. My heart starts racing, my body burning where his hands touch me. We begin to move, swaying and circling slowly to the music, and I try to ignore the slow fire spreading through every inch of me.

"How was the trip?" I ask.

"It was...fine," he says, his shoulders tensing beneath my touch for a moment. So, something had happened then. I won't push, not now. I just want to forget about everything else and just *be* for a little while longer. "Did you miss me?" he teases, the tension fading.

I roll my eyes and make a "psh," sound, but can't manage to put much bite into it.

"I knew it," he says, cocky grin sliding across his face.

"Oh fuck off." That only makes him smile wider and my own lips curl in response. He wraps his hand farther around my back and pulls me even closer. I try to ignore the fact that everyone seems to be staring at us...some with open hostility.

"Uh, I don't think *your girls* are too happy about us dancing," I say, cutting my eyes towards Destiny and Tricia, who are standing in the corner and glaring daggers at me. At least Robin, one of the less theatrical of his routine visitors, doesn't seem to care one way or another, dancing close with Johnson across the floor from us. She even gives me an encouraging smile that clearly says *get it, girl*. I like Robin a lot actually. Not only does she not scream like a banshee when she's in bed with Traeger, she makes the delicious bread that I've fallen in love with since coming here.

Traeger follows my gaze and hikes a shoulder.

"So what?" he asks, turning back to look at me again. I arch a brow in question and he holds my gaze before he answers. "I like to fuck, Melody." A swift wave of heat runs through me at his words and I barely stifle a gasp. "I won't deny that. And, despite what you think," he smirks, clearly remembering our conversation in his room before we were interrupted, "they like it too. But I have made it clear in no uncertain terms to each and every one of them, that it is only sex, nothing more. I've made no promises of anything other than something physical to any of them. Simple."

I cut my eyes to Destiny again, standing alone now. Guess Tricia left. Destiny still looks like she's plotting my murder.

"Maybe not as simple as you think," I mutter.

"I can't help it that I'm so damned lovable." He gives me that crooked grin again and I smack the back of his head. He chuckles lightly. "It's half true."

"Love and fear aren't the same thing," I say, and then wish I hadn't. He clenches his jaw but doesn't argue.

"For one, they don't fuck me out of fear, I promise you that. I wouldn't do that. And two: I'll take either. Love, fear, whatever keeps people safe. Despite whatever you might think, you have to at least know that that's what I want. I want those of us who have survived this long, against all odds, to be able to live with as little danger as possible. If I have to be hated and feared to do that, then so be it."

It's in this moment that a fundamental truth slides into place inside my mind and heart: Austin Traeger really is a good man. A good man who has to do terrible things and make impossible choices, but a good man, nonetheless.

"I do know that," I say quietly. Our gazes lock and the air seems to rush out of the room, but before I can do something terribly stupid like lean in and kiss him...or maybe jump into his arms and wrap my legs around his waist, not giving a shit who might be watching, the song ends. I blink, the bubble around us popping almost audibly, and step away.

"Melody..."

Before he can finish whatever he's going to say, Heather, one of the other women in the security group, approaches and asks if Traeger will spin her around the floor. He smiles and accepts and I nod, quickly scooting out of the way, laying a hand on Heather's shoulder in greeting as I shift. The other woman smiles in return, nothing predatory or jealous in her gaze. I like her, though we haven't gotten to know each other all that much yet. But she hates Jett as much as I do, so that automatically makes her alright in my book.

I walk to the other side of the room towards the table where the drinks are, and Renee's suddenly at my side, arm winding through mine.

"Oh my *God*," she gushes.

"Shut up," I say. "I know you don't know this, but I am an elite, highly trained government agent. I know fourteen different ways to kill someone with a corkscrew and I will use all of them if you don't zip it."

Renee laughs, having no idea that I'm actually semi-serious. It's actually twelve ways with the corkscrew, but an additional six with my bare hands, so, I think the exaggeration is fine.

"Ok, ok, fine, I'll shut up..." She makes the motion of zipping her lips, but as we grab some drinks, she adds, "But do you think he'll wind up at your door tonight?"

Fuck. Do I? Will he? Do I want him to? A big, big part of me does. I'm so on edge physically that he could probably look at me the right way and I'd get off. But another part of me isn't sure. He'd been insistent that everything that went on behind closed doors with him is purely physical...does that apply to me too? It doesn't feel like it, but I honestly don't know. As much as I'd like to pretend otherwise, I don't think I could just do a fuck buddy situation with Traeger. Aside from not wanting to just be one in the endless line up, I...fuck, I don't think I want something just physical with him. I don't think I could keep emotions separate. I...like him. I have feelings. I'm an utter idiot.

But it turns out, I don't have to worry about it. Traeger doesn't knock on my door that night. I would swear I heard him at our connecting door around midnight though, and I could picture him just outside it, raising his hand to knock and then dropping it. Maybe he's just as confused and torn as I am.

He does knock the next morning though.

"Supply run. You want in?"

"Do I get a gun?"

"Not yet."

I give him a dry look but nod. Even without a weapon, I like going out on runs and patrols. Neither of us bring up the previous night, but it isn't awkward thankfully. He gives me a smile that tells me that he didn't know how to handle it and so he didn't. I didn't either, so I can't really blame him. I was just as capable of knocking on *his* door and I didn't do it. I give him a smile in return that tells me we're good.

"Alright, we head out in a few hours. Gonna be gone for a few days, so head down to the commissary and Patrick will get you set with supplies." He looks like he might say something more, but instead he just slaps a hand on the door frame and nods before walking away.

"So, you've never hit this one before?" I ask from the backseat of the Jeep. I'm excited to be out of FOS, but the looks Jett has been giving me the past two nights on the road as we'd bunked down has a bad feeling settling in my stomach. The looks unmistakably said *soon*. He's just waiting for a moment when Traeger and Wynn aren't around, I know it. I figure that I'm on solid enough footing with Traeger after all these months that if I do retaliate against an attack by Jett or his little lackeys, he won't take any anger out on Jonah. But to be honest, I don't think he would mind if I fought Jett. I've gotten the distinct feeling that he doesn't care for his second in command all that much now that Jett's true colors have come out and rumors are swirling. I wonder why he hasn't done anything about it himself yet, but I'm trusting in the fact that he's a good man and is just coming up with a plan before acting.

"Nope," Traeger says. "Johnson took a small team and went through all of this area about a year ago, noting all of the small towns along the way that might be good to check for supplies as needs arose. We've been checking them out as necessary since then, but we've never been here before."

"Wouldn't it make sense for me to have a weapon then, since we don't know what we're walking into? A lot could have changed in the year since Johnson's team swept through."

"We'll have you covered, don't worry."

I roll my eyes and make a jerking off motion with my hand behind Traeger's back. Very mature, I know. Wynn catches it in the rearview and snorts, trying to cover it quickly with a cough. Traeger shifts in his seat to look between the two of us, brow quirked. I give him a doe-eyed look of innocence and Wynn laughs again, not bothering to hide it. Traeger's lips quirk and I find my own doing the same. Things are... I don't even know between us. Different, but not changed drastically. He didn't jump in my sleeping bag with me or anything these last two nights on the road, but he's made a point to brush my arm or put a hand on the small of my back when he's passing me. Little touches that feel stolen and somehow important. I don't mind that they're hidden and understated. I don't think of it as something that we're keeping hidden, but more like it's something just for us. It's no one else's business what we're doing or not doing. We'll figure it out when we're back from this run, but for now, I look forward to the stolen moments.

Wynn meets my gaze in the mirror.

"Wanna play?"

I look at Traeger, debating if I want to allow him into this part of my life. I decide that I…do. *Fuck me, I might be in trouble here.*

I shrug, going for nonchalance though I'm actually a little nervous. I don't open up to many people, and even these banal, stupid things are still things about me, the *real* me, and my past. But, I've decided that I'm going to try to let the walls keep coming down, so here we go.

"Sure."

"And what exactly are we playing?" Traeger asks.

"It's a game we started when we were on patrol shifts together," Wynn says.

"What We Miss about the BB—Before Bloody—world," I explain. "It can't be anything obvious like 'I miss not having zombies trying to eat me,' or anything like that—and it can't be people, either. It has to be just random things that you miss from the old world, things you never thought much about at the time, but now you'd give your left nut—metaphorical or otherwise—to have or see or experience again. Mundane, stupid shit."

"I'll go first," Wynn offers. "Onion rings. God, I loved some good beer-battered onion rings."

"Good one," I say. "I'll go with popcorn. The good kind from the big popper thing at the movie theater with all the melted butter on top." My mouth waters at the thought. Mitch and I used to go to this theater down the road from our first apartment that showed old movies every Thursday night. Tickets were five bucks and we'd mostly go just so we could gorge ourselves on popcorn and candy. My chest twists a little at the memory, one of those beautiful, bittersweet memories that make me so happy and so heartbroken all at once, even after all this time.

Traeger laughs lightly.

"Are they always food-related?"

"Usually," Wynn and I say at the same time, both laughing immediately after as we try to out-jinx each other. He wins, but I don't abide by the rules and keep talking anyway.

"Well? You're up," I say, eyeing Traeger, honestly curious what he might say.

He rubs his hand over his jaw as he thinks about the question.

"Superbowl commercials." I huff out a surprised laugh, and Traeger's lips curl. "Food wise, definitely the pulled pork from this little mom-and-pop place down the road from our house. Absolute best in the entire world."

"I love me some pulled pork," Wynn says with a wistful sigh.

"Concerts," I add after a few minutes. "I loved going to concerts."

"Shoe shopping," Wynn says, taking his turn. "I had a huge shoe collection, it was kind of my thing."

I look to Traeger, encouraging him to keep going.

"Days on the lake. Loading up the boat and being out on the water all day long. There were these little islands spread all throughout Lake Orion with little beaches. We'd anchor the boat and spend the after-noon lounging on the island, listening to music and tossing a football around." It reminds me of days that we used to have too, me and Mitch and Jonah and Sean, when we'd go to the lake house. It made me wonder how else our lives might have been similar. Would we have been friends if we'd met BB?

We play the game for a bit longer until we finally pull off the highway onto a small, two-lane road with not much of anything for miles and miles. Eventually, a little town emerges.

"Alright, game time is over," Traeger says. "Be alert."

Wynn nods, and we all transition easily into survival mode. Heads on swivels, ready for anything. We drove slowly, winding around abandoned cars. The town is tiny, even smaller than that last one I'd hit with Jonah and the Coveys before everything went to hell. It looks like everything had come to a grinding halt as soon as the Bloodies made their appearance in the world here. Thick layers of dirt and dust cover the storefronts and cars, and vines had grown over most of the build-ings and benches. It looks entirely abandoned.

"Ghost town," Wynn mutters, voicing my unspoken thought. We drive around the square that makes up the main part of the town several times to be sure there aren't any traps or anyone waiting to ambush us. With no signs of life, we decide it's safe enough to start exploring on foot. We park the vehicles at the end of one street leading out of the main square, towards what looks like some farmland maybe, and prepare for the first step of any run: Bloody clean up. We'd seen several wandering around and they're edging their way towards our group, drawn by the noise. They're slow moving, so they probably haven't fed in a while.

I hate being out in this with no weapons, but I have to trust Wynn and Traeger to keep me covered, as they'd promised. I know if I cooperate with his little probation period, Traeger will give me full privileges eventually. It grates on my nerves, but I understand his reasoning and I've even done the same thing to newcomers at The Cove. They had to pass tests and get my approval before they were allowed on security detail or to touch a weapon of any kind. So, I get it, and I'll do my time, but it doesn't mean that I like being a sitting duck.

The two other groups with us parked on other streets and we'll all meet in the middle of town square after we all clear our respective areas.

Traeger talks into his walkie. "Holloway, whatcha got?"

"Three in the street so far."

"Mendoza?"

"Eight on this end. A handful more trapped inside this coffee shop."

"Alright. Be fast and quiet."

He clips the walkie to his belt and checks his pistol, silencer attached, as Wynn grips a machete in his left hand. It's always better to try blades before bullets if possible, but Wynn and Traeger both have semi-automatic rifles strapped to their backs too, just in case. I ease out of the Jeep behind them and tug my backpack on my shoulders. Traeger eyes it and I give him a challenging look.

"Where I go, the bag goes," I say. It's my only absolute rule. "I've already told you this and if you want to argue about it, I will, but it will not be quiet and it will not be easy."

He holds up a hand in surrender. "I didn't say a thing," he says defensively, though his lips quirk up on one side. "Just want to make sure you can maneuver with that thing."

"I'm good." I'd spent months training with my pack, getting used to moving with the weight of it and accounting for the additional bulk when fighting. It might as well be a part of my body at this point. Traeger cuts his eyes to Wynn who hikes a shoulder. No one but Jonah knows how truly important having the pack with me at all times is, but everyone else just goes with it and assumes I like to be extra prepared to be on the run if it comes to that. One of the worst things you can do in the apocalypse is be caught on the run with no supplies.

Trager nods to both of us. "Alright, let's get this done."

The boys walk ahead of me and I go on scouting duty. As they take care of the few Bloodies roaming the street, I ease onto the sidewalk, checking in storefront windows for signs of life or the undead. I wipe dirt from a window and cup my hands around my eyes so I peer inside an ice cream parlor with cute little bears with overflowing cones painted on the walls.

"Front of this one looks clear!" I call over my shoulder. I continue on down the left side of the street, dubbing four out of the six shops clear, at least at first glance. The other two have bloodies inside and they'd begun clawing at the glass when they heard the commotion and saw me outside. There aren't enough to break through, so I'm not too concerned with them at the moment. We'll handle them once we get the street cleared. Easy day.

"Wynn, on your right!" Traeger shouts. Wynn quickly moves out of the reach of a Bloody who had managed to sneak up on that side and he takes her down. After confirming that Wynn is good, I jog towards the other side of the street to start my job over again. I squint at the glass of a little boutique as I approach, unable to see inside because of the glare from the sun, but once I'm close, I suck a breath and back hastily away.

"Fuck. This one is *full*," I say as Traeger takes out the last Bloody. Something cracks beneath my boot, broken glass or something, but when I glance down, the hair on the back of my neck stands on end. There are footprints within the dust and dirt on the sidewalk. *Fresh* footprints—and they aren't from Bloodies.

"Fuck, fuck, fuck," I mutter, looking up and down the sidewalk. There are prints *everywhere*. People had been here and recently. I can't believe I hadn't noticed them until now. My thoughts go into over-drive, and I jerk my head around, glancing upward. *Best vantage point is on the roofs. They'll be up there if they're still here...*

Sunlight glints off of a rifle scope and I scream "Down!" just as shots ring out. To their credit, both of the men listen to me without hesitation and it probably saves their lives. A bullet whizzes past Wynn and he rolls out of the way, quickly scrambling to his feet.

"Rooftop, my two o'clock!" I yell as I fling myself behind a big mail bin, more shots ringing out and pinging against the metal at my back. Others begin to pop on the other streets as well, yells echoing from all around. I tentatively peek my head around the corner and a bullet slams into the ground just a few feet away, sending rocks and dirt flying into the air. I grit my teeth.

"Melody!" Traeger yells from across the street. It looked like he and Wynn had managed to wedge themselves into a small alley between two shops from what I saw before someone tried to shoot me in the face, so I think they're relatively safe from fire. The gunmen are only on the roof on the left side of the street, so for now, I'm the easiest target, but I don't know how long that will last.

"Melody, I'm coming!" Traeger calls.

"No!" I shout. "I'm alright! Get the Jeep and get us the fuck out of here!"

"Fuck!" he yells in frustration, knowing damn well that I'm right. Getting to the Jeep is the better plan. We need to get out of the imme-diate line of fire and then we can regroup. Even so, I hear bullets spraying the asphalt and him returning fire with his pistol as the idiot sprints for the mail bin. He somehow makes it without being hit and I yank him down beside me.

"You are a fucking moron!" I hiss at him. He searches me over for injuries, as he if he doesn't even hear me, his jaw set into a hard line and his green eyes blazing and...frantic. He grips my shoulder before sliding his hand to the side of my neck in an almost tender gesture. I'm not sure he even realizes he's done it.

"Are you alright?" he asks me, voice rough. I blink at the intensity of it.

"I'm fine," I tell him. "I'm alright."

"I'll fucking kill them," he all but growls, eyes wild. This is…unexpected? He looks like a caged animal whose ready to tear the throat out of anyone who would dare get near him—or who would dare try to hurt me. Am I imagining all of this? Adrenaline mixed with pent up frustration mixed with all the feelings I'm having but trying not to admit to, all coming together to make me see what I want to see?

I shake myself as bullets ricochet off of the mailbox. *Not the time, Morales.*

"Hey," I say gently but firmly, holding his gaze and gripping his wrist, "*I'm ok.*" He blinks and shakes himself, as if coming out of a trance or something. He swallows hard and gives one hard jerk of his head that I'm taking for a nod of acceptance. "And they're a shit shot," I add with a rueful smile. "We can make it to the Jeep and then come up with a game plan. Alright?"

Traeger takes a deep, steadying breath and nods.

"On three."

We never make it past one. Wynn apparently has the same idea and makes a break for the Jeep. We peek around the mailbox to see him stumble back as the jeep is assaulted with gunfire. He bolts back to the safety of his alleyway.

"Stay there!" I yell to him. I glance back at the Jeep and grind my teeth. The tires are blown out, and I know without a doubt that the engine is shredded. Ok, plan B: take out the shooter, get to better cover, and find a car to steal. Easy peasy.

"Fuck!" Traeger grits out.

"Give me the God damn gun." I hold my hand out for the rifle. Traeger eyes me for a heartbeat and I snap, "We don't have time for this. They're going to move positions soon and our little safe island here will be compromised. You're just going to have to trust that I won't shoot you in the fucking skull, alright? Now, give me the gun so I can save our asses."

He quickly pulls the gun over his head and thrusts it into my hands.

"I trust you," he says simply.

I smile as I check the weapon. "Alright, on three I want you to pop around that side and fire off a couple of rounds. When they return fire, I'll light 'em up. Ready?" He nods. "One…two…three!"

Traeger does exactly as I instructed, and I ignore the flare of panic as our attackers fire at him. I pop up and quickly sight the target, taking out one and then a second. I duck back down as the third sends a spray of bullets our way. Traeger settles back beside me.

"Nice shooting," he pants.

"Duh," I say with a grin. I feel almost high, like I'm finally doing what I'd been made to do again. "Ok, now—"

Another round of bullets rains down but not at the mail bin. No, this time they fly into the window of the boutique just to our left, shattering the glass.

And they release a hungry horde of Bloodies not twenty feet from us.

CHAPTER THIRTEEN

TRAEGER

"GO!" I roar, dread coiling around my spine like an icy fist. I fire my pistol into the mass of rotting corpses spilling out of the broken storefront, some with bone showing through their ribcages, others with half-severed limbs hanging uselessly at their sides. The black blood oozes and drips from their gaping mouths, rotting teeth flashing in the sun. I shove Melody behind me. This wasn't how this was supposed to have gone down. She wasn't supposed to have been in danger, not like this. I know that in this world, nothing is completely safe anymore, but fuck, I really thought it would be fine. I shouldn't have brought her, not until she was allowed to have a weapon.

But my stupid fucking need to be near her won out over logic. Melody is becoming a problem. A problem I in no way want to be rid of, but a problem all the same. She's quickly upended everything that I've created and worked so hard to put into place over the last few years, and while I should be pissed about that, I'm not. I fucking love it. I crave it. I need more of it.

But now isn't the time to be worrying about any of that. Now, we need to get the fuck out of here.

We have no choice but to leave the cover of the mail bin, and as soon as we make a break for it, the gunman on the roof rains down bullets. By some miracle, we don't get hit—Mel was right: they are pretty shitty shots—and Landry bolts into the street and takes the guy out while he's distracted firing at us.

"Come on!" Melody yells. I run backwards trying to keep the Bloodies back as best as I can while we retreat. I cap a couple, clean shots right through the skull, and they drop, but the flood keeps coming, trampling right over their fallen brethren like they're nothing.

"Traeger, forget them and fucking RUN!" Mel screams. She latches a hand onto my arm and tugs, and I give in, turning to run flat out for our lives. We sprint down the street and turn, only to find another group of Bloodies coming towards us.

"Fuck!" I shift to place myself in front of Melody again, and I swear I can feel her roll her eyes from behind me. I'm not doing it because I think she's weak or can't defend herself, I'm doing it because…I don't want to think about it right now.

"This way!" Landry yells, nodding down an alley between two buildings that connects to the next street over. We're moving away from the main square, away from the rest of our people, but we have no choice. We'll circle back as soon as we can.

"We need wheels," I say and Melody nods in agreement.

"Looks like there's a parking lot full of cars behind that building," Landry says, nodding to a crumbling brick building in the distance. We just need to cross another street and a small field to get there. "Probably our best bet—" He cuts off with a yell as a shot rings out and he stumbles back into the wall. Melody and I both turn to find the shooter, but she's faster. Two more bodies drop. I knew that she was good, but *damn*. Seeing her in action is something else. It's fucking sexy. Don't ask me to explain.

Landry slumps against the side of the building, his left hand clamped over his right shoulder, and Mel takes up a protective position a few feet ahead of him, rifle at the ready and head on a swivel.

"Traeger, get him!" she demands. She doesn't turn to make sure I follow directions, just keeps scanning the street ahead and the buildings around us for threats, undead and otherwise. I honestly don't know whether to be annoyed or impressed that she's barking orders—maybe a combination of both. I drop down beside Landry and check his shoulder. He sucks in harsh breaths through his teeth, but nods, telling me that he's ok. Or ok enough to get the fuck out of here anyway.

Two Bloodies emerge from the end of the alley. Mel dispatches them quickly, but all the noise is going to bring more and soon.

"We gotta go," Mel says. "Wynn, you good?"

"Good," Wynn grits out.

"Mostly just a graze and bullet went straight through. He'll need stitches, but he's alright," I confirm. I tear a strip from the bottom of my shirt and wrap it around his arm. He hisses in quick breaths through clenched teeth, but holds still as I tie it as tightly as I can. It'll have to do for now. Mel glances over her shoulder as I help Wynn up. His arm is soaked with blood, but he's steady on his feet. He nods to Mel and the three of us sprint to the mouth of the alley, pausing just long enough to make sure there aren't Bloodies or gun-wielding assholes lying in wait, and quickly cross the cracked asphalt and the field beyond. The grass is thick and waist-high, so it's a bitch to run through, and I can only hope there aren't any Bloodies hiding within, like sharks lurking beneath the surface of the ocean.

We eventually make it to the parking lot on the other side with no surprise attacks. We scan the choices and Mel runs towards an old 4Runner in the corner.

"Seriously!?" she yells in frustration when she tugs on the door only to find it locked.

"Out of the way," I grunt, and she shifts, turning her head as I bring the butt of Landry's rifle down against the driver's side window. The glass shatters and I reach in to pop the locks. I hiss in pain as a shard of glass slices my forearm, but I don't have time to worry about it right now. I've most definitely had worse.

"Get him in the back," Mel says as she uses an old *For Sale* sign to brush the glass out of the driver's seat. She throws her pack into the passenger side and dives into the driver's side floor, yanking the panel off to access the wires beneath the steering wheel. I eye her with interest for a heartbeat, but she doesn't seem to notice. I get Landry into the backseat and then jump into the passenger seat, settling her pack on the floorboard between my feet.

"Come on, come on…" Mel begs quietly as she fiddles with the wires.

"Melody," I say, trying to keep my tone calm. There are at least twenty Bloodies closing in on us fast from three directions.

"I'm trying!" she grits. "Come on you piece of—hell yeah, baby!!" The engine roars to life and she sits up, smiling triumphantly with a hint of justified cocky thrown in, but it fades when she sees the Bloodies. "Oh *fuck*."

She throws the car into drive and slams on the accelerator, and I thank whoever might be listening that the SUV still has gas. Gravel flies as the tires spin, but a heartbeat later we're hauling ass around the group of Bloodies, clipping one and sending it sailing over the hood with a sickening *thunk*. Black blood streaks the windshield and a piece of a flannel shirt gets caught in the windshield wiper.

"Good work," I tell her after a few minutes, my heart still hammering inside my chest. I can see why she was the unofficial head of security and the point person on most runs back at The Cove. She's a huge asset, that's for damn sure.

And I almost lost her today.

I clench my hands into fists and force the thought away. She's not even mine to fucking lose because I haven't figured out how to navigate our situation, but still—it's been a long, long time since I've felt fear like I did today, and it had nothing to do with bullets raining down on me or flesh-eating zombies trying to get a taste.

"Thanks" Mel says, meeting my eyes for a moment and tucking some strands of hair that had escaped her braid behind her ear. It seems like there's so much more that she's not saying, but I could just be imagining it. I know that she's attracted to me. I know that she's thawing a bit, maybe even actually starting to like me. But could she ever actually *want* anything? Could I change everything if she did? Could she ever forgive me for taking her away from The Cove?

She clears her throat lightly and looks to the rearview mirror.

"Wynn, you alright back there?"

His dark skin looks a little gray and I know he's losing too much blood, but he smiles.

"Ça va, cher. Right as rain."

"I can't believe you got hit," Mel says with a grin. "Fucking couyon."

She's playing it off but I can tell that she's rattled. She drives like a bat out of hell a few miles out towards the farmland before deeming it safe enough to pull over and get a better assessment of Landry's wound. Mel checks him out while I sweep the area, but it looks like we're alone for now. She pulls out a first aid kit from her pack—I guess it's a good thing she keeps it on her at all times after all—and gets some QuikClot into Landry's arm. I wince when he yells through gritted teeth at the pain. I've been there and that shit fucking kills. I hand him a canteen and he takes a few big gulps. I squeeze his uninjured shoulder and he nods, letting me know he's alright. Melody gets a bandage over the wound and we make a makeshift sling out of an old sweatshirt from the back of the SUV.

"Holloway, how's it looking back there?" The voice that crackles through the walkie isn't Holloway.

"Ackers here, sir. Holloway...he didn't make it." I close my eyes and lean my forehead against the walkie for a heartbeat. Holloway was a good man. I say a silent goodbye and thanks and open my eyes. Melody eyes me but I continue on because that's what you fucking do in this world.

"Status."

"The hostiles have been taken care of. Bloodies are running rampant though." I hear gunfire in the background and my body tenses.

"On our way."

"I'm good," Landry assures us. "Let's get back and help the others."

We make our way cautiously back to the others and start clearing streets as we go. Melody is scarily efficient and I know when the time comes, she'll be a huge asset to our patrols and runs. We're dirty and exhausted and covered in thick, sludge-like blood when we finally rendezvous back in the middle of the town square like we originally planned.

"Report, Mendoza," I bark as we stride towards him. Helene jogs up and hands me a rag, then helps Melody get Landry over to a bench to rest and get looked at again. I wipe some of the worst grime from my face as he lays it out for me.

"Four dead, nine injured, sir. Most are gunshot wounds—two are pretty serious—but..." He clenches his jaw and I already know what he's going to say before the words pass over his lips. "O'Leary and Harrison were both bitten."

"Fuck," I grate.

"Harrison, uh, took care of herself as soon we got everything under control." I clench my jaw but nod. I can't say that I wouldn't have done the same if I were in her shoes. "O'Leary is around the back of the hardware store, sir. He requested you." I nod and steel myself for what I'm going to have to do next.

"I'll take care of them. Any survivors from the other side?"

"No, sir."

I honestly don't feel one way or another about that. I've been in this game too long and know that while the human part of me wants to save as many people as possible, the survivalist reasons that these people had attacked us and would have gladly killed us all. Tried their damndest to do just that, no questions asked. So, fuck them. In the end, I choose me and mine, just like they would choose them and theirs. Whether you're the hero of the story or the villain completely depends on which side of the line you're standing on. In this story, from my perspective, they're the bad guys who had tried to hurt my people and we're the heroes who fought back and won. The end.

I glance automatically to Melody and clench my jaw, replaying every second of this day over in my head, seeing all the ways it could have gone so, so wrong. Her features harden and her body goes tense as I watch and I frown at the sudden change. I follow her gaze and see Jett leaning against the end of the hardware store, half hidden in shadow. The look he's giving her makes my blood boil and a quiet fury begin to prowl inside my chest. I've heard the rumors. I've seen his true self slip to the surface a time or two when he thought I wasn't watching. He hides it fairly well around me, but I know the truth. I'll be taking care of this little situation soon enough, but it has to be done in the right way. There are always reasons and plots in everything I do.

I force myself to leave it for now. I know he won't do anything while I'm here, but as soon as he's given the chance, I know he'll make his move. *Soon, fucker. We're going to dance real fucking soon.*

I take a deep, settling breath and head to the back of the hardware store. I pull out my pistol as I go and check the chamber.

I'll only need one bullet for this part.

CHAPTER FOURTEEN

MELODY

"ALRIGHT!" Traeger calls, bringing everyone to attention after taking out O'Leary from what Helene told me. I admire him for being willing to handle things for his guys, but man, I can't imagine having that on my shoulders.

"Teams of four in each building, starting on this street and working our way North. Let's fuckin' get this done."

Now that the fighting is done and the aftermath and the Bloodies have been taken care of, it's time to do what we came here to do in the first place and scavenge for supplies. It's going to take a little longer than it originally would have since we lost so many to death and injury, but we'll get it handled.

Traeger strolls over to me as I stand to join my group and holds out his hand expectantly.

"Seriously?"

"It isn't that I don't trust you," he says, and I know it's true. It's the rule and, despite the emergency situation earlier, there's no reason for him to bend the rules for me. Again, I get it. I don't like it, but I get it. So I sigh and hand my—his—gun over. He takes it and starts to turn away, but I grab his wrist.

"You need a bandage." I look pointedly at his forearm and his brows draw down as he follows my gaze.

"Oh," he says, seemingly surprised to find that he's bleeding. "I'm fine." I give him a level look, he sighs. "Alright, play nurse if you must," he grumbles. He sits down on the curb and I grab supplies from the med kit Helene left out. She was an EMT back before the world ended, so she'd be much better at this than me, but I know enough. She has far worse injuries to attend to right now, so I can handle Traeger.

"Would be more fun if you had one of those outfits though," he adds when I come back and start cleaning his wound.

"Into role playing, huh? Wouldn't have guessed that based on everything I've heard."

He laughs and I give him a small smile before I get to work picking small pieces of glass out of his arm. He inhales sharply and clenches his jaw, but other than that doesn't react much.

"You shouldn't have come after me," I say quietly as I finish disinfecting and wrapping the cut with gauze and tape. "You could have gotten yourself killed." I glance up to meet his gaze and wonder if he can see the unasked question there: *why?* Why risk his life like that?

"I had to, Melody. I..." He swallows hard but before he can say more, someone calls his name. He sighs and stands, his shoulders tense and straining under the weight of the world suddenly resting there. *God, is he ever able to rest?*

I nod, telling him to go ahead and do what he needs to do. I inhale softly when he reaches out and wipes his thumb across my cheek.

"You had some dirt," he says in a low voice.

"Oh," is all I manage to get out before his name is being called again. He drops his hand and walks away, and I blink, telling myself to get a fucking grip. I check on Wynn, who promises he's fine, just tired and excited for the pain meds to kick in, and then join my assigned team to start sweeping buildings for supplies.

"Looks like there's a big closet in the back if you want to check that out," Wilson says a couple of hours later, nodding back towards the boutique he'd just exited, a box full of t-shirts and socks in his arms. I finished my assigned buildings, but don't mind helping out some of the other groups to try to get things done quicker. I duck inside and look over the clothes as I make my way towards the back of the store. Cute stuff. I eye some of the dresses, half tempted to snag a few to bring back with me to FOS. There's a "store" set up in the old gift shop where extra clothes are kept for anyone to take as needed. I decide to bring a bunch of stuff from this place back with me, knowing the female population of FOS would be very appreciative of some new cute items.

I finally make it to the closet Wilson mentioned and find a pretty good stash—paper towels, tissues, soap, toilet paper, a couple of cases of bottled water—when I hear someone else come inside the main door, the little bell still ringing happily to announce new visitors.

"There's a few things back here!" I call. "I need a box or maybe they have bags at the register—" I turn to find Jett leering at me from just outside the closet. Every muscle in my body goes rigid. It was too much to hope that a Bloody tore him to shreds during the fight. I'd even have settled for a good old fashioned bullet to the chest. But, alas, I'm not that lucky.

"Need some help?" he asks with a disgusting grin.

"I think I've got mouth breathing down, thanks," I say dryly.

His grin only widens as he swaggers towards me, rubbing his chin and shaking his head.

"I can't wait to put you in your place, little girl." He leans in close but I don't back away, only glare. The only thing I hate more than being told to behave is being called *little girl*. "Can't. Fucking. Wait."

"Mel?" Timmons calls from the front of the store.

"Back here," Jett calls back, holding my gaze before taking a few steps backwards, smirking. Timmons comes around the corner and smiles, not seeming to notice anything amiss.

"Wilson said you might need this," he says, holding up a big cardboard box.

"Yeah, uh, thanks. Got a few things in here," I say, taking the box but keeping my eyes on Jett until he's out of my line of sight. He's barely keeping himself from acting. He's like an addict jonesing for that next hit. He can only hold back for so long. Whatever he's planning, he's going to do it soon.

And when he does, I'll be fucking ready.

THREE DAYS LATER, we're stopping for the night before making it back to FOS tomorrow, maybe the next day depending on Bloody traffic and weather. It looks like a storm is rolling in, but I'm hoping it holds off until we're at least on the road tomorrow. I'm not in the mood to camp out in the fucking rain tonight.

This site is a large open clearing near the river. A small cabin used to be perched in the center, but it toppled what looks to be a long time ago. Now it's just a heap of time-worn wood that's probably a fantastic hiding spot for all kinds of critters I want nothing to do with. I make a mental note to set up my camping spot as far across the clearing from it as I can get.

The river runs on the southern edge, so it's a great spot for refilling our water containers, and through a small thicket of trees, there's a small offshoot that forms a small pool—perfect for bathing. And dear God do I want a rinse.

"How's the arm?" I ask Wynn as I help him spread out his bedroll.

"It's fine," he assures me. "Really," he adds when I give him a hard look. "Sore, but could have been much worse. I'll be back to my old self in a few weeks, and I've still got my shooting hand, so at least I'm not useless."

"Ehh, that's debatable." His mouth pops open in mock indignation and I snort.

"Mel!" Traeger calls over the rush of the river. "You're up." He hikes his thumb back towards the trees he just exited, telling me that it's my turn at the pool. He's been more tense than usual for the past couple of days, but we haven't had any time to talk. Every time I try, he's called away or needs to handle something. Part of me thinks he's avoiding me, but the other part thinks that one is just paranoid.

"Oh thank God," Wynn says, wrinkling his nose. "You smell terrible."

I punch him in his good arm and he laughs lightly. My gaze shifts to Traeger again, because when the fuck doesn't it lately? Johnson leans in to say something quietly in his ear. He tenses but nods.

"Landry! Wilson! Tucker! You're with me. We've got an issue at Checkpoint Romeo Eight to handle. Jett and Mendoza—you're in charge here for the night. Meet us there tomorrow." Traeger meets my gaze again and gives me an almost imperceptible nod, so small, I'm not entirely sure I actually saw it at all, but I can't shake the feeling that he's trying to tell me something. I want to ask him what's going on, but he seems to force himself to turn away without so much as a wave goodbye. I frown and shift my gaze to Wynn. He looks as confused as I feel, but hikes his uninjured shoulder.

"Well, guess I'll see you tomorrow, cher." He cuts a look at Jett and then adds, "Stick by Timmons for the night while I'm gone." I roll my eyes but agree when he gives me a dry look. He walks to the waiting Hummer and the five of them pile inside. I give the vehicle a wave in goodbye as it pulls away, and grab my pack. I work through different possibilities in my head as I walk through the trees towards the pool. Something is going on, I just know it. That look from Traeger, the nod...I know he was telling me something.

And then it clicks.

There's another smaller clearing once I break through the tree line. The river rushes by on the right, but straight ahead, a bit of the land juts out and creates a calmer pool. I drop my pack and fish out my soap, heading over to the pool for a quick wash down without getting undressed. I would love to dive in and take a proper bath, but I'm not about to be caught naked right about now—I have a good feeling that I'm going to have company very soon. *When the cat's away, the mouse will play, right?* As if on cue, I hear their heavy footfalls in the trees behind me. I guess they aren't worried about sneaking up on me. I take a deep breath and that familiar calm settles over me.

Here we go.

I straighten at the edge of the pool and turn to find Jett and his two fuckhead shadows making their way into the clearing.

"Well, well, well. Look what we have here, boys," Jett says, sounding extraordinarily proud of himself. I barely stop myself from rolling my eyes. Proud of himself for finding me...in the place where the whole camp knew I was going to? *Great job, idiot.* I really will be doing the world a favor by taking this oxygen thief out of rotation.

"Who goes first?" Bartlett sneers, his yellowed teeth making me curl lip in disgust.

"Well, by my count, there are three of us," Jett says, smirking, "and she's got three holes to fill."

The other two laugh like morons and move towards me while Jett gets sidetracked with my bag.

"I'm shocked you can count that high to be honest," I say in a bored voice. I'm not worried about Tweedle Dee and Tweedle Fuckface. I let them close in on me, but I do tilt my head ever so slightly and tense my muscles as Jett stoops to snatch up my pack. He strolls around the clearing as he digs through it, tossing things out. Bartlett and Meadows grin at me as I shift forward, watching Jett like a hawk. They came here to attack me, and that's all well and good. I was ready for it, welcomed it even, but I hadn't thought about them rifling through my shit. *If he touches Leo…*

He pulls out the stuffed dog and laughs darkly.

"*This* is what you carry around with you everywhere? This is what's so fucking important that you won't leave this pack behind?"

"Put. The Dog. Down," I say in a deadly cold voice. This had been a fun game before, a cat playing with the mice before the killing blows. Now, it's fucking serious.

Jett smiles at me, one of those sick, twisted smiles, and time seems to slow as I watch him toss the stuffed dog into the river. My world tilts on its axis and a red haze covers my vision, fury roaring to life in my chest and taking over my entire body. I sprint forward, thrusting an elbow into Bartlett's nose before spinning around Meadows, evading them both easily. I run towards Jett and slide beneath his outstretched meaty hand just as shots ring out. I don't give a shit. I hear shouts, maybe even my name being yelled, but I don't. Fucking. Care. None of it matters. I have to get to him. I fucking *have* to. He's my last piece of Gabby. I can't lose him. I won't lose him. I'd rather fucking die.

I dive into the river, and am immediately swept up in the current. I start to swim, faster than I ever have before, desperate to get to the dog. I can barely see him ahead in the fading sunlight, being pulled farther and farther away from me, but I refuse to give up. I push harder, force my body to move faster. I grit my teeth and the only thing I hear over the roaring water all around me is her name echoing in my head. *Gabby. Gabby. Gabby.* It's a mantra. It's a prayer. It's desperate plea. I scream a wordless threat to the world, telling it in no uncertain times to fuck right off. I will not lose him. I will not lose her, not again. I *will not lose.*

I fight and I fight and somehow, against all odds, I make it to him. I grab the dog like my life depends on it, holding him so tightly my fingers ache. I try to make my way towards the bank, but the current is so fucking strong, stronger than it had seemed before, and the surge of adrenaline that had gotten me through that rushing water to fight fate itself, is spent now. I kick and try to pull myself through the water, but I'm so fucking tired. I'm not going to make it. A very small, dark part of myself accepts my fate, welcomes it even. *Finally,* it thinks. *Finally time for no more fighting, no more pain. Finally time to rest.*

But the larger part of me rears up then to beat back the darkness. *No.* No, this can't be how it fucking ends. After everything that's happened, after everything I've lost and given up and fought for. A face flashes in my mind now. Not Gabby or Mitch or even Jonah. That face makes the voice scream in my head now. NO! I'm not ready. This is *not* how it ends. So, I fight. I fight against the current with strength I don't have.

"Melody!" Traeger's voice rings out and I realize that somehow, I've almost made it back to the bank. Traeger rushes to me, diving into the water and wrapping his arms around me. Holding me up and tugging back towards the shore. When we've mostly made it out, he lets me go and I collapse on hands and knees, sucking in ragged breaths in between coughing fits. Traeger drops to his knees beside me.

"Melody! What the fuck were you thinking?!" He grips my shoulders and hauls me up, his eyes desperately searching my own. "Are you alright? God, Melody…"

"Fine," I gasp, breathless. "I'm…fine…"

He clenches his jaw and someone else stomps through the shallow water to us. Wynn.

He mutters a string of insults and prayers and insults in Cajun and I manage a half-sob, half-laugh as he helps me stand. Traeger takes a few steps back. I want to pull him close again, but I realize that we're surrounded by a small group of people. We trudge out of the water and back onto dry land and Wilson throws a towel over my shoulders. The rush of everything that happened in the water finally starts to recede and a cold, burning fury fills my every nerve.

I meet Traeger's gaze so he knows that I'm deadly serious when I say, "I'm going to fucking kill him."

He doesn't argue, just leads the group back up the river bank—Jesus, how fucking far had I'd traveled down stream??—until we finally reach the cleaning again. Jett, Bartlett, and Meadows are there on their knees, hands bound behind their backs. The rest of the group stands around them in wearing looks of disgust and anger, a few of worry and confusion.

Traeger steps forward while I hang back beside Wynn, Wilson and Johnson flanking us.

"The three of you stand accused of conduct unbecoming of members of my fucking team," Traeger says, voice as hard and sharp as tempered steel and carrying through the clearing. He isn't yelling, but this is somehow worse. More intense. More menacing. His gaze skates over the rest of the group, a very clear warning there, and I see every single person acknowledge it very seriously. Here is the Traeger I'd heard rumors of, the one who was cold and ruthless and terrifying.

"I've been hearing things, boys," he says in that quiet, cold voice, "things that I don't fucking like. But it was all *hearsay* to use a pre-fucking apocalypse word, and I believe in innocent until proven guilty. But tonight, you were seen, by multiple witnesses, threatening Melody Morales. I'm paraphrasing here, but I heard something along the lines of there being a certain number of you and a certain number of holes to fill—does that sound about fucking right?" His jaw ticks and I can practically feel the anger radiating off of him in waves, hitting like lashes of a whip. "And I don't believe that Mel gave any invitations for such things."

He pauses for a tick, waiting to see if any of them are going to try to refute it. None of them do, of course.

"Alright then. Guilty it is." He turns to look at me. "Mel, the punishment is yours if you want it."

I don't say a word, just toss the towel to the ground and stride forward. I slip Traeger's knife free from his belt as I pass him in a smooth, practiced motion. He arches a brow but otherwise doesn't react. Bartlett whimpers when I approach, but he doesn't get a word out before I slide the blade across his throat. It glides through his flesh and muscle like a hot knife through butter. I would remember to commend Traeger for the quality of his blade later. A small gasp ripples through the group, but I barely hear it. I'm in a dark, cold place where there is nothing but me, and the blade, and the task at hand.

Bartlett gurgles and chokes as blood pours, soaking the ground. Collins shakes violently as he stares, horrified, as Bartlett's body slumps forward. He cuts his eyes back to me. They're wide and terrified and he tries to pull away, but he can't go anywhere.

"No, p-please, please just wait. I didn't want to! It was him, he—"

I flick my wrist again, gliding the blade across his jugular and bringing forth another fountain of blood. I feel it splash on my throat and chest, hot and wet, but I don't care. His body thuds to the ground beside Bartlett's. I move to stand before Jett. He doesn't whimper or cry, but he does close his eyes as I slash out with the knife, the deadly sharp blade whispering against his throat, a thin line of blood slowly blooming. Barely a scratch. A second later he pries his eyes open, blinks in stunned relief, and grins that stupid fucking grin.

"I think you missed, bitch," he sneers, but then gasps as I slip the knife into his side, sliding it up between his ribs in just the right spot, with the exact amount of pressure needed. Blood gushes over my hand, but I don't pull back. Not yet. His eyes fly wide in pain and surprise. I lean in close as he shifts forward, desperate to cover his wound, his instincts telling him to curl up and protect himself, but he can't do any of that. His hands are still bound and he's being held upright by Mendoza.

"That just pierced your lung," I say in a low voice, though loud enough for those closest to us to hear. "You don't get a quick death, you sadistic fuck. You're going to drown in your own blood, and it's going to take time. It's going to hurt. You're going to feel your life draining away as you choke and struggle for air. You were always going to die by my hand for what you did to Jonah, that was never in question, but I would have made it quick...well, quick*er*, anyway. I would have made it painful, don't get me wrong, but not like this. *This* you brought on yourself."

I pull back and cock my head to the side as he wheezes, the sound thick and wet.

"B...itch," he spits, though there's not as much venom behind the words as he'd like. I look at him impassively.

"I told you to put the fucking dog down."

I step back and Mendoza shoves him forward. He falls heavily on his face, rolling to the side and coughing up blood. I take another step away and look down. Blood coats my boots and arms and chest.

"Take the bodies into the woods," Traeger says before stepping towards me. "Chain that one up," he adds, jerking his head towards Jett. I wordlessly hand him the knife and he shoves it back into the sheath at his hip. He silently ushers me across the clearing and through the woods, back to the pool again. He tries to take Leo from my left hand and I yank him away, eyes blazing. I hadn't even realized I'd still been holding him. There's blood on his gray fur.

"Melody," Traeger says quietly. "Melody, it's alright. Look at me, it's me. I'm just going to help you get cleaned up, ok?" He's talking to me like I'm a trapped animal, and it helps to break through the haze I'm trapped in. I shake myself, trying to calm. I meet his gaze and there's a surprising gentleness there, in such contrast to the cold brutality from just a few minutes ago. I nod and let him take the dog, watching as he places it on top of my bag. Someone had gathered all of things that Jett had thrown out and piled them back by my pack. Traeger leads me to the edge of the water and eases me down to my knees. He kneels beside me and uses a cloth I hadn't even seen him grab to start scrubbing the blood away.

"I'm sorry," he says.

"I'm not," I reply, trying to stop my shaking. There's a chill in the air now, summer finally fading into deep fall, and being soaked to the bone isn't helping things. "It was a good plan." I was the bait to catch

Jett and his goons in the act. "Though, I admittedly hadn't anticipated going into the river."

Traeger pauses and gives me an assessing look. "You were never in any danger, I swear to you, Melody—well, until you jumped in the fucking water that is."

"I know."

"You knew we were watching?"

"I figured you were, but I wasn't worried about taking care of them. I figured you wouldn't have been too mad if I killed them outright, but having the public execution probably worked better."

He shakes his head and continues to clean me up. I let him, too exhausted and numb to think too much about it, and I'd be lying if I said a part of me didn't like it. It had been so long since anyone had… cared for me like this, Jonah notwithstanding, but of course, that's different.

"You probably think I'm pretty fucked up, killing them like that. Killing *Jett* like that."

He clenches his jaw. "No, I think he deserved worse. I wish I could have done so much fucking worse."

I meet his eyes and a poem in one of the books he'd given me springs to mind.

I love you as certain dark things are to be loved.

We share a darkness, an understanding of the world and what it means to survive in it. The sense of right and wrong that may seem skewed, but makes perfect sense to us. He sees my darkness and doesn't shy away from it. He accepts it as a part of me. I feel myself falling for him, right here and now, and I'm not sure what to do about it. I'll do a deep dive into it all later, but for now, I just swallow hard and let a long exhale.

"Thank you," I say quietly.

He clears his throat. "You should get into some dry clothes. I'll meet you back at the camp."

After he walks away, I rinse Leo off as best as I can before changing and heading back to the clearing. I frown when I get there, not finding my bedroll where I'd left it earlier. Wynn jogs up then and pulls me into a hug. I return it, mindful of his injured arm and trying not to jostle him too much.

"You alright?"

"I'm good, I promise." I really am. I feel no guilt about what I did to those men. In fact, I feel a sense of relief. I've been counting down to the day I finally ended Jett, so I'm glad to finally have my revenge. I don't know what that says about me but I honestly don't care. I'm far past the point of caring or worrying about the blood on my hands. I'd been rattled because of Leo, that's all.

"I'm good," I tell him again, "but, uh, where's my stuff?"

"Traeger moved you into the camper with him for the night, just to be safe." In a lower tone he adds, "we don't think Jett had any others in his little gang, but we're going to keep an eye on you and things for a bit, just as a precaution."

I nod and give him another hug before making my way to the camper. It's small, but plenty big for the two of us to sleep. Though, now that I think about it, I would bet that he won't actually sleep with me. He'll keep watch all night. When I climb inside, he's lounging on one of the bench seats, cleaning his knife.

"I'm told I'm bunking here tonight," I say in greeting.

"Just a precaution," he assures me, just as Wynn had said. "Bed is all yours."

I nod and sit on the edge, kicking my wet boots and socks off before pulling my legs up to rest my chin on my knees.

"You didn't ask," I say after a few minutes. He quirks a brow. "You didn't ask about the dog. Why I would risk my life for something so stupid."

He shrugs. "I figure you'll tell me if and when you want to." He stands and slides the knife into its sheath once more. "I'm sure you're tired of being asked, but are you alright?"

"I'm fine, I promise."

"Get some sleep, I'll be right outside." Our gazes catch and hold, and for a second, I think he might lean in...But then he turns and walks to the door. I'd be lying if I said I wasn't a little disappointed. It's a bad idea, sure—not the right time or place to be diving into all of that shit—but I wanted it all the same.

He stops when he reaches the door, bracing his hands on either side of the frame.

"Fuck it," he says, low and rough, and a second later, he's turned back, making it to the bed in three long strides. His hands slide across my cheeks, cradling my face as his lips meet mine. I gasp against his mouth, but fist my hands in the front of his shirt. Despite the fire just beneath the surface, the kiss is soft and gentle. Tender even. God, I've dreamed about this, imagined it too many times to count, and now I can't quite believe it's really happening. Maybe it isn't. Maybe it's a dream. Maybe I died in that river and this is some weird last ditch hallucination my brain is coming up with just before the last neuron fires…

But no. No, this has to be real. I couldn't hallucinate the feel of him, the softness of his lips, the heat of his body seeping into mine.

He presses his lips to mine, once, twice, before lightly sucking my bottom lip between his, making me moan softly and tighten my grasp on his shirt. He pulls back too soon, stroking his thumbs across my cheekbones as he holds my gaze for an endless moment, before dropping his hands and stepping away. I blink, feeling a little dazed, and wanting to yank him back to me for more, so much fucking more.

But he only nods and walks back to the door of the camper without a word, leaving me confused…and grinning like an idiot.

CHAPTER FIFTEEN
TRAEGER

WHY THE FUCK had I kissed Melody?

I know damn well why. Because she'd almost died multiple times in the past seventy-two hours, and I couldn't stand it anymore. I couldn't stop *not* touching her, not assuring myself that she was here and safe and whole. I couldn't stand the thought of wasting another second not kissing her, of not taking the chance and of risking never having it again. We live in a dangerous, fucked up world. Any of us could die any second.

So, yeah. I fucking kissed her because I couldn't not kiss her.

And kissing Melody had been like tasting heaven. It had barely even been a kiss, really, just a few brief touches of lips, but it had rocked me to my core. I have my girls and we have our fun, but this was something else entirely. This was deeper. This was connection. This was something real when so little else in this world is anymore. I saw into the depths of her tonight, into that darkness inside her that mirrors my own. She isn't afraid of mine and I'm not afraid of hers. We fit. We match. We understand each other in a way that's on a deep, cellular level. We do what has to be done. We protect. We terminate those who threaten what we care about. We feel no remorse for it. We even fucking delight in it when it's warranted.

I'm a fucking goner.

I don't know what the kiss means—or rather, what *she'll* allow it to mean. I know sure as shit what it means to me—but I'm not sorry that I did it.

I exhale roughly and settle into a chair outside the camper. I don't think anyone else would dare try anything, especially not after witnessing Melody's punishment, but I'm taking no chances. I hated the plan, but it was the best option, the only one I knew without a doubt would pull the snake out of hiding. Jett had been eyeing Melody since that day at The Cove and I knew he wouldn't pass up the opportunity that he'd been waiting to find for months. I'd been planning to take care of him here soon anyway after I'd gathered up all of my intel, but everything needs to be done strategically in this world.

Melody proved to be the perfect bait, and while I had no doubts that she could protect herself and that we would be there before anything could happen, walking away from her to set the trap was one of the hardest things I've ever had to do. When I think of watching them poise to attack, the things they said, the things I knew Jett planned to *do*, fury boils inside me so hot and volatile that I want to burn the entire fucking world down. I force myself to uncurl my fists, realizing now that I've got them clenched so tightly that my knuckles are turning white.

I force my breathing to slow, reminding myself that she's alright, that she's safe inside the camper a few feet from me. I should go back in. I should finish what I started with that kiss. I should make us both forget everything else for a while. I should…

No. No, I should definitely *not* do any of that right now. A time and a place and all that.

Landry comes over and hands me a few strips of jerky and a canteen.

"How she doing?" he asks, nodding towards the camper.

"She's alright. She's strong."

"No doubt about that," he agrees with a smile, but it fades quickly. "Wish she didn't have to be strong quite so often though. She's been through a lot. I mean, I know we all have but Mel…" He trails off and shakes his head. I wonder what he knows about her, what she's confided in him. I want her to trust me that way, to share all of herself.

"The bodies?"

"Burned. Jett finally stopped breathing, though it went too quick for the fucker if I do say so myself."

"Has he turned yet?"

"Not yet, but we're watching. He's chained up nice and tight."

I won't put that asshole out of his misery. He can live forever as a mindless, starving zombie. He'll be secured in a pin like the animal he is, and live in agony for the rest of his undead life. Even that's too good for him, honestly, but it's the best I can do.

"Sounds good. Make sure word spreads through the settlements."

"Of course, sir."

He updates me on the watch schedules for the rest of the night before heading back to get some sleep. I settle in, knowing I won't be sleeping at all, and replay the kiss over and over, hoping like hell it won't be our last.

CHAPTER SIXTEEN

MELODY

"WELL, I can't pretend like I'm sad he's gone. That *any* of them are gone," Renee amends. "They were all assholes, Jett was just the worst of them."

Word had quickly spread through FOS about what went down out on the road and Renee had found me the minute I'd gotten a hot shower and changed clothes, pulling me into a huge hug as soon as I opened my door. It surprised me how much I'd missed her over the week we were gone and I was beyond glad to be back. Somehow, FOS has become...maybe not quite home, but as close as I can get to it without Jonah.

"Everyone probably thinks I'm a full on psychopath now," I sigh, tucking my hands into the sleeves of my hoodie as we sit out beside the lake. Fall is settling over us and the air is getting cooler and cooler by the day, but the grounds of FOS are absolutely beautiful and I just can't seem to stay inside. The leaves have all fully changed now, the forest a kaleidoscope of reds and yellows and oranges surrounding us on all sides. I've always loved the fall, and I miss going to pumpkin patches and on hayrides and having horror movie marathons. I make a mental note to use those the next time we play *What Do You Miss?*

"Nah," Renee says. "And for any that do, that's probably a good thing anyway. Makes them a little scared of you. Fear is powerful these days."

"Are you afraid of me?" I tease.

"Oh absolutely terrified." We laugh a bit and then I chew on my lip. I could use some advice about a certain evil leader who isn't actually an evil leader who kissed me in the camper and seems to have been avoiding me ever since.

"So...something happened with Traeger," I finally say casually. Renee's mouth pops open and she punches me in the arm, surprisingly hard. "Ow!"

"How were those not the first words out of your mouth when I saw you earlier??" she demands, brushing hair angrily off of her face.

"Umm because the whole *we got ambushed and almost died and Wynn got shot and then Jett and his goons tried to attack me and I went cold-blooded killer on them all* seemed a little bit more important?" Renee isn't impressed and looks at me expectantly. "And it wasn't *really* something. Just a...sort of something."

"Would you just spill it already?"

"There were just a few *moments*. Like when I was pinned down by the gunfire and he charged over, all guns blazing like a fucking idiot—"

"A romantic fucking idiot," Renee counters.

I snort. "Like an idiot, but when he got there, he looked almost frantic. And then when I was in the river, the way he called my name and pulled me out...I don't know." I exhale. "Oh and then of course there was the kiss."

Renee screams. Literally *screams*, and I clamp my hands over my ears, though I can't help but laugh.

"Stop it. It was nothing. I mean, it wasn't nothing, it was..." I shake my head, not wanting to think about the kiss any more than I already am. It's been living rent free in my mind since the second it happened. "But it was just a kiss. A quick kiss and nothing more. And nothing since. He hasn't tried again or mentioned it, hasn't even acted like it happened. And I have no idea what that means, or if he's waiting for me to make a move, or what the fuck is going on, or if I even *want* something to be going on, annnnd my head hurts."

I groan and bury my head in the front of my sweatshirt. I sound like all those girls I'd always pitied, worrying about guys and thinking so much about the *what ifs*. I'd always been sure with this kind of thing. If I was into a guy, I told him. If it wasn't reciprocal, cool. I moved on. No harm, no foul, no big deal.

But with Traeger I'm...a fucking mess. I don't know what to think or feel or do. I can admit that I have feelings for him, strong ones, but...there's still a part of me that's holding myself back. Part of me that doesn't know if I can let go of the past. Part of me that's...fucking terrified. There, I said it. I'm terrified of what trying to be with Traeger might mean. I'm terrified of letting him in. I'm terrified of...loving anyone again.

"Have *you* tried again? Or said anything? Or acted like it happened?" Renee asks.

"Listen, no one asked you to be the voice of reason here..." She bumps my shoulder playfully and I let out a long exhale. "No, I haven't tried anything or said anything, and I definitely haven't acted like anything happened. But I don't know, Ren. I feel...connected to him in some really profound, intense way that I can't even explain. Which is ridiculous because we hardly even know each other, really."

I feel like I hardly know anything real about him other than the fact that he misses days on the lake and barbecue. And yet, somehow, I feel like I know him better than almost anyone else on the planet. It's just there. Just an understood, fundamental fact, that I *know* this man.

"I think you *do* know each other," Renee says, echoing my own thoughts. "Just because you don't know everything about each other's pasts doesn't mean you don't know each other." I start to argue, but Renee holds up her hand to stop me. "Listen, I don't know what's going on with you two, or what it all means, but I do know that in all the time I've been here, I've never seen him look at anyone the way he looks at you."

I take a long, deep breath and let it out slowly. Alright. Fine. Let's just pretend for a second I can let this happen.

"So, what do I do?"

"You stop being a baby, grow some lady balls, and talk to him about it."

I blink slowly. "Did you just tell me to grow some *lady balls*?"

"I did. Because you need to," Renee says primly before her lips curl into a smile.

CHAPTER SEVENTEEN

TRAEGER

I'VE BEEN AVOIDING Melody since we returned to FOS. I could blame it on all the housekeeping I needed to do after the ambush and Jett's untimely demise, which really had taken up a lot of my time, but in truth, I'm just being chicken shit. I have no idea what the right move is with Melody, which is actually new for me. I always seem to know what to do, what the best choice is in any given situation. It's one reason I've survived this long and that I'm even in the position I am, leading others. But with Melody? No fucking clue.

Despite really not knowing all that much about her, I'm damn near in love with Melody Morales. What the fuck is that about? How can you possibly feel so connected to someone without even knowing anything about their past? But it doesn't matter. I'm lost for the girl. Honestly, I have been basically since the moment I saw her. I don't want to throw around ridiculous shit like love at first sight, but there has always just been something about her, something that drew me to her in a way I can't explain.

So, I should just man the fuck up and say something, right?

When we both emerge from our rooms at the same time before dinner, I figure it might just be a sign from the universe.

"Hey," she says casually. She's in the hoodie that she almost always wears, the one that's a bit too big for her and I'm pretty sure was Jonah's, and her hair is loose and curling in long waves down her back. God I love her fucking hair. I don't know why, but it's like my Kryptonite. I want to run my fingers through it, wrap it around my fist and pull her face to mine, or maybe use it to tilt her head back, force her to look up at me from her knees—I cut the thoughts off before they can spiral.

"Hey yourself," I say, giving her an easy smile. I move closer and lean against the wall beside her door. "I'm sorry I've been a little MIA since we got back. I had a lot of shit to get situated with our, uh, change in leadership and everything."

"It's fine, I get it." She leans against the wall beside me and smirks. "Heavy is the crown and all that."

"Yeah, it really is." I mean for the words to come out light but there's a note of heaviness to them. It's true. It is fucking heavy and I've been carrying it for so long. I knew what I was getting myself into when I decided to step into this role, and I'm glad that I did it. I like to think that a whole lot of people are better off since I took control and I'm happy to shoulder the burden, but I wonder when it will be time to put it down, or hand it off to someone else.

She studies me for a long minute in that calculating way of hers, like she's seeing down to my soul and fettering out all of my darkest secrets. I wish I could read her mind. I'm desperate to know what she's thinking, what she wants.

She seems to make a decision, straightening and shifting her shoulders back.

"Listen, I'm too old for the worrying and the guessing and the are-we-aren't-we bullshit." My eyes widened slightly. "So, I'm going to ask the simple question, and you're going to give me the simple answer, deal?"

"Alright," I say, quirking a brow and holding my fucking breath. She inhales deeply and holds my gaze for a long minute. She exhales and her eyes dip to my lips.

"Oh fuck it," she mutters before reaching out and gripping the front of my shirt. She tugs me down and slams her lips to mine. I freeze for a heartbeat, but then give in completely, groaning and tunneling my hands through her hair like I've been dying to do. I bite gently at her bottom lip and she gasps, tightening her grip on my shirt. I tilt my head and deepen the kiss, thrusting my tongue against her own. This isn't like the soft kiss we'd shared in the camper. This is pure fire, threatening to consume us both. I need more. I don't know that I'll ever get enough.

She moans against my lips, and moves one hand to my hip, hooking a finger in my belt loop and using it to tug me forward. I turn us so that her back's against the wall, my body pressing fully against hers. God, the feel of her pinned beneath me is enough to make me lose my mind. She inches her fingers under the hem of my shirt and I shudder at the touch, my muscles clenching. She rocks her hips against me and I think she might just be as desperate as I am.

"I didn't hear a question in there, Melody," I rasp and she smiles against my lips.

"Why do you always call me that?" she asks as I kiss along her jaw.

At her ear, I whisper, "Well, it's your name, isn't it?" When I pull her earlobe through my teeth, she shudders, pulling me harder against her.

"You know…what I mean," she pants as I lick and kiss down her neck, across her collarbone and throat, and back up the other side. I want to kiss every inch of her, my blood on fire at the thought. I pull back and met her gaze.

"I just…like the way it sounds on my lips," I tell her honestly. I really can't explain it any other way. *Mel* fits her, but *Melody* just feels right for me. For us, together.

"I like the sound of it on your lips too," she says with a sultry smile that makes my cock throb. I'm so hard I swear to God I might bust through my jeans. I lean in and brush my nose against hers.

"So, about that question…?"

She laughs a little breathlessly and bites her lip. I'm just about to lean in and take over, maybe move things inside one of our rooms, when the door to the stairs flies open. We spring apart like we've been caught doing something we shouldn't be, which is ridiculous. I can do whatever the fuck I want, really, and no one with any kind of good sense will question it. But this is different than me with the other girls.

This is more than just getting laid. This is *more* everything, and I don't know how I want to handle sharing this more with anyone else yet.

So, I take another step away from Melody and try to act normal. I clear my throat and try to discretely adjust a few things. She pulls her lips in to hide her smile and I'm glad that she doesn't seem upset or like she's regretting what had just happened.

"Landry," I say, trying not to sound as annoyed as I feel at his sudden appearance. He doesn't typically end up on this hallway. He's part of my security team, but he was never put on guard duty up here, and that duty has all but been eliminated now anyway. I only had them for the first few weeks that Melody was here, just I case she got any crazy ideas like trying to stab me in my sleep or anything.

"Can I help you?" When I meet his eyes, worry unfurls in my stomach and I tense. Something is wrong "What happened?"

Wynn looks between me and Melody, and that worry turns into an icy ball of dread. She straightens, reading the situation as well as I have, knowing Wynn well enough to understand that something bad has happened and it has something to do with her.

"What?" she asks, stepping forward. "What's wrong, Wynn?"

"It's...It's Jonah."

CHAPTER EIGHTEEN

MELODY

MY BLOOD ROARS in my ears and I feel too cold and too hot all at once.

"What?" I bark. "What happened?" I glance at Traeger. A second ago, I'd felt a connection that I honestly never thought I'd feel again, along with all whole host of other, more carnal things. Now, when I look at him, all I feel is a hot, simmering rage.

"They were out on a run and he was trying to save a family…"

"Was he bitten?" I interrupt, my body going completely numb. *Say no. Say no. God, please say no.*

"No," Wynn assures me quickly. "No, he wasn't bitten. There was a family pinned down in a burned-out building. He fought his way through to them and a beam collapsed."

I blink rapidly, trying to stay upright. "How bad?" I ask, keeping my voice calm and even, but inside I'm screaming.

"Some broken ribs, broken leg. Doc Hastings thinks maybe a bruised spleen, but they're monitoring him closely…"

"Mel—"

I whirl on Traeger, fury burning everything else I feel for him away to ash.

"This is your fucking fault," I hiss, nearly snarling. His jaw clenches and his nostrils flare, but he doesn't say anything. I know somewhere deep down that, logically, it isn't actually his fault, but all of the anger and fear whirling inside me has to be directed at something, at someone.

And he's the fucking winner.

"I'm going," I say, daring him to tell me no. "Blindfold me, gag me, knock me out—whatever, but I have to see him. I'll keep all your fucking secrets, but I am going. You'll have to shoot me to stop me."

The muscle in his jaw ticks and I can't read the look in his eyes, or maybe I don't want to. He looks to Wynn and, after what feels like an entirety, he nods.

"Take her, just the two of you. Go now." He glances at me and then adds, "Take B route."

"You sure?" Wynn asks, brows rising. *B route? What the fuck does that mean and why does it have Wynn looking so surprised?*

Traeger holds my gaze, and without taking his eyes off me, he says to Wynn, "I trust her."

I refuse to thank him. I feel like this is all my fault somehow, like the universe is punishing me for deciding to try to be happy, for taking things with Traeger somewhere. For falling. *This is what I get. This is what I deserve.*

THE TRIP DOESN'T TAKE NEARLY AS long as it had when I'd first come to FOS, and Wynn explains that they have multiple routes to and from FOS from every other settlement. It's how they keep the location a secret. On the way there initially, we'd taken a route designed to take extra time and get me completely lost. Now I understand why Wynn had been surprised when Traeger told him to take Route B: this is a straight shot from FOS to The Cove. No backtracking, no detours, no doubts about where, exactly, I am. I could lead all of Haven directly to Traeger's front door now if I wanted.

I trust her, he'd said. I try not to think of it, or what had happened in the hallway or the things I'd been feeling. I try not to think of the flash of defeat I'd seen in his eyes when I'd glared at him, blaming him for Jonah's injuries, as if he knew in that instant that whatever had been building between us was crashing and burning and leaving him standing in the ashes alone. I try not to think of him at all.

Wynn and I don't talk much on the drive. It's taking all of my strength not to lash out and put my fist through the window. We finally get to The Cove and I jump out of the car before it's even fully stopped. Bret blinks at my sudden appearance.

"Mel?" he says, incredulous.

"Is he at our place or Doc's?" is all I say. Later, I'll apologize and give him a proper hug because I've missed him, but right now all I can think of is Jonah. I have to see him with my own eyes. I have to make sure he's ok. I can't do this again, I can't lose anyone else, I just *can't*.

"Oh, uh, yours," Bret says, clearly confused as he glances between me and Wynn. I take off towards the house that had once been mine. I barely hear Bret ask Wynn if anyone else is coming and if he needed to star rounding up weapons. I burst through the front door, and Mulligan leaps to his feet from the chair in the living room.

"Mel?" he gasps. He stumbles over and wraps me in a hug. I clutch at him, squeezing so tightly that I'm sure I'm probably hurting him, but I don't care. He doesn't seem to either, squeezing me right back. "God, how are you here? I never thought…Fuck, it doesn't matter." He holds me tighter, his body shuddering a little. I can tell how worried he is, how glad he is to have someone to share this with.

"Where is he? Is he ok?"

"I'm fine," comes the soothing, familiar voice that's been my anchor through virtually every storm in my life. *Jonah*. Tears sprang to my eyes and I feel like I can breathe for the first time since Wynn said those terrible words in that hallway. I disentangle myself from Mull and circle around the couch. Jonah lays there, a blanket up to waist and his flannel shirt open over his bandaged ribs. He has scrapes and bruises on his face, neck, and arms, but he smiles at me and it lights up his entire face.

"You idiot," I say before a sob breaks free. I sit on the edge of the couch, and hug him, trying to be careful of his injuries. He wraps his arms around me and strokes my back.

"Shhh, Mel, it's ok. I'm ok."

How is he the one consoling me? He's the one who's hurt, who had almost *died*. It only makes me cry harder. Jonah has always been the one to take care of me and I've missed him so fucking much. I hadn't let myself really feel the full force of it, but now, it's like I'm in the middle of the ocean during a hurricane. Wave after wave of raw emotion rushes over me, dragging me down only to hit me all over again as soon as I surface.

What feels like hours later, I finally pull away and scrub the tears from my eyes.

"Tell me."

He sighs but tells me the whole story as Mull presses a glass of scotch into my hand. I give him a grateful look, squeezing his forearm before he pulls away, and he smiles at me, looking exhausted but happy.

"I had to, Mel. You would have done the same thing." I wish I could argue with him, but I can't and he knows it. The asshole grins at me.

"You're still an idiot," I point out, taking another sip of my drink. The worst of the panic and pain is fading now and I'm finally finding my equilibrium.

"Well, you've known that for going on two decades," he jokes. "Enough about me and all of this," he says, gesturing to his chest and then waving it away like it isn't a big deal. "I'm fine and Doc is checking in every hour to be sure. So, we're shifting gears: How are you fucking here, Mel? Are you alright?"

"I'm good, I promise." I'll keep my word to Traeger and not give up any of his secrets, but I need to make sure that Jonah knows that I'm really and truly ok, to ease his mind and make sure he doesn't worry needlessly about me. He needs to focus on other things, like healing and resting for starters. "Really, J, I'm fine. I haven't been beaten or tortured—unless you count harvesting vegetables as torture."

"Well, I know how much you hate gardening."

We both smile and it feels so fucking good, like this is where I'm supposed to be. A nagging, stupid, annoying voice in the back of my mind tries to argue, to say that somewhere *else* feels more like home now, that someone else is who I want to be beside right now. But that isn't fucking happening, not anymore. I hadn't been here with Jonah when he needed me, and I'm placing the blame for that squarely on Traeger's shoulders—whether he deserves it or not.

"I don't think I can stay long," I say.

"The fact that he even let you come at all is a miracle. Even if it's only for five minutes, I'll take it." As if on cue, a soft knock on the door sounds. Mulligan gets up to answer it and I brace myself to be torn away from Jonah already. *It's not nearly enough time. I can't leave him yet.*

"Jonah," Wynn says, nodding in greeting as he steps inside the living room. "How you doing?"

"I'm alright. Tired of everyone hovering," he says pointedly at Mulligan, but he smiles. He loves how much Mull loves him. "But I'm ok. Doc thinks nothing bad internally, so just gotta wait for all the broken bones to heal."

"Good, good, I'm real happy to hear that, man."

"We have to go?" I ask, tensing.

Wynn shakes his head. "He's giving you three days."

Jonah and I both blink in surprise. Is Traeger trying to win me over? Make up for the blame I'm placing at his feet? Well, it won't fucking work, but I'm sure as shit not going to look this gift horse in the mouth. Mulligan steps forward.

"I've been sleeping down here with Jonah, so Mel can have our room and you can take Mel's," he offers. Usually a whole house is prepared for Traeger's men when they come to visit, but since this was kind of spur of the moment and it's late, I'm sure Wynn is perfectly happy to just bunk here. Mulligan meets my gaze and at my look adds, "But I do believe my spot on the couch is being commandeered this evening, so same plan except I'm taking our room I guess." I smile at him and he winks. He turns to Wynn. "I'll help you with the bags and get you situated."

Wynn nods to me, giving me a look that reminds me to keep my promise and tells me that he trusts me to do it. I nod back, letting him know I won't do anything stupid or that will put anything at risk. I know that Jonah and Mulligan wouldn't tell anyone, that they can be trusted with the secrets too, but it isn't my place to make that decision.

I hate keeping things from Jonah, but I'll do it. The important thing is that he knows that I'm safe.

"You both seem pretty buddy-buddy with Wynn," I say, arching a brow at Jonah after Wynn and Mulligan head outside to get my pack and whatever bag Wynn had apparently packed. I vaguely remember him helping me pack some things too, but it's all a blur.

"He's made it a point to come see us every time he rides through, to let us know that you're alright and everything. He's a good guy."

"He is," I agree. "We've become really good friends."

I gently lift his legs so I can slide beneath them, setting them down over my lap as I lean back against the cushions. When he winces and sucks in a harsh breath, I grind my teeth.

"I will never forgive him for this," I mutter quietly.

"Forgive who?"

"Traeger. If he hadn't taken me—"

"Technically you volunteered," Jonah interrupts, smirking when I glare at him.

"I should have been with you. I should have had your back." Tears burn my eyes again and Jonah's smirk fades.

"Mel, this could have happened whether you were with me or not. Hell, you could have been hurt right beside me if you'd been there. It's no one's fault, come on."

"It's his," I insist.

Jonah eyes me, that look in his eyes telling me he knows there's more that I'm holding back. I've never been good at lying to Jonah. Everyone else? Sure, no problem. Half of my job had literally been to lie, and I'd been damn good at my job, but Jonah has always known when I'm keeping things from him. Planning his surprise twenty-seventh birthday party had been nearly impossible. He claims he really had been shocked by the entire thing, but I have my doubts. I think he just maintains that story to make me feel better.

"I've been thinking that things aren't quite what they seem," he says slowly, telling me without telling me what he suspects. We've always been able to communicate like that, almost telepathically to a point. It used to drive Mitch and Sean crazy. I meet his gaze and decide that I'm not technically breaking my promise if I hint and he infers and reads between the lines.

"I can neither confirm nor deny..." I say quietly, cutting my eyes to the stairs. "But you might be correct in your line of thinking." He nods to himself, as if he's seeing everything click into place inside his mind, confirming what he thought might be the case.

"I'm ok, J. I promise you, I'm alright. Maybe even..." I shake myself, refusing to say the word *happy*. Maybe I had been, or at least getting close to it, but that was before.

"Oh my god," Jonah breathes, a smile tugging his lips upward and transforming him from handsome to downright gorgeous. Jonah smiles with his whole self somehow, like it comes from deep within his soul and lights up every inch of him.

"What?" I ask, confused. "What's that shit-eating grin about?"

"You're falling for him."

"What?? *That's* what you got from that? That's not—"

"Oh I know what you're saying," he says, cutting me off with a look that says I'm an idiot. He keeps his voice low as he continues, "I had my suspicions based on what Wynn was passing to us about you being ok, that fondness in his voice. I figured you weren't being tortured if he was buddying up to you and I can tell he's a good dude and wasn't just bullshitting." He quirks a brow, looking smug. "And he wasn't the only one assuring me that you were alright."

I frown. "Huh?"

"Doc Hastings told me that he has very reliable sources within FOS and promised me that you were alright, that things aren't necessarily what we think. That...FOS is a safe place. He gave me that look that told me it needed to remain between us, but you know how good Doc's instincts are with people. He knew within five minutes of meeting that Caitlin bitch that she was bad news, and then next thing we know, she's stealing and trying to kill Marcus. So, whoever his contacts are at FOS, he trusts them, and I trust Doc." He shrugs easily.

I blink, trying to figure out who Doc might know at FOS, and how he knows the truth, and why he would risk it—and Traeger's potential wrath—for sharing that knowledge with Jonah. I shake my head, deciding to think about that later.

"Plus, I'm a genius," Jonah adds. He grins and waggles his eyebrows and I roll my eyes. "But I stand by my initial response: *you're falling for him.*"

I narrow my eyes at him. This is the one time I curse the fact that he knows me better than I know myself.

"Wynn is a great guy but no, he's just a friend."

Jonah snorts and ignores me. "God, I can't believe it. I've been hoping for this for years…"

"Oh fuck off, Cothren."

He chuckles. "Go ahead and deny it but I think I'm right and I think *that's* why you're so pissed right now and blaming him with your whole fucking chest, Mel. You're looking for an excuse to cut and run because things were heading somewhere serious and your emotionally damaged self didn't know what to do with that."

"My *emotionally damaged self?*" I repeat slowly, mouth gaping. I refuse to even acknowledge anything else he's said because it *might* have the tiniest kernel of truth tucked in there somewhere.

"I love you, but you are so emotionally damaged, babe. Rightfully so, of course," he adds, still smiling, "but damaged all the same." After a moment he says softer, the grin fading a bit, "You're scared of losing anyone else."

I swallow past the lump in my throat. He's…maybe in the neighborhood of having me dead to fucking rights, like he always is, but I'm not about to admit it. I'm sticking to my guns. Jonah had almost been killed and it was Traeger's fault. End of discussion. Whatever had been happening between us was squashed now. I wrap my heart with the anger and fear, imagine heating it and forging it into impenetrable steel.

It's done.

"Let's not talk about it anymore right now," he says, letting me off easy. "Hell, I wasn't sure I'd ever get to see you again, so let's just be us for a bit, alright? I've missed the hell out of you, Mel." His eyes shine and mine water again.

"I've missed the hell out of you too. Even if you are kind of an ass."

He huffs out a laugh and then winces. I stiffen, reaching forward to try to do something. What, I have no idea, but I feel like I should do something to help. He waves me off.

"I'm fine, just sore. It's going to take time to heal. You know the drill—how many ribs have you broken by now? Seven? Nine?"

"We'll split the difference and call it eight," I say with a shrug. I know he's right: it's just going to take time, but he's ok. He's really and truly alright. I didn't lose him. I let the knowledge chase away some of the deadly cold from my veins. *He's ok.*

He smiles and I settle back into the cushions, playing with the hole in his sweatpants.

"Alright then, tell me everything that I've missed. Did Kelly ever tell Jack about Randy?"

CHAPTER NINETEEN

TRAEGER

THINGS WITH MELODY ARE FUCKED. I understand—somewhat—but at the same time, I want to put my fists through the walls in frustration. We'd been so close, *so fucking close*. But the minute Wynn delivered the news about Jonah, the minute I saw that look in her eyes, I knew any hope of it becoming what I wanted it so fucking desperately to become was gone. An ember snuffed out before it had time to grow into the fire it was meant to be. She blames me. She blames me because she wasn't there with him, to protect him. In her eyes, it's my fault that he was hurt and that's not something she can forgive.

I think there's more to it than that, but I'll keep my wishful thinking to myself for now.

Now she's closed herself off from me almost entirely. She answers questions when asked, nods in acknowledgment or greeting, but our days of talking or joking or playing *What Do You Miss?* are over. I even tried leaving books for her again, but after the third resounding thud, letting me know in no uncertain terms that she'd tried her level best to throw the damn things back at me *through* the wall, I stopped trying for the safety of the poor books.

"Melody, come on," I all but beg about a month after Jonah's accident, jogging to catch up to her near the greenhouse. I'd given her time, but I can't just give up. This thing between us is too real, too important, to just let it go without a fight.

So, I'll fucking fight.

She stops, shoulders tensing. She takes a deep breath, seeming to steel herself before turning to face me. Is it getting harder for her to keep this up? Or is that just more wishful thinking?

She turns and I try not to let the disappointment show: there isn't a hint of anything but cool indifference on her beautiful face. It feels like a punch right to my gut. She hikes a brow in question, though she doesn't look at me directly. She never does anymore. I exhale roughly and run a hand through my hair. This is useless. She isn't ready to let me fight for her, for us. Maybe she never will be. I don't like the cold pit that forms in my stomach at the thought. I push it away, refusing to look at it. I know she felt the same. I fucking *know* it. It wasn't just physical in that hallway, it was so much more than that. She couldn't have forgotten it so quickly, so she's forcing herself to act like she has.

That's what I'm telling myself anyway. Maybe I'm just a pathetic, love sick puppy who can't take a hint, but I'm not giving up, not yet.

But for now, instead of saying what I *want* to say, I just remind her about our upcoming trip. A few hours north of FOS, there was a small community out on what was essentially an island in the middle of a huge lake. It had been entirely cut off from the rest of the world right at the beginning of the end, the two bridges that stretched across the water on the south and north ends blown up by some over-zealous residents thinking they could save everyone on the island if they kept everyone else out. They'd even gone so far as to sink cars and other hunks of metal along the shoreline to keep boats from crossing over. It was a good plan, in theory, but they didn't realize that half of them on the island had already been infected. We knew so little in those early days, everyone was just grasping at straws and making rash, desperate decisions that they thought meant survival. It was fucking chaos. It's honestly a miracle any of us survived.

My guys have been working on repairing the bridge on the south side of the island for a few months now, and they've finally got it stable enough to cross on foot. Eventually, we'll get it to where vehicles can make the trek, but for now its foot traffic only. I gave the order that no one goes across until I come personally. I don't like watching from the sidelines with this kind of thing, especially if there are potentially new people to bring into Haven—or fight. Flashes of the ambush where Melody had nearly been killed flicker through my mind and I clench my fists at my sides.

Either way, I want to be there in person to clear the island, so we're taking a large team to do a massive sweep of the entire thing.

"Pack for a couple of weeks, just to be safe," I say and she nods. Neither of us move. She swallows hard and finally—*finally*—shifts her gaze to meet mine directly. There's a flash of something there. Pain? Longing? Regret?

"Is that all?" she asks quietly.

"Melody, I…" I search her eyes, trying to find something that tells me she still wants me, wants this. I shake my head. "Yeah, that's all."

She nods and walks away.

CHAPTER TWENTY

MELODY

LIFE AT FOS has gone from pretty good, verging on great, to complete shit. I hate how things are now, but I can't let go of my anger, can't just get over the fact that Jonah had almost died and I hadn't been there, and it was Traeger's fault. Jonah had tried his best to sway me before I left The Cove, telling me that I was essentially a giant idiot, but I refused to give in.

He was right: I got scared and now I'm using Jonah's accident as an excuse. I'm still scared, but I...fuck, I don't know *how* to let go of this fear and anger and uncertainty, even if I wanted to. I feel like I'm tangled in barbed wire with no hope of escape now. The more I struggle, the more ensnared I become, the more pain lashes through me from all directions.

I force all thoughts of Traeger and our relationship—or lack thereof, I guess—away and focus on the task at hand. We're about to embark into uncharted waters, so to speak. No one has been on this little island in almost a decade as far as we can tell, and we could be walking into an entire community full of Bloodies—or survivors who like their privacy and might not appreciate visitors.

I tell myself that if the latter is true, then they would have done something to our guys when they were working on the bridge, right?

So I'm assuming it's the former. Not necessarily a better option, but a somewhat easier one to deal with in a sense. Hordes of Bloodies can overrun you quick, sure, but at least they can't think and plan and coordinate attacks. I'd take the mindless zombies over calculating humans any day.

I have complete faith in the construction and engineering teams, but I still hold my breath as we cross the bridge, glancing over the edge to the water below. You could survive the fall, if you didn't land on a submerged car or something, but it wouldn't feel good.

"Half expected the whole damn thing to collapse, not gonna lie," Wynn says when we're back on solid ground on the island.

I grin at him. "Same though."

We all take a second to be still and scan the area in front of us, listening for anything. Bloodies, shouts, gunshots—anything. But if there's anything out there waiting, they're keeping it quiet.

One of the guys on the construction team used to live in this area and tells us that the island is mostly just houses—some absolutely huge ones—but it also had a convenience and bait store, a small medical clinic, and two little restaurants. The silver lining to the entire island being infected almost from the very start is that all of those houses and businesses are most likely still very ripe with supplies for the taking. Well, silver lining for us, anyway. Guess from the islander's perspective there isn't really shit to be happy about.

The plan is to split into five six-person teams and go house-by-house, making our way from one end of the island to the other. Once we clear everything, we'll work on going through and inventorying supplies. We'll be out on the island for a week, at least, so my pack is a bit heavier than usual to include extra clothes, gear, and provisions. Once we get the initial area cleared and find some working vehicles, the group staying back to guard the bridge will bring over the rest of our bags and drive them to wherever we decide to camp for the night. For the most part, our day will be spent on foot though. It'll avoid unnecessary noise, plus hopping in and out every few feet like kids Trick-or-Teating seems more annoying than just huffing it to me. Guess Traeger agrees.

Thankfully, the rain had stopped on the drive here so we aren't getting drenched right now, but the ground is completely soaked and muddy from the weeks' worth of storms that had hit this area.

"Alright, you know your jobs. Be safe and vigilant," Traeger says before we all split off into our assigned teams. I tell myself not to notice how good he looks in his tactical gear, the tight black long-sleeve thermal molding to his chest and arms, the weapons strapped all over him giving him a lethal and sexy vibe that I'm inwardly drooling over. Just because I'm not letting myself try anything again doesn't mean I went blind and can't see how attractive he is. Too fucking attractive.

He shifts his gaze to mine and holds there for too long before he says, "Let's move out."

I swallow hard and adjust the straps on my pack just to give me something to do with my hands. It's getting harder and harder to ignore him, to ignore the things that I still want, despite still being so fucking angry.

Of course, I'm on his team. I don't bother putting up a fuss about it. Part of me is even happy about it. That part needs to shut the fuck up.

"Get some," Wynn says, holding out his fist towards me. I grin and bump my fist to his. I can't deny that I'm excited. I need some action to take my mind off of everything else.

"Laissez les bons temps rouler, baby."

WE MAKE it most of the day without much incident. A few Bloodies inside some of the houses, but overall nothing too crazy. Without even really looking too deeply, I know that we'll get tons of great stuff from these houses, and, Traeger assures me without me asking, it will be spread equally throughout the settlements.

The properties here are good size, the houses a little more spread out than we originally thought, so we have to hike a good bit between some of them. I hate hiking. Running is fine, but traversing through mud and downed trees and overgrowth like a fucking frontiersman is not my idea of fun.

The three groups that are working this side of the island take a break. The mud and slippery terrain is making it hard for everyone, so we can all use some water and rest. We find a a spot where the trees are a bit thinner, not quite a full clearing, but only smaller trees dotting the landscape. It honestly looks a little creepy with the thin layer of fog hanging around because of all the rain and I rub the back of my neck at the prickling of unease that skitters up my spine. I don't like not being able to see clearly around us.

Wynn holds out his canteen and I take it gratefully, not wanting to dig through my own pack to find mine. I take a long sip and wipe my mouth with the back of my hand before holding it back out. I jut my chin to the edge of the trees.

"How far you think that drop is?"

This part of the island is elevated above the water and an inlet from the lake runs between two small-ish...I guess cliffs is about the closest thing to a right term for them, though it feels like a gross exaggeration.

"Sixty feet at least probably," Wynn says following my gaze. I nod and he takes another drink. "This is gonna be a huge haul when it's all said and don—" He breaks off when screams ring out. I spring up from my perch on a half-rotten log, muscles tense and ready. I grab my gun, just as everyone around me does the same. The only good thing that's happened since Jonah is that my probationary period was lifted and now I can have weapons.

"Horde!" someone yells and then a group of Bloodies seems to materialize from the trees, as if they'd appeared out of thin air. They look creepy as absolute fuck lurching out of the fog and my heart thunders in my chest.

"What the fuck?!" I yell, catching Traeger's eyes across the small space. Shots begin to ring out as everyone starts fighting for their lives. The Bloodies keep coming and coming. Ten, twenty, maybe more. How had a group this big crept up on us so quickly? Whoever had been scouting ahead must have been slacking...or they got taken out before they knew what hit them. *Shit, shit, shit.*

I start taking them out as fast as I can, but we're in relatively close quarters and I don't want to risk hitting any of our own people. I grit my teeth in frustration and sling my rifle over my back, reaching for one of the many blades I have within easy reach instead. Knives are riskier since I have to get closer to the Bloodies to make the kill, but they're safer for everyone else in the long run. I stab and slice and duck and spin, my knife and body coated in thick, sludgy blood soon enough.

"Melody!" Traeger bellows my name as I bolt forward to take out a Bloody who has Martin pinned, barely keeping the thing's snapping jaws from his throat. I sink the blade into the Bloody's temple and it goes limp. I help shove it off of Martin and yank him upward, nodding before sprinting for the next one, then the next. A blood-curdling scream rings out to my left and I whip my head that direction only to see a Bloody tearing out Amber's throat. Her scream cuts off in a low, wet gurgle, and blood pours down her chest. The Bloody follows her body down as it slumps to the ground, feasting. Another joins and I grimace as the stomach-churning sounds of wet flesh being torn apart. I grit my teeth but force myself to move on: there's no help for her now. I can only hope that they finish the job enough that she doesn't rise again.

I keep an eye on Wynn and Traeger as I fight, needing them to be alright. As complicated as my feelings are for Traeger, I don't want to think about him being hurt or worse. I refuse to think about it or think about what that means, so instead, I take out my frustrations on the undead all around me. God, there are so fucking many of them. I scream through gritted teeth as one gets so close that I can see the bits of rotting flesh hanging from his gaping jaw—singular I suppose, since the entire bottom half of it is missing. He forces the full weight of his desperate body on me and I nearly topple backward. My boots slip in the mud, but even as we slide backwards, I keep my arms against the Bloody's chest, pushing back against it with all my strength. He may not be able to chomp down with only half a face, but if he gets his top teeth into me at all, I'm done for.

I scream again and shift my weight, spinning and following the Bloody down as his momentum takes him to the ground. I slam my knife into his skull and he stops struggling. I roll off of him, breathing hard, but only allow myself a heartbeat to lie there before springing up to find my next target.

Traeger somehow ended up on the edge of the clearing, near the drop off and three Bloodies are gunning for him. My heart clenches, panic taking hold and strangling me. I fight my way to him, desperate to get there in time, but by the time I do, he's already taken all three of them out. He turns towards me and arches a brow, asking if I'm alright. I nod before I freeze, icy cold fear skittering up my spine as I look just over his shoulder. Another Bloody lurches towards him, faster than the others. It must have fed on one of our people already, the boost of fresh blood making it stronger, faster, more volatile and frenzied. Traeger won't have time to turn and get his gun up. The thing is already almost on him.

No.

Without thinking, I raise my arm, blade in hand. Traeger's eyes go wide, actual fear and confusion and a bit of hurt flashing in the green depths. I let the knife fly and he barely has time to flinch before the blade sinks into the Bloody's eye, mere feet behind him. He whirls just as the body slumps to the ground, and stares dumbfounded for a second. I close the distance between us and yanked my knife free, wiping the blade on the Bloody's shirt. I glance around and see that most of them have been handled. I try not to look too closely at the bodies of our own littering the ground among the monsters. Wynn is still standing and uninjured from what I can tell, so the fear clenching my heart eases up a fraction.

"Holy shit," Traeger breathes as I straighten. "How…" He cuts off as the ground beneath us shifts. He grabs me, and I meet his gaze for a heartbeat before everything gives way and we tumble down the embankment.

CHAPTER TWENTY-ONE

TRAEGER

MEL SCREAMS as we fall and my heart ends up in my throat. We both try to grab onto anything to slow our descent, desperately scraping and clawing at the earth, but there's nothing but mud and wet leaves. I hold onto her arm, refusing to let go of her. The whole thing only takes seconds, I know, but it feels like an eternity. Rocks and twigs scrap against my hands and face, but I barely notice. We finally hit the bottom with jarring force, and I lose my grip on Melody. She screams again as she lurches sideways, and we both tumble and roll across the small sandy bank in opposite directions.

"Melody!" I yell, scrambling through the damp sand towards her. "Melody, are you ok?" I reach down to help her up, but her leg nearly gives out and she cries out in pain, quickly clamping her lips together to stop the sound. I keep her upright, but she keeps weight off of her right foot.

"My ankle," she gasps. "Might be broken, not sure."

"Mel! Traeger!" Landry calls from above us. He holds onto a tree, probably worried about another landslide, and leans out over the edge as far as he can.

"We're ok!" Mel calls. "Be careful at the edge! Looks like more could give way any second."

"Yeahhh," he says, eyeing the ground warily. "We'll find a safe way down, just sit tight for a bit."

I hear the unmistakable groans then and whip my head to our left. *Fuck.*

"We don't have a bit," I say, trying to keep my voice even. Mel follows my gaze and curses. A whole group of Bloodies is coming around the curve of the bank right for us. This whole fucking area is apparently infested. I shift Melody so we can head the opposite directly, only to find another group closing in from that direction.

"You have got to be kidding me!" Mel groans.

"Fuck, fuck, fuck," I grate, glancing back up the embankment. Maybe there's a way we can climb...but no, it's pointless. No way in hell we're going up. Which only leaves one other option. I look across the small inlet to the other bank. It's clear of Bloodies, at least for the time being, and it's our only chance. Melody seems to come to the same realization, but doesn't look too thrilled by the idea. We haven't cleared anything on the other side of yet, there's no telling what we might be walking into, and that water is going to be cold as fuck.

"It's the only option," I say. "There's no way we make it out with this many." We could get a little cover from above, but with no one able to get too close to the edge, it won't be enough. She glances back and forth between the hordes closing in on us and I know she knows that I'm right.

"Go!" Landry yells. "We'll be there as soon as we can find our way around. Fucking GO!"

"Give me the pack." I hold my hand out towards her. She starts to argue, but I snap, "We're about to have to swim every bit of eighty yards, maybe more, in freezing water and then huff it, and you've got a potentially broken ankle. You don't need the extra weight. Give me the fucking pack, Melody."

She presses her lips into a hard line, but slides the bag from her shoulders and hands it to me. I pull it on and she grabs the walkie talkie from my belt, spinning me around and shoving it inside the pack.

"The pack is waterproof," she says in quick explanation and I nod, glad she thought to put our only form of communication somewhere safe. Melody is good in stressful situations, that's for damn sure.

"If you lose that bag…" she warns.

"I won't, now fucking *come on.*" I take her hand and yank her towards the water. I brace myself but gasp when we hit the water, the temperature a complete shock to my system. It must have been much colder up here than back at FOS, the storms bringing in a cold front.

"Fuck that's cold," I pant between clenched teeth.

"Full send," Melody groans. "It's the best way." She takes a quick breath and then dives into the water. Well shit. I take three quick breaths and force myself to dive headlong beneath the surface just as the first of the Bloodies reach the bank just behind us. My chest constricts as the cold envelops me, feeling like an icy fist squeezing my entire body. My muscles all feel like they're made of stone, but somehow, I make progress through the water. I keep an eye on Melody, but she's keeping pace just fine. It's not *that* far across, relatively speaking, but fuck it feels like we're swimming across the whole of the Mississippi. But we keep going, neither of us daring to stop to rest.

I finally make it to the other side and trudge up the bank, helping Melody to stand when she reaches it just behind me. She sucks in a harsh breath as she puts weight on her foot and I eye her worriedly. This isn't going to be fun for her. Maybe I can carry her? But before I can offer, she seems to physically push the pain away, separating herself from it completely. She nods.

"I'm good…but we have to go," she grits out. More Bloodies are making their way down this side of the bank now as well from our left. They're like ants flooding out of a hill that's been stepped on, so many more than you ever realized were there pouring out like lava. I jerk my chin towards a path that leads up the side of the embankment on this side and she nods. I pull my knife and pistol, both ready for whatever might be waiting for us, and keep a close eye on Melody as we run for our lives. I know she's hurting but she doesn't say a word, just keeps pushing. She might just be one of the toughest people I've ever fucking met.

Cold is seeping straight into my bones and Melody's teeth are chattering. We need to get somewhere safe, and preferably warm, as soon as fucking possible. We run as fast as we can through the trees, but she slips more than once between the wet ground and her ankle and I clench my teeth, knowing I need to get her off of that foot. We only run into a handful of Bloodies on this side and I dispatch them quickly, but the ones from the bank are following our path and soon the area will be overflowing. We've got some distance between us, but we can't stop out here in the open or they'll be on us too quickly.

"Is that a house ahead?" Mel pants, and I know she's only upright now by sheer force of will. I squint and can make out what looks like some kind of structure behind the thick trees ahead. Whatever it is will have to do.

"Yeah, looks like it, come on."

We finally make it into what was once a back yard. The house itself is mostly destroyed, only a couple of partial walls remaining of the burned-out shell. But, by a stroke of fucking luck, there's big barn-like building off to the right that had escaped the fire completely. Maybe one of those barndominiums that were all the rage for a while there? I can't imagine it was an actual barn with horses or anything out here in the woods, but what the fuck do I know? It has big actual barn doors on the front, but they've been boarded up, so we head towards a smaller door on the side. I take a quick breath and push open the door, ready for whatever might be lurking inside.

We wait on the threshold for a few seconds before charging inside, listening. Melody shakes her head, saying silently that she doesn't hear anything either, and we ease inside. It's dark, the windows mostly covered and only the faintest light sneaking in from the edges or in places where whatever is covering it—boards probably—have fallen away. I slide my knife back into the sheath at my hip and pull the flashlight from my belt instead, clicking it on. I sweep the beam through the room. It looks like some sort of workshop, with tables lining the walls and a huge workbench taking up the middle of the room. Tools and sawdust cover most the surfaces, and giant stacks of wood on the shelves along the back wall beside giant storage lockers that probably hold even more tools or wood. Some half-finished pieces of furniture—a rocking chair, a crib maybe, a small table—are piled in one corner. Not many places for anything to hide, thankfully.

"Looks clear," I say, moving further into the room. Melody follows and closes the door behind us.

"We need to block this," she says, gesturing towards the door as she limps forward. I hand her my pistol and flashlight, and shove one of the tables over so it blocks the door. It'll have to be enough for now.

"You need to get off that foot," I say, taking my things back from her. I shine the flashlight around the room again, deciding what the best spot for her will be. The workbench will work, though it won't be very comfortable.

"Wait," she says, putting her arm on my wrist and directing the light back where I'd just swept from. "There's s-s-stairs back there." She's starting to shake harder and I'm far from warm either. The temperature had dropped a good bit even since we started out this morning, and it's getting closer to sunset, so it's getting even colder now. Being drenched in nearly freezing water isn't helping a damn bit. We need to get warm and we need to do it now. I shine the beam higher, following the stairs as they disappear into the ceiling.

"An office maybe? Or an upstairs apartment?"

"Yeah, could be."

"Well, let's see if anyone's home," I say. If it's an apartment, it might have some food and blankets at least, and being on the second floor will give us an extra layer of security, so up it is. I help Melody hop up the stairs and at the top, we repeat the process from before: open the door, wait a tick for anything inside to hear us and come running—or to open fire on us, if it's someone of the breathing variety.

Nothing.

Melody practically melts with relief and I know she's gotta be nearing the end of her mind-over-matter capabilities. We step inside and I quickly sweep the room. It's much brighter up here, the late afternoon light shining in through the windows and sliding glass door to the small balcony that juts out from the back of the building. It's an apartment, like we guessed, with a large open space that makes up the living room, kitchen, and dining room, and a hallway leading towards the back of the place with a few doors branching off of it. Melody is pale and shivering nearly uncontrollably, and worry spears through my chest. Was it cold enough for hypothermia to set it? I don't fucking know, but I'm not taking any chances.

"Need t-t-to clear the r-rooms," she gets out through chattering teeth. I nod and lead her to the couch.

"I'll clear, you sit."

She doesn't argue, which tells me all I need to know: she's absolutely hitting a wall and is going to crash out soon. I make quick work of clearing the rest of the apartment. There's a small bathroom, bedroom, and closet off of the hallway, with the larger master bedroom and adjourning bathroom at the end. No threats to speak of. I'll do a deeper dive and explore more later, but for now, I need to make sure Melody's ok.

She'd shed her wet jacket and managed to get one boot off by the time I get back. I drop her pack and kneel down in front of the couch. I reach out and unlace her other boot with numb fingers, but force my body to obey. She clenches her fingers into the couch cushion as I ease her shoe off, pulling her sock off right after. I whistle low. Her ankle is already bruising and swollen. I can't tell if it's actually broken or just really badly sprained, but either way, I know that it must hurt like hell.

"I can't believe you ran on this," I mutter, my muscles suddenly clenching up as the cold hits me hard. I guess I've been running on adrenaline too, blocking out the worst of it, but now it's coming on strong. A violent shudder racks Melody's slim frame. *Fuck, fuck, fuck.*

Fire. We need a fire. I glance around to find something I can burn in the grate, beyond thankful the apartment has a fireplace.

"Clothes off. N-now," Mel says effectively stopping my search of something to start a fire with. I pull back to look up at her, arching a brow. She rolls her eyes. "Body heat, you j-j-jackass."

Oh. Right. Of course. I try not to think about the fact that that means I'm about to be up close and personal with a naked—or at least *nearly* naked—Melody, our bodies pressed together...

She shoves me away and stands, keeping the weight off her injured foot. She unbuttons her jeans and I rise to my feet, pulling off my shirt and tossing the wet fabric aside. I yank my boots and socks off, and start on my pants, a tiny thrill of nervousness running through me.

"If your boxers come off, I s-swear to God I will castrate you," she says and I huff out a laugh.

"Boxer briefs, actually," I correct as I work on getting the wet tactical pants off. "And, ok, they stay on."

I grab a blanket from a stack in the corner and when I turn back, all thoughts of being cold fly from my head. Melody stands in nothing but her underwear. Black, lacy boyshorts with a matching bra that make my mouth fucking water. The top of a tattoo peeks from the beneath the lace at her right hip bone and I need to know what the rest of it look like, just how low it dips down...

I shake myself. *Doesn't fucking matter right now. Focus.*

Despite the situation, I swear her eyes blaze for a second when she takes me in, her gaze traveling down my bare chest and stomach, further still...I swallow hard and mentally slap myself. *How about make sure that neither one of you are going to lose any extremities due to frostbite before you worry about eye fucking each other, you asshole.*

I throw the blanket around my shoulders and pull her close, wrapping the blanket around her as she snakes her arms around me. Already the heat within the blanket feels like heaven. I try to ignore how close we are, how much of our skin is touching, how little fabric separates us. I ease us down onto the couch, shifting so that she's in my lap, keeping us as close as possible. I think she's going to argue, but she sighs in relief, and rests her head in the crook of my neck.

We stay that way for a long time, neither of us saying a word, just letting the heat fill us. After a while, her shivering slows, and I'm hit with the painful sensation of numb fingers and toes regaining feeling.

"Don't read anything into this, Traeger," she says against my throat. "This is about my desire not to freeze to death. Nothing more."

"Wouldn't dream of it," I say. "Though, you know this is more effective if we're *completely* naked..."

"Don't press your luck." I swear there's a smile in her voice and I laugh lightly. I tighten my arms around her and she settles more firmly against me. Despite everything that had happened between us, despite the fact that, as she said, this has nothing to do with anything but our bodies' needs and survival, I can't help but feel so fucking content with her in my arms.

"Better?" I ask after what feels like hours.

She exhales and nods. "Better."

"I'm going to start a fire, and we need to get your ankle wrapped and you in some dry clothes."

As much as I hate to do it, I ease her off of me, maneuvering out from under the blanket and tucking the edges back tightly around her. I poke around in her pack, eyeing the stuffed dog that she risked her damn life for, and look for clothes. I highly doubt she'll want to put on jeans right now. "Let me check the bedroom, see if there's some sweats or something so you don't have to worry with real clothes right now."

"Thanks," she sighs, and I can see the pain and exhaustion hitting her hard. I dig through the dresser and find a goldmine. I tug on some dry clothes myself and come back, holding up sweatpants, a t-shirt, and a hoodie, smiling.

"Jackpot. Got plenty of dry, warm stuff for both of us." I toss the clothes to her. "You change while I grab wood from downstairs to burn."

I freeze when I reach the bottom of the stairs. I can hear them outside, the screeching and moaning and dragging sounds of Bloodies. The fucking soundtrack that's constantly playing in the background of this world. I tread lightly to one of the windows where the bottom corner of the wood had broken away. I peek outside and watch as a small herd ambles by. They're not paying much attention to the barn, so they don't seem to realize anything is inside, they're just following along the path they were already on in following us. They'll move off soon enough, I'm sure, but I'll keep an eye out once I get back upstairs just to be safe. I quietly grab a small stack of wood and head back up the stairs.

I manage to get a fire going pretty easily. I worry for a second about the smoke being seen by anyone still alive out here, but know that we have to risk it. We're fairly secure up in the apartment, so if someone does come to call, I'll be able to handle it easily. I check out the window and am happy to report that the Bloodies have made their way past the barn already. One less thing to worry about for tonight. I wrap Mel's ankle, give her a protein bar, water, and Advil, and then fish the walkie out of the pack.

"Landry, you there?"

The answer comes almost immediately and my muscles relax a fraction. I'd been worried about the rest of the group.

"Yes, sir," Landry's voice comes through the static, clearly relieved. "Are you and Mel alright?"

"Yeah, we're good. We found a place to hunker down."

"Thank God. We backtracked to one of the cleared houses and are safe for the night here too."

"Good work." I clench my jaw and then ask the question I'm dreading hearing the answer to. I'd seen the blood, the bodies littering the ground, the pieces of my people strewn around that fucking clearing. "How many?" Melody sits up straighter and leans forward. I hold her gaze as we wait for the answer. Despite the distance that's grown between us over these past weeks, we're united in this, in our worry for our people, in the regret for the loss of life.

"Six dead, sir." *Fuck.* I sit down on the coffee table and hang my head, closing my eyes. I feel like a failure. It's my job to keep them safe and I didn't fucking do it. Melody puts her hand on my forearm and I sigh before opening my eyes again. That one touch says so much: *It isn't your fault. This is the world we live in. You did your best. You have to keep going.*

"Mel's ankle is hurt pretty bad, so we won't be able to hike out again just yet."

"We'll try to find a way to that side of the island tomorrow."

Mel shakes her head and I quirk a brow.

"They should keep clearing houses. If I can't walk anyway, they might as well use the time to complete the mission. Everyone can use those supplies, Traeger. This is for all of Haven."

Well, I can't argue with that, and I decide not to point out that this means that we'll be stuck together in this apartment for at least a couple of days.

"Negative," I finally say into the walkie. "Go ahead and stick to the plan. Clear the houses and you'll get to us eventually."

"You're sure?"

"That's an order, Landry," I say, though it isn't with any real kind of command.

"Yes, sir. I'll check in tomorrow as we progress."

"Sounds good. Be safe."

I toss the walkie into the chair and rise to put another piece of wood on the fire. I wander back to the bedroom to see about sleeping arrangements, but it's damn near freezing. The temperature dropped like crazy when the sun set, and the fireplace doesn't really provide much heat this far back.

"Living room camp out it is," I call out from the bedroom. The couch is small, really just a loveseat. I know she could fit fine, but it won't be the most comfortable of sleeping arrangements and I don't want her sleeping on the damn floor either. So I heft the mattress from bed and, after some rearranging and a few half-hearted protests from Melody, settle it right in front of the fireplace. She still looks too pale, though there's a flush in her cheeks that I don't like, and another spike of worry slashes through my gut. She could easily get sick being that cold and wet and pushing herself too hard.

"Get some rest, I'll take first watch."

She looks like she might want to argue but I give her a pointed look and she relents. She really must be hurting. I help get her settled onto the mattress and covered in as many blankets as I can find. I pull a chair from the dining table over towards one of the windows and settle in.

"Thank you," she whispers softly, surprising me, before passing out completely. My lips curl up a tiny bit. It's a simple thank you. Nothing more.

But I'll take it.

CHAPTER TWENTY-TWO

MELODY

I'M ninety-percent sure that my ankle isn't broken, just really, *really* sprained. I woke up this morning to find it completely black and blue and swollen to twice its normal size. It reminds me a little of how both ankles had looked almost every day at the end of my pregnancy, minus the bruising, of course. But they were *huge,* like ham hocks with bunny slippers stuck on the ends. I smile a little at the memories before forcing them away. I'd been able to run on it yesterday thanks to adrenaline and my keen eagerness to not end up a Happy Meal, but thinking about putting weight on it now makes me want to cry.

So, as much as I hate to, I accept that I'm going to be mostly a bump on a log for at least the next day or two. I feel a little off, too, like maybe I have the beginnings of the flu, but I figure it's probably just from being drenched and freezing yesterday, plus exhausted. So, it's probably fine. I'll just rest and feel better later. Not much else to do, after all.

I frown when I realize that Traeger's gone.

"Traeger?" I call, but no answer. I actually wonder for a heartbeat if he's finally gotten tired of me hating him and decided to leave me behind. I honestly wouldn't blame him if he has. I know deep down that it hasn't really been fair how I've been treating him since Jonah, but…well, J had called me out perfectly: I am entirely emotionally damaged. Jonah being hurt had scared me to my core, but it had also given me an excuse to close Traeger out and not have to face any of the fucking terrifying things I'm feeling for him.

Because, yes, I'm still feeling them. I was able to cover them in anger there for a bit, but that stopped working pretty quickly. I still ignore them and shove them away every time they try to peek their little heads out…ok, so more like I pummel them with a hammer when that happens, like a giant game of Whack-a-Mole: Emotions Edition, but it's getting harder to keep that up. Despite being afraid of what I'm feeling for him, I'm getting so tired of fighting it.

And, yet, I keep on doing it. I don't know how to make myself do anything else, to just let it fucking go and dig myself out of the cold, walled up cocoon I've wrapped myself in. I put my head in my hands and groan, but then I hear noise outside and put the pity party on hold for now.

I heave myself off of the mattress, presumably looking *super* cool and not at all ridiculous, and hop on one foot to the window. I look out to find Traeger tying ropes between the line of trees surrounding the workshop-slash-apartment. I squint and see that there are cans and bottles hanging from the rope, clinking and banging together as he works.

"He's creating a warning system," I say to the empty room, nodding in approval. "Smart man."

I watch him as he works, but I'm really thinking about how he looked yesterday, stripped down to nothing but his tight black boxer-briefs; the way the water droplets clung to his muscles; the way all that ink danced over his skin and made me want to trace every pattern with my tongue; how it felt to be wrapped up with him in that blanket, skin on skin.

In that moment, I'd completely forgotten about trying to hate him and all of my admittedly misplaced anger. I'd forgotten about every-thing outside of the two of us. It didn't matter how we'd gotten here or everything that had gone wrong. All that mattered was that we were here, together, wrapped up in each other and hidden away from the world.

I sigh and turn away from the window to survey the apartment. The furnishings are worn, but nice, lots of rich wood and soft leather. Sports memorabilia and triathlon awards—Charlie Rocker was really fucking good, apparently—line the walls and sit on shelves, giving it a very bachelor-pad feeling, but there are homey touches too: handmade quilts stacked in the corner, a *World's Best Uncle* trophy on the mantle beside a picture of a handsome man with a gap-toothed little girl in pig tails and a little boy with red hair and freckles at a baseball game.

I hop through the living room and into the kitchen. I figure I might as well make myself useful and check out the food situation while Traeger works on security. I glance out onto the small balcony and nearly choke in surprise, barely stifling a scream before it tears free from my throat. In the chair, there's a fucking *body*. Not a Bloody, just a run of the mill dead person. I ease forward to get a better look through the glass. He's been dead for a long while by the looks of it, and by his own hand, judging by the pistol lying on the wood beneath his decomposing hand and the gaping hole in his temple. A twinge of sorrow rushes through my chest. This must be the World's Best Uncle.

"Rest in peace, Uncle Charlie," I say quietly.

I wonder who Charlie was. Why did he live up here above a workshop? Who lived in the big house before it burned? What had made him take the road out instead of trying to survive? To be fair, he could just as easily ask me why I *hadn't*, why I even worried about surviving at all. For a long, long time, there wasn't much hope. There was only fear and death and surviving day-to-day, hour-to-hour. So why had I kept going? I...don't know, really. For Jonah, of course, but beyond that, I'm not sure why I fought so hard all this time. Jonah would say it's just because I'm a stubborn asshole, and I guess part of that is right. Even so, I never would have survived long enough to finally see some good in the world again at Haven without Jonah. He kept me going, he pulled me out of the deepest darkness a person can be lost in. I miss him so much and wonder if there's ever a chance of us being together again. I really don't know, so I don't dwell on it for now, instead focusing back on my original mission: food.

I leave Charlie on the balcony and hobble the rest of the way to the kitchen, poking around in the cabinets and the small pantry. There's a decent amount of non-perishable stuff still here, so I'm relieved we won't be surviving solely on jerky and protein bars for the next couple of days. There's a large bedroom decorated half in dinosaurs, half in princesses, with a twin bed on either side. My heart twists. He must have had this set up for his niece and nephew. I try not to wonder what happened to them. I gently close the door and poke my head into the other doorways down the hall: a bathroom and a closet. I hop to the master bedroom at the end of the hall and cock my head as I read what's scrawled across the wall above the now empty-bed frame in sharpie:

I COULDN'T GO ON WITHOUT THEM.
CRACK THE CODE AND YOU DESERVE MY STASH.
GOD SPEED.
MMBBKGJGMJRNR

"What the fuck?" I mutter. I shake my head, not in the mood to deal with this bit of crazy right now. I'm still not feeling one hundred percent, my ankle is throbbing like a bitch, and I'm freezing even in the hoodie and sweats Traeger found for me. I move to the walk-in closet. There are a handful of clothes hanging on a short rack, shoes lined up neatly underneath, but the majority of the closet is taken up by floor to ceiling cabinets. I open one and gape before smiling widely.

"*Jackpot.*"

"Melody?" Traeger calls from the living room.

"Back here!" I yell, throwing open the next cabinet and the next.

"What are you doing in there? You shouldn't be up."

He stands just outside the closet, arms crossed over his chest.

"I'm fine," I say, rolling my eyes, but I can't stop smiling.

"What's with the grin?" he asks slowly, sounding a little confused and a lot apprehensive. I guess that's fair.

"I'm grinning because Uncle Charlie out there—dead guy on the balcony, by the way if you hadn't noticed yet—had a Bulk-N-Buy membership and he went *shoppin'*." I beckon him inside and he strides forward, eyes sparkling with excitement. He sucks in a harsh breath when he steps up beside me and I glance up at him.

"Holy fuck. Tell me this isn't what I think it is," he says quietly, eyes sliding closed and head bowing.

"Are you praying?" I ask with a laugh, so giddy by what I've stumbled upon that any trace of anger or any of that bullshit that I've been holding onto for all these weeks is nowhere to be found.

"You bet your ass I am," he says, and, after finishing apparently, opens his eyes. He reaches forward to grab one of several white boxes from the middle shelf. "Twinkies, Melody. *FUCKING TWINKIES.*"

I laugh again, shaking my head, and he grins back. There's an entire shelf of Twinkie boxes, another of soups and other canned stuff —veggies and fruits, and corned beef hash, which most people find disgusting but I happen to fucking *love.* Another shelf is full of chips and trail mix and beef jerky. *So* much food, the kind I wasn't sure I'd ever see again.

I hop as gracefully as I can to the next cabinet and throw it open.

"Oh my God! Pop Tarts!!" I cry. "AND SODA!"

"Shut the fuck up." Traeger rushes over and stands just behind me. "They're probably flat as hell..."

"One way to find out." I reach in and tear open one of the cases like a feral animal, clawing at the cardboard in desperation. I grab two cans and turn, handing one to Traeger. "Cheers."

"Slàinte Mhath," he says, making me arch a brow. He merely gives me a sly look and takes a long sip. "Fuck that's good. Or it probably isn't *really,* but it is. It soooo is." His eyes slide shut again and he shudders in pleasure, a low groan rumbling in his chest. I take a sip and understand exactly what he means, nearly whimpering when the first heavenly taste touches my tongue. I don't care if it's expired. I don't care if it isn't as bubbly as should be. It's sweet and a little fizzy and brings on a heavy helping of nostalgia.

"Best. Day. Ever."

He laughs and snatches my can from me before I know what he's doing and can stop him.

"Hey!"

"You get your ass back in bed and get your foot elevated. I'll bring a picnic."

CHAPTER TWENTY-THREE

TRAEGER

IT'S PROBABLY stupid and selfish and wasteful, but I can't quite make myself give a fuck. We absolutely gorge ourselves on all of the snacks from the Closet of Wonders as Melody keeps calling it. We eat and eat until we both feel sick, but man does it feel good. Melody is in such a good mood after the discovery, it's almost as if the past month never happened. The hostility's gone, and she's acting like she had before Jonah had been hurt. It feels good. It feels more than good: it feels *right*, like this is how we're supposed to be. Laughing and eating and talking by the fire, feeling so totally at ease, as if the outside world doesn't exist at all.

"The bottles and cans outside were smart. Early warning system," Melody says, shifting to lie on the foot of the bed so she's closer to the fire. Despite being in a great mood and eating her weight in chips and cookies, I'm still worried that she's coming down with something. Her skin is still pallid, but her cheeks are flushed and she's got that glassy look in her eyes, the one that comes with fever. She can't seem to get warm no matter how many blankets she piles on or how close she gets to the flames. She keeps assuring me she's fine, just tired from yesterday and that her ankle hurts, but I'm not sure that I believe her.

"Well, Uncle Charlie gets the credit there. Looked like he'd had them rigged a long time ago but they'd fallen at some point, probably during a storm or something. Now we'll hear anyone coming though."

"Kudos to Uncle Charlie then. So, what do you think the gibberish on the wall in there is about?" she asks, jutting her chin towards the bedroom.

"I think it's a way to figure out the combination to the locks on the cabinets downstairs, but I have no fucking clue what it might mean or what might be in there."

"Guns maybe? Ammo? More Twinkies?" she suggests with a grin before yawning widely. "Did you talk to Wynn?"

"Yeah, everything is going good. No more herds, and they cleared three more houses this morning. They should make it here in another day or so probably." She nods and her lids start to droop. "Why don't you take a nap? I'll check the snares I set up earlier and be back in a bit." She'd been out cold still this morning after the sun came up, so I'd taken the time to scope out the perimeter, take care of a few rogue Bloodies, get the security lines in place, and set a dozen snares in hopes of getting us some fresh meat. Of course, that was before I knew about all the stores Uncle Charlie had waiting for us, but either way, fresh meat was always a good idea.

"No, I'm fine. You need to sleep, you stayed up all night."

"I wasn't injured," I point out. "I'll nap after I get back, promise."

Before she can argue, I hoist myself off the mattress and gesture for her to settle back down. She sighs but maneuvers herself back up to the pillows and I pull the blankets over her, adding an extra throw to be safe. I set another soda and a canteen of water on the floor where she can reach them easily, and she's already asleep by the time I pull on my jacket and boots.

CHAPTER TWENTY-FOUR
MELODY

"MELODY??"

My eyes fly open as I'm pulled from my nightmare, and Traeger's face hovers in front of my face. I blink, and the room seems to spin. I'm covered in sweat, my hair stuck to my temples and back my neck with it, but so cold that I'm shaking, my teeth clattering so hard my jaw hurts.

"Fuck," he grates. "You're burning up. Why didn't you tell me??"

How long had I been asleep? I was supposed to take watch so he could nap, wasn't I? Fuck, he must be so exhausted. I know that I'm not supposed to care, that I'm supposed to hate him, but right now, I can't really remember why. Everything is fuzzy, my head feeling like it's stuffed with cotton and the size of one of those big balloons people ride in...what are they called? Why can't I think of the word? It doesn't matter. My head feels too big and too blurry and all I know is that I don't want to push Traeger away right now. No, I want to pull him down to lie next to me, want him to wrap his arms around me and pull me in tight against his chest, want him to kiss my forehead and chase the nightmares away. I blink, trying so hard to force everything into focus, but it won't cooperate. Everything stays a little wobbly, like she I'm looking at everything through water.

"I'm...fine..." I say. Or try to say. I can barely keep my eyes open and I'm honestly not sure the words I'm thinking are actually making it out of my mouth right. There's a very good chance that everything is coming out as slurred, garbled nonsense. God, I'm so hot, but somehow freezing at the same time. How does that work?

"Fuck, fuck, fuck. I fucking knew that something was wrong, I should have pushed more, I should have..." he trails off and I hear him digging around in the cabinets in the kitchen, but somehow a heartbeat later, I feel the mattress sink beside me when he sits down on the edge. What the hell? Had I fallen asleep again? I swear I just blinked. I don't know what's happening. I've had the flu before but never this bad.

"Melody, listen to me. I need you to open your eyes and take this medicine, alright?" I manage to pry them open again and he helps me rise enough to get some pills down. "Christ, Melody, I get that you're mad at me, but you could have told me you were fucking sick."

Mad? Am I mad at him? Why would I be? No, that doesn't seem right. I think I'm the opposite of mad at him...

"...mad?" I ask, but the word is slow and slurred. A few seconds later, the darkness jerks me under again.

I WAKE up later having no idea how much time has passed. I feel much better than I did before and I know my fever has finally broken, but my memories of the last...however long are distorted and convoluted. I'd seen Gabby, over and over, a thousand memories flashing through my mind like a flipbook. Some were real things that had actually happened—her first day of preschool, smiling like a ray of sunshine in her yellow polka dot dress; passed out cold on Mitch's shoulders after a very long day at Disney; learning to swim in the lake; catching her first fish. But others were scenarios that I *wished* we'd gotten to experience together, Gabby at ages she never made it to—Gabby learning to drive a car; Gabby going to her first prom; moving into her college dorm; walking down an aisle in a beautiful white gown; glowing as she held a newborn in her arms. I'd been so happy in the false memories, but I was also screaming in utter agony, knowing it wasn't real, clawing at my chest trying to rip my own heart out. How could dreams hurt so fucking much?

The past and the present all melded together in ways that I knew couldn't be real, but all seemed like they were. They seemed *so fucking real*. I saw Mitch and Jonah and Sean and Mulligan...and *Traeger*. Traeger always seemed to shine brighter in every single image in my mind, like a spotlight followed him through the ever-changing scenes. He always seemed to be drifting away from me though, and no matter how hard I tried, I couldn't call out to make him stop. The others encouraged me to go, to run after him before it was too late. *It's time, Mel. You need him,* Mitch had said with a smile, giving me a playful shove forward. *Go, mommy. Go,* Gabby said, letting go of my hand just before I pried my eyes open.

I finally understand where the term *fever dream* comes from. I'd always kind of thought it was bullshit, but now I get it. I sit up groggily and shove hair from my face, grimacing. I feel sticky and grimy with sweat and I've never wanted to brush my teeth more than I do in this moment.

"She lives," Traeger's voice rings out from somewhere behind me. I turn to find him walking back into the living room from the kitchen. He hands me a cup of water and I empty it in three long gulps, gasping quietly when I'm done. I probably should have taken that a little easier, but my throat feels raw. Had I been screaming? *Fuck.*

"How long was I out?" I ask, voice raspy.

"Couple of days."

"*Days*?" I repeat, eyes bulging. He must have woken me several times for more medicine—another thing Uncle Charlie had stocked, thank God—but I have zero recollection of it.

"Days," he confirms, eyeing me.

"Wynn and the others?"

"They're alright. Ran into a bit of a snag with a washed out road, so they're a little behind schedule, but they're good and still trying to find their way here."

I nod and we sit in silence for a few minutes.

"Who's Gabby?" he asks finally and my breath catches in my

throat. "You were saying her name over and over when you were sleeping. Screaming it sometimes," he adds softly. He keeps his gaze trained on me, that calculating look in his eyes that always makes me feel like he sees too much, but right now, it makes me feel like he can see straight through to the very darkest parts of me. I clench my jaw and let him know silently that I won't be answering. I might have been debating on axing this whole hating him thing, but right now I'm too exhausted and raw to let him into this part of my life. Maybe never. I haven't decided yet.

He hikes a shoulder, letting it go for the time being, and I relax a fraction.

"I was busy while you were out," he says leaning back in the chair and stretching his long legs out in front of him, the picture of ease. "Do you want the good news, the bad news, or the other good news?"

"Bad news sandwich, I guess." His lips curl and I give him a half smile in return.

"Good news: I got the solar panels back up and running. Bad news: looks like Uncle Charlie was replacing the HVAC system when the world went to hell, so still no central heat, but," he rises from the chair and moves to the wall beside the doorway, "good news: we got this." He flips the switch on the wall and lights flare to life. We'd been relying on firelight and a few camping lanterns he'd found down in the workshop until now.

"Shut the fuck up!"

"Yep. Shower is working too. It'll be pretty cold still, but it's running water at least. Looks like Uncle Charlie and whoever lived in the big house before it burned were kind of off-the-grid survivalist types. Solar panels, their own water system, all that good stuff."

I grin but the familiar war starts up inside me again, despite everything: *hate him, hate him, hate him. Love him, love him, love him.* Because yes, I *could* love him...maybe even already do. He seems to see the inner battle, to see me pulling down the barriers between us again.

"*Come on*, Melody."

"What?"

"Are you seriously going to keep doing this? Hasn't it been long enough? Jesus, haven't I been punished enough?"

I shoot up off the mattress, the rage suddenly boiling over, honestly surprising me. I guess I've been keeping it all bottled up for too long, never really addressing anything. I don't know if it's the fever I just got over or the pain now radiating up my ankle and making me grit my teeth to keep from crying out, but whatever the reason, I'm apparently done keeping everything in.

"Enough!? *Never.* You will never be punished enough! Jonah was hurt, he could have *died*, and I wasn't there! Because of you!"

"That's bullshit and you know it!"

"What!?" I bark, incredulous.

"Even if you had been there with him, Jonah still could have been hurt in that building! You could have been hurt right beside him. You could have fucking died. Who the hell knows! This is the world we fucking live in, Melody. Hell, it was the world before, too. You couldn't protect everyone all the time! There were no guarantees!"

I know he's right, but I refuse to let logic enter the conversation. Or screaming match, I guess is more of an accurate description.

"I should have been there! You took me away from him!!"

There it is. I guess *everything's* coming out. All of the fear and anger and resentment and sorrow from all these months, back to the beginning. It's all coming to a head now.

"I'm fucking sorry!" he roars. "Actually, you know what, that's not true. I'm *not* sorry. Not even a fucking little bit!" I blink, unbelieving he's really saying this shit. "I'm sorry that you had to leave people that you care about, but I'm not fucking sorry that you came to FOS, because from the minute I fucking met you, I knew there was something between us. And you fucking know it too. You can't deny it, Melody. You're just scared. You're scared shitless to admit it, for reasons I don't fucking know because you won't tell me anything about your past—and that's fine. I get it. But you're afraid of letting yourself be with me, of seeing what this could be. So you jumped at the chance to have something to hold onto, a reason to hate me and put up this wall back up between us, because you knew that things were moving somewhere new and serious and fucking good. It could be *so fucking good*," he says, huffing out an almost hysterical laugh before shaking his head. "But it's a bullshit reason and you fucking know it!"

I stand there, breathing hard, not able to say a word because I have no idea what to say. I want to argue. I want to tell him that he's wrong, that every single thing he said is wrong, but I can't. I can't say or do a damn thing because he's fucking *right*. Every damn word out of his mouth was right. I am scared. I did use Jonah as an excuse. And it could be good with us. It could be great. It could be damn near perfect.

He runs his hand roughly through his hair and shakes his head, clenching and unclenching his jaw.

"I'm going to check the perimeter. Take a shower. There's cooked rabbit on the counter."

With that, he yanks a coat off of a peg on the wall, tugs a ballcap on is head roughly, and pulls the door open. He pauses and without looking at me says, "You were saying *my* name over and over too, you know."

I inhale quickly but he stalks out, slamming the door behind him. I stand there, staring at the closed door for a long time after he leaves, his words echoing in my ears. I eventually let out a long, shuddering breath, and grab my pack, digging around for clean underwear. I hobble to the bathroom, wincing as I put weight on my foot. My ankle is still hurting, but it's not nearly as bad as it was...fuck, how many days have we been here now? Three? Four?

There's shampoo, conditioner, and soap in the shower already, and though the water is definitely cold, I don't mind. It helps clear my head. I scrub the sweat and grime away and wash my hair, all the while thinking about everything Traeger said. I am afraid. I'd been afraid before, but had decided to leap...and just after, I'd found out about Jonah and it had felt like a sign—or an excuse, really—to cling to the fear. If I never actually jumped, I couldn't fall, and if I didn't fall, I couldn't get hurt.

And that's the real issue.

Because if I'm being honest with myself, really, completely honest for the first time in a long time, I'm terrified of loving Traeger because I know if I lose him, it'll be a hurt I can't survive.

CHAPTER TWENTY-FIVE

TRAEGER

I WAKE WITH A JERK, as I often do. Mel's sitting in the chair by the window, rifle leaning against the sill beside her. We haven't talked since the fight yesterday. I'd gone out and roamed around the woods for a good hour trying to work through all of the shit going through my head. I'd checked the perimeter, finding no signs of life or the undead, tagged a few more rabbits, and came back with bitter cold seeping into my bones. The temperature had plummeted drastically in just a couple of days, and I thank whoever or whatever might be out there listening that we'd made our escape when we did. If we'd gone into the water now…well things could have ended very, very differently. It always amazes me how quickly things can change, how a matter of days or even hours or minutes can make such a huge difference in the outcome of things.

If we hadn't been delayed coming back from that tournament at the beginning of all of this…I shake the thoughts away, not liking to think about how things had been in those early days of the end of the world. It had been a time when people had been terrified, and fear made people do terrible and desperate things.

I sit up and rub my eyes, swinging my legs over the edge of the mattress on the floor. The fire's roaring, the pops and crackles a soothing background soundtrack to our time in this little apartment, and the room is bright, but the light looks odd somehow. Off. I frown.

"So, do you want the bad news or the good news or the other bad news?"

Taking her answer from before, I say, "Bad news sandwich."

"Bad news: A snowstorm rolled in during the night and dumped about four feet of snow on us."

My eyes bulge and I lurch to the window. That's why the light looked strange: the sun is flittering in through a thick waterfall of snow, reflecting brightly off the piles of it.

"Shit," I mutter.

"Good news: Wynn and the others are alright. Wilson had one of his weird feelings about the weather and they decided to backtrack to one of the better equipped houses, just to be safe. Turns out, Wilson's bad shoulder is a better meteorologist than the guy who used to be on Channel 9. He's been in touch with Zimmer back at FOS, and everything is all good there. The other settlements too. Snow hasn't hit them yet, but there's a good chance it's headed that way, so they're all preparing just in case. Everything is all good."

I rub the back of my neck. At least everyone was alright. Not the most ideal situation, but we'll figure it out. Then I remember…

"And the other bad news?" I ask warily.

She sighs "It doesn't look like it's going to stop any time soon. We are good and snowed-in. Probably for at least a week, maybe more."

"Jesus Christ."

I hate the idea of being stuck out here, cut off from everyone and everything. I hate the idea of not being back at FOS if anything goes wrong. I…don't hate the idea of being snowed in with Melody. But I quickly push those thoughts away.

"Yeahhhh. So, it's a good thing Uncle Charlie was stocked up and you caught all those rabbits."

I exhale a long, slow breath, collecting my thoughts and making plans and backup plans.

"I'll bring up some more wood from the workshop and pack those other rabbits in some ice to cook in a few days. We should be alright on power for a few more days too and I'll go try to clear off the panels." She nods. She looks like she might say something else, but turns to look back out the window.

This is going to be the longest week of my life.

CHAPTER TWENTY-SIX

MELODY

THE FIRST DAY of Snowmaggedon is...tense. We both seem to be at a loss for how to handle the situation or how to address the giant elephant in the room after our fight. I should tell him he was right. I should tell him that I'm sorry. I should just give in to everything clawing to come out, but I can't. I don't know why but I can't make myself take that step off the ledge into the unknown.

So, instead of coming up with any kind of solution, we just stay tense and quiet all day, reading or trying to crack Uncle Charlie's weird code on the wall.

"Fuck this," Traeger finally grates, tossing an empty can at the writing and leaving the bedroom without a word. I frown, but when I hear banging and cursing from downstairs, I assume he's gone to try to force the cabinets open. He comes back sweaty and in a worse mood than before, and takes a long shower after that. I slip out of the room to give him some space and make us both a plate of food.

The snow let up for a little bit in the late morning, but starts again in earnest by late-afternoon, dumping another two feet at least.

"We're never getting out of here," I groan. Traeger eyes the sky through the window, not arguing, which doesn't make me feel any better. There's no reason for either of us to keep watch during the night now—Bloodies don't do well in snow and there's no way anyone living could make it through this shit.

"So, guess we can both sleep now," I say. We stare at each other for a long moment, then both shift our gaze to the mattress. I swallow hard but before I can say or do anything, Traeger grabs a blanket from the stack and a pillow from the couch, and settles on the floor beside the mattress.

"Traeger, you—"

"Goodnight, Melody," he says quietly. His tone isn't entirely unkind, but it tells me loud and clear that he doesn't want to discuss this and just wants to go to sleep. I sigh and snuggle down beneath my blankets.

"Goodnight," I say softly before rolling over and trying and failing to ignore the fact that he's so close...and that I want him closer.

I'M RUMMAGING through the closet in the hall when he comes back from grabbing more wood for the fire.

"What are you looking for?" he asks.

I turn and hold up the stack I found.

"We have Uno, Trivial Pursuit, Monopoly, a deck of cards, or a Disney Princess memory matching game."

He arches a brow but otherwise hides his surprise at my (sort of lame) attempt at an icebreaker. I'm tired of being cooped up in this apartment and acting like two gun slingers in the wild west, ready to draw and fire any second.

"Do you know how to play Rummy?"

I smile. "Rummy it is."

I head back over to the mattress and settle on one side, eyeing the spot across from me until he sits down, leaning back against the couch. I look up at him from under my lashes as I shuffle.

"Don't read anything into it," I say, but flash him a tiny smile.

His lips twitch. "Wouldn't dream of it."

And so, we play. All day long we play, pausing occasionally to get snacks or to build up the fire. We don't talk much, but it's better than it has been in weeks and I feel much lighter when I drift off to sleep that night. He sleeps on the floor again, but I lie closer to the edge this time. The next day is pretty much the same, but we switch up the games. We finally start to talk. Just random things at first, nothing too heavy, but eventually, we start to dip into *real* conversation. My pulse quickens, but I find that it's only partly in fear, the rest is in anticipation and excitement to learn more about him…and maybe it's even a little from excitement of sharing my life with him.

"Where were you?" I ask as I throw down a Draw Two card. He gives me a look that says there will be payback as he grabs his extra cards. "On Day Zero?" Though it was quietly going on for a few weeks before news officially broke, most people considered the day they started dropping bombs as Day Zero, the start of the Bloody Apocalypse.

He takes a deep breath, holding it for a few seconds before letting it out slowly. I get the feeling he doesn't talk about this much…or ever. Because, I realize in this moment, who the fuck would he talk to about it? He has plenty of people surrounding him almost constantly, but I don't think he confides in most of them, at least not about personal things. It must be lonely. *Heavy is the crown…*

He plays a blue card and though his shoulders are tense, his voice is clear and even when he speaks.

"I was on a bus with a bunch of high school baseball players." I quirk a brow. "I was the head coach—varsity baseball, football, and for one ill-fated but fun as hell season, girls volleyball. That's a story for another time," he says with a grin but then it fades. "I was also an English and shop teacher, while we're on the subject. Anyway, we were playing in a tournament a few hours away. We were supposed to have gotten back a day earlier, but games got delayed and we ended up staying an extra night and then news started to break about the virus and a few people at the tournament started to show symptoms and they called the game, right in the middle of an inning. It was crazy." Something flashes over his face at that, pain and regret and guilt, I think, but it's gone quickly.

"So we were headed back that day. We lived in a small town on the outskirts of Atlanta, but had to drive through the heart of it to get home. We were on the highway and could see the city in the distance… and then we saw the first of the bombs explode." I inhale sharply. Of course I knew that bombs had been dropped on the bigger cities, but I couldn't imagine seeing it happen from a distance. Watching, knowing your family and friends were out there and there was nothing you could do to help them, to stop what was coming for them. "It was… bad. Chaos. The kids were freaking out and we didn't know what was happening, we thought a terrorist attack or something maybe, but had no idea what it really was. I mean, none of us connected the virus outbreak that had stopped the tournament with explosions in the city, ya know? We had no idea how bad the outbreak was, what was really happening with the Bloodies. Our driver said he'd heard rumors from a buddy up in the Capital, but none of us knew anything for sure. They kept it all so quiet until it was too late."

A lump forms in my throat, thick and heavy and threatening to choke me. I'd known. I'd known in time to get my family somewhere safe, but Traeger and all those kids on the bus, thousands upon thousands of others—they hadn't been given any warning at all. They hadn't even been able to tell their families goodbye. I know they originally had plans to evacuate healthy people from the big cities and spread warnings across the country, but then Bloodies started popping up out in the world and it started spreading like wildfire, and someone with a finger on the End of Days button got a little trigger happy I guess. No one had any warning. No one had any idea what was happening.

Except me.

My eyes burn. Will he hate me when I tell him the truth? I want to ask what happened after that, what the first days and weeks and months had been like for him, what had happened to his team, but I stop myself. I'll let him tell me as much as he wants for now, I won't push. He's looking at the wall over my shoulder but I know he's seeing something else entirely.

"So a baseball coach and a teacher, huh?" I say with a smirk, trying to change the subject and get that horrible haunted look out of his eyes. "Told you I had your number. That first night at FOS, remember? I said you worked with kids."

"Speaking of that night," he says, a cunning look in his green eyes. He leans forward. "What exactly did you do in the old world, Melody?" I force myself not to shiver when he says my name like that, low and smooth and full of so many dark promises. "And none of this 'a little of this a little of that' bullshit." I eye him, impressed that he remembered exactly what I'd said all those months ago. A lifetime ago. I take a deep breath. This is the first big reveal, the first step in letting him know the real me. Or, rather, the old me. I somehow feel like he knows the real me better than I even know myself most days. And, yes, I'm very aware of how big a green flag that is, but I've been choosing to be colorblind. Sue me.

"First off, the shrimp boat and the Hooters stories were completely true." He gives me a look that says he'll want more on those later, but waits patiently for the real answer. *Alright. Here we go.*

"Officially, I worked for an agency of the government that went by three letters. Pick any three, it doesn't really matter in the end." His eyes widen, brows inching upward toward his messy hair.

"And...unofficially?"

"I worked for an agency of the government that didn't exist at all. Very, very deep, off the books, Blackwater on steroids kind of missions. Things that didn't ever *officially* happen in places no U.S. government agents were ever *officially* in."

"Jesus Christ," he says, exhaling roughly. "Seriously?" I hike a shoulder and nod.

"I was only out in the field for a few years before...before I transitioned back to a more, uh, tame job as a profiler mostly behind a desk."

He stares at me for a long moment, taking it all in. The card game's completely forgotten—which is really a shame because I'm sitting on three Draw Four Wilds and two Skips and could already see the look on his face when I hit him with that epic combo for my finale. C'est la vie, I guess.

"So...you're telling me that you were some super secret government agent that went on crazy covert missions and was essentially... what? A spy?"

"Unofficially, yep."

"So the ace shooting skills, throwing that knife within an inch of my face without hesitation and nailing that Bloody dead on, all the security knowledge, you *profiling* me...Fuck, it makes so much sense." He scrubs a hand over his jaw, his stubble so thick after a week of not shaving that it's graduated to a beard and stache. It looks really damn good.

I shrug and he shakes his head, running a hand through his hair.

"All that time, you could have taken me out so fucking easily." It isn't a question.

"Yep." No reason to lie.

"Why didn't you?"

"At first it was because I couldn't risk Jonah and the others. I assumed if I took you out, Jett would just retaliate even harder—and I didn't want to take a chance on him becoming the new leader. You were the lesser of two evils." I smile at him and he bobs his head, acknowledging that that was, in fact, the case. "But then...well, I started to like you. Even when I was trying to hate you, I couldn't. And I didn't want to kill you anymore."

"Jesus," he breathes. "Thanks for that, by the way." I laugh lightly and he grins. "That's pretty fucking cool, you know that, right?"

"I'm well aware of how cool I am." Our gazes lock, amusement dancing in his eyes, and the room suddenly feels very small and very hot. I clear my throat. "We should, uh, probably hit the hay."

"Yeah, you're probably right."

Neither of us move though, and after a long moment, I finally ask, "Kevin's son. Why did you kill him? Was it really just an example killing?"

He tenses, clearly caught off guard by the question, and for a second I'm not sure if he's going to answer. I'm pretty certain there's more to it than that—there always is with him. Everything is always calculated, always with a purpose—but I'm not sure what.

"His son killed two women at Greenbrier and four more at The Farm."

"What?!" I gasp, and Traeger nods.

"Butchered more like. He hid it well, at least at first. The first woman's death at the farm was put down as a machinery accident out in the field. It tracked with how...mangled her body was when it was found." I fight back bile and rage, my hands clenching into fists. "The second woman was thought to have been attacked by Bloodies, and the third just disappeared—but when the reports showed that Brad had been the last person seen with each of the women, I started watching him closely. He went to Greenbrier to help out with some mechanical issues they were having and in the time he was there, two women went missing. No one else really saw the connection since they didn't know about the girls out at The Farm, but I knew. I fucking *knew*. I…caught him in the act on the fourth woman back at The Farm. It was like something out of a horror movie, Melody, just sick, twisted shit. He confessed then, but it wasn't like he was begging for his life. No, he was *gloating*, like he was proud of everything he'd done." He curls his lip in disgust and then shakes himself, pulling his mind from that terrible memory.

"But you didn't tell anyone?"

He shakes his head. "No. If it happened now, I probably would, but at the time, everyone needed to buy into the Traeger-is-a-psycho-dictator bit. Different times, different situations, call for different narratives."

"Like with Jett," I say, realizing the difference between the two situations. With Brad, Traeger needed everyone to think he killed anyone who didn't obey him and fall in line, he needed that blood to paint a picture of fear to help maintain order among the settlements. With Jett…

Traeger finishes my silent train of thought. "With Jett, it showed everyone that certain things will *not* be tolerated, that the rules apply to everyone and that no one is above them, even those high up in my command. Things have shifted from when we were first trying to wrangle all of Haven, weed out the bad apples and make it somewhere that people could finally start living instead of surviving. So now, I don't need them to cower in fear at the mention of my name. Now, I need them to see that everyone is safe within Haven, that no one is above the laws." He runs his hands through his hair and lets out a long slow exhale before meeting my eyes.

"I had to do things in the beginning that still make me sick to think about. I have blood on my hands that will never, ever wash away, but they were things that *had* to be done to keep everyone safe. I didn't want to be the leader, but it just...happened. I did bad things to stop worse ones from happening. I killed bad people to stop them from killing innocent ones. It isn't an excuse; it's just the facts. People started following me, looking to me for guidance and protection. They needed a safe place, they *deserved* a safe place. So, I gave them one. I found a way. I did what had to be done. I don't regret it, but it wasn't something that was easy and it isn't something that doesn't weigh on me every fucking day."

Something surges up in my chest then, hot and fast and undeniable: Respect. Empathy. Maybe something else.

He glances up at me from beneath his lashes, as if he isn't sure he wants to see my reaction.

"Let's go to bed," I whisper. His shoulders slump, as if he's failed, as if he's broken the first few steps of the bridge we're building back towards each other. He nods and shifts to move off of the mattress, but I grab his forearm. He stiffens, like his entire body has been electrified.

"The floor can't be comfortable. We can share the mattress." His brows wing upward but I only roll my eyes and start moving the cards out of the way. He puts another piece of wood on the fire and then climbs beneath the covers on the other side of the mattress.

"Don't read anything into it," I say again, fighting to keep my lips from curling into a grin.

I can hear the smile in his voice when he replies.

"Wouldn't dream of it."

CHAPTER TWENTY-SEVEN

TRAEGER

SO, maybe being snowed in with Melody isn't so bad. Now that she's lowering the walls again and letting me back in, that is. It was hard talking about the beginning, about that night when I watched the city burn, and I realize that it's been years since I've told anyone about it. Years since I had anyone—other than Doc—that I could really talk to about much of anything deeper than patrol schedules and supply inventories. No one else knows my past. No one else has ever wanted to.

Sleeping beside her had been a special kind of torture, but one that I'll gladly take every night for the rest of my life if she lets me. It had taken all of my self-control not to slide across the mattress, wrap her in my arms and hold her through the night. I refuse to think about everything else I'd wanted to do in that damn bed.

The snow had stopped falling early this morning, but the feet upon feet of it that had piled up wasn't going anywhere for a good long while. I've been in contact with Landry and Johnson, and they were able to get off the island and on the road back to FOS before the worst of the snow stranded them. Haven got hit with the storm too, but not quite as bad as we did here. All of the settlements are good—plenty of supplies and there were protocols in place for events like this. Everything is good on all fronts, so I try not to worry. Not like I can do anything even if something is wrong, but I have faith that my people can handle it if and when something comes up.

I kind of hope that this is another sign that I'm no longer needed as the leader of Haven. I'll be more than happy to step away from it. The evil, sadistic king persona had only been necessary in those first few years to get everything under control and settled. I've let it fade a bit over the years, and I rarely have to "prove" myself anymore to make a point. The threat of me is mostly enough. But now, I wonder if maybe even that isn't necessary. We handled all of the people who wanted to pretend that the end of the world meant they got to just run wild with no rules and do whatever they wanted. We established trustworthy leadership and processes for supply distribution and growing food. We have a solid security force in each settlement and protocols in place for almost every situation you can think of.

Haven is running like a well-oiled machine. So maybe I really can just leave it all behind. Maybe I can put the mask down for good and start my real life again.

"What about your wife?" Melody asks, pulling me from my thoughts. She looks pointedly at my hand where I'm rubbing my thumb over my ring finger, where a silver band once sat. I always do it when I'm thinking and I guess she's noticed. Of course she has. She sees everything. We're playing the princess matching game, both lounging across the mattress.

I tense and clench my jaw. I know this is a good sign, that we're finally talking and really getting to know each other. Or learning about each other's pasts anyway. I feel like I know Melody better than anyone else somehow, despite not even knowing half of what her past is hiding, and that she can see straight through to the very heart of me.

But still, some memories are harder to talk about than others.

"She was my best friend's little sister, actually. We were high school sweethearts, but ended things when we both went off to college. Wanted to sow those wild oats and all that." I shoot her the crooked smile that she pretends to hate, but I know damn well works its magic on her. It had gotten me out of trouble more times than I could count in my younger days. "But we ended up reconnecting years later at a retirement party for a mutual friend's father. Both of our life plans had gotten a little derailed—my baseball career ended in the minors after a blown rotator cuff, and she'd followed a guy across the country and it didn't pan out—and we ended up back at home. Got married three months later."

"And the guilt?" she asks. "I'm sure part of it was that you weren't with her when it happened, but...I think there's more to it than that." Sometimes I wish she wasn't *quite* so good at what had apparently been her fucking job: reading me like a fucking book.

"We were fighting. Before I mean. Things had been rough for a while. She...cheated on me with a coworker, but wanted to work things out. I told her I would try but I knew deep down that I couldn't get past it, that we were done. So, things were pretty miserable. But she was trying so hard and it was destroying her. And I still couldn't just man up and tell her it was over." I stare at the wall, remembering the last time I saw her so clearly. "She wanted to come with us to the tournament, thought it would be good for us, time out of the house and out of the town with too many ghosts following us around all the time. But I said no. When I left that day, she just stood in the doorway and watched me go, tears in her eyes. I think...I think she knew it then. She knew that we were done and that I could never find my way back to her. I should have just *told* her though. She messed up and broke things, yeah, but I still owed it to her to tell her the truth, to not drag her along with hope when I knew damn well there wasn't any."

Melody is quiet for a long minute, so long that I finally turn to look at her, letting the vision of Emily crying in the doorway fall away.

"I'm sorry," is all she says and somehow, it's enough.

I shrug. "It was a long time ago, I just...I wish things could have ended differently. I'll never get the chance to make it right."

"I get that."

"I managed to keep my best friend through it all though—the cheating, the terrible home life award, the zombie damn apocalypse—so that's a silver lining I guess." Her brows lift and I smirk, anticipating her face when I drop this bomb. "Doc Hastings."

She blinks. And then blinks again.

"Doc Hastings is your *brother-in-law*!?"

"Yep. He actually stepped in for the school's athletic trainer for that tournament for us—she'd come down with food poisoning the day we were leaving and Doc volunteered to go in her place. I think he was happy for an excuse to get out of town for a while too. All of the issues with me and Em stressed him out. Neither of us ever tried to make him pick a side or anything of course, it wasn't like that, but he felt torn in two either way. Two people he loved, both hurting, both needing him to lean on. Anyway, he's been with me since Day Zero. When we first started working on pulling all the settlements together to create Haven, there were three pregnant women at The Cove. I knew he needed to be there for them and...well, I was stepping into my Emmy-winning role as Traeger, so, it was better that no one really knew he was related to me."

She shakes her head, laughing, but then her eyes fly wide like something is clicking.

"You told him to let Jonah know I was alright? To tell him...the truth about FOS?" I nod. She looks like she wants to say more, but doesn't, just turns her thoughts inward, working everything out herself. I know she'll arrive at the right answer without me having to explain it. I swallow hard and decide to shift gears, to see if she'll let me in a little bit farther.

"Am I pressing my luck if I ask about your husband?"

She takes a long breath in, twirling one of the cardboard squares in her fingers as she mulls it over.

"Mitch," she finally says. "His name was Mitch." Her throat bobs and there's a small, sad smile on her face as she dives back into her memories. "He was great. We met at a hot wing eating contest—I wiped the floor with him, of course." She grins. "He said it was the sexiest thing he'd ever seen and that he had to get the number of a goddess among mortals." She rolls her eyes, still smiling, but then it slowly fades.

"He was killed overseas a few years before the end of the world. He and Jonah's husband, Sean were in the same truck when they hit an IED. We lost them together, somehow kept ourselves from falling apart together, survived the apocalypse together, survived..." She trails off, eyes watering. She scrunches her nose, trying not to let the tears fall and something inside my chest twists painfully. I would do damn near anything to keep her from crying, to hold any pain at bay or take it from her and shoulder it myself.

"What if he came to FOS?" I offer. "Him and Mulligan both."

"You would do that?"

"Of course. I...I want you happy, Melody. That's all. If having them at FOS would make you happy, then it's a done deal."

She studies me for a long time. So long, I start to feel a little self-conscious.

Finally she says, "I'm pretty tired," letting the topic of her past and of Jonah relocating fall away for now.

I nod and scoop the game pieces back into the box and set it on the side table. We both settle into our respective sides of the bed. I lie on my back and put one hand behind my head, staring at the ceiling, my other hand resting on my chest. I blink in surprise when Melody reaches over and grabs my arm, tugging me towards her. I don't know exactly what's happening, but I know better than to look a gift horse in the mouth. I close the distance between us, rolling onto my side, and she pulls my arm around her. My eyes slid shut in bliss as she snuggles back against me, pulling my arm tighter around her stomach and putting her back firmly against my chest.

"Don't read anything into it," she says quietly, the smile obvious in her voice.

I'm not going to press my luck for anything more than this for tonight, but I can't stop myself from leaning down and whispering low in her ear, "Wouldn't dream of it."

She inhales quietly and a slow shiver works its way through her body, but I just chuckle and lay my head down. I honestly figure I'll stay up all night, strung too tightly with our bodies so close, with her wrapped in my arms, with her smell enveloping me. But within minutes, I feel so relaxed, more relaxed than I have in damn near ten years, that I drift off into a deep, blissful sleep.

CHAPTER TWENTY-EIGHT

MELODY

THAT WAS the best sleep I've gotten in years. I'm not actually sure how I'd managed to sleep with Traeger without, well, *sleeping* with him, but it seemed like both of us had needed the closeness and vulnerability of lying with someone through the night more than anything else, and we'd both drifted off before anything could even start to move towards more.

We'd shifted at some point during the night, and I woke with my head on his chest, one leg thrown over his thigh. His arm is still wrapped around me, holding me tightly against him even in sleep. I take the opportunity to study him as he sleeps, and am struck all over again how damn handsome he is. I study the hard line of his jaw; the small scar above his eyebrow that you have to be very, very close to even notice; the soft curve of his lips as they part slightly. I remember what they felt like against mine, soft and warm, but demanding and sure, and promising so much more with every touch. I barely stop myself from leaning in and kissing him again now. I also barely stop myself from waking him up with a good old fashioned morning blow job, but quickly slide from the bed quietly before I decide to just say fuck it.

I shake myself, forcing all dirty thoughts away...or at least, to the side. They're still *very* much there. I make my way down the stairs, shivering in the cold of the workshop. My ankle is mostly fine now, still a little sore and stiff, but I can walk again, so now the only thing keeping us here is the snow. If I'm being honest, I really don't mind. I even kind of wish that the snow would never melt. Things are becoming so easy here between us, shut away from the world, free from all the expectations and responsibilities waiting for us back home.

I head outside, walking around the small area that Traeger had cleared the day after the snow had stopped. The plumbing is working fine for the shower, but neither of us want to risk trying to flush the toilet and fucking things up royally. So, after those first few days of the lovely bucket-in-the-bathroom situation while my ankle healed enough that I could easily go up and down the stairs, we'd carved out a little area outside in the snow to take care of business. I do my thing, surrounded by walls of white, and then dart back inside. I hop up on top of the workbench in the middle of the room and bring the walkie up to my mouth.

"Wynn? You awake?" A few seconds later his voice crackles over the line.

"Hey Mel. You holding up ok out there in the cabin in the woods that is definitely not something out of a horror movie?"

"Har har. And it's more of an apartment over a barn than a cabin, thank you very much. But we're good. Ankle is sore but not too bad. Are y'all ok?"

"We're good here too. Trying to make our way back there to get you and the supplies, but scouts are saying snow is still pretty piled up on the roads farther north."

"Yeah, we're still pretty much buried out here."

"Well...maybe that's not such a bad thing."

"And what exactly is *that* supposed to mean? Don't you miss me, Landry?" I ask with mock indignation.

"Oh you know damn well what it means, couyon."

My mouth pops open. "I am not!"

"You are," he says simply, but I can hear the smile in his voice.

"I'm going to smother you with a pillow when I get back."

He laughs and I smile, kicking my legs back and forth over the edge of the table.

"Look, I'm just saying, maybe this little romance novel-esque snowed in scenario might be just what you needed to get over your little hissy fit."

"*My hissy*—Ok you are definitely getting smothered. Maybe even stabbed. Don't worry, it won't be fatal, but it'll hurt like a bitch. It was *not* a hissy fit. I had very valid reasons to be upset."

"That's true, but you know damn well that all that anger and blame was a little misplaced."

I roll my eyes and pick up a scrap piece of wood from the table, drumming it lightly on my knee.

"You sound just like Jonah, you know that? You're not allowed to hang out with him when you go to The Cove anymore."

"Uh huh, you're telling me that *nothing* has happened?"

"I..." I bite my lip. "We're not fighting anymore," I hedge.

"Ahhhhh sookie sookie now," he says in a sing-song voice and I can just see him in my mind, grinning and dancing like an idiot.

"Ok I'm going now because I'm cold and you're an idiot. Mostly the latter part."

He starts singing for real now. "I've been really tryin' babyyyyyy—"

"GOODBYE."

I turn the walkie off and shake my head, but laugh. I hop off the table, clip the walkie onto the waistband of my sweats, and blow into my hands, rubbing them together to ward off the chill. I grab one of the big spaghetti pots from the workbench and head back out into the cold, filling it to the brim with snow. Again, the taps are working—and we left one trickling this whole time to keep the pipes from freezing—but there's no reason to waste the resource when we can just as easily boil the snow.

I jog up the stairs and find Traeger up and making coffee when I come through the door. I inhale the rich, familiar scent that I never thought I'd smell again. It's nostalgia and heartbreak and heaven all wrapped up in one delicious aroma. There are still three entire bulk-sized boxes of K-Cups in the closet, but I'm already mourning the day when those run out and we're thrust back into the world where coffee is a rarity. *RIP*.

"Smells good," I say when he looks up, that slow, crooked grin spreading across his face and a glint of mischief in his green eyes. I sit the pot down by the fireplace and cross to the counter that separates the kitchen from the living room. He slides the mug over and I wrap my hands around it, enjoying the pleasure-pain sensation as the warmth seeps into my chilled skin. I raise it to my mouth and blow lightly across the surface.

"Sleep ok?" I ask nonchalantly.

He scrubs a hand across his jaw, looking unhappy and my brow furrows.

"Well, I *would* have, but a large, Melody-shaped octopus seemed to have wrapped itself around me during the night."

I narrow my eyes and thin my lips, though I'm fighting a smile.

"Oh fuck off."

"It's true. I was nearly strangled multiple times. I feared for my life."

"No one likes you," I tell him as I take a tentative sip of my coffee. A long time ago, I would have had it filled with so much creamer and syrup that it really wouldn't even have resembled coffee anymore, but I'll take what I can get these days. At least Uncle Charlie still had sugar, and Traeger already knows exactly how much to add for my liking. It's all so...domestic. Intimate. Nice.

I barely suppress a moan at the taste, and I continue, "I took a poll of everyone left on Earth and the decision was unanimous."

"Well that's just plain mean, Melody," he says with a grin, leaning his forearms on the counter. He looks rumpled and sleepy, his hair a mess and his beard thick and scruffy. He's in a pair of gray sweatpants and even as I tell them not to, my eyes dart downward. The counter blocks that particular area and I yank my gaze upward again. What is wrong with me? He's got one of those tight black t-shirts of his on with a zip-up hoodie thrown over top, the sleeves pushed back showing off some of his tattoos. He looks...fuck, he looks *sexy*. Extremely sexy. Too sexy. The tiny thread of self-control I'm clinging to is fraying faster and faster by the second. I clear my throat and take another sip.

"I talked to Wynn. Everything is all good back home. Er, at FOS."

He nods, not saying anything about me calling FOS home, but giving me a knowing smile all the same.

"I have good news," he says.

"No bad news to go with it?" I ask, quirking a brow.

"For once, only good." He takes a drink of his own coffee—black. *Blech.* I would rather be torn apart by Bloodies than drink that—and smiles a very self-satisfied smile. "I got the TV working."

"Shut the fuck up!"

"Feel free to bask in my glory. Or worship at my feet. Whatever you prefer."

I grab a pen off the counter and toss it at him before leaping off the stool and hurrying to the cabinet below the TV. It houses a small Blue Ray collection—thank God Uncle Charlie hadn't joined the times and moved to streaming everything—and start perusing the titles. A familiar popping sound fills the air and I whirl back to him. He's waiting in front of the small microwave. He must have found a few bags of popcorn in one of the cabinets. I don't even fight the smile blooming across my face, and grab two cases from the shelf.

I stand and hold them up. "Do we want action—" I shake the movie in my left hand, "—or comedy?" I shake the one in my right.

"Comedy first, action second," he says with a shrug. Apparently he has no plans other than to veg out for the next few hours and I am completely on board.

"Good choice."

Traeger adds another log to the fire before we settle on the mattress, backs pressed against the front of the couch with a bowl of popcorn between us.

"Not as good as the popcorn back at FOS, but not too bad," he says, shoving a handful into his mouth. I look at him sidelong, warmth flooding through my stomach. He'd scoured town after town to find that popcorn machine. For *me*. Because I'd said I missed movie theater popcorn. My chest gives a little twist. I'd nearly forgotten about it in my determination to be angry and hate him lately. He'd done that for me, for no other reason than to make me happy. *Could he...I think maybe he...*

I clear my throat and grab a handful of popcorn from the bowl, and we spend the morning pretending that the world outside doesn't exist.

THAT EVENING, I take a quick shower and eye my clothes, biting my lip. That thread of self-control that had been fraying all day? Yeah. It's gone. Snapped clean fucking off when Traeger had come out of the bedroom earlier, toweling his wet hair as he told me that it was all mine. His shirt had ridden up, giving me a peek at his lean stomach, the dips and ridges of his abs, those fucking indentions at his hips...I'd had to squeeze my hands into fists so tightly my knuckles ached to stop myself from grabbing him. I'd sped into the bedroom like my ass was on fire, quickly shutting the door behind me and ignoring his look of confusion. I'd leaned back against it, banging the back of my head lightly against it several times, trying desperately to get a hold of myself. It had barely worked and I knew it would only last long enough to shower and change. The second I see him again in the living room, I know that all bets are off.

Hey, at least I'm honest with myself.

I gather up my hair and wrap the long strands into a knot at the top of my head, sliding a pen through it to hold it in place. I tug on the tank top, foregoing a bra underneath, and slip into the lacy boyshorts. I leave the sweatpants sitting on the dresser, take a deep breath, and quietly open the door. Traeger is standing by the fireplace, one arm resting on the stone mantle, staring into the flames and looking lost in thought. He didn't even seem to hear the door open, so I pad across the kitchen, silent as a cat, and pause just behind the couch to study him. He'd trimmed his beard and mustache, back to that sexy manicured stubble stage that looks far too good on him. His hair is almost dry, the strands curling up against the back of his neck. *He needs a trim,* I think with a smile.

The lights are low, only the fire and a lantern on in the corner illuminating the space. We figured we'd used enough electricity binging movies all day and should conserve for the evening. He looks so handsome in the firelight that it makes my breath hitch and my stomach dip, heat scorching through my veins. I want him and nothing is standing in my way now…namely myself. The steel wall I'd put around my heart that night after Jonah's accident, the one forged of hate and anger and fear, had fallen away. Little by little over the past few weeks, sure, but it had all but collapsed in a shower of rubble during these days in the apartment with him. I'm still afraid, but I'm not going to let the fear stop me anymore.

I make my way towards him and he finally realizes I'm there, turning towards me with a smile. A smile that fades into a look that's half confusion, half hope, and one hundred percent desire as his eyes skate over my thin tank top and bare legs. His throat bobs as I stalk closer.

"Melody…?"

"Don't read anything into it," I say with a sultry smile as I step into his open arms and wrap my own around his neck. I'm not even sure he realized that he'd opened them, beckoning and begging me to move within them. I turn my face up and see his lips curl at the corners before I go up on my toes and press my lips to his. He inhales sharply, but doesn't hesitate to wrap his arms around my waist and pull me tight against his body. The second our lips touch, my entire body is on fire, every nerve ending sparking to life and begging for more. His lips are as soft and warm as I remember, moving gently, but urgently against my own. I moan quietly when he thrusts his tongue against mine, his fingers clenching on my hips before moving beneath my tank, up my back, tracing the line of my spine and making me shudder and arch into his touch like a cat.

I toy with the edges of his hair with one hand and slide my other down his chest and stomach until I can tunnel my fingers beneath the hem of his shirt. I glide my palm over his stomach and he gasps quietly against my lips. His skin is hot from the fire and his muscles jump beneath my touch. He tilts his head and deepens the kiss as my fingers move along his abs, up his chest. His heart thunders against my palm and I know mine's beating just as hard.

"Wouldn't dream of it," he murmurs against my lips, making me huff out a laugh—before he nips at my bottom lip and the laugh becomes a semi-embarrassing moan. He kisses along my jaw and I move my hand to his hip, holding tight to steady myself before my legs give out. He's driving me absolutely *crazy*. Every lap of his tongue, every graze of his teeth, every whisper of his fingers along my back, is like some new delicious torture that I never want to end.

I want more. I *need* more. I need it in a way I haven't in so damn long. It's an all-consuming need, erasing everything else. My entire world shifts so that this moment, this touch, this kiss, this man— they're the only things that exist, the only things that matter.

He pulls back and cups my face, holding my gaze for an endless moment. Searching. Finding. Connecting on some level I can't even understand. Eventually, he smiles, a heartbreaking, breath-stealing smile, and then reaches behind me, snagging the pen and tossing it aside. My hair tumbles down my back and he tunnels his fingers through it like he's been dying to do it for months.

"I love your hair," he mutters, leaning in to kiss me again.

I smile against his lips and tug at the bottom of his shirt, pushing it up over his chest. He reluctantly pulls his hands free from my hair and reaches behind him, tugging the shirt up and over before tossing it away. Why the hell is that so sexy?

And why the hell had I stayed mad at him for so long and missed out on seeing *this* every fucking day?

Austin Traeger shirtless, his tattoos standing out darkly in the firelight and his sweats hanging low on his hips, is fucking criminal. His skin is far from flawless, but every line of ink, every single scar, tells the story of who he is and where he's been. They tell me that he's strong, and kind, and selfless. They tell me that he's brave and vulnerable and human. They tell me that I'm a fucking goner.

I slam my lips back to his again, a new urgency burning through me. I throw my arms around his neck and jump. He doesn't miss a beat, grabbing my ass as I wrap my legs around his waist. Our bodies are completely in synch, as if we've done this a thousand times. I dig one hand into his hair, tugging hard on the strands as everything burns out of control, a spark to kindling.

He seems to sense my rising desperation, groaning into my mouth as he turns, slamming me against the wall beside the fireplace and pinning me there with his body, hard against mine. I gasp and dig my fingers into his shoulder, into his scalp, needing him closer, needing him to kiss me harder, needing everything.

"God, Melody," he groans, grinding his hips against me. He's hard, so fucking hard, and I whimper at the thought of him slamming deep, driving me to the brink over and over.

"Please, Traeger. *Please*," I beg. As so often happens between us, he seems to know exactly what I'm thinking, exactly what I need without saying the words. He presses his hips harder against me, holding me to the wall as he tears my cami off.

"*Fuck*," he whispers as he glances down. I pant as he stares, licking his bottom lip before biting down. *Dear God* that's fucking sexy. I want his lips on me. His tongue, his teeth, his hands—fucking everything. I can't even think, can barely breathe. I'm practically quivering by the time he grips my wrists, moving my hands from his shoulders to the wall on either side of my head, and pinning them there. I gasp quietly, that simple act turning me on far more than it should. He holds my gaze, his green eyes burning as he says the next words slowly. Deliberately.

"Melody, you are fucking gorgeous," he rasps. "I've dreamed about you, just like this…" His gaze shifts, eyes slowly traveling from my eyes, to my lips, down my throat, to my breasts. God, how can a look *feel* so good? He pulls his gaze back up again until our eyes meet. "But my dreams could never do you justice." I swallow hard, panting quietly. I can't stop myself from arching my hips against him where he still has me pinned. He clenches his jaw when I grind over his cock, the feel of him hard and ready against me so intense that I swear to God I could come just from this. I try to move my hands, desperate to touch him, but he holds fast, his fingers like shackles on my wrists.

And fuck is it hot.

"Traeger," I say, half plea, half command.

His green eyes blaze. "Austin," he says gruffly. "Call me Austin. *Please*."

I understand his plea and my heart twists. With me, he doesn't want to be Traeger, the leader of Haven that does whatever has to be done to keep people safe, the man who's despised by many for who he has to pretend to be, the man who I know without a doubt is tired of carrying the weight of it all on his shoulders. With me, he only wants to be Austin, the man he probably thought he'd lost for good all those years ago. I know it now, beyond a shadow of a doubt. Despite all of my fighting and all of my fear, I've fallen completely in love with him.

"Austin," I whisper, putting everything I have into the word, and his eyes slide closed, as if hearing his name on my lips is the answer to a prayer. His hands tighten my wrists and when he opens his eyes again, they're blazing with a desire so deep and primal that it turns my blood to pure fire in my veins. I can't wait anymore. I need him so badly that the force of it startles me.

I give him a sultry look as I learn forward and bite his lip, pulling it gently with my teeth before letting it go. He groans.

"I believe once upon a time, you promised to earn my screams *all—night—long*..." I whisper. He smiles the sexiest crooked grin I've ever seen and my stomach clenches, my core throbbing with anticipation.

"Well, in that case, I guess I better get started then..."

CHAPTER TWENTY-NINE

AUSTIN

I'VE BEEN with many women in my life. Some might say *too* many. But being with Melody, feeling her lips and body against mine, feeling her soft curves and heated skin…Well, it makes me forget every single one before her. I thought maybe I'd been dreaming when I saw her walking towards me, an unmistakable look in her eyes, and wearing nothing but a tank top—a very thin, didn't-leave-much-to-the-imagination tank top to be more accurate—and lacy panties that barely cover her ass.

I've been dying for this moment. She's spent months pulling away and putting a wall between us. I've been trying to hold out hope that we could somehow find our way back together, to really start this again like we'd been so damn close to doing before. And now the moment is here. She's finally let me back in and I'll do damn near anything to keep it that way.

She wiggles her hips, pressing herself harder against my aching cock, seemingly as desperate for me as I am for her. I release her wrists and she wraps her arms around my neck again, tunneling her hands through my hair as I kiss her, rolling my tongue against hers. Hard. Demanding. Dominating. I shift us away from the wall and grip her perfect fucking ass again. I turn and walk across the room to the dining table and sit her down on the edge.

She runs her hands over my chest and stomach. My abs clench as her fingers skate even lower, trailing down, down...

"*Fuck*," I rasp, hissing in a sharp breath when she brushes her fingers over my cock. Even over the sweats, it's fucking ecstasy. I swear to God I might die if I don't have her hands on me, skin on skin, but that has to wait. I have other plans...but even so, I clench my teeth and arch my hips forward as she continues to stroke.

"Melody," I grate, somewhere between a prayer and a warning. "You keep that up and this is going to be over before it starts."

She pulls back and arches a playful brow at me, her hair tumbling over one shoulder.

"Mr. I Have A Different Girl In My Bed Every Night is going to come already from a little over-the-clothes fondling?"

"First off, it isn't *every* night—and it's been weeks, thank you very much." I tried to fall back into the old familiar habits, but figured out pretty quickly it wasn't going to work. So, I've been very busy with other things and have promised so many rainchecks that I'd be cashing them out until I die—if I ever actually planned to do that, which of course I don't. But Melody was all I wanted, all I could see. It felt wrong to be with any of the others, even when she was shutting me out.

She rolls her eyes, but smiles and leans in to kiss my neck. I'm momentarily distracted, completely forgetting what else I was going to say. There was...something...else...*Fuck that feels good.* Her fingers continue to glide over my shaft, and her tongue darts out to lick lightly before she pressed her lips to the base of my throat, just over my hammering pulse point. I tilt my head back, giving her better access. I tunnel one hand in her hair, holding her to me, begging her silently not to stop. I finally muster enough strength to gather my thoughts, and remember what I was going to add to the conversation.

"And secondly—" I say a little gruffly as I reach down to place my hand over hers, pressing her palm harder against my cock, and moving our hands together. She makes a sexy little half gasp-half moaning sound. "—*You* touching me is entirely different, Melody."

She pulls back and meet my eyes, looking for the lie, searching for the line that any guy would say in this moment, but there's no lie to be found. It isn't just a fucking line. It's the truest thing I've ever said. Sure, I had plenty of fun with the other girls, but it was *nothing* like this. As fucking corny as it sounds, I know that it's different because I'm in love with Melody. I have been for a long time, and it makes everything different. Every touch, every tease, every breath, every whisper—it's all different. It's all *more*.

"I could come just like this," I tell her, continuing to move our hands together, stroking. She inhales sharply, her pupils expanding before my eyes. *Hmm, I think Melody might like a vocal man.* Which is fucking perfect, because I love to talk. I hold her gaze as I say, "Feel how hard you make me, Melody?"

She whimpers quietly and her pulse quickens, the beat thrumming wildly at the base of her throat. I would bet good money that she'd love to see me to come like this and the idea makes me even harder. *Maybe another time*, I think with a smile. I have so many ideas for us, so many things I want to do and experience with her, but for now, I need to earn her screams, as she'd so kindly reminded me.

I gently move her hand away through some kind of Herculean effort that I honestly didn't know I possessed, and lean in to give her another kiss before she can pout about it. She lets her head fall back as I kiss down her neck, knowing the spots that make her shiver and moan already. I suck gently at her pulse point and she widens her knees, shifting her hips closer to the edge of the table and tugging me forward to settle between her thighs.

"Mmmm," I rumble against her skin as I kiss across her collar bone and lower, over the swell of her breast before flicking my tongue over one jutting nipple.

"Fuck!" she cries. I close my lips around the peak and suck hard, and she groans loudly, digging her fingers into my hair and holding me to her. As if I'd ever fucking leave. "Oh God, that feels *good*," she moans. I suck and twirl my tongue around and around, and soon she's writhing against me, bucking her hips and digging her nails into my scalp. I can feel the wet heat of her through my sweats and I groan around her nipple.

"Jesus Christ, Melody," I grunt, shoving my hips forward against her, unable to stop myself. I pull away from her breast, but she quickly grasps the other with one hand and guides my head down with the other. I grin. My girl knows exactly what she wants and how she wants it. I obey without question, hell bent on doing anything and everything she desires. I lick and nip and suck, moving one hand downward and running my fingers along the lace of her panties—her fucking *soaked* lace panties. *Jesus. Fuck.*

I don't waste any time. I honestly don't think I could tease her right now even if I wanted to. I need to touch her too fucking badly. I pull the lace aside and thrust a finger deep inside her. She gasps loudly, digging her nails into the back of my head. I pull back and hold her gaze as I slowly move my finger, in and out, in and out, making her pant.

"So wet for me, Melody?" I ask, leaning in to bite at her lower lip. "That's my fucking girl," I whisper.

"*Oh God,*" she gasps on a breathy moan, jerking her hips forward, sending me deeper. "More," she demands. "More, Austin."

A shudder works its way down my spine at the sound of my name —my real fucking name—on her lips, her commanding me, begging me, needing me. *Me.* Austin, not Traeger. Not the persona I have to wear like a mask. She's doing all of this for the real me, the one that so few people know anymore. But Melody *knows* me. Whether she knows every detail from my past or not, she knows me in a way that no one ever has.

I add another finger, groaning at the tight fit. She rocks her hips, arching them in time with my thrusts, fucking herself on my fingers. If that's not the sexiest fucking thing...I gnash my teeth, the desire hitting me like a fucking Mac truck. I curl my fingers as I pull them back, hitting that spot that should—

"*Fuckkkk,*" she moans and I can't help my smirk. I know a thing or two about these things. But I need more. I withdraw my fingers and grip the edges of her panties.

"These need to go," I nearly growl, voice low and rough. I tug them down as she lifts her ass, and toss them aside. I step back and hold her gaze as I slowly sink to my knees in front of her. Her eyes are wide, her entire body trembling. "Show me, Melody. Show me just how fucking wet you are for me."

She bites her bottom lip and then with the sexiest, sultriest look I've ever seen, slowly spreads her knees.

Fuck. Me.

I scrub a hand over my mouth as I take her in, the sight so fucking sexy I nearly lose it right here and now like a fucking teenager.

"Mm, mm, *mmm*. The term *mouthwatering* comes to mind, Melody."

She inhales quietly, but quirks a brow in challenge and presses her knees even further apart in clear invitation.

"Have a taste then," she says in a breathy whisper. *Jesus Christ.*

"With fucking pleasure."

CHAPTER THIRTY

MELODY

I'M GOING to fucking combust just from the way Traeger—no, not Traeger. *Austin.* I smile inwardly, loving the fact that he wants me to call him by his real name, like I'm the only one who gets to know that man, like he belongs to me and me alone.

So, I'm going to combust just from the way *Austin* is looking at me. I can feel his stare in every inch of my body, every nerve on fire. My heart is thundering in my ears, beating so fast that I worry it might just give out, but dear God, I've never been so aroused in my fucking life, never wanted anything so badly.

When he sank to his knees in front of me, I almost stopped breathing. When he'd asked me to show him how wet I was for him, his voice pitched low and so sexy it should be illegal, I thought I might come right then and there. Now, as he leans in and places a soft kiss to my inner thigh, my entire body feels like I've been electrified. When was the last time someone kissed me like that? Touched me? *Too fucking long.* He places another, and another, slowly working his way upward until I'm trembling, so on edge that I swear to God he could probably just look at me the right way and I'd come harder than I have in my entire life.

"I've been dreaming about finding out what this tattoo was," he whispers as he runs a finger lightly over the ink on my hip. He plants another kiss on my thigh. Higher. Almost where I need him. "I have to admit, the dagger and rose is sexy as hell." Another kiss. *So. Fucking. Close.*

I hold my breath, locking my muscles in place and not daring to move as I wait…

And then pure *ecstasy* rips through me like a strike of lightning at the first lap of his tongue. I cry out, somewhere between a scream and a gasp, and Austin groans in what sounds to be approval. He reaches up and grips my thighs.

"Mouthwatering was the understatement of the fucking century," he rasps before dipping his head again and giving a slow, long lick up my pussy.

"Jesus," I moan, not even caring that it's obscenely loud. There's no one to hear us out here. I can scream all I fucking want. He settles my knees over his shoulders and grips my ass, pulling me closer to the edge of the table. He works his tongue like it's his fucking job, every lick somehow more pleasurable than the last. I collapse back on the table, my back bowing at the pleasure and my eyes sliding closed, only to have him pull away, tsking.

"Ah, ah, ah. Don't you dare stop watching this, Melody. Eyes right fucking here."

My eyes fly open as I inhale sharply. How can he be this fucking hot, this fucking perfect? I've always liked a talker but dear God, Austin is an expert that's blowing my mind. I'm more than happy to obey, so I prop myself up on my elbows and meet his gaze. Watching is sexy as hell. He grins.

"That's my good girl."

"*Fucking hell…*" I whisper, barely able to speak. It's all too much, but not nearly enough. He leans in and flicks his tongue over my clit, before closing his lips and sucking hard, never taking his eyes from mine. It's official: Austin Traeger might just be the sexiest man on the planet.

"Don't stop," I pant as he alternates between licking and sucking on the tight bud, and then moving down to lick me long and slow again. I dig my ankles into his back, urging him onward. I'm already close. Hell, I was close the second he started, but I've been keeping my climax at bay by sheer force of will. I never want this to stop.

"God, I could do this all night, Melody," he whispers. "Could have you ride my tongue until you couldn't fucking move..." I whimper. "Could lick this pretty pussy for hours..."

"Austin," I gasp, not sure if I'm cursing him or begging him or sending his name up as a prayer.

"One day I'd love to make you beg me to let you come," he says, eyes still locked on mine as he slides two fingers inside me. I groan and my hips arch upward. His words make delicious images flash through my mind, and I plan to make sure he makes good on that promise. How can we fit this perfectly? Be this in sync?

His lips curl at the corners. "But today is not that day, sweetheart," he says softly. "Today, I want to give you anything and everything you want. I want you to come so many times you lose count, until you can't walk, until you can barely remember your own name."

He slowly thrust his fingers as he speaks, curling them just right and soon my hips are rolling in time with his motions, pleading and desperate. He rests his other hand on my lower stomach, his big hands splaying across my body and holding me in place.

"So," he says in that deep, velvety voice, "come for me, Melody."

He twirls his tongue over my clit again, faster now, licking and sucking as he works his fingers. *Oh God.* I feel the tension coiling, tighter and tighter, until I'm right on the edge, ready to free fall.

"So close," I pant, "don't stop."

He presses down with his hand on my stomach just as he sucks on my clit, and I careen over the edge of that imaginary cliff. My orgasm rocks through me, so hard it makes my entire body shudder violently. Stars flash behind my eyes and I collapse back on the table again, no longer able to hold myself up. I roll my hips, riding his tongue just like he'd said I would. He removes his fingers and presses his tongue deep inside as I ride out the waves ricocheting through me. He seems to be relishing it, like it's the greatest prize, one he doesn't ever want to give up.

My legs are shaking, but he doesn't stop licking.

"A-Austin," I gasp, "you can stop."

"Oh no, Melody, I really don't think I can."

It feels too damn good to really put up much of a fight, so I don't. I feel like the two of us have been traveling down this road for so long, meeting roadblock after roadblock, having to take too many detours, but we've finally made it where we're supposed to be. He's been my destination this entire time, since the beginning. He's the reason I never stopped fighting.

So, yeah, I'm going to enjoy the hell out of this for as long as I can. He slows things down, licking gently against my sensitive skin, and every lap of his tongue sends ripples of pleasure through my entire body.

"Mmm that feels so good." I push myself up so I'm sitting and tunnel my hands in his hair. He meets my gaze through his long lashes while he licks me. God the sight of him, face buried between my thighs, his eyes intent on mine. *It's so fucking hot.* "I love seeing you eat my pussy, Austin," I rasp, gently rocking my hips. His eyes flash and then slide shut, a shudder running through him and a soft groan rumbling against me. He reaches down and by the way the muscles in his bicep and chest move, I know he's stroking himself. Talk about fucking sexy.

"Oh God," I whisper. I'm already getting close again, a slower build this time, but more power behind it. "Don't stop...just like that... *don't stop.*" He doesn't, bless him, and I ignite all over again, throwing my head back to cry out. Shudders rack my body, little aftershocks feeling like tiny explosions.

I tug at his hair, urging him upward. His skin is flushed, sweat dampening the hair around his temples. I wrap one hand around the back of his neck and slam my lips to his. I can taste myself on his tongue but I don't care. Truth be told, it's kind of hot. I don't waste time, my need is riding me too fucking hard. I shove my other hand down the front of his sweats. He hisses against my lips as I wrap my fingers around his shaft, his skin hot and smooth beneath my palm as I stroke his straining erection—his very *large* straining erection. *Fuck me.* I have a moment of trepidation. It's been years since I've slept with anyone. I might as well be a fucking virgin again at this point...and Austin Traeger is packing some serious heat.

Either way, I can't wait any more. I shove at his sweats, wanting them off so I can have my turn to play, but before I can get what I want, he lifts me off the table. I yelp, the sound giving way to a giggle as he carries me back to the mattress. He lays me down and stands, hooking his thumbs in the waistband of his pants. I push up on my elbows, biting my lip and arching a brow.

"Well, come on then. Don't keep me waiting."

He laughs, low and husky, shaking his head.

"As you wish," he says with a wink. I grin, the fact that he remembered one of my favorite movies sending a stupid little flutter through my stomach, but the smile fades as I watch the material slide away.

Holy. Fuck.

I jolt upright, my entire body going somehow rigid and boneless all at once. Austin's cock is practically pulsing. Thick and hard, straining forward. I can't decide what I want more: to suck him or fuck him.

He grips his cock, slowly stroking his shaft as I watch, and I can only imagine what I look like right now. I figure it's something akin to one of those cartoon dogs who sees a giant steak, all giant heart eyes and drool. Might as well have *AWOOGA!* flashing over my head like a neon sign.

"Get your ass down here right now Austin Traeger."

He flashes me that cocky grin that I love and crawls towards me across the mattress. He leans in and kisses me, slow and deep. I run my hands over his arms and chest, down his back, wanting to learn every inch of him, the story behind every scar, the meaning behind every tattoo, the places that make him shiver when touched.

He pulls back and gives me a serious look.

"You aren't going to try some secret spy moves on me, are you? This isn't all some very elaborate long con to take me out?"

I laugh and walk my fingers up his chest. "Would you feel safer if my hands were tied?"

He closes his eyes and groans.

"Don't you tempt me, Melody…"

I grin, pulling him down to kiss me again. I'll never get tired of kissing this man. I snake my hand between us, wrapping my hand around his cock again. I shift so that he's cradled between my thighs and guide him to the right spot. He hisses in a breath between clenched teeth and levers himself up on straightened arms. He stares down at me, waiting, and when I nod, he slowly shifts his hips forward and I gasp.

Holllllly shit. He's big. Too big. Fuck I don't know if I can do this.

He holds himself still.

"Oh God, I don't think...I don't know if I can..."

"Look at me," he commands gently. I pry my eyes open and meet his stare. "You can. Just breathe, baby." I take a deep breath, nodding, and he slides in another inch. "That's it." I take measured breaths as he eases his way forward. It's easier now, and him talking me through it isn't just helpful—it's extremely hot. I get wetter, more turned on than I've ever been, and he glides in another couple of inches. "That's my girl. I knew you could take it. Fuck, Melody..."

He thrusts his hips and he's as far as he can go. He groans, almost a growl, deep in his chest, and I make some unintelligible sound that definitely isn't English. My back bows and I dig my nails into the small of his back. It's tight, but not painful, more just the feeling of pressure and being *so. Fucking. Full.* He waits, not moving while I adjust.

"Alright?" His voice is strained, his muscles rigid as he waits.

I shift my ass a little and things are golden.

"Ohh yeah," I moan, "*so* fucking good." I hike my thigh over his hip and urge him to keep going, needing him to move, needing him to fuck me the way I've been dreaming of for months. He draws his hips back and rocks them forward again, sliding even deeper than before. It's beyond pleasure. It's a bliss that's so intense it's almost painful, and I'll never, ever get enough. He starts to move, *really* move, pounding in a punishing rhythm.

"So fucking tight," he grits as he slams into me. "God, Melody..."

"Don't stop," I pant, "Harder, Austin."

"Oh, my girl wants harder?" *His girl.* Another stupid little flip of my stomach, but it's quickly forgotten when he shifts back on his knees. He hooks his elbows under my knees and lifts me up, slamming his hips forward over and over and over. My head thrashes and it feels so good I think I might die from the pleasure of it. Is that possible? *What a way to fucking go.* I realize with a semi-annoying jolt that maybe all the girls back at FOS *hadn't* been acting after all. They may have been playing it up a bit to stroke the HMFIC's ego, sure, but he really is *that* fucking good. The way he moves his body, the way he works his fingers and tongue, the way he seems to know exactly what I need, where I need it, and when. He's a certified sex god.

I reach up and rake my nails down his stomach. His skin is hot, slicked with sweat, his hair plastered to his forehead and temples. He shifts us again so that my right foot rests on his shoulder. The new angle has him hitting spots I didn't even know could be touched, and soon I'm almost to the tipping point.

"Oh God, I'm close. Don't stop. Just...like...that..." He reaches down and gently massages my clit and another orgasm rips through me like wildfire. "OH GOD!" I clench my thighs around him as I come hard, my eyes nearly rolling back in my head. Austin keeps pounding, never slowing his relentless rhythm.

"Fuck, Melody. I can feel you coming, can feel that tight little pussy clenching me...AH FUCK!" he bellows as he follows me over the edge. He collapses on top of me, still gently thrusting his hips as the after-shocks rock through us both. He buries his face in the crook of my neck, kissing me there and whispering my name over and over, so low that I can barely hear it over the roaring in my ears. I run my hands up and down his spine, loving the feel of his heart thundering against my chest, a mirror of my own.

I'm not sure how long we lay here this way, wrapped up in each other, catching our breath and trying to come back down to earth. Hours maybe. Days. However long it is, it's not long enough.

I could stay just like this forever.

CHAPTER THIRTY-ONE

MELODY

I ACCEPT the glass of water from Austin and gulp the contents down in record time. I scooch to the top of the mattress, sitting up to rest my back against the front of the couch. He flops down across the bottom, cocking his elbow and resting his head in his hand. His eyes darken as he watches me scoop my hair up and hold it on the top of my head, rubbing the back of my neck. I smile at him, remembering how much he said he loves my hair, how sexy it was when he'd yanked it down earlier to run his fingers through it.

His eyes slowly trail down from my hair, linger on my lips for a second before tracing down the column of my throat and landing squarely on my breasts. He runs his tongue along his bottom lip, subbing his hand across his jaw.

"Do you, uh, want the blanket? To cover up?"

I arch a brow. "Do you *want* me to cover up?"

"Never," he says immediately, making me laugh. I'm not shy about my body, especially not when he looks at me like *that*. A slow shiver runs down my spine at that look, and my own eyes drift down his own still-uncovered body. God, he's gorgeous. Strong and cut, the tattoos giving him that touch of danger that elevates him from handsome to devastating. I don't try to stop my gaze from heading lower and my eyes widen when I see that he's already getting hard again.

"Oh really?" I ask, brows hiking upward. His rebound time is pretty damn impressive.

"Don't blame me, Melody. *Look* at you." His voice is low and gruff, and my stomach clenches. "Do you know how often I walk around FOS with a raging fucking hardon just thinking about you? Every damn time I see you…"

He trails off as I crawl towards him across the mattress. I'd gotten to do one of the things I'd wanted earlier. Now, I want the other. I lean down and kiss his chest, and a low rumble of appreciation vibrates against my lips. He tangles his hands in my hair again as I move downward, kissing a long scar that runs across his ribs—knife wound, I think—and over the ridges and dips of his abs. I lick along the indention beside his hip as I wrap my fingers around his cock. His hips buck and his breath hitches. I grin as I stroke slowly, glancing up at him as I plant another kiss on his hip bone.

"What do you want, Austin?" I whisper, holding his gaze as I blow lightly over the head of his cock. He makes some unintelligible sound and jerks his hips again. I grin but don't let up. "Tell me."

He eyes me with a mix of challenge and amusement and desire. He shifts so quickly that I gasp in surprise and then he's standing beside the mattress. I raise up onto my knees as he reaches out and slides two fingers beneath my chin, gently forcing my head back so that I meet his stare. I inhale sharply at the look in his eyes, something so intensely dirty and dangerous stirring there that my pulse races and my blood turns to molten lava.

Ohhh fuck. This plan backfired—in the best possible way.

"I want those pretty lips of yours around my cock, Melody," he says, voice a sultry rumble that makes my toes curl and my nipples harden. He notices and his lips quirk up into a sexy half-smirk. He grips the base of his cock with one hand and the back of my head with the other. Gently, giving me every opportunity to tell him that I'm not into it or to stop, he guides the thick head to my mouth, his eyes never leaving mine. I open my mouth obediently, more turned on than I've ever been. He slowly feeds his cock between my lips.

"Ah *fuck*. That's right, baby. Take my cock, nice and slow…"

Jesus, this is hot. Too hot. I've never experienced anything quite like this before but I'm officially fucking addicted. I'm already wet again, aching, needing him so badly a faint tremble racks my body. He slides over my tongue, down my throat, and I'm thankful I've never had a problem with my gag reflex because *dear God* he can get deep.

I start to move my head, letting his slick shaft glide in and out, twirling my tongue around the head.

"Christ, Melody," he groans.

I grip his hips as I lick and suck, dipping my tongue into the slit on the head and tasting the bit of salt. I moan around his cock, digging my fingers roughly into his skin. He doesn't seem to mind. In fact, he seems to like it, tightening his grip in my hair and gently thrusting his hips. He stills, silently asking if that was alright. I pull his hips forward, begging him to do it again. Another low moan rumbles through his chest, like me giving him this permission is the sexiest thing in the world. He does it again, and again, and I take everything he gives me, needing more, my thoughts becoming a little…feral.

I look up to meet his gaze again.

"God, look at you. You so look so fucking pretty while I fuck your mouth, Melody." *Fucking. Hell.* He thrusts again while he holds my gaze and my entire body convulses, my own hips subtly arching forward, needing something, anything. I can't take it anymore. I slide one hand downward, moaning as I slide my fingers over my own slick flesh.

"Melody," he gasps quietly, "are you…Jesus fucking Christ, you are." He wipes his hand over his mouth as he watches, wide eyed as I suck him so fucking deep. His eyes slide closed and a shudder works its way through his body. When he opens them again, they're absolutely blazing, a sexy determination shining in the deep green. "Are you wet, sweetheart?" he asks. I whimper and releases his cock long enough to answer.

"*Soaked.*" I hold his gaze as I run my tongue along the underside of his shaft, from base to tip. I grip him, hot and wet in my palm, and glide my fist up and down. He grits out an appreciative grunt and I run my tongue around and around the head while I pump my fist, stroking him while I rub my clit.

"I'm going to come, Melody. Fuck, I'm close."

I close my lips over him again, taking his shaft deep over and over, harder and faster. His muscles shake and I thrust my fingers into my pussy, moving in time with the movements of my mouth. I'm close too. So close. I spread my knees wider, thrusting harder. Deeper.

"That's right. Take my cock, Melody. Take it like a good fucking girl."

That's it. I'm fucking done for. I cry out a muffled scream around his cock as I come on my own fingers.

"Oh fuckkkk," he groans and thrusts his hips forward again, fingers tightening in my hair. Once. Twice. "I need to know where…" I glare at him, arching my brow and somehow conveying *where the fuck do you think, idiot?* without words. He pulls my arm upward, forcing my hand from between my legs, and bends his head. He sucks my fingers, moaning as he moves his hips faster and how is every new thing he does sexier than the last?? I suck him harder and a moment later, he roars my name as he comes in a rush. I swallow him down, eyes sliding closed in utter ecstasy. Who knew that blowing someone could be so fucking hot? *Not this girl.* I've never minded giving head before, had fun with it usually, but it had never been *sexy* to me before this moment.

I collapse backward onto the mattress and Austin joins me, breathing hard and limbs sprawling. I throw my legs over his stomach, and he rests one hand on my thigh.

"And here I thought I'd be out of practice," I quip, breathless. He huffs out a laugh.

"If that is you out of practice, I am in big, *big* fucking trouble."

I chuckle, grabbing a pillow and shoving it behind my head.

After a while, when I've come down from that absolute high, I say, "alright, so tell me."

"Tell you what?"

"Everything," I breathe. I want to know everything about this man, the one who has somehow managed to light the spark inside me again, the one I thought was gone forever. The man who seems to know me on a level that I didn't even know existed. The man who can work my body like a fucking nine-to-five. The man who it might just kill me to lose. I push that thought away and just focus on the here and now.

He smiles, a slow, sexy curl of his lips, as if he's been waiting for me to say that single word, for me to want to let him in completely, no more secrets or walls between us.

And so we talk. For hours and hours, all through the night. We talk about our lives before, our childhoods and jobs and everything in between. We talk about our lives after the end of the world, how we got to where we are now. We take breaks in between the talking sometimes to do other things. To be fair, there's still talking involved, just a dirtier kind…and afterwards we talk some more.

"And the dog?" he finally asks just as the sun's rising, glancing towards the stuffed dog standing watch on the side table. I'm lying on my stomach with my head resting on my folded arms, looking at him. He's propped on his side, staring down at me and running his fingers up and down my spine. I take a deep breath and prepare myself to tell the story. I think he knew this would be the hardest one, why he didn't bring it up before now. I've never told *anyone*. The only other person on the planet who knows about this part of my life is Jonah. Even Mull doesn't know it all, at least not from my perspective. Jonah was like a father to Gabby, so he had every right to talk to Mull about losing her from his eyes, but I've never told my story to anyone.

But I want to share it with Austin. I want him to know me in a way that no one else does except Jonah, but this is different than even that. Jonah had been there with me through it all, he'd lived it too. Sharing it with Austin is choosing to give him a piece of me that no one else has.

"His name is Leo," I say quietly, and though I'm prepared for it, the pain makes my breath catch, memories rearing up out of the pit I keep them in inside my chest. It feels like a line of spikes being slowly dragged down my body, each inch sending new shocks of agony ripping through me. It's been so long since I let myself really look, that I let myself remember…

But I swallow hard and keep going.

"And he belonged to my daughter, Gabby."

Austin inhales quietly. I know that he probably suspected who the stuffed animal had belonged to, at least a vague idea, and that he assumed that I'd lost a child after that first night at FOS when I'd told him how I was sure he hadn't had children, but hearing it confirmed is different, I guess.

"Was it…was it Bloodies?" he asks gently.

"No, nothing like that. I was losing her before the end of the world. She was diagnosed with acute myeloid leukemia a few months before everything went to hell."

"Oh God, Melody, I'm so sorry."

I give him a sad smile, that one that you give people when they tell you that they're sorry for your loss. The one that says *it's ok* even though it's far, far from ok, but it's all you can offer them.

But no, it isn't all I can offer, not this time. I reach over and take his hand in mine, and he squeezes it gently.

"She was only six and it was…aggressive. Even with treatment, the odds weren't in our favor. So…well, we were on borrowed time." Tears burn my eyes but I don't want to stop. "A good friend from the bureau found out about what was happening with the Bloodies before news broke, before everything got so out of hand and the bombs dropped and—" I take a deep breath, forcing myself not to spiral. "He shouldn't have told me, but he did and he's the reason I'm still here. He warned us about what was coming—the outbreak and the zombies and the bombs that they planned to use to try to contain everything—and told us to get as far from D.C. as we could. Mitch and Sean—that was Jonah's husband—died years before that, so it was just me and Jonah and Gabby against the apocalypse." I cast my mind back to the very beginning again, letting all of the memories hit me.

"We gathered as many supplies as we could and we went to Jonah's lake house out in the middle of nowhere. That's where we spent the first few years after the end. It's where…it's where Gabby died." A tear rolls down my cheek and Austin reaches out to wipe it away before pulling me against his chest. With his arms wrapped around me, I can keep going. He's here to hold me together, giving me permission to break if I need to.

"We were able to shield her from everything out there, so she had no idea what was going on in the world. Thankfully, the property was pretty secluded, so we didn't have to worry about many Bloodies or other people wandering in. She just thought we were having a great family vacation," I say with a laugh that fades quickly. "She was happy. She spent her last month on earth happy and that's all I can ask for, especially given the state of the world. She started to decline pretty quickly after those first few weeks, and we knew it was time. It was... peaceful. We had a lot of pain medicine and we were able to make the end bearable for her. She went to sleep in my lap, one arm wrapped around Leo and holding my hand. And that was it."

I can't speak for a long time as I let the pain wash through me, letting myself really feel it for the first time in years. Maybe for the first time ever. I barely remember the days afterwards. I remember Jonah digging a grave beside Gabby's beloved swing, the one Mitch had built for her by hand. He'd carved their initials into the seat and it was her special place, especially after Mitch died. I remember kissing her forehead one last time and Jonah taking her from my arms because I couldn't be the one to put her in the ground. I remember kneeling in the mud as the rain pelted down on me, feeling completely numb and utter agony all at once, and I remember screaming.

But after that, it's just darkness. It's like I went to sleep for months, not really seeing or feeling anything at all, not truly accepting everything. I knew that Gabby was gone. I wasn't in denial, exactly, but it was like when I thought about it, it seemed like a dream, or like I was looking at it through a pane of warped glass. Everything was there but also...not.

Austin gives me as much time as I need, just holds me as I cry and reassures me without words that he's there. After a while, I find my voice again.

"After that, everything became about survival, about keeping Jonah alive and safe, and that was it. I went to a very, very dark place that really, I probably shouldn't have made it back out of. I was ruthless. I was cruel. I was brutal. I did anything and everything in my power to keep Jonah safe and I didn't care if that took every drop of humanity out of me. He was all I had left and I wouldn't...I *couldn't* lose him." Austin flinches ever so slightly, understanding now why Jonah is so important to me, why leaving him at The Cove meant so much. I squeeze him reassuringly. "I eventually came back, piece by piece, but that had taken me years, and even then, it's like I kept this wall around myself, letting very few people inside. Mull, Renee, Wynn, Abuela— and you."

I lean back to look at him and slide one hand over his cheek, gently stroking my thumb over his cheekbone. I lean in and kiss him, slow and deep and saying all the rest of the things that I can't say out loud right now. I shift on his lap and lose myself in him for a while.

"THANK you for telling me all of this," he says quietly, hours later as we're finally drifting off to sleep in the middle of the afternoon. My head's on his chest and I'm wrapped around him, pressing my body as close to his as I can. His fingers play in my hair and my eyelids droop.

"Thank you for...everything," I whisper.

"Melody?"

"Hmm?" I murmur, sleep pulling me under like a riptide. I'm not even sure if what I hear next is real, but I fall asleep with a smile on my lips.

"I think I've gone and fallen in love with you."

CHAPTER THIRTY-TWO

MELODY

IT'S weird being back at FOS. We just got back a few minutes ago, and while my heart actually leapt when we made our way over the now-familiar road through the woods thinking of seeing Renee and Abuela again and a sense of returning home settled over me, a part of me mourned the loss of the apartment. Being there with Austin was like some secret, perfect bubble where we could just be us. Where no one had any expectations of either of us, where there weren't zombies trying to rip us to shreds, where he didn't have to wear that mask and pretend to be a person he wasn't—an act that I know is slowly starting to kill him.

It took a week for the snow to finally melt and Wynn and the others to make their way back to us, and it was one of the best weeks of my life. We talked, and laughed, and cried. We shared things that neither of us had ever shared with another person. We connected in a way that I thought was gone from my life forever. And *dear God* had we done everything you can imagine in the physical department—and probably a handful that you really can't. Mind-blowing. Life-altering. More pleasure than any single person should ever have.

We'd even cracked the code on the armory. We'd tried and failed to figure it out too many times to count and both of us were pretty much resigned to the fact that it was a lost cause. We'd searched every book in the place, thinking it had to be a cipher of some sort, the letters corresponding to ones within a text maybe, but had no luck. We'd been just lying on the mattress, watching another movie, when Austin had jolted upright, nearly spilling all the popcorn.

"What?? What's wrong?" I'd asked, alarmed, looking around for some threat I'd managed to miss, half expecting to see a Bloody scaling the balcony or something.

"I got it," he'd said with a grin, pointing at one of the frames on the wall and then snapping his fingers. It was a signed ticket stub of some sort, but I had no idea how in the hell that helped our cause. He'd run back into the bedroom like a little kid running downstairs on Christmas morning, and I'd rolled my eyes, pausing the movie and setting the popcorn bowl on the table before joining him.

He was staring at the wall, nodding to himself, lips moving as he said God knew what so quietly that only he could hear it. Then he grinned, clapping his hands and whooping.

"Yeah baby! I fucking got it!"

He kissed me hard and then he was gone again.

"Ok this getting left in the dust thing is getting old!" I'd called as he'd torn through the apartment and down the stairs. I followed and he was already working on the lock when I made my way into the workshop.

"MMBBKGJGMJRNR," he said as I hopped up onto the workbench to watch. He was pretty cute when he was all giddy and excited, I had to admit.

"Try again, in English this time?"

"I can't believe it took me so long to see it. They're baseball players, arguably some of the best in history. I guess that's why Uncle Charlie chose them. But anyway, the combination is their jersey numbers— well, I'm like ninety percent sure, anyway." I saw the string of letters in my mind and he started to rattle them off. "Mickey Mantle, Barry Bonds, Ken Griffey Jr., Greg Maddox, Jackie Robinson, and Nolan Ryan."

"Holy shit," I breathed, knowing immediately that he had to be right. "But wait, how do you know MM isn't Mark McGwire?" I didn't know a ton about old baseball players, but my uncle owned a memorabilia store and had a bunch of stuff from that big home run race that happened way back in the late nineties.

He looks thoughtful and then shrugs. "I just think Uncle Charlie was a Mantle fan." I get the feeling that he's saying *he's* a Mantle fan and hopes Charlie was too. He frowns. "Wait, shit, it's not enough numbers."

"What do you mean?"

"We're one off. 7-24-25-31-42-34. I need one more."

"Try zero seven."

He did and when the familiar click of the lock releasing echoed through the room, he met my gaze, smiling widely.

"Let's see what's in the treasure chest, shall we?"

I'd hopped off of the workbench and stood beside him as he pulled open the first cabinet and *holy fucking shit*. It was stocked to the brim with weapons—everything from guns to knifes to throwing stars for fuck's sake—and enough ammo to start a small war.

"Yeah, baby!" Austin had cheered again, picking me up and twirling me around in triumph and excitement. And then we celebrated in a whole different way that involved me being bent over a workbench. All in all, it was a great fucking day.

I hadn't been sure how to act when the rescue party arrived, but it had been such a whirlwind of Austin getting caught up on everything going on across Haven and making plans to start transporting supplies back, that I ended up not really having to worry about it much. He had to fall back into King of the World duties and I had to let him. I was plenty busy helping Wynn and Johnson on the supply side of things too, so it wasn't like I was just sitting on the sidelines, pining and pouting or anything.

"Holy fuck," Wynn had whistled low when I'd showed him the arsenal. He fist bumped me with a huge grin on his face. There was enough weapons and ammo to keep everyone safe for a good long while. *Thank you, Uncle Charlie.* "So, uh…are you two like…a thing?" he'd asked me quietly as we walked back across the bridge behind a flat bed trailer that we'd loaded down with the first round of supplies and the engineers had rigged to be pulled across by some fancy pulleys. It beat having to bring it all across by the wagonful, so I wasn't complaining one bit. A few trailer loads and we'd have our trucks full, and another team would come back in a couple of weeks for more.

I'd glanced ahead at Austin, walking slowly in front of the trailer and keeping a close eye on things.

"I...don't know. Yes?" I hadn't meant for it be a question, but I honestly wasn't sure what the right term for us was. We were obviously together. There was no going back now, for either of us. I'd even admitted to the jerk—who gloated in an admittedly adorable way—that I loved him.

"Say it again, Morales. I didn't hear you the first time," he'd said, grinning and dancing around the kitchen. Literally dancing. I'd thrown a dish cloth at him. He'd rolled it up deftly and popped my ass with it, making me yelp and laugh like an idiot. "Come on now, don't be shy. What did you say?"

"I take it back," I'd grumbled but I couldn't seem to wipe the smile from my face. He'd tugged me to him then, kissing me like I've never been kissed before.

He'd whispered against my lips, all joking gone, though I could feel the smile as he said, "say it again, Melody. Please. I don't think I can ever hear those three words enough."

"I love you," I whispered just before I kissed him again, something inside of me breaking and healing at the same time. I never thought I'd feel this again. I never thought I'd say those words to anyone after Mitch, but definitely not after everything else that had happened. I never thought I could be this happy again. He'd lifted me onto the kitchen counter and we'd celebrated properly.

Now, we're back to the real world and I don't know what that looks like, but I'm not letting myself worry about it too much. We stroll down our hallway now, hand in hand. No less than ten people had been waiting to jump on him the minute we all walked inside the lobby. Renee had flown at me, pulling me into a bearhug and I'd returned it, only to get the same treatment from Abuela a second later. Austin met my eyes across the crowd now separating us, and whatever he saw there had him telling everyone in a booming, though not unkind voice, that we were exhausted and needed rest. Everything could wait for the next day. Renee had given me a look that said *we will be talking in detail soon* and Abuela had simply winked as Austin and I had walked towards the stairs.

"So, are you really exhausted?" I ask, rubbing my thumb across the back of his hand in small circles. He glances at me and his lips curl up.

"I will never, ever be too exhausted for that."

I huff out a laugh but just as we reach his door, it flies open. I jerk back, surprised, and automatically drop Austin's hand. Destiny stands on the threshold, dressed in a lace dress that's more empty-space than fabric. My brows hike upward and I blink several times.

"Oh thank God you're back," she sighs heavily, giving Traeger a coy, suggestive smile. "I've been missing you like crazy…"

Austin is still as a statue beside me. I glance to him, waiting for him to tell her no, that their arrangement is finished, that we're together now…but he doesn't and my heart clenches in my chest. I know he wasn't lying about how he felt about me, but…well, things are different here, aren't they? He has a reputation to maintain, a mask to display for the world—and that mask doesn't include me. I don't know why I didn't think of it before now, and suddenly it's hard to breathe. I don't want to have to hide this. I don't want to be his secret. I get it, but I don't know how to navigate this—and I sure as shit can't stand the thought of him keeping up his little appointments with his girls. The mere thought of Destiny's hands on him makes me want to vomit. And, ok, yeah, it also makes me want to do her serious bodily harm in a variety of ways.

It feels like it's been hours, but really it's only been a few seconds. I turn to walk away, my blood pumping loudly in my ears, but only make it a step before his hand is on my wrist, stopping me.

I glance down to where his fingers are firm on me and then meet his eyes.

"Don't even think about it, Melody." His voice is a soft rumble, and I feel a shudder of relief make its way through my body. He turns back to Destiny.

"Destiny, this, uh, arrangement of ours—all of the girls—will be ending."

Her eyes bulge and as they shift to where Austin still holds onto my wrist, her look of incredulity changes to one of outrage.

"Her?? You have got to be kidding me!"

"I assure you that I'm not." His tone isn't harsh, but firm and the touch of authority in it reminds Destiny of who he is. She looks like she wants to argue, but doesn't. She glares daggers at me and then, surprisingly, at Austin. I narrow my eyes a fraction, tracking something in her eyes that I don't like, and making a note. She isn't going to take this lightly, no matter what she might pretend otherwise. She smooths out her features, a sharp smile settling over her face.

"Your loss," she says, hiking a shoulder and waltzing past us down the hallway, putting a little extra roll in her hips. We watch her go and after the door slams shut, Austin lets out a long sigh.

"Probably could have handled that better," he says, rubbing the back of his neck and looking so tired and weary that I want nothing more than to take all of this from his shoulders. It's too fucking much. We've only been back for twenty minutes and already the weight of it all is bearing down on him, his mask shifting more firmly into place and tearing away the man I know and love.

"You'll want to watch your back with that one now," I tell him, and then purse my lips. "Well, both of us actually. I know murderous intent when I see it." I reach out and run my hand along his cheek and he closes his eyes, leaning into the touch.

"I'm not worried." He opens his eyes and gives me a crooked smile. "My girl is a secret ninja assassin." I giggle as he picks me up and tosses me over his shoulder. He takes a second to swat my ass, as expected and appreciated, and then he walks us into his room, kicking the door closed behind him. Once we're in the bedroom, he slides me slowly down his body until I'm on unsteady feet, and brushes the hair from my face.

"How about a hot bath?" I bite my lip. A hot bath sounds like absolute heaven, but I feel like an asshole using that much heated water. As if reading my mind, he adds, "I can do whatever I want. I'm the King of this little kingdom, remember?" He says it playfully, but there's a strain behind the words. I decide to say fuck it and indulge for the night.

"A bath sounds fantastic." I lean up to kiss him, and add quietly against his lips, "And I think the king is in need of a little...stress relief." He groans before kissing me again. He scoops me up in his arms and carries me to the bathroom.

"I WISH we were still at the apartment," Austin says quietly later as we lounge in the oversized tub, sated and luxuriating in the warmth. My back is to his chest, his legs on the outside of my own and his arms wrapped tightly around me. "Everything was just so...easy there. Here it's nothing but complicated and..." He seems to be casting around for the right word.

"Heavy?"

He sighs. "Yes. Fucking heavy. Too heavy." My heart clenches. Coming back is going to be much harder for him than I originally thought. Finally being able to be himself out on the island broke something free inside him. Now he's having to shove it back down and hide it, and I don't think it's as easy as he hoped it would be. I lean up and kiss him, desperate to erase his worry, desperate to shoulder some of his burden for him.

We lie in bed together a little bit later, both of us starting to nod off.

"Maybe it's finally time," he whispers.

"For what?"

"For Traeger's time to be done."

CHAPTER THIRTY-THREE

AUSTIN

THE FIRST ATTEMPT on Melody's life comes two weeks later. As she suspected, Destiny was enraged at her sudden and, in her opinion, completely ridiculous dismissal from my bed. I think it wasn't even just that I didn't want to fuck her anymore, I think it was that I'd made it clear around FOS that Melody and I were together. A couple. That I loved her. Despite my best efforts and what I genuinely believed up until that night I first danced with Melody, apparently the arrangements with the girls hadn't been purely physical like I thought. Feelings had been caught. Or at least, a claim of sorts? They were *Traeger's Girls*. They had their own reputations and "status" as they saw it with that title. I never looked at it that way, which I know was really fucking stupid of me. Melody has reminded me that I'm the biggest idiot more than once on the matter.

Melody easily handled Destiny's attempt—an ambush near the greenhouses late one night with a dagger that she had no idea how to even hold, let alone do damage to anyone but herself with—and, surprisingly, tells me to go easy on her when it comes time for punishment. She had to be punished, of course, there was no way around that. We have rules, and attacks of any kind, no matter who they were on, aren't tolerated within FOS. And as much as I understand where

Destiny is coming from to an extent, and a part of me agrees with the need for leniency, the other, louder part of me is absolutely raging at the threat to Melody's life. Destiny had tried to take what was *mine*, to hurt the woman I love more than anything on this fucking planet. *How fucking dare she??*

"Let's take a drive," Melody says quietly, seeing the fury in my eyes, the tight coil of my muscles as I fight to maintain control. "I get it, I do, trust me, but let's take a drive and cool off." I know that she's right. I can't even speak around the anger, the thick, clawing lump it has wedged in my throat, so I just nod and stride off to the cabinet to get the keys to something fucking *fast*. Melody follows me and her eyes lit up like I just brought her to Disneyworld.

"Oh hell yeah, baby," she says with a grin, running a reverent hand down the length of the Indian. Are motorcycles practical in the zombie apocalypse? Not exactly. They're loud and offer zero protection. But did I still have to bring this beauty back with me from a run a year ago? Abso-fucking-lutely. It reminded me too much of one I'd had not long after Em and I had gotten married. It was my baby, truth be told, but I sold it when times got hard and we needed the money. It had damn near killed me to do it, but it was the right thing.

I'm still fuming but I manage a small smile for her. I hop on the bike and Melody eases on behind me, settling her hands on my hips. When we finally get out onto the main road, I put the pedal to the absolute fucking metal. Melody whoops behind me, and I smile, feeling the rage easing with every mile we get farther from FOS. Eighty. Ninety. Melody yells for me to go faster, and I grin, hitting one-ten. We just ride for a long time, flying through the empty roads and letting the freedom of it fill me up and push out everything else. Eventually I pull off the highway into a gravel parking area for one of the many nature trails that dot this stretch of the road. I park the bike and Melody slides off. I throw my leg over and lean against the seat as Melody steps in between my legs. I grip her hips and pull her in for a long, deep kiss.

Without saying a word, she settles me. Just holding her in my arms chases the worst of the fury away. I'm still pissed as fuck, but I don't want to murder Destiny anymore at least. She pulls back, leaning her forehead against mine and I sigh heavily.

"You good?" she asks.

"Yeah, I'm good. I...shit, Melody, I was ready to kill her. I can't..." I press my lips into a hard line, not able to give the words life. *I can't lose you.*

"Hey, I'm alright, Austin." I look away and she grips my chin and forces my gaze back to hers. That shouldn't be so hot, should it? "It's going to take a lot more than a terrible assassination attempt by Destiny to take me out, baby. Trust me on that."

"I love you," I tell her, reaching out to tuck a lock of hair behind her ear.

"I love you too."

"It was worth it, you know." She frowns, brow furrowing. "The end of the world. All the pain and destruction and death. It all led me to you. I never would have found you if not for it. Or even if I did, we wouldn't be the people we are now, the ones whose broken pieces somehow fit together so fucking perfectly. So, as fucked up as it is to say, it was worth all the ruin, Melody. I would watch the world burn all over again—I would fucking burn what's left of it myself—for this. For us."

She blinks and her eyes are glassy. She punches me in the chest playfully.

"Stop trying to make me cry, asshole."

I chuckle at that and pull her into a tight hug.

"You're worth it too, you know," she whispers.

———

ABUELA, Mickens, and I, as the judicial committee, vote for two lashes and a week in confinement for Destiny after Melody and I come back. I let Johnson handle the lashing and bury myself in Melody instead, needing to prove that she's alright, that Destiny's stupid fucking attempt to take her from me had failed. Melody understands exactly what's happening, letting me do what I need to do, taking her hard and fast, losing myself. She murmurs all the while that she's here, that she's ok, that she loves me.

I take Melody back to The Cove with us the next time go, breaking my own rules and frankly not giving a fuck anymore. She deserves to see Jonah and Mulligan, she deserves to move freely through Haven like the rest of the security team. I know it's a dangerous line to walk— Melody would still keep the secrets of FOS, of course, but even her presence here, us being together, will be enough for some people to start questioning. But maybe that's ok. Maybe it's time that people know the truth. Maybe it's finally time for Traeger to be put away, like a suit shoved in the back of a closet.

I can't help but smile as I watch Melody light up being around Jonah and Mulligan again. I watch her laugh harder than I've ever seen as we eat dinner together, but I don't feel like I'm on the outside, a stranger trespassing on their lives. No, she makes me feel like I'm a part of it all—and so do the guys. Jonah gives me a warm but somewhat sheepish smile.

"So, we kind of figured it out months ago, honestly."

"Yeah, he's just a big ole softie," Melody adds, winking at me.

"Ok, ok, I didn't say that," Jonah assures me, rolling his eyes. "I just know that…well, you do what has to be done to protect people, and I'm on board with that. I respect the hell out of it and know it can't have been easy, even if the intentions—and outcome—were all good."

I incline my head in acknowledgment and thanks. Later, I help him clear the dishes from the table while Melody and Mulligan talk animatedly about someone else in town that apparently has a wild dating history.

"I'm glad she found you," Jonah says quietly, startling me a little. "I was scared for so long that Mel would never let anyone else in, that she'd walled herself up too damn well and that no one could ever break through it. I think…I think she didn't think she deserved to be happy again, like she had to punish herself for the things she'd done, or like being happy again would be some kind of betrayal to Mitch and Gabby."

"I can understand that," I tell him honestly, voice low.

"I thought you might." He gives me a sad smile. "Anyway, I know that this whole thing—" he gestures between me and the dining room where Melody laughs so hard she snorts, "—can't be easy given your position. Complicated seems like the understatement of the century." I huff out a laugh. "But thank you for it. She's happier than I've seen her in so damn long. If we can help with anything, just let us know."

I nod and shake his outstretched hand. We head back into the dining room and find Mulligan wiping away tears from laughing so hard. Jonah arches a brow and Melody gets out of her chair and slides into my lap as soon as I sit, like we've been doing this for years. Mull tries to fill us in on whatever had started the laughfest, and I feel the tiny flames of hope spring to life in my chest that I've found a little family around this small dining table.

And then the second attempt on Melody's life happens.

CHAPTER THIRTY-FOUR

MELODY

WORD SPREADS quicker than wildfire about our relationship. It's only been a month or so, but every single person in Haven knows damn well that Traeger and I are together. Some people look at me in confusion, probably wondering if Austin is forcing me to be with him. Some people smile warmly, seemingly happy, or at least accepting. And there are plenty that look with downright hostility. I don't know if they're pissed that I slept my way to the top—in their opinion—or if they don't think Austin deserves any kind of happiness. Probably a combination of both plus a host of other things.

But I couldn't care less. I've jumped headlong into this thing with Austin, letting myself be completely all in. No walls. No fears. No hesitations. If there's one thing we both know, it's that life is too fucking short, especially in this world. Every heartbeat is a gift and we don't want to waste a single one.

"There you go, much better!" I say, smiling and nodding encouragingly at Jenna. I'd volunteered to help train some new members of the security team out at The Farm. Jenna had asked if I could teach her how to throw knives because she'd heard rumors that I was really damn good at it and she thought it would be a handy skill to have. I'd agreed easily, wondering who had spread that particular rumor. Probably Wynn.

"Thanks," Jenna says, smiling a little shyly, but there's pride in her eyes when she glances back at the row of practice dummies—burlap sacks stuffed with straw to vaguely resemble a person and targets painted on their—across the field beside the barn where we've been practicing.

"Ok, this time, try releasing just a little bit later—"

"Help!!" someone cries. Jenna and I both turn towards the sound, my hand flying to the pistol at my hip and Jenna tightening her grip on her knife. A man is sprinting towards us, looking panicked.

"What's wrong?" I ask, stepping forward. I can't remember his name, but I know I've seen him around The Farm before. Paul maybe?

"She fell," he pants. "Out in the woods just past Field Eight." He points over his shoulder to the trees in the near distance. "It must be an old storm cellar or something, but she fell through and I think she's really hurt." He's frantic, eyes wild.

"Who fell?" I ask.

"Sarah," he chokes out.

"Oh God," Jenna gasps beside me. "That's Terry's daughter. She's only ten."

I'm already grabbing the guy—*Preston?*—by the shoulder and running towards the field and the trees beyond.

"Go get more help!" I call to Jenna over my shoulder. She nods and takes off in the opposite direction, back towards the big farm house.

"Hurry. Oh fuck, fuck, fuck. She's just a kid. I think she's hurt, she wasn't moving…"

"It's ok, she'll be alright." I'm not really one to pray much these days, but I send one out into the universe all the same that my words aren't complete and total bullshit. *Not a kid. Come on, not a little girl…*

We run across one of the field, trying not to trample whatever's growing—I honestly can't remember what Field Eight is set up for, though I know I've seen the list and map a handful of times—and through the trees lining the other side. My lungs are burning a bit by the time I see an old truck and a couple of other guys standing around a hole in the ground, splintered wood sticking up from the edges like jagged fingernails reaching out of the earth.

"There!" the guy pants. *Fuck what is his name?* "She fell through right there!"

I dash to the edge, barely sparing a glance at the other guys. I look down into the hole, bracing myself for what I might find, but...there's nothing there.

Searing hot pain erupts through my skull, turning my vision to a blinding white for one terrible, intense heartbeat before everything goes dark.

"I don't like this."

The voice is male, low, and anxious. My head is throbbing, a burning pain still radiating through my entire skull, and something coats the left side of my face. Blood. My head is bowed, chin leaning on my chest, and I keep it that way, keeping my eyes closed as I take a few deep breaths through my nose and figure out what the fuck is going on. I clear my head, forcing the pain to quiet and take a back seat while I inventory everything I know:

I was attacked.

Reason? Unclear.

I'm in a chair. Wood. Like the kind you'd have at your kitchen table.

I'm not tied to the chair, but my hands are secured behind my back with no shit handcuffs. *Where the hell had they gotten these things?* The metal bites into my wrists.

I'm inside, but the way the sounds are shifting around me, I don't think it's a house. The space feels too big, too open. A barn maybe.

It smells dank and musty, not horrible, but like somewhere that hasn't been cleaned in a while.

"Pipe down, Dominic. You knew what you were signing up for."

Another man.

"You said we'd use her to get his attention," Dominic hisses quietly. "Not...not *this*."

"You've got a problem with it? Fuck off then, pussy."

"Fuck you, Manny." Dominic doesn't leave, so he must decide that he doesn't want to be seen as a pussy, or maybe he's just afraid of this Manny guy. Who knows.

"Message has been delivered and Craig just checked in." I know this voice. Pete. That's his fucking name. The asshole who lured me into a trap, pretending a little girl was hurt. *Fucking prick.* "She awake yet?"

"Not yet," Manny says.

"Well, let's just move this along, shall we? Our guest will be arriving shortly."

I hear him walking closer and then my cheek explodes with pain. The fucker backhanded me. My eyes pop open as my head rocks to the side. It feels like fire licking across my face and I clench my jaw, tasting blood. I turn back to face him and he smiles. A sick, twisted smile.

"Welcome back, sleepy head," he mocks.

"You hit like a bitch," I say, spitting blood on the floor—a mix of rotted straw and mud. Pete huffs out a small laugh at that. I glance around. It's an old barn, just like I'd thought, with boards missing from the roof here and there. The large doors at the end have seen better days: one is rotted almost completely through at the bottom and the other hangs crookedly on its hinges, like it might give up its fight and finally collapse at any second.

And to the left, beside a young guy with dark red hair who must be Dominic, stands a table laid out with a variety of knives, tools, and even an old blow torch.

You said we'd use her to get his attention.

Oh. It all clicks. They plan to use me to hurt Austin.

Well, this should be fucking fun. Pete's still smiling when I meet his gaze again.

"Let me guess, use me to get to Traeger?" I say, quirking a brow in a derisive way that tells him I think he's an idiot. Pete crosses his arms over his chest, but clenches his jaw. I snort and shake my head. "Trade my life for his maybe? It's a stupid fucking plan. We might be together, but he wouldn't risk his life for me, you idiots." I say the lie as smooth as butter, knowing how fucking wrong it is. He will burn this entire fucking world down to get to me. "You really think that he'll…what, exactly? Give you Haven? Is that what you want?"

"I don't give a shit about Haven," Pete growls. He leans down and braces his hands on the armrests of the chair, getting right in my face. I don't flinch away and a flash of surprise flits through his eyes. They're such a dark brown that they look black, and there is an intense, cold hatred there. He blames Austin for something terrible, I know that much, though I have no idea what.

"I want him to suffer. I want him to die screaming while I fucking laugh."

My nostrils flare and heat rises in my chest, that red haze threatening at the corner of my vision. No one threatens what's *mine*. Pete takes my reaction to mean fear, I guess, because he smirks and pushes himself away.

"And you're going to help us with that. It's nothing personal, Mel. He cares about you—as much as a monster like that can care about anyone, I guess—so, we're going to have a little fun with you first to fuck with his head, and then when he comes to trade his life for yours, we'll start the real party."

"He won't come, you prick," I spit.

"Of course he will. He's already on his way. Craig has him trussed up like a Thanksgiving turkey for us and they're headed here now. So, we better get started."

He walks to the table and trails his fingers along the line of instruments. He picks up a boning knife, the blade long and thin, and twirls it in his hand.

"That's going to go through your left eye before this is all said and done. Just a warning."

Dominic looks spooked, eyes wide as he glances between me and the other two men, taking one small step backwards. I feel bad for the kid—it's obvious he doesn't really want to be a part of this, but he's still here and not stepping in to stop it so…well, whatever happens, happens, I guess. He made his bed and now he'll have to lie in it. Manny quirks a brow, not fear, but interest in his eyes, and Pete just laughs.

Pete turns from the table and walks back towards me, knife in hand.

CHAPTER THIRTY-FIVE

AUSTIN

I'M SITTING in Yvonne's office, going through some supply requests with the leader of The Farm. I like Yvonne. She's tough but fair, firm but kind. She doesn't take bullshit but she isn't an asshole just to be an asshole. She'd been running this place for years before the end of the world, and keeping a farm of this size going back then was no easy feat.

"So, if your people come across anything like this—"

A knock on the door sounds through the room, but before either of us can say anything, the door bursts open. Yvonne bolts to her feet.

"Jenna? What's wrong?"

"I'm sorry to barge in, ma'am," she shifts her gaze to me, cheeks heating and looking downright terrified, "sir," she adds inclining her head. "But...something's happened."

"What's wrong?" Yvonne asks, coming around the desk towards Jenna, and I rise from my own chair.

"We were working on knife throwing and Pete came up, frantic, saying that Sarah had falling down through some old storm cellar or something out in the woods."

"Sarah is the daughter of one of our nurse's," Yvonne explains quickly.

"Right. She's only ten. Anyway, Mel ran off with him and told me to get more help. So, I did, but when we got to the spot…" She bites her lip and her eyes water. Something cold and uncomfortable unfurls in my stomach. Had Melody been hurt? Had she fallen down into the cellar too and gotten injured or…or worse? The thought steals the air from my lungs but I shove it away as forcefully as I can. I won't go there. Not until…No. Just fucking no.

"What?" I ask, trying to keep from snapping at the girl.

"Craig was there waiting but no one else was there. No Sarah, no Pete, no Mel. He said that we needed to get Traeger and bring him there…" She swallows hard and twists her hands together in front of her. "And fast if you ever wanted to see Mel alive again."

Yvonne sucks in a harsh breath and everything around me seems to tilt for a long moment. Someone has Melody. Someone is threatening her life, possibly hurting her…because of me. I easily—and happily—slip fully into Traeger, the ruthless, merciless, cold-blooded killer. My chest feels like it's on fire, hot, burning claws of rage slashing and scraping, desperate to escape.

"We'll take one of the ATVs," Yvonne says. I nod and we rush down the hallway.

"Landry, Johnson, with me," I snap. "Mendoza, I want this entire fucking farm locked down *now*."

Yvonne barks orders to her own people as we move out of the big farm house and to the waiting vehicles in the makeshift parking lot to the left of the house. We load into something that looks like a golf cart on steroids, one made for rough terrain, and take off. Yvonne is tense beside me, and I can tell she's upset about Melody, pissed at her own people, and terrified that I'll retaliate against all of the The Farm for this. I might. I haven't fucking decided yet and I can't think straight right now.

The drive doesn't take long, but it feels like an eternity. I try to stop my mind from flashing a thousand different scenarios behind my eyes, like a horrific, morbid flipbook of torture. She's been tortured before, I know. The stories she's shared with me…I shudder just thinking about them, bile rising in my throat and my fury spiking so high that it makes it hard to breath.

So I know she can handle far more than she should ever have to but so help me if they lay a single fucking hand on her...

Yvonne slams the ATV to a few yards away from a guy leaning against the hood of an old truck. Craig, I'm assuming. I see a gaping hole in the ground to the right of the truck, broken boards sticking up around the edges like rotten teeth. Guess they hadn't been lying about the old storm cellar or whatever the hell this thing was. Craig has a shit eating smirk on his face and that red haze starts to creep into my vision, filling everything with the need to punish. I jump out of the cart and stride towards him.

"You kill me, and she dies," he warns, a triumphant look in his eyes, that smirk growing. I nod and keep coming at him. His smirk falters when he realizes that I'm not stopping, that his threat didn't work the way he thought it would. He straightens and pushes himself away from the truck, taking a small step backwards. "I mean it. If I don't check in, they'll—"

I'm on him then, hand around his throat as I force him backwards. His eyes fly wide in terror and he tries to push me away, shoving at my arm. It's no use. Nothing on this earth could stop me right now. I slam his back against a tree and lift, holding him a few feet above the ground so that the toes of his boots barely scrap the leaves. He gasps and claws at my wrist, but I barely feel it. I only feel the cold fury filling every inch of my body, so cold it burns. I bare my teeth at him, feeling more animal than man. I lean in close.

"Where the fuck is my wife?" I growl.

CHAPTER THIRTY-SIX
MELODY

PETE STALKS TOWARDS ME.

"I'm really sorry about this," he says, still slowly twirling that knife, but that unmistakable gleam in his says otherwise. I've seen that look too many times in my life. It's the kind of look I'd expected to see in Austin's all those months ago when he'd been about to kill Kevin. No, that look doesn't say *I'm really sorry about this*. That look says *I can't fucking wait*. So, yeah, Pete is full of shit.

"Not as sorry as you're gonna be in about two minutes," I tell him. He smirks and turns back to look at Manny and Dominic. Manny grins, shoulders shaking with quiet laughter, and Dominic looks like he might throw up, refusing to look at anything but his shoes. I take one quick breath, bite the inside of my cheek, and yank my left thumb upward with my right hand, dislocating the joint. White hot pain spears through me and I swallow my scream, clamping my lips firmly closed. I take a few quick, quiet breaths through my nose to steady myself, and force the pain into a little box inside my mind, closing it tightly to be dealt with later. I slip my left hand from the cuff and wait, keeping them both behind me as if I'm still shackled.

Pete turns back to me, still smiling, and takes the last few steps to stand just in front of the chair. He leans down.

"I think I'll take my chances."

"I was hoping you'd say that." I slam the heel of my right hand up into his nose. I feel bone and cartilage crack and the sound is so grotesquely satisfying that I grin.

"Fuck!" he roars, one hand flying to his face as blood spurts. Manny yells something about me being a crazy bitch, but I'll deal with him in a second. I spring up from the chair and arch backward as Pete slashes out wildly with the knife, still trying to staunch the blood from his nose with his other hand. On his next swipe I grab his wrist and twist it at an unnatural angle, squeezing to put pressure on his radial nerve. He cries out in pain and the knife falls from his useless fingers. He yanks savagely at my hair with his other hand, so hard that my eyes water, but I jam my elbow into his already broken nose and he releases me as he howls in pain again.

I stoop to grab the knife but a wave of dizziness crashes through me and I stagger, blinking away black spots. The momentary distraction is enough for Pete to tackle me from the side. The air whooshes from my lungs as we hit the ground and Pete rolls on top of me, straddling my hips and pinning me down. His blood is still flowing and heavy drops land on my chest. He slaps me again and I see stars, but when he comes back down for a second strike, this time with the knife in his hand once more, I throw my hands up to block his descent. He bares his teeth and digs the fingers of his other hand into the ground beside my head as he tries to force the blade towards my throat, inch by inch.

"You bitch," Pete growls.

"Fuck you," I spit back, gritting my teeth as I fight to keep the knife from plunging downward.

Commotion erupts outside, screams and gunshots, and I know that something serious is going down out there. I know in my gut that it's Austin and pure love floods my chest like lava, warming every inch of me. He managed to get out of whatever bonds they'd put on him and now, they were paying for it. *That's my man.*

"See what the fuck is going on!" Pete roars and Manny dashes to one of the windows that still miraculously has glass in it.

"Oh *fuck*," Manny manages to get out just before the door to the barn flies open. I turn my head, still pushing desperately against Pete's wrist as he forces it downward, and watch as Austin steps through. *Holy shit.* He looks like some kind of avenging angel with the sunlight filtering down on him from a hole in the roof, the blood splattered all over his chest and arms and face, and the absolute blazing fury in his eyes. He might as well have a sword of fire, dark wings flaring out behind his back.

"MELODY!" he roars and my chest twists. The fear. The worry. The fury. But despite all of that, I grin up at Pete savagely, letting him know without words that he and his friends are all as good as dead.

Manny attacks Austin with the machete in his hand and my heart stops being for a second. Austin grips his hatchet with both hands, throwing it up in front of him like a baton to block the blow. I wonder for a second why he didn't come in with guns blazing but the answer crystallizes in my mind almost as soon as the question forms itself: he didn't want the cold detachment of a gun. He wanted this to be up close and personal, he *needed* it to be. The dark, twisted part of me delights in that fact, mirroring the sentiment.

I love you as certain dark things are to be loved.

"You stupid bitch," Pete grits out. "You stupid fucking bitch. This isn't how it was supposed to go. I'll fucking kill you! And then I'll kill him! I'll gut that fucker and dance on his fucking grave, do you hear me?" He's maniacal now, nearly insane, and I wonder what in the fuck Austin did to this man to make him act this way, to need revenge this fucking badly. No matter what it is, I don't care.

"That," I say in a deadly quiet voice, "was the very, *very* wrong thing to say to me."

I bring up a knee as hard as I can and he cries out in agony when I make contact with his balls. I arch my hips and roll to the right and his body tumbles off of mine as we roll. I spring up and he pushes to his knees, screaming some mix of profanities and unintelligible nonsense, spit flying, eyes wide and crazed. I spare a glance towards the door and see that Austin and Manny are still very much locked in their fight. *Fuck, fuck, fuck.*

Pete manages to hold on to the knife and he slashes out at me again. I catch his wrist easily and grab his elbow with my other hand, bringing his forearm down hard over my own knee as I thrust it upward. An unholy scream fills the air as his bone snaps, the jagged edge piercing through his skin. Blood spurts and he cradles his ruined arm. I hear someone vomit not far away—Dominic I guess.

I kick him in the chest, sending him sprawling backwards, landing hard on the ground with his arms splayed out beside him. I bring down a booted foot on his broken arm, and he screams so loudly it feels like my eardrums might burst. I don't hesitate, just bring the knife down and slam it through his left eye, as promised.

"I told you it was going through your eye," I whisper. "I'm a woman of my word."

His screams turn into quiet gasps as he convulses. I yank the knife back and turn to back to Manny and Austin—only to find Manny in *pieces* all around Austin's feet. He meets my gaze and his eyes are absolutely blazing with lethal fury.

He shifts his gaze behind me, and I follow it to find Dominic cowering under the table. Austin doesn't seem too concerned about him and crosses to me in a few long strides. He drops the bloody hatchet to the ground and cradles my face between his big hands.

"Tell me you're alright," he says and it sounds like he's so close to breaking, barely keeping everything under control. I grip his wrists.

"I'm alright. Not a scratch on me." He clenches his jaw, and gently, but deliberately, runs one across my cheek. He holds it up in front of my face to show me the blood that must have dripped from my forehead. "Ok, *hardly* a scratch on me," I amend. "But I'm fine, baby. I promise."

He closes his eyes and leans his forehead against mine, letting out a long, shuddering breath. My eyes water and my chest aches knowing how worried he must have been, all of the possibilities running through his head. If the roles had been reversed...well, no one would be left alive, that's for fucking sure.

"Are you ok? Is any of this blood yours?" I ask quietly.

"Fine," he rumbles, and I honestly don't know that he can say much more than that right now. He pulls away as Wynn, Johnson, and a few other people from The Farm pour into the barn, all looking fresh from battle, though none nearly as bloody as Austin.

"That one?" Austin asks, voice low and gruff. He tilts his head towards the table and I turn to look at the kid beneath it, rocking gently back and forth as he stares unblinking at the carnage around him. Part of me wants to let Dominic share Pete and Manny's fate. He was part of this after all. He chose to follow these idiots and not do a thing to stop the terrible things about to happen. But I know that he doesn't really deserve that. He deserves to be punished, no doubt about that, but not in the way Austin clearly has in mind.

"He didn't want things to go down this way. He wasn't like the others." Dominic snaps his gaze to mine at that, his blue eyes finally focusing. He looks like he might cry and his mouth pops open in shock.

"Alright," Austin says, but then I feel his entire body go rigid. My brow furrows...until I realize what he's staring at: the table full of things they'd planned to use on me, all the ways they planned to hurt me to hurt him. I put a palm on his cheek and force his face back to mine.

"Let's get out of here, ok?" He seems to barely hear me and I know all too well what he must be seeing and hearing: a red haze of rage and the roaring of his blood in his ears. I tug him towards the door.

"Mel?" Wynn asks. I nod, telling him I'm alright.

"Uh, hey, can you find the keys for these things?" I ask, holding up my right hand and jangling the cuffs still attached there. Wynn's face darkens, realizing that I'd been restrained that way. He nods and I tug Austin outside.

It's an absolute bloodbath. At least ten people dead, most from bullets, but there are plenty of other injuries—stab wounds and severed limbs, even a head lying a few feet from its body. *Jesus fuck.* We walk through the battlefield, my boots squishing in muddy, blood-filled earth. Austin's still on edge, still lost in that dark, rage-filled place that I know all too well. He leads me to a group of vehicles hidden in the woods a few hundred yards away from the barn. We hop in an old Jeep, the suped up kind people used to take mudding with big ass tires and lights mounted along the top.

He floors it and we shoot off through the trees, bumping over the rough terrain, until we hit an open field. I can just spy the farmhouse in the distance, looking tiny it's so far off, and I realize that we're still on The Farm property, just way in the back of it. Austin hits a worn road that I guess is for farm vehicles, and we head down it a ways, driving behind the back of the field in silence for what feels like hours. Finally, Austin throws the Jeep into park.

He grips the steering wheel so tightly that his knuckles turn white, his jaw clenching and unclenching, and his breathing is choppy and ragged. His eyes are squeezed shut, and I know what's going through his head: all the what-ifs, all the questions he doesn't have answers to yet, all of the fear and the rage. The blistering hot, rabid, clawing rage that makes it hard to see or hear or feel anything else.

I start to reach out to pry his hands from the wheel but stop, realizing my thumb is still dislocated. I clench my teeth and pop the joint back into socket, hissing in a quick breath. He snaps his eyes open and turns to me, murder and questions and terror mixing in those green eyes that have somehow become the center of my world.

"I'm fine," I assure him, wiggling my thumb. "Popped it out to slip the cuffs, but it's fine now. It's not the first time it's happened, so it's really not a big deal." The cuffs in question still dangle from my right wrist and his nostrils flare when he notices. I reach over with my left hand and grip his chin, gently forcing his eyes from the cuffs to my face. "Hey," I say softly.

He takes one long, deep, breath, like it's the deepest one he's taken in his entire life, and a shudder rocks through his body as he lets it out. It takes him a few more seconds, but he finally seems to claw his way out of the darkness. He leans in and kisses me, but instead of the desperate, frenzied kiss I'm expecting, it's so soft and tender that it nearly breaks my heart. He pulls away, leaning his forehead against mine for another heartbeat before pulling away.

"Stay here." He hops out of the car and opens the back, fumbling around before coming around to the passenger side. He opens the door and I twist to face him so that my feet rest on the running boards. He pours some water from a bottle onto a rag and wipes the blood off of my cheek and temple, moving gently when he reaches my forehead. I wince and he grinds his teeth.

"This might need stitches," he says gruffly, studying the gash where Pete or one of the other goons had slammed the butt of a rifle to knock me out. "What else?" he asks.

"Nothing. I busted loose and you rode in like the White Knight before they could do anything else. I promise."

He reaches over my head and grips the top of the Jeep, his whole body tense and rigid, and stares up at the sky as if holds all the answers. I shouldn't notice how his shirt rides up, revealing a strip of smooth, toned skin, the bottom edges of his snake and dagger tattoo peeking out from below the hem, but I do and I reach out and settle my hands there, needing his skin against mine. He exhales roughly before tilting his head back down to meet my gaze.

"I'm ok, Austin. I'm here and I'm ok and everything is fine."

"God, Melody, I thought…"

He makes a choking sound, like he can't get enough air into his lungs, and suddenly his lips are on mine again, hard and desperate this time. I welcome it, running my hands up his stomach and chest, around to the small of his back and pull him closer to me, settling his hips between my own. I don't know how long we kiss for, but it feels like forever. It could be forever and I'd die happy. In his arms, his lips on mine, is exactly where I want to spend the rest of my life.

Which is why, when he'd told me he had a really crazy question to ask me, I'd grinned like a lunatic, knowing exactly what he was going to say and exactly what my answer was going to be. I didn't care that we'd only been "together" for a couple of months. I didn't care that people might think it was crazy or that he was forcing me or who knows what else. I didn't care about anything but marrying Austin Traeger.

So, that's what we did. There are no rules for marriages in the apocalypse—no licenses or witness requirements or ceremonies, unless you want them, of course. So, we'd just made the decision that we wanted to be husband and wife, and so we were. We'd found rings at a jewelry store in the town down the road from The Cove, and that was that. We're married. We're together, forever, in every way possible. I'm his and he's mine, and I never thought I'd feel like this again.

But more importantly, I fucking refuse to give it up. He said that we were worth all the ruin of this world, and I happen to fucking agree. He is worth everything.

We finally pull away and I ask, "How did you get away from Craig?"

He arches a brow. "Didn't have to."

"But they said..."

"Craig was all too happy to play along and tell those fuckers whatever I told him to once I cut the first finger off. So, he told Pete that I was under control, but really, the calvary was riding in the whole time."

"That's my guy," I say, leaning in to kiss him softly again, going for levity.

"This can't keep happening," Austin whispers against my lips.

"I'm fine," I tell him again, pulling back.

"For now. Christ, Melody, you can't keep being put in the crosshairs because of me, because of my past actions." He runs a hand roughly through his hair.

"Everything you did, you did for them," I say fiercely, fire roaring in my belly.

"I know that. You know that. No one else does and trust me, most of them wouldn't give a shit even if they did." He shakes his head, staring off into the middle distance somewhere. "I thought maybe..."

"What?" I ask, pulling his face back towards mine, making him focus on me again. "What did you think?"

"I just thought that maybe we could have a normal fucking life together, Melody. I knew people would never love me, but I thought that maybe they could just...let me *be*. Let me quietly fade into the background while others took up the mantle and could just move on. I sure as shit never thought they'd go after you. If I had known, Melody, I never would have—"

"Never would have...what? Decided to marry me?" I ask with a pointed look.

"No, of course not." He rubs his eyes in frustration and I wish I help him somehow. "I just...I don't know, maybe I shouldn't have let people see? Maybe we should have kept things quiet?"

"I don't want to skulk around in the shadows, Austin. For the first time in so fucking long I am *happy,* and I don't want that happiness marred with darkness and secrets."

"So instead it should be marred by people trying to fucking *kill you*??" His voice rises and I can tell that he's struggling to keep his emotions under control.

"I'll deal with it." I shrug and his eyes bulge, incredulous that I'm being so cavalier about everything I guess. "In case you forgot, I'm pretty capable of defending myself."

"I know that. Christ, I know that, Melody, but come on. We can't constantly have you looking over your shoulder, but it's also not fair to you to be cooped up at FOS forever. Hell, even there there's always a chance that someone could decide to have a go. Someone I took from another settlement or something, finally sick of being away from their families. I just..."

He swallows hard and reaches out to rest his palm against my cheek, the ends of his long fingers tunneling into my hair.

"I cannot lose you, Melody. I love you more than I've ever loved anyone, in a whole different and new way that I didn't even know existed. I am only myself when I'm with you. I don't have to hide anything from you. Good, bad, ugly—you never flinch from any of it. I need you and I love you and I *can't* lose you." His voice breaks at the end and so does my heart a little bit. This man. There is so much more to him than anyone could possibly understand. I lurch forward to press my lips to his, tears burning my eyes. I pour as much as I can into the kiss, needing him to understand how much I love him, how much he means to me.

Eventually we pull apart and he leans his forehead against mine, taking slow, deep breaths.

"We'll figure something out," I assure him.

"I think the only way we get a fresh start is with me in a body bag."

CHAPTER THIRTY-SEVEN
AUSTIN

THREE WEEKS LATER, it's time. I'm still not sure how I feel about all of this, but…here goes nothing.

I drag Jonah out of the clubhouse at The Cove by the back of his shirt and toss him unceremoniously to the ground. He grunts in pain and rolls, and a collective gasp runs through the crowd waiting outside. A surprise, mandatory meeting of every member of The Cove had been announced just a few hours ago, and no one had any idea what was happening. We'd made sure that everyone understood that it was nothing good though.

Melody races out of the clubhouse doors behind us, screaming.

"Don't you fucking dare!!" she screeches. "Leave him alone!!"

I don't take my gaze from Jonah's prone body, but I see Johnson grab Melody and drag her to my right. She kicks and flails, but he keeps a firm hold. Mulligan is dragged to the other side, restrained by Landry and Mendoza. He's struggling, but in a more understated, terrified way than Melody, like he's in shock. Melody is like a spitting, wild wolf caught in a trap.

"Everyone listen the fuck up!" I roar to the crowd in front of me. Most of them cower back at the furious authority resonating in my words. My heart is thundering in my ears, my pulse racing and my palms sweating. There are too many fucking emotions roiling through me right now, but I try to focus. Everyone exchanges worried glances, not understanding. "This piece of shit tried to have me killed." I spit beside Jonah and I throw out a hand, pointing to Melody. I curl my lip in disgusted rage. "And this *bitch* pretended to want to be with me to help him do it. Pretended to fucking *marry me* for fuck's sake.' I bark out a humorless, hysterical laugh that makes a few people in the crowd flinch backward. "The long fucking con, I guess and I only have myself to blame for falling for it. But damn, quite the little pet you've got there, Jonah, slutting herself up real fucking good for this little plan of yours." I hate the words. They taste like acid rolling off of my tongue, but I tell myself it's what has to happen.

I pull my leg back and kick Jonah hard in the stomach, and Melody screams again. Jonah curls in on himself protectively, groaning.

"Stop!!" Melody shrieks again. "You fucking prick!!"

I turn to look at her finally, and she actually flinches back from my stare. My stomach churns at that flinch, at the way she's looking at me. I push on.

"Go on, Mel. Tell them how you gave yourself to me like a good fucking whore, how you crawled and begged, how you screamed my name…" She doesn't say a word, just grits her teeth and glares at me, not denying a thing. I smirk at her and huff out a mocking laugh. I turn back to the crowd. "Now, as you all might remember, I don't take too kindly to having my life fucking threatened. So, we're going to take care of this right now."

I pull a hunting knife from my belt and hold it up, admiring it. The sun glints off of the blade in a strangely beautiful way. Mulligan bellows, the crowd gasps and whispers, some even cry out in alarm, and Melody's struggles grow more frantic.

"Let me go!!" she screams, baring her teeth at Johnson.

I twirl the knife in my hands, smiling a cold smile, slipping on this mask that I've worn so fucking well over the years. I turn my gaze back to the crowd and throw my arms out wide dramatically. Might as well be theatrical, right?

"Should we make it quick and painless? Or slow and agonizing? What do you think?" The crowd remains silent, eyeing each other uneasily. "Oh come on, we'll do it up Gladiator style: thumbs up for slow; thumbs down for quick." I hold out my hand and alternate between the two. Up, down, up, down.

And then the wind is knocked out of my lungs as Jonah springs up and barrels into me. Melody cries out, and Jonah and I go down in a heap, rolling and scrambling and both trying to get the upper hand. Jonah lands a solid punch and I taste blood in my mouth.

"Jonah!" Mulligan yells. My guys keep the crowd back and under control, though I don't think anyone would dare try to intervene right now, not with tensions roiling so high.

I land a kidney shot and when Jonah huffs out a pained breath, I take advantage and roll once more, pinning him beneath me. I turn my head to spit blood before wiping my mouth with the back of my hand. I grab up the knife again and raise it high…waiting…

Out of the corner of my eye, I see Melody go limp in Johnson's arms. He stumbles trying to account for her now dead weight, and she takes the opportunity to slam her fist into his nose. She spins, jerking the pistol from his hip as she does. I turn to meet her gaze and she aims the barrel directly at my chest.

"Go to hell," she sneers, gray eyes flashing with too many things to track.

And then she pulls the trigger.

Everything slows down, just like in a fucking movie. The force of the impact sends me flying backwards, and I watch as another shot rings out, this one from Landry. Jonah lets out a guttural, agonized scream that twists my heart. Melody stumbles backwards, hand flying to her stomach where a patch of red seeps from between her fingers, growing and growing…

She collapses. *Wrong, wrong, wrong!* my mind screams, but the only way out is through. A puddle of blood pools out around Melody's still form, and more gushes down my own chest, soaking me in seconds. Everyone is screaming now, confusion and terror and heartbreak permeating the air like a storm. I collapse back onto the ground, arms splayed out to my sides.

"Get the fucking doc up here!!" Johnson bellows amid the chaos. Doc's face comes into view above me as he puts two fingers on my neck to check my pulse. I reach up weakly to clutch at his arm and his lips twitch in amusement. I cough and sticky, wet crimson leaks from the corner of my mouth, down my chin. It tastes like shit.

"We need to get him to the hospital. Now!" Doc yells, looking to the FOSers around him. Someone grabs me beneath my arms, someone else my legs, and then I'm hoisted into the air. My head lolls as they hurry me down the street.

"Mel?" Doc shouts. Johnson crouches by Melody's side, fingers to her throat, and shakes his head. Gone. Everything about this feels so wrong.

"Damn it. Someone grab the body."

"You three, get everyone back to their homes and in lockdown! NOW!" Landry yells from behind us. Johnson runs behind us, cradling Melody's body to his chest. I close my eyes as they rush me to the hospital that won't do a damn bit of good.

CHAPTER THIRTY-EIGHT

MELODY

"AUSTIN TRAEGER IS DEAD," Wynn's voice rings out over the gathered crowd a few hours later. "Melody Morales too." Murmurs ripple through the crowd. I'm listening from my hiding spot in the back of one of the covered trucks not far away, wishing I could peek outside and watch.

"So, by my count, you called me a bitch, a slut, *and* a whore," I whisper. Austin smiles at me, tucked in beside me behind the crates of supplies. His shirt is still covered in the fake blood, and though I know damn well that it was all bullshit, the sight still sends a ripple of unease through me. I'd pulled that trigger. I'd shot him. It wasn't real, but still, the act had felt so fucking wrong it made me physically sick.

Of course, pretending to get shot myself wasn't all that much fun either. My own shirt is stiff with the dried corn syrup and food coloring concoction.

When I'd first had the insane plan, Austin had been skeptical, but he started to come around when I laid it all out. How we could make blood bags and have them burst to mimic blood spatter; how we could use a rubber bullet in place of the real one—which would hurt like fucking hell, but wouldn't do any lasting damage—and how I happened to know exactly where a whole stash of them was; how we could even make a capsule that he could break with his teeth that would make it look like he was coughing up blood to really sell the whole thing.

The more we talked about it, I saw the hope start to build inside him. Slowly, at first, but then, he really started to believe that maybe this could work, maybe this was finally the way out. It had made my throat feel thick. All he wanted was to be free of this, to be with me and live in peace after so fucking long of doing anything and everything that was needed of him in order to keep so many people safe. He deserves this. He deserves his happiness.

And I fucking do too. Maybe that's selfish. I know at this point, almost everyone still breathing has gone through a lot, but I feel like I had more than my fair share. So, yeah, I deserve this second chance at life and peace and love too.

"Technically, I said you acted in a slutty manner. I didn't directly *call* you one," Austin says with a smirk, and I snort, rolling my eyes. "I think a deserve an Oscar, honestly." He reaches out and tucks a strand of hair behind my ear before cradling my cheek with his palm. I turn and kiss the center before lowering it to intertwine our fingers while we wait for Wynn to finish the big finale.

With Traeger dead, those that had never wanted to follow him to begin with would usher in a new era. No more ruling with fear and pain and intimidation. Instead, it would be done with understanding and cooperation, a joint governing body made up of leaders from each settlement that collectively decided what was best for all of Haven. I really think it can work, and I know Austin does too or he never would have thought it was time for him to step down. I know that he would have played that role until it killed him if it was what Haven needed, if it kept everyone safe.

After a lot of talking and a lot of questions, I finally hear the front door open and slam shut. The truck starts and pulls out of The Cove, and I let out a long, slow breath once we're out on the highway.

"It actually fucking worked," I say, a little astonished. "I mean, I know there are lots of steps left and things to sort out, but Phase 1: Kill Traeger *actually fucking worked, baby.*" I grin and Austin chuckles.

"I can't say that I'll miss him."

He sighs heavily, and I swear I can actually see the weight of it lifting from his shoulders finally. The window in the partition between the front of the truck and the covered back slides open and Wynn's face appears. He grins like a lunatic.

"Ok, that was fucking fun. Batshit crazy, but *fun*. You really are a couyon, Mel."

"You were pretty good," Austin says, inclining his head. "A solid B+." Wynn and I both laugh.

"Hey, I helped!" Johnson adds from the drivers side, his head popping into view for just a second. I wince when I see his swollen nose, bits of dried blood still crusted above his lip and across his cheek.

"I'm sorry I hit you so hard, I was a little caught up in the moment."

He waves me off. "All good. I probably deserved it on some cosmic level from all the practical jokes I used to pull back in the day. We'll call it karma. But come on, have you ever heard a more dramatic performance? *Get the fucking doc up here!* Fucking classic."

"Yes, yes, everyone did phenomenal and we should start doing traveling plays all through Haven," I say with a roll of my eyes.

"Well, you're technically dead, so that would be weird…Oh, unless we did Hamlet. You could play the ghost of the dad and *really* freak everyone out."

I pinch the bridge of my nose, but I can't actually be annoyed by anything right now. I feel like I'm cloud nine. Higher than fucking cloud nine, the highest of the highs. Even so, I have fun and pretend.

"For the love of God, can we please get back to business?" I beg. Austin chuckles low, rubbing his thumb across my thigh before squeezing it lightly.

"Is Jonah alright? I might have gone a little heavy with a few of the licks out there," Austin asks, but he rubs his jaw where Jonah clocked him pretty good in return. I'd say they're even.

Wynn waves him off. "Yeah, he's fine. A busted lip and probably some sore abs in the morning, but he's great." I squeeze Austin's hand as Wynn continues on. "Everything is in place. Andrews and his team are headed to The Farm and Stoker and his to Greenbrier to spread the word and start working on plans, and Renee has everything set up at on the island for ya. You're sure you don't want one of those other giant houses out there?" He eyes us skeptically like we might have some screws loose.

Austin and I share a look. We could have had our pick of any house out there, but neither of us wanted anything but that apartment back. We might rebuild the main house one day, or maybe turn the workshop into a first floor and turn the whole thing into a barndo, but for now, the apartment is home. It's where he finally broke through every wall I tried to put in his path. It's where we finally found what we'd both been looking for all this time. It's where we both showed each other all of our dark and twisted and broken pieces and neither of us flinched away. No, we saw that all of those pieces fit together and made us whole in a way that we could never be alone.

"We're sure," I confirm, not taking my eyes from Austin's, his smile matching mine.

"Can you cool with the gooey eyes shit? I'm going to lose my lunch, I swear to God..."

"Don't make me come up there," I say, giving him a look that tells him I'll happily kick his ass if I need to. It only makes him grin wider, but he holds up his hands in surrender.

"Ok, well Renee has the apartment all ready for you. She and Zimmer got all of the stuff from your rooms—literally an entire truck load of nothing but books for fuck's sake—and enough supplies to set you up for a bit. Plus, there are still plenty of houses on that side of the island that haven't been scavenged yet, so you've got tons to pick through if you need something before someone can get back to you. Renee and Zimmer picked a house on that side too, but you've still each got plenty of, um...privacy," he says with a suggestive waggle of his dark brows. Austin chuckles, but tries to hide it with a cough. He does a terrible job and I give him a dry look. Wynn continues on, "No idea what Jonah and Mulligan will pick yet, but I already called dibs on the big cabin near the inlet where you two took your little tumble."

Renee had leapt at the chance to relocate to the island with me and Austin, and when I'd first brought up my plan to Jonah, he and Mulligan said they'd join us too with no hesitation. When Wynn said he would like the opportunity to relocate too, my heart had felt so full I had to walk away so no one could see me cry. Having all of my family back together again was more than I could ever have hoped for. Jonah and Mull are going to get things settled in Haven first, help get everyone eased into the new system and find a replacement for Jonah on the council. He's going to be "too bereaved" from my death to continue on, and he and Mulligan are going to strike out on their own. Doc said he couldn't leave the people who needed him, but promised to come visit soon and often. He's excited at the prospect of raiding the small doctor's office we'd found on the island for new supplies and equipment, but I think he's even more excited to have his best friend back—*really* back, for the first time in almost a decade.

"Got it, I'll make sure they know that one is spoken for," I assure Wynn. He nods and we all settle in for the long drive towards our new life. Austin rearranges the crates and rolls out the sleeping bags Wynn stashed back here for us. We highly doubt anyone will be watching, but we aren't taking any chances on this plan right now, so we're hiding out back here for the duration. He lays back with his arm behind his head and I snuggle in beside him, head on his chest.

"I shot you," I whisper.

"Yep, you did. Just swear to never do it for real, and I think I can forgive you this once." I can hear the smile in his voice.

"I make no promises," I say with a grin, wondering if I'll ever stop.

EPILOGUE
MELODY - EIGHT MONTHS LATER

"HAPPY TO REPORT that Haven is adapting well to the new government situation," Doc tells us over dinner. He'd fabricated a medical emergency at FOS that he'd need to monitor for a few weeks as an excuse to get away and come visit. The island is still mostly off of everyone's radar, except a small number of people at FOS, plus Doc. I feel a little bad sometimes keeping it a secret, but it's for the best for now, and if anyone ever needed sanctuary here, of course we would offer it. Maybe in a few years, no one will care whether Austin Traeger still lives or not, but for now, we're happy to keep playing dead out here in our weird little piece of heaven in the middle of the apocalypse.

We haven't only been hiding out and playing house. We repaired the bridge on the other side of the island and started exploring that area. We found more supplies, took out a shit ton of Bloodies, dealt with some inhuman humans who were sacrificing women to Bloody hordes kept in pits like some freak ass religious cult, but also saved a handful of good ones. Those we made sure found their way to safety in Haven.

I have this perfect balance of still helping people and making the world safer, while also getting to have an amazing life with the man I love. Adventure and an anchor, what I've been craving for so long.

Doc has been regaling me with stories of Austin as a teenager and then young twenty-something idiot, and my cheeks hurt from smiling and my stomach from laughing. Austin acts indignant during some of the more embarrassing stories, but overall, he's a good sport and I know it makes him happy to finally be able to talk about his past, to relive good memories without guilt or fear.

"You know, that reminds me of a time when Mitch and Mel got themselves trapped under a desk in Senator Braden's office when they snuck in there to hook up," Jonah adds with a grin.

"Ok, first off, *your* husband was the one who dared us in the first place! And you were encouraging it, so don't even act like you couldn't control what he did. And secondly, how were we supposed to know that he was going to come in there and take a fucking nap on his couch for two hours!!"

Austin and Doc roar with laughter, and I throw a green bean at Jonah. He catches it and tosses it in his mouth, smirking at me. Mulligan comes in and I leap up.

"Gimme, gimme, gimme!" I exclaim, reaching my hands out to the wiggling baby in his arms. Doc watches on, a bittersweet smile on his face. He'd tried so hard to save the baby's mother—a young girl we'd found out on the road, eight months pregnant and not doing well—but there's only so much he can do these days. She would have needed specialists and an OR back in the real world, and even then, her chances would have been slim. So, Doc had been left with a newborn who needed a home, and he'd immediately sent word to Jonah and Mulligan to see if they'd be interested. They jumped at the chance. Jonah had always wanted kids but then Sean's death and the end of the world and losing Gabby had put those plans on hold.

Mull hands baby Elliot over, and he smiles and giggles, reaching a chubby hand out to my cheek. Being around Elliot has helped me heal in ways I didn't expect. Holding him, I allow myself to remember my own daughter like I haven't in almost a decade. It still hurts, of course, it always will, but it also makes me smile. Austin meets my eyes, knowing exactly what's going on in my head like he always does, and gives me a look, asking if I'm good. I smile and nod as I rest Elliot's head oh my shoulder and kiss his soft chocolate brown curls, rocking from foot to foot.

"Did we wake you up, little buddy?" I ask.

"Nah," Mull assures us, leaning in to kiss Jonah before settling into my vacated chair, looking tired and worn, but happy. Austin fixes him a plate of food and slides it over. "He was out like a light, just decided he'd had enough sleep for now."

"Doc, you need anything before we head out?" I ask, reluctantly relinquishing my nephew to Jonah.

"Nah, I'm all good here." He's staying here at Jonah and Mulligan's since they chose one of the larger houses and Austin and I are still living happily in our little apartment. Well, more space is really only half of the reason he chose to stay with Jonah instead. He'd bunked down with us for a night but apparently Austin and I can't keep quiet enough for his tastes. Yes, I'm aware of the irony of that after my annoyance of how loud Austin and his girls were when I was in the suite next to his at FOS.

Austin gets up and wraps Doc in a hug, slapping him on the back a few times before doing the same to the other two men.

"I'll see you two in the morning before I head back. I'll make sure to send Wynn back with some of the Oreos we found." My mouth practically waters at that. Wynn is out working on supply distributions and I made him promise to visit Abulea's grave for me while was back at FOS. She'd passed peacefully in her sleep about a month after our big fake shootout, but she knew the truth and I like to think that she died happy for us both.

I sing to doc, "Did you ever know that you're my hero?"

Jonah covers his ears, and Mull covers Elliot's. Doc and Austin wince dramatically.

"Very funny." I roll my eyes but kiss all of the boys except Austin on the cheek—him I punch playfully in the stomach—before we head towards the door.

"Good night!" we all call to each other as Austin and I pull out of the driveway. We make our way back home, windows down and breathing in the late summer air. The oppressive heat finally broke about a week ago and now it's damn near perfect. I straighten when we pass Renee's house and Austin slows the car.

"Hey!" I call out the window. Renee waddles down the driveway to my window, grinning.

"Hey yourself." She waves to Austin and he asks how she's feeling. "Like a whale," she sighs, "but good. Doc checked me out earlier and said everything is looking great and on schedule."

"You missed dinner, I'm sorry."

She waves me off. "Not your fault I passed out for a nap at 4:30 in the afternoon"

"Well there's plenty of food left, I'll have Jonah bring some down for you."

"He doesn't have to—"

"Oh stop it. Food will be delivered soon, now get off your feet and rest."

"Jackson is putting the crib together right now. I better go supervise."

"I'll come over tomorrow. Love you."

"Love y'all too." She steps away from the car and waves as we drive off.

"Did you ever think about it? Having kids again I mean?" he asks.

"Sometimes," I admit. "Not in any real concrete way since I was very anti-relationship and happiness and all of that for so long." He grins. "But yeah, I always wondered what it might be like to have that in my life again. What about you? Did you want kids?"

"I always did, but it wasn't in the cards for me and Emily. Before the end of the world, I filled that place in my heart with all my students and players. Since then…I don't know, I guess it's still there."

"Well," I say slowly, letting the picture in my head settle a little more firmly. "I can't have kids myself, but…if we ever came across a child who needed a home, I wouldn't be opposed to giving that to them." I peek at him, biting my lip. He turns to me and beams, reaching out to squeeze my hand.

"I like that plan."

We pull up to the barn and he kills the engine. We cleared away the burned skeleton of the main house but we haven't quite figured out what we want to do yet. We head upstairs, Austin's fingers curled into the back pocket of my jeans, and I'm suddenly very much in the mood to play. My lips curl as I kick off my shoes in the living room the way Austin hates, purposefully kicking them away from the bin. I smile wider when I hear him exhale in exasperation behind me. Things are amazing with us, but not perfect by any means. We still argue and do things that drive each other crazy—sometimes on purpose because it's oh so fun, and the "punishments" are so damn delicious—but I'm so incredibly happy it makes me sick sometimes.

"Melody," he says, tone half warning, half sensual. I shiver at the sound. *Speaking of those punishments...*

I turn and walk backwards as he slowly stalks towards me, tugging his shirt off as he does. He knows exactly what game I'm playing and he's all too happy to join in. I bite my lip at the sight, still as turned on by it now as I was the first time I ever saw it what feels like a lifetime ago.

"Yes?" I ask sweetly, unbuttoning my shorts and shimmying out of my cut offs without slowing my steps.

"Your shoes..." He eyes me, a sexy glint of mischief in the green that makes my stomach clench.

"Oh, silly me, did I leave those in the middle of the floor again?" I ask, tapping my chin. I'm to the bedroom now, still slowly making my way backwards as he follows. He unbuckles his belt with one hand, unbuttoning his jeans and unzipping his fly quickly after. My ass hits the bed and he grips my waist, lifting me easily atop it. He yanks my tank top off over my head and makes quick work of my bra before kissing me deeply as he moves me up the bed. I'm breathless and writhing by the time he pins my hands above my head, quickly securing my wrists with the straps attached to the headboard. We've made quite a few modifications to the apartment since moving in— floor to ceiling bookshelves, Polaroids of our family and friends in frames on the walls, a few new pieces of furniture pilfered from the other houses on the island—but this might just be one of my favorites.

He kisses down my throat and chest, purposefully ignoring my aching nipples before continuing downward, trailing kisses over my stomach and waist. I wiggle and arch my hips, desperate for his tongue, but he only chuckles low.

"Oh no, sweetheart. Not yet." His words are a rough caress that sends a deep shiver running up my spine. The dirty, dangerous promises that voice makes to my body...

He tugs my panties down my thighs and then secures each of my ankles to more straps connected to the footboard. Now I'm pinned, wide open, ready to be used however he sees fit. All of the possibilities flash through my mind and my body trembles. I subtly rock my hips, needing him so fucking badly. He studies me, a low moan rumbling through his chest.

"Already fucking wet for me, Melody?" he rasps, eyes locked between my thighs. "Hmmm..." He reaches to the straps and pulls them tighter, spreading my legs farther apart. I gasp. "There were go," he rumbles. "Now, what am I going to do with you, baby?" He reaches out and runs a finger lightly down my pussy, making me moan loudly. I try to buck. I try to move. But the straps hold me tightly in place. It's torture. It's ecstasy. I can't ever get enough of this, of Austin.

"Hmmm, I think maybe we need some help tonight." My stomach clenches. We may or may not have raided a sex shop a couple of months ago when we'd ventured off of the other side of the island, and come home with quite a few new, uh, *friends* for the bedroom. He goes to the closet, and I smile in anticipation waiting to see what he comes back with. This is going to be a long, long night.

My smile only widens at the thought.

Hours later, I'm a boneless, sweaty mess sprawled across the bed on my stomach. Austin slowly kisses up my spine before settling in beside me, rubbing my wrists gently where they're red from the straps. I don't mind, but I love how he always takes care of me like this afterwards. I think that he likes that I do it for him too. I've come to learn that Austin is not a man who is used to being put first and taken care of. It's understandable with how he's had to live his life for the last decade, but I make a point to take care of him every chance I get. He deserves it. He deserves so much more for everything he sacrificed to make sure so many people were safe.

"Ok?" he asks, voice a little hoarse.

"Better than ok," I whisper, still a little breathless. "But I'm still not putting my shoes in your dumb little bin." He laughs lightly and kisses my shoulder.

"I would be devastated if you did." I smile and muster the strength to roll onto my side so I can look at him. "There's my girl," he says quietly, brushing damn hair from my forehead.

"Always," I assure him. I shift and settle my head on his chest, the steady beat of his heart quickly starting to lull me to sleep. He wraps an arm around my, pulling me tight against his side.

"Don't read anything into this…" I tell him and I can feel more than hear his low chuckle. He kisses my head and I smile a soft, easy smile that I thought I'd lost for good all those years ago. I can hear the smile in his own voice when he responds.

"Wouldn't dream of it, Melody Traeger. Wouldn't fucking dream of it, baby."

ACKNOWLEDGMENTS

As usual, this book wouldn't have been possible without a whole host of people, so I need to thank:

- My husband, for always supporting me in this crazy hobby. I like you and I love you.

- Jeffrey Dean Morgan for making the character of Negan come to life in a way that 1) inspired this book and 2) made me question my morality. #DADDYWINCHESTERFORLIFE

- Lexie, Kayleigh, and Kala (forever funny) for being the best cheerleaders and bullies ever. Jeff beans. Get the pudding. Book Babes 4 life (and no, Timmy, you can't join the chat)

- My amazing PA, Nancy, who I couldn't survive without and who never bats an eye when I come up with crazy ideas.

- My awesome ARC readers and Street Team

- All of you reading this right this second. I adore every single one of you! Thank you for taking a chance on a no-name indie author like me.

ALSO BY K. D. MILLER

Adult Contemporary Romance

- Carpe F*cking Diem
- Wrong Place. Wrong Time. Right Viscount.
- Puck the Holidays (Vipers Sin Bin - Book 1)
- Puck of the Irish (Vipers Sin Bin - Book 2)
- The Pieces You Kept

Adult Paranormal Romance

- Red
- Dark Burning (Veracity of the Gods - Book 1)
- Sweet Tempest (Veracity of the Gods - Book 2)
- Untamed Fate (Veracity of the Gods - Book 2.5)
- Vows Forged in Blood

Young Adult Sci-Fi/Fantasy

- Titan Rising (Outliers Series - Book 1)
- Titan Unleashed (Outliers Series - Book 2)
- Titan Reckoning (Outliers Series - Book 3)
- Evansfire

www.ingramcontent.com/pod-product-compliance
Lightning Source LLC
Chambersburg PA
CBHW030347120726
47901CB00007B/1942